The Tinker Girl

By

Mhari Matheson

Published in the United Kingdom in 2013 by
Cambria Books; Carmarthenshire, Wales, United Kingdom

Acknowledgements

The author's name may be on the cover but numerous people have helped along the way. The journey began with Kevin who held my hand as he pulled me through the intricacies of laptop, printer and Internet as I wrote, and then designed the wonderful cover.

The readers of my drafts: Haig and Margaret; Christine, Dick and Trishia; Pat, Tracey and Chris; Gwen; Elizabeth and John, and David, whose feedback eliminated early errors.

To the tutors and fellow MA students of Trinity, whose workshops identified the weaknesses, bolstered my confidence in the strengths, and bore me towards my final draft, and to Mari, Iau and Nick who read it. To Craig whose continued reading, encouragement and specialist knowledge was always only a phone call away.

Particular thanks are due to Menna, Helen and Jeni for their belief in the book and their valued advice and enthusiasm in urging me to publication. This would not have happened without Cambria agreeing to publish and guiding me through the process.

Finally, to John, my initial reader, who allowed a cast of characters to sit round the table and invade our life. His constant support, confidence and critical eye propelled me onwards. To all of the above I am truly grateful.

For my

Beloved Bwana

My amanuensis

CHAPTERS

Prologue

1889

The wailing notes of the fiddle were dragged beyond the tinker campfire by the gusty Highland wind. The three men round the embers knew by the silence from within the covered cart that the ordeal was over.

As more wood was thrown on, two figures descending from the cart were visible in the renewed flames. The youngest man at the fire rose to greet them. Their words, though expected, bent him more forcibly than the stormy night. Shoulders bowed he reached inside the tarpaulin and clasped the newly shrouded body in his arms. The two women followed in his wake as he led them, past the flickering fire and bent heads of his companions, on into the darkness with only the clang of spade on Scottish mountain stone to guide them.

The diggers' heather torches lit the last few paces and there he laid the body of his love in the shallow grave. Standing but for a moment, he turned and strode back past the fire, unheeding of the pleading men still seated there, on into the blackness with no thought of ever returning.

The keening of the women's Gaelic lament from the grave cut through the darkness, and the fiddler took up his instrument to echo it, ceasing only when they returned to the cart. Now a second bundle was brought from within, barely visible as it was passed from the one old woman to the other. A clasped handshake, a nod of the head, and the figure with the scrap of life in her arms turned and was soon lost to the night.

The two men by the fire watched the tinker matriarch clamber back inside the cart, and only then did they rise and douse it. Death had taken one of their tinker clan, grief had robbed them of another, and no doubt the minute spark of life in the tiny body, torn from the dead woman, would soon be quenched as effectively as the fire.

Part One

The Mountain

1899

1

She was so busy on her knees, gathering bilberries for the Cailleach that Cate didn't know anyone was there until she saw the boots on the next set of berries. Basket in hand she stood and faced them. The biggest tinker boy, owner of the outsize footwear, took a step forward and she guessed she was in for a hiding. Flight was the only escape. She flung the almost full basket of berries at them and ran.

Cate knew, even at ten, she was quicker than most of the tinker youths, but today the big one had joined in and he was the worst bully of the lot As she was with the tinkers for only part of the year, he was the one who encouraged the others to target her, saying she didn't belong. The moor on this side of the Kevinishe village made speed difficult. It was soggy underfoot. She wouldn't sink so far as the heavier boys, but they had the strength to pull their feet out faster. A quick look over her shoulder showed her that one of them had stayed to rescue the basket from the heather. Pity it hadn't been the big one.

Looking for the drier grass patches, only once or twice did she become mired in the boggy peat. As the first sheltering rocks appeared, Cate dodged between them, leading her attackers to the other side of the mountain, knowing she had to lose them before scurrying back to the waterfall and the cave behind it.

As the rocks became big enough to hide her she knelt and scanned the hillside below. The tinker boys were still bearing left.

She'd tricked them. Keeping out of sight, Cate turned to the right, climbing until she struck the old track, and then, as fast as she could, made for the waterfall. Edging her way behind it, along the familiar narrow ledge, she dropped into the opening and crawled to the old heather bed at the back. Safe now, she lay trembling, lungs burning. Slowly her breathing returned to normal. As the minutes went by, she felt she must be safe. Tiredness and relief swamped her. She slept.

The picture was quite clear. *She was in a large town, overwhelmed by noise, people, and buildings: this time she couldn't get away. She was climbing stairs, not rocks, bent double with pain, frightened!* Then the picture faded.

The noise of the waterfall beyond steadied her. She'd been listening to it as she woke. Had she been awake? What did that strange picture in her mind mean? Less frightened now, she rose, tidying the rough heather bed. Determined to forget, she left.

Wearing an assortment of boy's clothing on her skinny frame, a flat cap concealing her red hair, Cate eased her way from behind the curtain of water and stood looking down the mountain, her beloved Beinn Nishe. The early mist was lifting and there in one of the breaks stood a stag. Crouching behind the nearest boulder, squinting over the top, she smiled. The beast moved his great head from side to side, as if saying 'look at me', so sure of his own importance, just like the tinker bullyboys. Well she'd outrun them, but now she was hungry. A movement below set the stag running, and she did the same, scrambling lightly through the scree, down to the heather moor, and on till she saw the peat smoke from the village chimneys with the sea beyond.

This was her world for part of the year: Kevinishe. During the summer she travelled with the tinkers. In the winter months she lived here with the Cailleach, the Gaelic name for an old woman, in the tiny Black House on the edge of the moor. The village itself was small enough to be almost hidden by distillery and mountain. Tiny estate houses hugged the shore and, beyond the woods, concealed by tall conifers and oaks, was the Laird's home, Kevinishe House.

Being an orphan, splitting her year between tinkers and village, belonging to neither, meant both groups were as wary of her as they were of the Cailleach. Indeed some of the villagers thought of the

12

old woman as a witch, though they were glad enough of her herbs and potions when they were sick. And there was *The Sight*: stories told of the Cailleach warning of disasters, like the blow-out in the distillery and the great fire, many years before. Cate also saw pictures in her head, but never spoke of them. Sometimes they frightened her. At other times a *red-headed woman* appeared and she liked that: the woman seemed friendly.

A rumble from her stomach reminded her she was hungry and set her feet running downwards to the lower slopes of the moor, but the stray bramble bushes had few of the late autumn berries. Moving into the woodland through a gap in the fence, Cate searched in the odd spaces left by fallen trees, but with little success. She knew she was trespassing, because this was private ground and, somewhere hidden behind all the trees, was the Laird's home. Part curiosity and part hunger made her continue, and her persistence was rewarded when the trees thinned and she saw a scraggy hedge of bramble bushes. Pushing her way through, she could just see a big bunch of brambles. One last stretch and her fingers touched the fruit, but she slipped and crashed through the hedge behind. Only the fiery hair escaping from the cap, knocked sideways in the fall, threatened to betray the girl within the boy's clothing. Tucking her hair back under the cap, she looked around.

Cate felt as though she'd fallen into another world. Never had she seen such a wide expanse of smooth green grass, for it was nothing like the rough greeny-brown stuff on the sandy soil by the shore—the communal grazing they called the machair. Nor was it the normal scrubby vegetation that surrounded heather moors and peat bogs. Shiny evergreen bushes hedged the green, and beyond there were other pretty bushes, tall trees, and a glimpse of the building. A child of the mountains, moors, lochs and sea, it was not the size so much that astonished her as the tidiness. No straggling dunes of grass. No hotchpotch of animals, carts or hovels.

"So this house, as big as the mountain, is the Laird's: The MacNishe!" She'd spoken out loud, before she remembered where she was. It wouldn't do to be spotted. Stepping back against the hedge, Cate wondered about The MacNishe. He must be a very important man to need a house this size and to own everything: river, loch, village and distillery, all named for him.

Something moved to her right, so she squeezed beneath the green bushes and hid. A young woman wearing a grey dress with white cuffs and apron pushed a pram, that seemed as big as the carter's wagon, into the centre of the green. Glancing over her shoulder, she pulled on the brake, checked the pram, and disappeared into the bushes.

Now it was time to go. Cate turned to search for an opening, but hid again as a boy slouched onto the green, kicking his toes into the surface and leaving pockmarks in it. From the shelter of the hedge her watchful eyes raged at this unnecessary spoiling. The boy seemed suddenly to see the pram and, after a brief look around, ran towards it. Grasping the handle he began rocking it up and down, then side to side. Before long the wails of the frightened infant in the pram broke the silence. Yet the boy continued.

Memories of cruelty by older children and villagers were too much for her. With no thought to trespassing or danger she ran and hurled herself at the boy. "Stop that now! The bairn's hurt! Leave it be!" Using all her strength she pushed him to the ground, screaming at him to stop while scratching and kicking any part of him she could. The bullying tinker boys had her well prepared for this sort of thing, and her ready temper gave her strength. Caught unaware, the boy bellowed for help as he fell. Soon figures appeared from everywhere: the Laird's grandsons were in trouble and woe-betide a servant who didn't respond. Cate continued her attack until the screams and shouts of grownups reached her. Suddenly aware of danger, she fled.

Still lying on the grass, Bruce put his hands to his face and shrugged in pretend sobs. "He was attacking David. I tried my best to stop him but…" What a piece of luck that the disgusting tinker boy had been the only one to see him! He allowed the gardeners to help him to his feet. "Quick—after him! Don't let him get away! He was trying to steal the child. I stopped him." Soon his hated stepmother was there, cradling the miserable baby, and his father too, barking orders to the battalion of servants to fetch the doctor and search the grounds. As the nursery maid reappeared, she was dismissed on the spot for her negligence. The thought that her life would now be in ruins pleased Bruce and he only wished he could have hurt the horrid child in the pram as well. How dare the infant's mother think she could replace his own!

As he watched Fisher, the Laird's stillman from the distillery, go in search of the escaping figure, Bruce wondered why his grandfather allowed the tinkers, to over-winter in the long field. No one really knew the answer, though the Lairds had always done so.

With Lady Sarah tearful in the nursery, her husband, Bruce's father Rab, went to the Laird's quarters to tell him what all the commotion was about. Young Bruce held court in the kitchen, while Mrs. Mac, the housekeeper, bathed his face and Cook produced a tray of shortbread and hot sweet tea as they waited for the arrival of the doctor. Then the scullery door opened to admit Fisher, holding a struggling figure in the air in front of him. Bruce leapt to his feet. "That's him! Ought to be in jail, trying to steal our David."

Now, the others knew that 'our David' was hardly how Bruce thought of his stepbrother.

"Come on then, Fisher, get him locked up until they come from Fort William for him. What are you waiting for?" Bruce demanded.

"Yes, Fisher, lock him up in one of the cellars." Rab MacNishe echoed his son's demand as he entered the kitchen. The heir apparent was an impressive figure, master of the estate in everything but title. His father might be Laird but, as his only son, Rab saw to the day-to-day running of things, though he found the old man's reluctance to relinquish all power irksome. Hearing the Laird's steps on the flags in the corridor, he braced himself.

"Even a beggar or a thief, never mind a child, is surely allowed to protest their innocence, Rab. There's something not right here." Allowing no time for Rab to argue, MacNishe continued. "Put the boy down, Fisher."

The stillman dropped the struggling figure on the kitchen floor and, before any one could move, it flew at Bruce.

"Liar. I did no harm to the bairn and fine well you know it"

In the surprise attack the words were lost to all but Bruce. Pandemonium erupted, and, as Fisher rescued Bruce and MacNishe herded the women out of the way, the attacker vanished through the open kitchen door.

"After him," roared Rab. "There's no doubt of his guilt now! Come on, Fisher get the grooms and gardeners searching the estate. I want that wretch caught and this time thrown in the cellar immediately."

"Sir. Sir the…" Mrs. Mac intervened.

"Speak up woman! Now what's the matter? Can't you see we're busy?"

"Rab. I think the doctor…". His father motioned to the front door bell ringing on the wall.

"What? Oh right. Go and show him upstairs, Mrs. Mac."

"Right away, sir."

"Now, Father…"

"Yes I know, Rab, but somehow…Oh well, get on with your search."

Later, seated in his study, MacNishe poured the drinks as he tried to guess what the doctor was about to tell him. But impatience got the better of him. "Come on, Calumn, tell me. How bad is the wee fellow?"

"Bruised, as you would expect, from the shaking in the pram."

"But, not enough to…"

"MacNishe, you and I have grown old together…"

"So. The news is not good then?"

"Ach! I don't have the expertise for this disorder. Why don't you take him to one of the new-fangled chaps from Glasgow or Edinburgh?"

"Will they cure the child?"

"You know they can't do that, MacNishe. It may be 1899, but medical expertise still has few answers. All you can do is keep the boy from harm. See he takes no more knocks and hope to God there's no internal bleeding. I warned you in his first year. He'll be lucky to reach manhood."

"Lady Sarah?"

"I've given her a draught. It's hard for her."

"There's no chance another child without…?" The old man knew the answer, but the ache in his heart made him ask anyway.

"A girl perhaps, but with another boy I could never guarantee it. A double load would be over heavy for her, MacNishe."

"Aye, you're right. We must be thankful for Bruce." The old man wondered if he really was.

Bruce sat scowling in his room. It had all gone wrong. He hadn't believed his luck when he'd seen the pram left unattended. 'A blow could be the end of him', that's what the doctor had told his father and her. Listening outside doors had always been useful. That conversation had shown him how to make an end of the brat and then perhaps the mother would go. He'd just begun to bang him about in the pram when that screaming fiend had come flying at him.

He got up to look at the scratches on his face. Nobody had ever hurt him like that. Wait till they found that dirty tinker brat. And yet—that could be dangerous. He screwed his face up as he thought hard. He hadn't liked his grandfather's appearance. The old man seemed to know what he, Bruce, was about before he knew it himself. Yes. Maybe it would be better if they didn't find the tinker. That way no one would ever know what really happened.

Feeling more cheerful, he decided to return to the kitchen and see if Cook was making something special for his supper. As he was only twelve he still had to have it in the schoolroom with the governess, but since she was afraid of being replaced by a tutor, she was sure to be extra nice to him after his brave 'rescue' of his stepbrother. Smiling, he pretended to limp as he went down the stairs.

In the evening the Laird and his son ate alone in the dining room. Although Kevinishe House had plenty of smaller rooms for informal dining, it would never have occurred to either man not to change for dinner or to dine elsewhere. So they sat at the long table, as every MacNishe male over the age of fourteen had done since the present house had been rebuilt. Jessie, the parlour maid, served their meal and busied herself at the great oak sideboard between courses, while the ancient stags' heads dominated one wall and the fierce gaze of MacNishe ancestors glowered at them from the other. Only the glowing peat fire and the candles in the clan sconces spoke of warmth and comfort.

Since Lady Sarah was not present the talk was mainly of estate business and the distillery. It was one of the great stories of the glen: how a past MacNishe had won an illicit still in a bet and the hand of the daughter of the chief of the Clan Craig all in one year, thus providing a source of income as well as a 'royal' bride. This particular princess had been shipwrecked on her way to visit her Irish grandparents. It had been quite a coup for a minor Highland laird living on the isolated west coast of Scotland.

The after dinner dram, their own Craeg Dhu single malt, named after an earlier Laird, 'Black Craig', was interrupted by the parlour maid.

"What now, Jessie?"

"It's Fisher, sir. He's brought yon tinker back and says what's he to be doing with him?"

Rab spoke before his father could. "I'll deal with it, Jessie. Make sure Fisher gets a meal and a dram in the kitchen. He'll need it after searching the moors. I'll lock the brat in the cellar."

"Yes, sir. I'll just away an tell him."

"Don't look at me like that, Father. It's the only place for him. More like an animal than a human with all that wild behaviour."

"Perhaps, Rab, but still a child for all that."

"Man, you're going soft in your old age."

"Care for a young one has nothing to do with age, Rab. So mind your tongue in my house." MacNishe could see his words had annoyed Rab, reminding him that he would have to wait some years yet before he became Laird. True his son had other problems that made him short tempered, what with his baby son's haemophilia, and Bruce's reluctance to accept his step-mother. Their difference of opinion now over the tinker boy wasn't helping.

18

The struggling dawn had barely penetrated the tower room. The night chill slid off the rough stone walls enveloping the old man huddled in his chair. He knew the cold was not responsible for his dark mood. The events of yesterday had robbed him of sleep, but the real trouble was that, with Rab snapping at his heels, chafing under his authority, and his grandson Bruce not the kindred spirit he had hoped for, his old age was a lonely place. Bah! What a miserable old booger he was becoming. He'd tackle the narrow stairs, light a candle and have himself an early dram. That'd chase the chill.

Hand over the decanter he hesitated. In the distance he caught the sound of one of the old Gaelic laments. No one in the house was astir and yet it was in the house. Warily, MacNishe returned to the great hall. The sound was below him and in it was the echo of the Highlands, the very essence of the landscape. He placed it now. It was in the cellar.

He took the steep descent carefully, as much for the wariness of his mind as for the condition of his bones. The old fifteenth-century dungeon, now divided into cellars, still had the original iron gratings in the top part of the door. Peering in his flickering candlelight he saw the tinker boy, body pressed hard to the stones, head outstretched to the tiny grating high up in the wall.

He shivered as the mournful tune drew to an end. Although he made no sound, the tinker boy seemed to be aware of his presence and turned towards him.

"You have the Gaelic then?"

A brief shake of the young head was the only reply.

"Look here, I mean you no harm, but I need to know what happened out there with the pram. What were you doing?" In the silence MacNishe sensed the wariness of a fawn on the hill, aware of an approach but unsure how to deal with it.

"I fell."

"Fell, eh?" He understood he'd have to drag every word from the shadowy figure. This whole business was wrong. Nothing fitted. He'd dealt with the tinkers all his life. Oh they'd go the wrong side of the law easily enough, but taking a child from the Big House would mean prison for sure, and they were cunning, not stupid. His silence seemed to have an effect.

"From the brambles I fell, so I did."

"And the child in the pram?"

"It was not me made the bairn cry."

"Who then?" A shrug of the shoulders and MacNishe realised it was not defiance or guilt he was dealing with but an acceptance that the blame would be apportioned whatever was said. He would have to try something else.

"If I open this door and come in I'll not have you running away again, because I mean you no harm." Slowly he turned the key, keeping a watchful eye on the child. Once inside, steadying the wavering candlelight, he pulled the heavy door shut and leant against it. Closer now he realised the boy was shivering.

Trying again, he asked "Are you cold?"

"It's not cold, just…"

"What is it then?" the child really was trembling and the voice, when it came, was full of fear.

"It's the fire above you. Can you no smell it? The smoke—I canna get my breath. The place is burning. Let me oot". The child screamed, trying to push past him.

Placing his hands on the shaking shoulders, MacNishe was affected by the eerie atmosphere the child had created. "Calm yourself, now. There's no fire here. No smoke."

"No. No. I see. It's gone."

MacNishe stared as the boy moved back and shrank against the wall, head down.

"So what was all that about?" The child's stubborn silence gave him the answer. He knew there was no fire or smoke, but there had been a century ago. How did this child know of the fire that had ravaged the house, leaving the dungeon untouched? So this was why he'd felt uneasy. Was the child a *seer*? In that moment, whatever the boy was, MacNishe knew he would protect him. "Well, I'm shivering and that makes no sense when I've a nice warm kitchen above. A few bits of kindling on the fire, kettle on the hob and we'll soon be ready for a hot strupach. You could do with a cup of tea, now couldn't you?" He watched and waited as the child considered his words, but the longing for escape from the dark place was difficult to conceal.

"Now we could have a bargain here. You know what that is?"

"Mebbe."

"If you were to give me your word you'd not run away, we could both go up to the warmth." Slowly he turned and opened the door a crack. "What do you say? Have I your word?" MacNishe deliberately kept his back to the tinker and, holding his breath, waited for the next move. Years of dealing with men and animals had taught him that, irksome though it was, patience was often the only way. Eventually a sharp tug on his clothing told him he'd won. Turning, he saw the outstretched hand. Spitting on his own hand, to show a deal had been done, he grasped it and together they made their way to the kitchen.

With hot cups of tea in their hands, fire roaring at their backs, and sitting among numerous copper pans and utensils glimmering in the candlelight, MacNishe began the questioning again. "Why was my younger grandchild crying?"

"He was hurting and feart."

"Come now, why would he be afraid, lying quiet in his own pram?"

"The big boy was..." Here words seemed to fail and the small hands took the back of the spindle chair and rocked it up and down and side to side. The movement completed, the tinker turned to the Laird.

Even with all the accumulated dirt on the face, the candid gaze surprised him. Somehow he knew those extraordinary green eyes were telling the truth, and this knowledge disturbed him: so, it had been Bruce, trying to damage his stepbrother! Well, he'd known somehow it hadn't been right. Dammit, now what was to be done? Rab would never believe it and Bruce would only deny it. His thoughts were interrupted by the arrival of Cook ready for a hot cup of tea before beginning her day's work

"Sir, what's to do in here now? Och it's more trouble is it?"

"No, no, Cook. Come away in. We're..." MacNishe stood open-mouthed. At the sight of Cook the tinker had tried to hide behind him and the flat cap on the child's head had caught on the deer horn button of his dressing gown sleeve. The tinker now stood with a tangle of dirty red hair falling below the waist.

21

"It's a lassie, sir! It's a wee lassie!" cried Cook.

2

As she sat in her sitting room, Lady Sarah smiled at the commotion coming from the nursery. Quite why her father-in-law had been drinking tea in the kitchen with the supposed felon she'd no idea. Nor did she understand why Bruce had thought it was a boy. MacNishe's instructions were that she was to have a clean girl brought to her, and she supposed that he would then clear up the mystery, and tell her what his plans were. No doubt these would involve more argument with Rab.

Thoughts of the nursery reminded her of the bruises on baby David's body and the pain she carried daily. A brief knock and the housekeeper's entrance prevented her dwelling on these.

"Oh, My Lady, would you just look at me."

"Poor Mrs Mac. You are well and truly damp. Is she clean?"

"She's not only clean, but—she's—well, she's—och you'll see for yourself. Shall I bring her to you?"

"Yes, do that, Mrs. Mac. What about clothing?"

"We've brought a trunk of clothes from the attics, My Lady, and dressed her in those."

Waiting for the girl, Lady Sarah's thoughts returned to the immediate problem. Fond of her father-in-law as she was, his interference would infuriate dear Rab and as usual she would have to keep the peace. Yet how could she tell her husband that Bruce was determined to harm David? She'd seen it from the beginning. Rab had laughed, putting it down to normal childish jealousy and then to a woman's fancy. Now here was MacNishe telling her the fears were well founded. Rab could never be told. It would break his heart, if he could even be made to believe it. He'd gone to the distillery, but they would have to get the child away before he returned. Thankfully she could hear the housekeeper's voice.

"In with you now. Just you mind and be respectful to the mistress. She's a great lady so she is." With that Mrs. Mac pushed her charge into the room.

"Here she is, My Lady."

"Good gracious, she's…"

"Just so, My Lady. Who'd have believed it from the dirty wretch she was?"

"Come here, child. Don't push her, Mrs. Mac."

"Well she's that thrawn. For a wee one I've never known the like."

"That's alright. Why don't you leave us? I'm sure you have things to do."

"We-ell, if you're sure. She's a temper on her so she has."

"Leave us now, Mrs. Mac. I'll ring when I'm ready." Waiting for the door to close, Lady Sarah studied the child in front of her. She'd not seen the state she was in when captured but could quite understand the housekeeper's bewilderment. The child was striking. By some lucky accident they'd dressed her lean figure in a long green gown and the newly brushed red hair now hung down her back like a flame. True the face was crimson, but when the result of all that scrubbing had faded, she would no doubt have the creaminess of skin that usually accompanied the hair. The only harsh note was the expression on the child's face. It reminded her of long gone days when her younger brother had been dragged indoors, hurriedly scrubbed and paraded before relations. 'Mutinous' did not begin to describe it. Whatever her background, those green eyes were bold.

The girl meanwhile stayed where she'd been pushed. How strange it must be for the child. The morning's events had to have left her bewildered.

"You've been in the nursery? Seen the baby?" Acknowledging the stiff nod, Lady Sarah continued. "His name is David, after my father. He is very dear to me and we have to take great care of him."

"He was all by himself out there."

"I know, but that was an error." And one she determined would not be repeated. "The nursery maid should not have left him alone." Watching as she spoke, she felt, rather than saw, the tension slacken in the small body. Rising, she moved to the window. "Look, you can see where the pram was." She'd had plenty of practice cajoling her brother all those years ago. Give him a command and he'd do the opposite. Look as if you didn't care and curiosity usually won. She continued with her back to the girl. "What a lovely morning it's turning out to be. Beinn Nishe is almost clear of the mists." Turning back to the child she could see talking of the mountain seemed to set up some kind of struggle within her.

Cate moved slowly forward, reached for and held onto the curtain, before looking out. She could see the mountain now, but it looked different from up here. Turning her head she began to pick out the familiar landmarks. Her world was still there, but like a ghost, too quiet. She couldn't hear the sea splashing, or the wind in the trees. There was no smell of heather or peat. "It's no real up here. Can I go now? I want my own place."

"Who are you, child? What's your name and where do you live?"

"Cate." This was accompanied by a shrug of the thin shoulders. "Sometimes I'm with the tinkers and sometimes with the Cailleach on the moors. I'm an orphan. Am I to go then?" The Lady was frowning at her. Mebbe it was time to run again. Mind, how could she run anywhere in this? She tugged at the long skirts of the dress in disgust. Run along the shore? She could hardly walk without tripping over. Now it was her turn to frown.

"No. No. I was thinking." Lady Sarah studied the child as the small hands fiddled with the dress.

"Mind I'm no to go withoot my clothes. This'll no do in the wet heather. I canna be gathering the seaweed for the Cailleach in this." Could this Lady no see the sense of it?

"I'm afraid I can't let you go yet. We have to wait for the Laird." Seating herself on the chaise longue, Lady Sarah patted the space beside her. "Come, sit for a moment. I would like to tell you about David, my baby boy."

The girl's eyes widened in horror as the woman spoke quietly on. Death was no stranger, either in the tinker camp or in the village, but that was from cold or hunger or lung disease, never from bruising. This shaking of the pram by the boy was just cruelty. And to a brother!

"It's him should be in the jail!" Then a thought struck her. "Why does yon one no have the running blood?"

"Because Bruce is not my son. His mother died when he was five." Seeing the puzzled look she forced herself to say the words she loathed so much. "You see it's my fault David has this blood disorder."

"What did you do?"

"That's the point: I've done nothing to deserve this. You see it's a disease that certain women carry and hand down to their children, at least to the boys."

"What's the name of this running blood thing then?" The Cailleach had taught her about lots of diseases, but this blood thing was new. Fancy a mother giving it to her sons!

"Its proper name is very long, but it means David bleeds easily and then it doesn't stop. You see why that could be very dangerous," Lady Sarah answered

"Like when the Cailleach puts spit on the moss and covers the cut to make a crust, his cut would still bleed?"

"Is that what they do, the tinkers?"

"Sometimes, but the Cailleach—she's the old woman in the Black House on the moors—she does all the medicines, from herbs, leaves and berries. She's no a tinker".

Their conversation was interrupted by the arrival of the Laird. "Sarah, my dear, I—Damn me! My apologies, Sarah."

"It's alright, MacNishe, I was equally amazed." She looked at him with undisguised affection.

"Now then, I've racked my brain, but I can't for the life of me think what to do with her." MacNishe shook his head.

"Mmmm, I was wondering, MacNishe if…?"

"Spit it out, Sarah, if you've a germ of a plan. We'll need to be ready when Rab comes back."

"You know David should soon be walking, so I wondered…"

"What now, Sarah?"

"The problems with him will only increase as he gets older, so I thought—I mean he has Nanny but she cannot be with him every minute. What he needs is constant attention."

"You mean her?" The Laird nodded at the child.

"Yes. Why not? She's already come to his rescue. Perhaps it was meant."

"Now you're talking like a Highlander and a woman! You know very well Rab'd never agree."

"But, MacNishe…"

"No, Sarah. He's told us all, servants included, what's to be done and he'll not back down. Never!" MacNishe walked to the window wishing himself elsewhere. Sighing he turned once again to listen to his daughter-in-law.

"But I have to see to the caring of the house and of my child, and I want this, MacNishe. I need to know David's safe, and, if I can't do that here, I shall return to my father."

"Sarah, I'm getting too old for this upheaval, but I can see you're troubled. I'll tackle Rab. Though I have to say I'll never understand you ladies. It seems you're biddable on the whole, but every now and again—rude though it may seem—you're like horses when they dig their heels in: there's no moving you."

Meanwhile the child had tired of the adult conversation and wanted to leave. It would be too difficult to find her way out by herself. Help would have to come from the grown-ups, so she brought their attention back to her.

"I need to be away. Yon man's coming and I'll be for the jail. You'll no see me in jail?"

MacNishe had no immediate answer. "Keep her here, Sarah, and I'll see Rab downstairs. I suggest you be indisposed for the rest of the day. Jessie can bring your food. She knows how to hold her tongue".

The child had been ravenous yet curious during the breakfast that Jessie brought. The snippets of ham, cheese and scrambled egg accompanied by flaky rolls spread with salt butter and whisky marmalade must all have been new to her, though it seemed to be the setting on the silver trays twinkling in the weak autumn sunlight that held her attention. Lady Sarah let her admire, explore, taste and touch while she ate her own normal light breakfast, which had been later this morning because of the upset. Not for her the full bowls of steaming porridge, followed by a daunting array of meat and fish, washed down by strong black tea, that the men consumed early in the morning.

"Well, child, is that better?" The girl had not bolted everything in sight, which is what the older woman had expected. Indeed it was almost as though she'd deliberately set out to imitate, eyes ever watchful, quickly adapting to the style set for her.

"Aye. I was hungry, so I was, and I've never seen—such…" the small hands indicating the remains—"things."

"What was the best?" She smiled as the forehead puckered while the girl considered the question.

"Was that bread?" she asked, pointing to the scattered crumbs on the tray.

"Those are Aberdeen Butteries. Like bread, but soft rolls really. We have them in the morning, hot like that, although the men have toast as well."

"I like it better than crowdie. With the butter and yon stuff."

"Oh that's marmalade. Not ordinary marmalade of course because it has Craeg Dhu in it."

"But that's whisky." The child picked up the empty marmalade dish and smelt it. "Aye so it is."

How did this child of the wilds know and recognise whisky she wondered? Her thoughts were interrupted by a knock at the door and Jessie entered.

"Ah, Jessie, we've finished here, so you may clear. Don't forget—I'm indisposed."

"Yes, My Lady."

As he crossed the hall, MacNishe heard Rab outside, talking to the groom. He waited till his son entered the house.

"Have you a minute, Rab, for a dram in the gunroom?"

"Yes, if you want."

"I want a word about the tinker, " MacNishe began as he poured them both a dram.

"Father, as soon as I've downed this I'll get a message to Fort William and they'll deal with the thieving wretch."

"I don't think that would be advisable, Son."

"I don't give a damn what you think. I've…"

"Listen to me Rab. Sarah…" This was a waste of time. He'd never listen.

"Let's not bring her into this, Father. The matter is settled."

"I'm sorry, but that's where you're wrong. You know I don't agree with you, but this suggestion is Sarah's. She wants to keep the lass as a companion for David. No, not wants—is determined to do so."

"No, Father! No! Never. You can't give me charge over everything and then countermand my instructions. I thought that would be obvious to you. In fact I don't know why you did turn the management of the estate and the distillery over to me."

"Dammit, you know fine well. You needed the distraction when our wives died on the moorland road. I didn't have the heart for it then anyway." Why wouldn't he listen to reason?

"And now you fancy the reins again, eh?" Rab taunted his father.

" If you'd let me finish about the tinker."

"No! I've had enough. The tinker goes to prison and be damned to you."

With that Rab made for the great oak door, flinging it open as if it were made of balsa wood and nearly knocking Jessie over into the bargain. She watched as he bellowed for his horse and, once astride, rode down the long drive as if Auld Nick himself was after him. Sighing, she opened the gunroom door, stared for a moment and ran screaming from the room.

The women of the house gathered in the gunroom, staring at the sight of the Laird lying on the floor, face pale, blue lipped, creased in pain, and his breathing laboured. Lady Sarah was the first to recover from the shock.

"Ride for the doctor. Quickly! My husband, Jessie, where is he? Jessie! Think! Where is Master Rab?" She shook the wailing maid until she began to make sense.

"His horse. He went to…"

"Of course—the distillery. Someone run to fetch him." She stared at the Laird on the floor and couldn't think what to do for him. A tug at her skirt made her aware that the child had run downstairs with her. "Not now. I must think what to do."

"That's it. The Laird canna get breath. Open his collar. The Cailleach would raise his head to help with the breath."

"She has the right of it, My Lady. We must try to make him comfortable till the doctor comes." The housekeeper appeared, confirming the child's instructions.

"Yes. Yes, of course. Thank you, Mrs. Mac. I'm afraid for him. He's an old man and this house has had more than its fair share of grief these past years. This is the worst possible thing to happen."

As they tried to aid the Laird, the door opened and the large reassuring figure of Fisher appeared. As one the women folk breathed easier. Only Lady Sarah was aware of the grim look on his face.

"My husband—I sent for him."

"I know, my Lady, but he's no at the distillery. He was seen heading up the glen in a fair old hurry."

"He must have gone for the doctor himself."

"He'll no have much luck. The good man is away to an important medical conference in Glasgow. He called in for a jar to take with him. Said he'd be away for the two weeks."

Slipping away, since the adults were all occupied, the child was glad to see the open door leading to the outside. She hesitated, began to run and promptly fell over. Muttering, she gathered up the long skirts knotting them round her waist. With legs unrestricted she set off across the grass pushing her way through the laurel hedge.

The 'soft rain' of the deep Highland mist soaked her lithe body as she struggled through the sodden heather that caught and felled her time and again. The old man was her only hope and the Cailleach must save him. Would she go to the Big House though? Could she get there in time?

As Cate stumbled through the door into the gloom she hesitated. This same door had been her earliest memory, the gaunt black figure stirring a pot on the open hearth her only toddler contact. The first winter she could remember she did nothing more than bring in peat for the fire, stir the porridge and wash the bowls in the burn. The old woman had but little English and rarely spoke, so Cate had watched and learned.

One spring day the old tinker woman, who visited now and again, came to collect medicines and this time had taken her to the tinker camp and then to travelling with them. After that the pattern was set: travelling with the tinkers in the summer months and in the winter living with the Cailleach. No one answered her questions about her missing mother and father or about much else for that matter. 'Wheesht now' was the usual reply, so she stopped asking, accepting she was a nobody, and ranged between the two old women, belonging to neither and treated with suspicion by the villagers, who thought her a changeling.

"MacNishe. He's—at the Big House." Throwing herself to the floor the child mimicked the stricken man. It seemed to be enough for the old woman, who began collecting sundry small pots woven from strands of dried heather. Putting these into an old tartan plaid, she reached for her black shawl.

Horse's hooves drummed outside the door. A hurried knocking and Fisher stooped as he entered the Black House. A brief conversation in the Gaelic and he turned to stare at the girl. By now the old woman was ready and, with much scuffling and pulling, they were both mounted and away. Free at last, the girl resumed her usual daily tasks.

Meanwhile back at Kevinishe House the Cailleach had Fisher summon a groom and together they carried the Laird to a first floor bedroom. Untying the plaid the old woman laid out her heather pots while giving instructions in the Gaelic, which Fisher duly translated for Mrs. Mac. By the time the housekeeper brought the boiling water, bowls and night attire required, Fisher had undressed the Laird and once the nightshirt was in place, he ushered Mrs. Mac out of the room and stood back by the door while the Cailleach took over. From her pots she made an infusion of foxglove leaves in the boiling water in one bowl: these she usually used on skin wounds to help them heal but she had tried them before to help heart muscles work better in someone with heart pains and that had worked. She repeated this with an infusion of hawthorn leaves and flowers in the other bowl. She understood that the flowers were more potent than the berries and infused with the leaves they increased the blood flow to the heart. Then she strained the mixtures through muslin taken from one of her numerous pockets in her old black gown. Once these cooled she used a horn spoon to drip first the foxglove and then the hawthorn between the Laird's lips. Satisfied now she turned to Fisher, said "Chi sinn marbhitheas" and sat by the Laird.

Hand on the doorknob the stillman nodded. It was all they could do now. In the old woman's words, 'we'll see how it goes'. He left her to her vigil and went to inform the others. All any of them could do was wait.

3

On his return to the glen the doctor made his way to the distillery to settle his account with Fisher. Business concluded, the usual dram was offered. The doctor watched the remaining whisky as it slid back down the glass, nodding in approval as it took its time gathering again at the bottom. "Aye, this one's got good 'legs', Fisher. Glasgow has nothing to beat this, despite all their shouting about blends."

"Well they're maybe alright for lowlanders, Calumn. They can do with a softer, milder dram. Once you've got the taste for the heavier peat with the harsher whiff of the sea salt, yon blends taste like tea next to Craeg Dhu!"

"Now then, what's this I hear about MacNishe? Not another row with Rab?"

"One of the worst, from what Jessie said, and it's a wonder yon great oak door's still standing, never mind the state of the stallion when he came back to the distillery."

"Well, but what brought it on?"

While Fisher recounted the events of the days in question, the doctor supped his dram, shaking his head as the details emerged.

"So you see, Calumn," Fisher finished, "it was one push too far from Himself and one decision too hasty from Rab. Throw in the worry over the wee bairn, the Lady's sorrow and the fact that young Bruce is as nasty a lad as I've ever known, and there you have it."

"He's that bad then—Bruce? It's no just losing his mother?"

"No, no. Young Bruce is like Red Roddy, evil old booger that he is. His mother was the only jewel in that clan's crown by a long way, Callumn."

"The tinker business, Fisher? Surely Rab knows how touchy the old man is about them? I've often wondered about that."

"You and half the glen. The old ones speak of closeness and mystery, but the Cailleach's possibly the only one with the truth and I'll tell you now, you'll get very little out of her."

"Aye, your right there, Fisher. She's the only female I've ever come across who barely needs a tongue!"

"He'll mend though, Calumn?"

"Thanks to the Cailleach's prompt arrival, he will."

"The tinker lass, according to Jessie, was the only one with sense when they found MacNishe. By her running across the moors the old woman was ready when I got there."

"I thought the tinker was in the cellar, Fisher? Och man I'll away to the Cailleach before you confuse me even more. I need to thank her for saving my patient. Her infusions, the enforced bed rest, and perhaps her Gaelic company and their shared history steadied him till I returned. I've seen to him since and he's out of any immediate danger, though he'll bear watching for a while, just in case, and he needs no more emotional upsets. "

Rab watched the doctor leave the distillery and guessed he'd been with Fisher. Those two, with his father, had been part of his life since he'd left the nursery. His mother used to call them, 'The Highland Musketeers'. He stifled a sigh as he looked at the portrait of his mother on the far wall. He'd always been closer to her than to his father, but she'd understood and loved them both. Any conflict between them and she'd laugh them out of it. Laughter: they'd seen little of that lately.

Well something would have to be done or the old man would go to his grave. Rab looked over the sheets of figures on his desk but couldn't settle. Turning to the big window behind, he looked out at Loch Nishe. His father had rearranged the office in his time to keep his back to the window, saying his own father had spent too much time looking at his estate instead of working to save it. The distillery had nearly gone under during his grandfather's reign. Drink, cards, women and neglect of the workings had eaten away at the money. Only his grandfather drowning during an inebriated fishing trip on the loch had stopped bankruptcy. Luckily for the estate, MacNishe had proved to be an excellent businessman. He and Fisher restored Kevinishe to prosperity. A knock on the door brought him back to the present, as Fisher entered.

"You'll have had a craic with the doctor then, Fisher?"

"He was worrying about your father and easing his guilt with a dram."

"Guilt?"

"Aye, Rab, he was thrown by the fact that the one time he was needed he wasn't here."

"That would have saddened him. They're close those two."

"Been right the way since the schoolroom, Rab."

"What did he say?"

"He's trying to find an answer, same as us."

"What do you think?" Rab knew what Fisher thought but needed to hear it out loud.

"You'll no like it, Rab."

"So he's to come back? Come on, out with it, man."

"MacNishe is a distillery man. Dammit he saved the place from ruin. He thought only of you after the accident. It helped you but was the worst thing for him."

"That's what I thought you'd say."

"Look here now, I'm no saying you're doing a bad job, Rab. It's just another pair of hands could lighten your load and maybe give him back something to occupy himself. He's gone from a full life to that of an old woman."

In spite of himself Rab felt the laughter bubbling up. "God, Fisher, I'd like to hear you say that to his face!"

"Well you may laugh. He'd have the head bitten off me!"

"You know it might not be very comfortable—the two of us here."

"Aye, I was considering that. How about he came back to the stillroom with me, once Callum gives his permission? That would ease him in gently like and give you a bit more time for your own worries."

"You miss nothing, Fisher."

"Man, it's no trouble for me to be here day or night, for I've no ties, but a family man has aye to keep his eye on things. The Lady Sarah is far from home, and you and she have worries over the bairn. No wishing to speak out of turn, but the extra time could be useful."

"See that." Rab pointed up the glen. "The doctor must have a thirst on him—he's on his way back."

Nodding in agreement, Fisher said, "The Cailleach was likely no at home."

"Now there's a strange connection: a modern man of learning and an old woman full of hocus-pocus. Born sooner and she'd have been burnt as a witch!"

"Well now, Rab, the witch was the saving of MacNishe in the absence of the doctor, and I heard tell it was likely the same herbs she gave him as the doctor's pills and potions."

"We'll never know I suppose, but, whatever, I'm indebted to her."

On arrival at Kevinishe House later the same day the doctor found the Laird trimming his beard. Callumn busied himself with his case while remarking, "I know it's only October but it feels cold enough for snow out there this morning."

"There now, Calumn, I'm done." MacNishe ignored his friend's weather warning. "Since you're here, you can clear this lot to the table," he said, "and then come out with whatever you're thinking." The wry smile on the doctor's face showed MacNishe he'd guessed right. He listened carefully to the doctor's advice, annoyed that he'd not been part of the various discussions at the distillery, but honest enough to see that all three men were acting for the best.

"So that's the recipe for my future health is it? How do you know it'll work? Rab and I will then have two places to square up to one another."

"True enough, MacNishe, but then I don't really think that either of you want yourself in the grave, so you'll both have to try to see the other's point of view."

"It would be preferable to being at loggerheads with him."

"Good. That's the main problem, MacNishe, but you've others on your mind I'm thinking."

"Well there's David and…"

"Lady Sarah and the tinker?"

"Precisely, Calumn. She's got it into her head that the girl was 'sent' to help her keep young David from harm. It makes no sense, but she'll not see reason."

"Does Bruce really wish his stepbrother harm?"

"I think it's more jealousy than anything else, but it needs watching. So there you have it. I've told her she can have as many new nursemaids as she likes and Rab would accept anyone but the tinker girl. There's no sensible way out."

"There might just be."

"Let's hear it then, Calumn. I'm sick of the whole business."

"As I understand it, Rab decided on the jail when he thought he was dealing with a tinker lad—by all accounts an honest mistake. He'd not lose face now if he changed his mind on account of her turning out to be a lassie. Then there's the thought of her being another interest for Lady Sarah. A sick wee bairn can be very wearing. Perhaps the lass could cheer her up."

"That makes good sense, Calumn. It's neat. A way out for everyone."

"Well, I'll leave you to sort it. You can get up now but don't overdo it. I'll see you in a few days."

Jessie bustled in with the laden tea tray, placing it carefully on the sturdy low table in front of the fire, where two massive logs were spitting and crackling away. Logs were burning today, as Lady Sarah was taking tea with the men and she disliked peat smoke. Like all the other main rooms on the ground floor, the drawing room was furnished with substantial oak furniture hewn from the lower reaches of the estate and carved by the distillery coopers. Jessie ran her hand over one of the two massive sideboards flanking the walls, waxed till you could see your face in it. She checked the decanters and crystal glasses were all in order. No MacNishe wife had yet succeeded in removing the masculine feel of the room. At the sound of the front door she made a quick check of her tray and went to tell the mistress tea was served. Crossing the hall, she saw that the doctor and Fisher were with Rab and the now recovered Laird; so more china would be needed.

The four men settled themselves, leaving the fireside seat for Lady Sarah, who felt the cold.

"A dram to put a cinder in your tea, Calumn?"

"I can't think why not, MacNishe. It's a rough day out there. I'll not be the only one surely?"

"Not at all. We'll gladly join you." MacNishe studied the three men while he poured the whisky. He was lucky in his companions: Calumn and Fisher always there for him and Rab a son to be proud of, even if they did disagree on many topics. Good strong Highland men all of them, though Calumn was a mite scrawny. Fisher now was like one of the ancient firs that adorned the hillside behind the house. Hair not quite as black as in his youth but still thick, features that looked as though they'd been hewn from Beinn Nishe, and still no sign of a stoop on those massive shoulders that had allowed him to win throwing events in the Highland Games. MacNishe felt, if he could just get past this last hurdle, things might settle down; Lady Sarah entered the room.

"Ah, just in time, my dear. Is Jessie with—need I ask, there you are, Jessie. We're ready and waiting for you both, and I trust Cook has catered for our appetites?"

"As if she wouldna, sir. When have you ever gone hungry? Not even when you were small and a nursery tea not five minutes away."

"You see what comes to a man when all about him have shared his childhood. Sarah, my dear, lend your backing for a sick man."

"I do believe, MacNishe, you are trading on the 'sick'. You seem to have recovered both your health and your good humour." Lady Sarah smiled as she spoke.

"Now when am I ever…? Jessie, was that a sneeze I heard?"

"No, Father, Jessie just spoke for us all with the most expressive snort. Come on, Jessie let's get this tea on the go. All this talking has given me an appetite."

"Have you had a lot of business to discuss today then, MacNishe?" Lady Sarah had been primed and gave him the prompt he required.

"Not business as such. Just thrashing out a few problems to make the future easier and to settle the worries of these three old women here."

"Now what have you been up to?"

"Calumn here says I'm getting lazy and need some exercise and interest to keep my heart up to scratch. Not that I'd agree, but Rab has suggested I come back to the distillery as long as I keep out of his way." Smiling at his son, MacNishe felt that this modest explanation would save Rab's pride, and he could see that the two older men were nodding appreciatively. A little humbling might help the process.

"It won't be too much for you?"

"No, not a bit, Lady Sarah. As his doctor, I positively commend it."

"Now the rest is, perhaps, trickier," MacNishe continued.

"The rest, Father?"

"Rab, it's nothing to do with the distillery. But awkward for all that." MacNishe knew, by the sullen expression on Rab's face, how difficult it was going to be. Actually he could almost feel sorry for his son, but this whole thing had to be put to rest.

"MacNishe now, no more disagreements. Mind what happened last time." The doctor, having played his part, turned his attention to the tea, accepting a second scone from Jessie, and ladling on the salt butter and homemade bramble jam.

"Calumn, you can't blame Rab for his decision. He thought we were dealing with some rough tinker lad, who'd attacked Bruce, and he did what any father would have done. After all the lad was trespassing and..."

"But—but it was a little girl."

"Quite right, Sarah my dear, though Rab didn't know that when he decided on the jail and you have to admit, when the culprit ran a second time, his fate was sealed. Of course, if Rab had known it was a girl, he'd have given no such order." MacNishe felt that, since he'd humbled himself over the return to the distillery, Rab now had a way of backing down without losing face, so it would be a fair exchange.

"Being a girl certainly clouds the issue, though she was still trespassing, Father."

"Children can be thoughtless, Rab, and it's not as though she was thieving—a few brambles from the outer hedge."

"Quite, but it had better not happen again."

"As I said, youngsters, and that includes Bruce, simply don't think their actions through. Playing with the pram and rocking it were surely no more than high spirits, but I agree with you. No more child's play. It's too dangerous for David. Luckily this time we got away with it."

"What about another time?" Lady Sarah asked

"That's what I'm determined to avoid, my dear. The incident has shown us two things. David must never be left unguarded from others or even from himself as he starts to walk. Bruce and the tinker—what's her name, Fisher?"

"Cate."

"The parents?"

"Dead, I believe, MacNishe."

"Anyway, as I was saying, there's bad feeling between Bruce and the girl, and, at the same time, Rab, you and I would have wished Bruce to land the boy, as we thought, as good if not better than he got."

"That's hardly fair, Father. You don't learn to fight on your own."

"Exactly so, Rab. That's the first thing. We're being unfair to Bruce keeping him here on his own. What about Fettes School for him after Christmas? Give it some thought."

"Now then, Sarah, more tea I think."

"You've settled everything, MacNishe?"

"That we have, Sarah. Jessie, more tea if you please. Another snifter in yours, Calumn?"

Apart from MacNishe, the others were all surprised when Lady Sarah rose, excused herself, and left them. All but the Laird could see no sense in her abrupt departure.

"Sarah? Now then what's the matter?" Rab called after his wife.

"Rab, the second thing is a domestic matter between the pair of you," MacNishe answered for her.

"I've no idea…"

"You've not forgotten she wanted the lass as a sort of companion for David? Now it's not for the likes of us to make that sort of decision. You'd better go to her and we'll finish the boiled-up cake and shortbread on your behalf. No need upsetting, Cook." MacNishe almost felt sorry for his son as they watched him follow his wife from the room.

"You'll have pushed him too far, MacNishe"

"I'm having no part in it, Calumn."

"Mebbe so, but you'll be betting on Lady Sarah delivering, if I'm no mistaken," Fisher stated quietly.

"One of these days, Fisher, that cunning mind of yours will get you into trouble. For now, save Jessie's hands and put more wood on the fire for us. You're right of course. Once Rab has been persuaded, I know the old woman will be only too glad to let the lass come into service. It's no life for her on the road with the tinkers or holed up in The Black House, what with the language barrier and the lack of company. Rest assured, if Rab is persuaded, young David will have his nursemaid, and then a measure of peace should return to this house."

4

It was 10, March 1903 and David's fourth birthday. The late winter sun shone through Lady Sarah's sitting room bathing her in a shaft of light as she listened to David and Cate playing together in the corridor. She'd been right. The girl had joined the household instead of being sent to jail, and David adored her. The only problem, as usual, had been Bruce. Actually it was Rab's fault. Having given in over the girl, he'd refused to send Bruce to school until he was older. Instead he'd eventually installed a tutor, Mr. Wilkins. Bruce was no scholar, and during the last year and a half the poor man had done nothing but complain to Rab. MacNishe was now becoming irritated with the three of them. Cate also had a hard time. Bruce made a terrible fuss when she became nursemaid, and then he'd taken every opportunity to bully her. It was as though he'd turned his antagonism from David to Cate. Lady Sarah sighed. She knew the girl was being bullied, but at least David was safe with her around. A knock on the door interrupted her thoughts and she turned as MacNishe joined her.

"I've just seen the youngsters on their way out."

"Yes, MacNishe. Cate's arrival has changed our lives. Though she's a strange girl—not at all what I supposed a tinker to be."

"Indeed, there's something about her—her interest in reading for instance, Sarah. Who'd have thought it? Someone with her background!"

"Yes, she seemed to like words from the very beginning, listening while I read David his nursery rhymes at bedtime and saying them word perfect to him during the day. Then, when I started the alphabet, she wanted to know more."

"And I found her in the library not long after she arrived."

"What was she doing?"

"That's what I asked her and she gave me that look of hers, as if I should have known better. Said the covers were soft and smelt like saddles and she'd like to be inside that world."

"So she couldn't actually read?"

"No. I remember it was Robert Louis Stevenson's *Catriona*—apt I thought, for Cate can be an abbreviation for that. So I read her the first few chapters and she was enthralled. Sarah, I don't mind admitting her joy in the reading has brought me pleasure ever since."

"She gives me pleasure too—in so many ways." Lady Sarah rose and crossed to the window. "Let's see where they go—the loch probably. Oh, I see Bruce has come out."

"Does he still torment her?" MacNishe asked as he joined his daughter-in-law at the window.

"Oh yes: a knock, a bruise, a nip, a locked door to make her late, a disappearing item to land her in trouble. It goes on I'm afraid. Watch—he'll check up here. If he sees me at the window he'll go the other way."

"You're right. Off he goes to the stables. Damn me. It's time his devilment was stopped. Rab must see that."

"No, MacNishe. He doesn't see. Bruce may not be clever in the schoolroom, but he's very cunning outside it. He knows his father believes in him, and why wouldn't he? Bruce is always perfectly behaved in front of him, but avoids you because he knows you see through him."

"Well, that's the truth of it, Sarah, and it makes my heart sore to say it. But I'll tackle Rab nonetheless."

"You'll make yourself ill if you start quarrelling with Rab again. No, you must let Bruce alone. One day he'll go too far."

"But you were the one who used to worry about him, Sarah."

"That was when David was in danger, but now I know he's safe. It's hard on the girl, but she was hired as a watchdog, and it works. It'll be something else that brings Bruce down. He just can't help being downright nasty to someone or something. It's his nature. By the way, are you certain about the dog? Won't he be too boisterous for David? And what about Bruce, MacNishe?"

"It's time the little lad had an animal, and this breed is good with youngsters. Bruce has the gun dogs, so I doubt there'll be any ill feeling. Anyway, he's not much better with animals than he is with people."

"Well, if you're sure, MacNishe. The gamekeeper has gone to fetch it?"

"Should be here for the birthday tea—an extra surprise after all the presents this morning, and a sensible time."

"Sensible?"

"The pup will be tired after the journey. David will be ready for sleep after his exciting day, so they can have a play and then Cate can take charge. She's a way with animals. Gregor says she's often in the stables with the other dogs and even the horses don't mind her being close, unlike Bruce."

"I'm sure David will love it. Thank you for thinking of it."

"It's time he started to have some of the normal estate pursuits. Rest assured it will cause David no harm. At his age he should have a pony, but that's not possible for him. He deserves whatever happiness he can get." MacNishe made to take his leave, hesitated and turned back.

"You know, Sarah, it worries me. I can see the fecklessness of my father in young Bruce. Mind you, as Fisher keeps reminding me, there are two sides to heredity, and Red Rhoddy McPhail, Bruce's maternal grandfather, is as evil an old booger as you could find. Feckless and evil—what a package for a future Laird! Thank God I'll not be here to see him let loose on my beloved estate. I'm off to the study. A good dram should chase these depressing thoughts away".

When Cate brought her charge back to the nursery that afternoon, both of them cold now from the snow underfoot, Nanny had tea laid out.

"Now then, Master David, what do you mean you can't eat any tea?"

"Nanny, I'm too 'cited. What is Gramps bringing?"

"And what makes you think he's bringing anything?"

"He said this morning there was another surprise for tea."

"Haven't you just had that, with this fancy tea all laid out? Look—your favourites: salmon with baby tatties and then clootie dumpling with cream." Probably up half the night with that rich fare if he ate it all. Nanny, Miss Mary Richards, had seen it all before. Many's a time she'd had to mop up after Master Rab and that wee devil Bruce, and, if the Laird was bringing more excitement at this time of day, there'd be trouble in the night. That was not the nursery way. The knock on the door and David's excited cries brought her to her feet as MacNishe entered.

"Not disturbing you, Nanny?"

"No, no." She was relieved to see he'd come empty-handed, though the wee lad would be fair disappointed.

"Gramps, Gramps, where's my surprise? You promised."

"Why don't you open the door, and your surprise just might come in."

At his words the other three looked at him in astonishment. What sort of present was this? The two children were puzzled, and Nanny hoped her guess was mistaken. It would never do—not right in her nursery. Not right at all!

'Go on then, David. Open the door, lad, and see for yourself."

Cate took David's hand and together they slowly opened the door. Nothing happened.

"Gramps?" David turned a puzzled frown to his grandfather and just then felt something soft and wet on his legs. Looking down he saw a bundle of yellow fur. "For me, Gramps? For my very own?"

"Yours indeed. Cate will help. Now you'll have two playmates. Happy fourth birthday, David! I'll leave you to it, Nanny. He's to be a pet, remember—stay in the nursery. He'll never be a gun dog.

"Come now, David, what do you say?"

"Thank you, Gramps."

"There we are then. He's a fine yellow Labrador pup, and all for your very own. He'll need his own bed and things."

"I'll see to that, sir. I'll take care of it for Master David."

"Well, I'll leave you to it, Nanny. Good night to you all."

On one of their daily walks, Cate holding David's hand, they made their way round to the front of the house, Rory lolloping on behind, paws still too big for his body, and now a devoted member of the trio. Since Bruce was on his way to the loch they'd take their walk in the other direction today, down the main drive. Not too far, of course. David's legs couldn't manage much. Funny that. The tinker bairns used to waddle around all day. But then David was different in so many ways. She didn't know why, but she feared for him, though not because of Bruce, who didn't bother with his stepbrother now that he had her to bully. Remembering the times she had to run from the tinker boys, it didn't seem so bad when she had Bruce's nastiness to put up with, except she couldn't get away from him here.

She did have a day, now and again, to go and see the Cailleach. And that was the other thing that bothered her. Before, she could roam the moors, shore and mountain whenever she liked. Here the walls of the Big House seemed sometimes like the jail she'd nearly been sent to. Turning back to the house, she thought it was no wonder she'd been amazed when she'd first seen it. The drive, as she'd learnt to call it, was long, with its twists and turns hiding the house from the road. She liked the crunchy sound of the wee stones under her feet, but was wary of them if horses or carriage wheels went by. The drive was bordered with rhododendrons. They had big purple, pink or white flowers in the late spring and early summer. Shame none of them had scents. Behind them were pines that nodded at the November sky heavy with the threat of snow. The other walk she liked was over the rolling lawns that led to the loch, where all their fish were caught.

Kevinishe House, however, just sat there big and solid like Beinn Nishe, but the mountain welcomed you in all its coats. It could be green, or a sea of purple when the heather was out, or black with the sleeting rain, or, like now, with the winter snows, whiter than the white basins in the nursery. She loved it. The grey house, though, always looked the same: big and cold.

Mind, if the outside of the house wasn't to her liking, the inside was worse. Even after all this time she'd trouble finding her way, with all the different stairs and rooms. Mostly she kept to the nursery floor and Lady Sarah's sitting room. She'd always liked that room. Maybe one day she'd have something like it somewhere. Sometimes she went to the Laird's tower room, to read to him. She liked that too, and the library with its walls lined with books. The stories and pictures they held! Though hard to understand all the words, they took her far away from the glen, further than she'd ever travelled with the tinkers. It was a great joy, tucked up in a bed of her own with her book and candle. There she found another world.

"Cate, my legs are all tired." David pulled at her hand for attention.

"We're on our way, Davy lad. Home for tea, eh?" Looking down at the boy, she smiled. Davy was the first person she'd ever loved, and she knew he loved her. They spent all their days together. Outside, whenever the weather allowed, they wandered through the gardens, woods and stables close to the house. She wasn't supposed to take him further for fear of him falling, but she was always careful. No hurt would come to him as long as he was with her. At the thought of it she knelt down beside him and smiled. He was such a bonnie wee lad and he was nearly all hers. "Come away, my wee laddie. It's time for tea, so it is. No, Rory, no jumping. Sit! There's a good wee dog."

"Tea for Nanny, David, Cate and Rory. No tea for Bruce." The boy's shake of his golden head said much more than his words.

"Don't you worry yourself, Bruce gets no nursery tea with us, and we're no to feed Rory either, or we'll both be in trouble."

" 'Nasty horrid things, dogs'. "

"Aye, David, that's exactly what Nanny will say. Come on now, there she is."

Waiting at the front door, watching the pair of them, Nanny knew she was grateful for the peace of the last two years. They'd all thought her Ladyship was mad to bring that filthy tinker into the nursery but she had the right of it. That wee lass never took her eyes off young Master David and she was far more help than any nursemaid had ever been. Quick, she was. Only ever needed telling once. She was good company in the evenings, making the burden of that precious wee boy lighter to bear somehow. What a shame there'd be no more bairns in the nursery. Well it would be some years before this one was grown, and then when she was no longer needed, she'd just away to her sister in Glasgow, but she'd miss her comforts here.

Another Christmas had come and gone and January brought storms and trials to Kevinishe House. Now in March young David had succumbed to the croup. In the nursery, Cate, sharing the constant night watch over the sick boy, eased her cramped bones, eyes ever watchful of Davy's frail fretful body in the bed, ears poised for the choking cough that, when it came, would blot out the juddering rise and fall of Nanny's snores. Somehow Cate knew the crisis was near, and feared it. As the child's whistled breathing turned once more to frightened gasps for air, Cate was on her feet.

Cradling the weak body upright she massaged the back, putting all her pent-up love into the movement, knowing all she could do now was provide a comforting pair of arms. He was beyond mending. "Nanny', she whispered. Then louder, "Nanny, get Lady Sarah." Feeling Davy's body slackening, she shouted, "Naaanniiee!"

Jerking awake from the deep sleep of exhaustion, the woman tottered to her feet, took one look at the frightened girl, and scurried to do her bidding.

A week later, Cate shivered as a gust of wind stole under the cover of her black cape. Most of the other women, including Lady Sarah, had stayed behind, as tradition demanded, but she refused to let wee Davy go to his grave without her. After his death that night she'd sat by the coffin in Kevinishe House as the tiny body was 'waked' and all the customary measures had been taken: curtains drawn, mirrors covered, clocks stopped, everything done to protect the living from the soul of the dead returning. As if that poor wee boy's soul could bring grief to anyone! With Rory whining softly at her side, she clutched the cape to her body, defying the wind, and shrank against the graveyard gate. Only the men were allowed beyond this. She waited as the tiny coffin was lowered into the ground and the chief mourners sprinkled earth on it, turned and walked away.

Cate watched them leaving, villagers parting to make a respectful pathway. Leading them was MacNishe, in full Highland dress with a black sash, looking the Laird he was, fond of the dead child yet unable to accept weakness in his line. Hurrying to comfort his grieving wife was Master Rab all in black, wanting his turn at the Lairdship, at odds with his father, but thankful still to have one living son. They all passed her except Fisher, who halted and patted her on the shoulder before carrying on, and then Bruce, who stopped and stared.

Cate understood the gloating look he threw her. She wished she could shout to the world that this evil booger was no true mourner, but hiding his joy behind the funeral face: at last the unwanted stepbrother gone, herself no longer needed at the Big House, and Lady Sarah, like as not away back to her father in England, weeping for her dead child and nursing the knowledge there'd be no more babies.

"Oh yes, Master Bruce, I know your thoughts," she whispered to herself as she watched him, solemn faced, shaking hands. Cate could feel her rage increase as he made his way to the dark plumed carriage. One day, one day, she'd—her fourteen year old mind could only think of scratching his eyes out, but that would do for now.

She waited as the villagers drifted through the gates in ones and twos to make their way to the wake in the old barn by the distillery. Thinking less now about the dead child they hardly knew but more of the weighty hams, sides of beef, bannocks and the right to several legal drams in a proper glass to mark the sad occasion. Oh aye, rivers of Craeg Dhu they'd drink today and tomorrow they'd have sore heads when they got back to the making of that same malt which fed and clothed them all, and to the quiet thieving of it whenever they could.

50

As the stragglers left, and the gravediggers squabbled over shovels, Cate moved towards the open grave and knelt by the damp side, the dog sitting with her.

"Oh, Davy lad, you're safe now, but what of me?" At last the horror of the past few days seemed real: the nights she, Lady Sarah and Nanny had wiped the sweating brow, eased him into dry clothing, held the steaming kettles by the bed to help the choking, made the bread poultices for his chest, and all for nothing. The bad lungs, that neither the doctor nor the Cailleach could cure, had taken her beloved Davy.

"Rory, what're we going to do? What'll happen to us both? Where will we find someone to love us the way yon wee fellow did?"

The arrival of the diggers, ready to cover the grave, set her feet running with no thought as to where she was going. As the rain grew heavier Cate made for the cave, dog, as always, at heel. Sitting behind the curtain of water she seemed to hear Davy's name in every splash. For almost four years now she'd been at his side every waking moment: time that had changed her life, taken her from a ragged tinker girl to Davy's nursemaid. And what good was that now? Her fine uniform dresses and, when she remembered, her fine speaking, the learning and the books she'd begun to love: what use were they all after today? She hadn't wanted to leave her old roaming life, and now she didn't want to go back to it.

"Come on, dog, we'll settle here. I've no wish to join the wake." As she sought comfort from the animal's warm body her mind drifted to the time she'd found the cave, tucked into her beloved mountain. She'd followed the deer that day to the pools below, where an eagle had spooked them. With nothing better to do, she'd climbed higher, guided by the sound of the rushing water. A wee brown bird had caught her eye and she'd watched it bobbing up and down as it disappeared behind the curtain of water. Tracking it she'd discovered the ledge that ran right behind the waterfall and opened out into the small cave, with the remains of an old heather bed. Ever since then, whenever she could, she'd hidden up here. But that was in her old tinker days. Davy too was now in the past. Finally her tears came. Sensing her distress, Rory licked her cheek reminding her of a problem. "Rory, you'll have to go back to the Laird. I'll be for the jail for stealing otherwise. That's how I first saw Davy". Saying his name was too much for girl and dog. They clung together grieving, while far below in the cemetery the gravediggers wiped their shovels.

Breakfast the following day in Kevinishe House was a sombre affair. MacNishe sat watching Jessie bringing in the food, before he questioned the maid. "Is Lady Sarah breakfasting upstairs today?"

"Yes, sir. She's that upset, what with the funeral yesterday and then Cate disappearing."

"We could certainly have done without that. I can understand why the girl was distraught—might want time to herself. But overnight…?"

"She's no with the Cailleach then, Sir?"

"No, I rode up there early this morning, before breakfast. She suggested asking the diggers."

"You'll get little sense there, I'm afraid," Rab commented as he entered the room. "The distillery is manned by waxen-faced ghosts of men this morning. Unable to remember their names, never mind what happened yesterday. Fisher and I are the only two with clear heads. I've left him to take over while I have my breakfast."

"I'll go to the long field and see the tinkers when I've finished mine, Rab. That's where she'll be, most likely," MacNishe said hopefully.

"Look, Father, perhaps we…"

"Should leave her there? Is that what you're thinking, Rab? Cast her out now she's no longer any use to us?"

"That's a harsh way of putting it."

"No doubt, but it's a harsh thought to have, and perhaps you agree with Bruce that she's stolen the dog too."

"Now I didn't say that. The animal probably wandered away during the service. After all, none of us noticed much yesterday. Neither the girl nor the dog were at the wake in the barn, you said, Jessie?"

"That's right, Master Rab. I looked for her special like. She'd had precious little food or sleep, come to that, in the days leading up to…well she definitely wasna there."

"Right then, Jessie, get Cook to make us something light for lunch and send it over to the distillery. If all and sundry are worse than useless today we'd better keep an eye on things, Rab, we don't want them scorching the malt or falling into the mash tun."

Later, riding to the distillery after his visit to the Long Field, the Laird's thoughts were jumbled. Did he believe the tinkers? He didn't know. There'd definitely been no sign of either the girl or the dog in or around the camp, and he'd spoken loud enough for Cate to hear, had she been there. The tinkers' indifference to her whereabouts seemed genuine enough. Still, now they knew the dog was missing, they might just put themselves about to find it and claim the reward. But it was a sad state of things when a lively, intelligent young girl was of less value than a pampered household pet.

He would certainly miss her if she left. He'd taught her to ride, perhaps foolishly in view of Bruce's anger, but riding was one of his own great pleasures and he no longer rode with his grandson. He simply couldn't abide the way the boy treated animals, and their outings inevitably ended up with him disciplining the boy. That led to ill feeling between Rab and himself. So Cate had filled the gap, and she'd shown him things he'd forgotten about the estate: where the golden eagles nested, which hills the old stag was roaming at any one time, and when the salmon had returned to spawn. He often felt that, much as she loved David, she'd rather have been free to roam the mountain. Perhaps that's what she'd done yesterday, and the dog would have followed her.

She'd be safe enough as long as she stayed within the estate boundaries, but he'd heard that some industrial fellow, up from London, was at Laggan House with a shooting party and, God knows, some of them knew little or nothing about shooting. According to the ghillies that took them out, one of them all but shot the ear off a beater, who was more than happy, once Calumn had stitched him up, with the silver that crossed his palm for his unfortunate accident! Well, it was too late to look further. He'd have to wait and see if the tinkers came up with anything. With his workforce hung over, he needed to be at the distillery. Rab could ride out later for another look if the girl was still missing.

Back in the kitchen at Kevinishe House Bruce was delivering his thoughts on the missing girl. "I told them at breakfast she'd stolen the dog. It's what tinkers do. By now she'll have sold it to one of those men at the camp and he'll sell it on away from the glen." Bruce munched away at his shortbread completely unaware that his audience was staring at him in disgust.

"Well now, Master Bruce, I think Cate loved the dog."

"Rubbish, she's a tinker brat. They don't have feelings."

"If you're going to be nasty, Master Bruce, I'll thank you to get out of my kitchen. Family meals are served upstairs, so they are." Today of all days, Cook simply couldn't abide the boy.

Looking at the others, Mrs. Mac the housekeeper, fat old Cook and the equally ancient Nanny, as they supped their mid-morning tea, Bruce became aware that for once he was no longer being indulged. They were actually taking the tinker's side. "Now look here, she's just a filthy…."

"Master Bruce, if you were still in my nursery I'd get you to wash your mouth out with soap. It's horrid you are about Cate. Don't forget we all know how you bullied her: you twice her size, and her never telling. I've seen the bruises and the harm you've done her. Right careful of David…" Nanny wiped her tears at the mention of his name.

"You may well start snivelling, Nanny. I'll tell you this." He glared at the three accusing faces. "When I'm Laird I'll see to it none of you will be here. Anyway, with an empty nursery, Nanny, you'll be gone by the end of the week, so there." That said, he deliberately emptied the dregs of his tea on the table and sauntered out of the room.

As he left, Cook looked round her beloved kitchen. She'd been there so long she barely remembered her life before. Ten she'd been, and so frightened of the then Cook. Hard it was at first, all day scrubbing at the sinks. How many years of her life had she done nothing but scrub? Well, God willing, she'd be in her grave before Bruce ever became Laird. This large old room was her home now. The huge range gleaming in the chimneybreast had replaced the big open fire and roasting spits they'd had when she'd started. The copper pans gleaming on the walls, dressers filled with good china and plate racks stacked with everyday crockery had never changed. No, there was no other life for her than here. God willing, the next move would be to meet her maker.

"There, there, Nanny, don't let him upset you. We all know what he's like, and Jessie said that even Master Rab looked displeased when he'd gone on about Cate at breakfast time," Mrs. Mac said, breaking the awkward silence.

"Well," Nanny sniffed. "Well, Mrs. Mac, it's not before time if you ask me. Many's a day I've told them all he was a bad boy in the nursery, but then he'd be nice as one of Cook's pies in front of them. Mind you, he has the rights of it. There's no job for me now."

"There could be more babies. Lady Sarah still has time."

"No, Cook, there'll be no more. They'll take no chances." Nanny answered.

"I think we must wait and see. It's too soon, with everyone grieving, to think about what happens next. We'll all know in good time." Mrs. Mac, having given what comfort she could, left the two older women to their fears and went to check on their mistress. With Cate missing, Lady Sarah would need help, as she'd come to depend on the girl in so many ways.

Rab, annoyed that to please his father he too was now searching for the girl, rode as if the faster he went the easier it would be to forget the sight of that tiny oak box being lowered into the grave the day before. It had all been so quick. A cough, a cold, a few days of high fever, and his younger son was gone. How cruel fate was, after all the care they'd taken of him! What use had it been? The old man had taken it hard, Sarah was distraught, and now Cate was missing.

He could see the irony in his searching for her, but he'd long forgotten the jail episode. She'd done exactly what Sarah had said she'd do. David had been safe and happy with Cate, and for that he'd easily forgotten his initial misgivings. Still, here she was being a problem again. It was Gregor at the stables who'd noticed the absence of the dog. The thought of the animal brought the breakfast conversation and its unpleasant aftermath back. Had Bruce been serious when he'd suggested that Cate had stolen the dog? Serious or not, it had set the old man off, and even Jessie, serving them breakfast, had had her say.

Though he was loath to admit it, this was not the first time he'd been uneasy about one of Bruce's comments. Perhaps his father's advice about sending Bruce away to school had been right after all. Mind you, with David gone, would Sarah need Cate anymore, or even Nanny, come to that? In fact maybe now was the time for him to take Sarah to Edinburgh for a break and let Bruce finish his education there? Make a fresh start all round.

They'd always known death was a possibility for David because of the haemophilia, but not so young and not from a bloody cold! Distraught, he rode on, his anguish masked with anger at having to search for the girl, however devoted she'd been to David.

Making her way back to Kevinishe House, Cate was so deep in thought about her next move she never heard the hooves until it was too late. She looked up frozen in horror as Bruce rode straight at her. Only Rory's wild barking made her move, but she stumbled and fell and, though the horse attempted to jump over her, its back hooves caught her outstretched leg. The pain was intense as she struggled to get up, but it was no use. As she sank into unconsciousness, she sensed rather than heard Bruce's satisfied snigger.

Whether it was cold or pain or the dog's tongue on her face that brought her round she didn't know, but it was pain she felt now. By hanging onto the dog's collar she tried to ease her body up but let go quickly when blackness threatened. Later, when she came to again, she tried to remember through the pain. Yes, the funeral, lack of food and sleep during Davy's last days: no wonder she felt faint. Though struggling with pain, she knew she must return to Kevinishe House with the dog, to say goodbye to those who had been kind to her. Afterwards it would be back to the Cailleach until summer came. Slowly she slipped into darkness again.

She was cold. Where was she? Oh yes, summer and the tinkers. It would soon be time to sell the clothes pegs and heather bunches with the tinker women while the men traded horses, mending pots and pans between bouts of drinking and having the odd boxing match if they could get good odds. Her body hurt. She couldn't go with the tinkers. No. No. She wasn't going anywhere with the tinkers. She'd been dreaming. Had it all been a bad dream? Surely even Bruce wouldn't have ridden her down deliberately? But he had. How was she to get back to Kevinishe House? What would they think of her? She drifted away again. *There was the red-headed woman with the plaid running down the hill towards her. She could hear the soft-spoken words of comfort and the love that came with them and soon the pain was not so bad.* Rory's soft whining brought her round again, and she shifted her arm to gather him close for warmth.

On the adjoining estate, Laggan House was in turmoil. Not only had two of their daft English guests got themselves lost on the hillside but they'd also returned with a wounded girl and her dog. Dinwoodie was furious. The last thing he needed was to upset the local gentry, and that young idiot, Lord Abermarle, had strayed onto Kevinishe land. Dinwoodie began to wish he'd never rented the Laggan estate. It was all fine and grand for his wife to set her sights on the young Lord for their daughter, Vicky, but, damn it all, he was a buffoon, as well as penniless! They'd insisted they hadn't ridden the young girl down, although with hoof marks on her, somebody obviously had. Perhaps the doctor, when he came, would know who she was.

As Dinwoodie watched the doctor, having splinted the leg, ride away, he cursed under his breath. He'd have to send the groom over to Kevinishe House to explain why their nursemaid was lying upstairs. Ordinarily it would have been a good means of introduction to the local Laird, but, according to the doctor, they'd just buried the younger son of the house, so calling was out of the question. Still, they needed to be told of the girl's whereabouts and a message of condolence could accompany the note.

Sighing, he turned indoors. The late Queen had started something with this craze for all things Scottish. It might have suited her and Prince Albert in the mountainous Highlands, but he missed the foundry and his own comfortable homes in Glasgow and London. Of course, Gwennie was hell bent on doing 'the right thing' for their beloved daughter. Shouldn't have called her Victoria though. Gave the women in his life snobbish ideas and he had to fend off too many useless aristocratic fops. All they wanted to do was go clambering across the countryside shooting things or chasing them on horseback. They'd be far better off looking after their fortunes—of course that's where he came in.

Well he'd be damned if he'd sit back and watch any one of them squander his hard-earned wealth. When the women finally made their choice he'd see to it that Vick's share was firmly tied up and hope to God that his son Michael would find himself a sensible young woman and wouldn't take up with all this club and gaming business like these lordly young fools.

How different his own youth had been! Finding no work in Glasgow he and his father had trekked south to England. There they'd worked long hours in the charcoal industry in the Weald, before joining a friend in his blacksmith's shop. When the friend died they'd inherited the smithy. He'd continued working with his father, developing his own skills, finding his true calling in the wrought iron work for ornate gates and railings. He'd started with an order here and there, still in the blacksmith's shop. Then slowly his part of the business had increased and he'd employed other craftsmen as the desire for fancy railings and iron decoration became fashionable. Finally putting it on an industrial footing had been challenging, but he'd had the right idea at the right time and he'd prospered beyond all his dreams. Now he was determined the fruits of all that toil were not going to go into the pockets of some high-faluting toff.

Indeed, it was time they all went back to London. Mind you, maybe it would suit them to go to Glasgow for a bit. The young Lords preferred Edinburgh, but he still had a fondness for his birthplace. Yes, that's what they'd do, as soon as possible. The rental was up to the end of August, so that would give the girl time to recover and the Laggan staff could earn their keep looking after her. As far as he was concerned the Highland estates were too remote and wet for his liking, and most definitely not for the Dinwoodie family. He hoped he'd never set foot in them again.

5

MacNishe watched Cate as she climbed the stairs to the library. Her accident last Autumn had never been accounted for. Lord Abermarle was most insistent they'd found her unconscious. From his description, they could well have been trespassing. Still, the Dinwoodie fellow had been a good sort, paying Callumn to attend her and ordering his staff to care for her, until she could be moved.

Much had happened at Kevinishe House while Cate was laid up at Laggan. Rab and Sarah had gone to Edinburgh for an extended visit, taking young Bruce to finish his education at Fettes College. Nanny, now pensioned off, had settled with her sister in Glasgow. He'd found the old house too quiet. Even the dog had been reduced to an occasional melancholy whine as it tried to make sense of the rapid changes. Then Cate had returned to collect her few belongings and bid them all farewell, but he'd insisted she stayed for a bit, at least until Christmas was over. Then he'd pressed her to stay on.

"Now then, are you resting, or just looking?" he asked as he joined her on the gallery landing where portraits of MacNishe Lairds and Ladies and even some Irish Craigs lined the walls. The balustrade, like all the woodwork in Kevinishe House, was of oak, lovingly carved with intricate designs of thistle and heather, bulbous finials hanging down into the hall. The old house had seen some great ceilidhs and Highland balls, and he'd often watched from there, the kilted figures and their partners dancing. The house had been full of laughter then.

He realised he'd become lost in his own thoughts and turned to find Cate watching him. "Well then, what's your answer?"

"I was looking at them," she replied, sweeping her arm around the gallery. "Are they all yours?"

"That they are. The good, the beautiful, the handsome and…"

"That ugly one," Cate smiled as she interrupted, pointing at the furthermost one.

"Ah well, he was one of the Irish Craigs, so we can't really be held responsible for him!"

"But to know who you are and where you belong: that must be very fine."

"Well it is and it isn't." Seeing the puzzled look on her face, he carried on. "Sometimes it's a burden if you try to live up to ancestral reputations. At other times you worry that you might have inherited some of their worst points. Then, of course, you have no choice."

"But you do all the choosing—no one tells you what to do."

"What I meant was that, suppose I'd wanted to be, let's say, a sailor. As the only son of the Laird, I too had to be a Laird. I couldn't have run away to sea as I'd dreamed. Oh no. I inherited a big old stone house, a run-down distillery, a parcel of debts, and a bad reputation. I had no choice." MacNishe could see that, as a wandering child, this might not seem too hard an imposition, and he wondered how he could explain that other people's lives always seemed to be better than one's own.

"Well, I wish I had some of them. I've nobody." Moving on, her glance rested on a young woman with red hair. "Who's that one then?"

"Ah. That's part of an old family tale."

"A story? About her?" Cate moved closer to the portrait.

"Come, sit here. I'll tell you about it." MacNishe nodded at the chaise longue.

"The story." Cate prompted, impatient as usual.

"In the Forty-Five Rebellion, trying to put the young Prince Charles Stuart on the throne, there was a final battle at Culloden Moor, where the Highlanders were routed by the English. The MacNishe heir at the time, who'd been wounded in the fighting, was smuggled to safety by that woman."

"She was brave. Why did she do that? Surely it was dangerous? She must have been well rewarded by the family."

"I'm afraid not, you see it was a puzzle. She hid him, nursed him till he was well, but let no one know about it. Everyone thought he'd been butchered by Cumberland."

"So what happened?" Excited at the thought of a story, Cate stood as if to urge the Laird on.

"Come, sit again, and let me finish." MacNishe studied her as she sat. There was a quality about Cate, with her love of words and stories, her quick intelligence, that warmed his heart. He decided then and there to keep her at Kevinishe till she was full-grown. Wilkins could continue to tutor her in his spare time from the cataloguing, and she would be excellent company for himself and Fisher at the distillery. When she was older they'd find a governess or companion position for her.

"Sir, the story—they're lost."

"No, Cate, not lost—just not found. I suspect that was quite deliberate." He'd better get out of this quickly: she was too young for him to go into what had gone on in that cave. "In the end they both returned to Kevinishe."

"And they took her into the house?"

"No, child, the family threw her out."

"What! After saving him? They couldna be so cruel! But about the picture, sir?"

"Oh that. She returned to the house with it one day, saw the son, and bade him hang it on the wall"

"So why did he— if they didna like her?"

"With the picture, the woman laid a curse on the house of MacNishe, saying that the picture must hang, never to be removed, or the MacNishe line would fail."

"But, who was she then? Where did she belong?"

"My family would never say. I believe it had something to do with the Cailleach's, but words from her are like rays of sun in a wet Highland summer."

"She says little. It's always quiet in the Black House."

"Here we are quiet too. Come, if it's stories you want, you can read to me". Seeing her gaze lingering on the portraits, he understood her concern about not belonging, and tried to reassure her. "Now then, what you must believe is that all this family thing, good or bad, needn't be important. You're the beginning of anything you want to be. You're young, pretty and intelligent. I know women aren't supposed to worry about anything other than marriage and babies, but my Margaret was an enormous help to me when I set about turning the family fortunes around. She'd a way with people and a good keen brain I was glad of."

"You miss her, don't you?"

"Oh yes. I've never quite become used to it. When you're all grown up you'll find someone, and it'll be the best feeling in the world. Nothing will be too bad to handle when you've that special person by your side. Without them life loses its flavour." Sentimental old fool, he thought, though the words were true enough.

"But you weren't really poor then, were you? When it was your turn to be the Laird?"

"Ah, but you see, for a Laird I was poor. If you've nothing, you need very little to be better off. I on the other hand had to find enormous sums just to keep the house and the distillery going."

"So if I work hard, get a good position, will I make something of myself?"

"Don't forget the learning. In fact—how would you like to come to the distillery with me tomorrow, see what goes on in the office? It'll be a change for you. While we're there, I can show you something older than most of these." He swept his arm, encompassing the rows of portraits. "We'll have to get up early though. The men won't like it if you're seen in the heart of the distillery." MacNishe rested his hand on her head, in a brief show of affection, as they moved away. He admired her spirit.

The outline of the distillery and the smell of the malting had always been part of Cate's life. To her, as to all of Kevinishe, it sat there on the edge of the burn, sheltered from the north wind by Beinn Nishe, looking almost as big as the mountain next to the huddle of tiny village houses strung along the shoreline.

The man sweeping the distillery yard greeted the Laird and eyed Cate suspiciously. A boy, collecting old staves from a pile in the yard, stuck his tongue out at her. Then they climbed an outside stairs into a room that looked a bit like the library at first sight. There, through the window in the 'office', as MacNishe called it, she could see Beinn Nishe, her mountain, its upper slopes clad in the winter cloak of white, the glint of water sparkling in the snow as it tumbled over rocks, and the occasional movement of deer or sheep as they searched for food.

"Now then, just follow me and I'll show you real history. Ah, here's Fisher. Is the entrance clear?"

"Aye, apart from Angus and the lad in the yard."

"Right then, let's take her to our bit of history, Fisher."

Cate followed the two men, down stairs, up other stairs, in and out of doors, machines clanking, smell overpowering, till at last they were in a sort of hall. The men stopped by a nook in one of the walls and pointed. Cate stood on her tiptoes and all she could see was a scruffy old clay pot. She turned puzzled eyes to MacNishe. "What is it?"

"A whisky jar." Fisher answered her question.

"It's a dirty looking thing, so it is." Cate took another good look at it. By the way the men were standing and the tone in Fisher's voice, she knew there must be something special about it. Still, however long she looked at it—well, it was still just an old pot!

"The outside might look nothing much, Cate, but inside that old jar is the whisky from the original illegal still—the beginning of our own Craeg Dhu. Come." MacNishe turned, Cate and Fisher followed, and they made their way back to the office.

"A dram then, Fisher, for the story?"

"Indeed why not, MacNishe." Fisher pointed to the mountain as he began to speak. "Cate. A long, long time ago, in the depths of Beinn Nishe there was a hidden cave where they made whisky. The Laird at that time was a great gambling man and he won this illicit still in a bet. Later, someone took the excise silver to lead the officers to it. Though the excise men broke everything up before they left, the MacNishe, at the time, followed them and found that old jar they'd overlooked. Over the years the story was added to, a twist here and there no doubt, but it's always had a kind of magic about it. Two disasters we've had here at the distillery, and in neither one has it been damaged. So now everyone believes that the distillery will prosper as long as that jar is with us."

"So there you have it, Cate," MacNishe took on the tale, "and now and again, Fisher and myself have a dram, think of how far we've come, and salute the mountain with our whisky."

Cate studied the men as they faced the mountain and drank, ideas tumbling in her head. Was it her cave the old still had been in? Was the woman in the picture, the one who'd laid the curse, the *red-headed woman* she saw in her mind? When the men finished, Fisher returned to his stillroom and MacNishe settled her on a stool at a small table in the corner of the room, her back to the window.

She spent the rest of the morning at the distillery, copying down names and figures, much as she did with Wilkins in the library. Here it was into a 'daybook', so they'd know what was sold and what was paid. When she thought MacNishe wasn't looking, she couldn't resist stealing a glance at the mountain. Cate looked at her entries and smiled. Neat and tidy, no blots, though her hand and pen wipe were blotched. Yes, she would like this distillery work. Maybe if she tried very hard the Laird would give her a position here. Mind, there were no women or girls in the distillery, so maybe not. Would she ever find a place where she really belonged? With Davy she thought she'd found her life's work, but then he'd died. Look at Nanny. Kevinishe had been her home since Master Rab was born and now she'd to live in Glasgow. Not because she wanted to—it just happened. Well she wasn't going to let things 'just happen' to her and spoil her life. One day she would belong.

Cate rode across the summer moors, thinking of her busy days. She'd never been idle when she was younger, always tasks to be done for the Cailleach or tinker matriarch, but now, aged fifteen, to her joy her life was full of learning. Mornings were spent in the distillery office; afternoons cataloguing with Wilkins; and evenings with Cook and Mrs. Mac, sewing the fine stitches Lady Sarah had taught her, writing down all the old recipes Cook remembered and trying them out for kitchen meals. Slowing the mare as they neared the strewn stones at the base of the mountain, she turned homeward. At the stables she dismounted as Gregor appeared from the tack room. Like most of the Kevinishe staff, he was getting old and this summer rain wasn't helping his rheumatism.

"The bones no so good today, Gregor? Are you rubbing them as I told you?"

"Well and no good it would be doing for me, young Cate, when it's the power of your hands that works the magic."

"Gregor, you must care for yourself as well as the horses."

"Aye, aye, but they don't like this rain any better than we do. It's sun on our backs we're after needing. What's the use of Lady Sarah coming back for the summers if they're to be wet all the time? Where's the sense in that? Soon she'll no bother coming at all, and then what'll master Rab do?"

Cate was fond of the grumpy old man. Short though he was with people, always ready with a moan, she knew he would give his life to protect his charges. The present problem was that the horses were not being exercised enough. The big mounts, like the stallion, were too strong for her and even Gregor seemed to work them less now because of his rheumatism.

" Mr. Rab, Lady Sarah and Bruce, with house-guests, will be here tomorrow for the holidays, so we could do with some dry weather," Cate said as she handed him her reins and watched as he walked the mare to cool her. The man was limping badly and Cate understood his grumpiness.

The next morning Jessie picked up the mail Wullie the Post had brought and took it into the morning room.

"That the mail, Jessie?"

"It is that, Mr. Rab. I'll away and bring the breakfasts. It's just yourselves. The guests will be down with Lady Sarah later, and Master Bruce hasn't stirred."

"Time he was up. Give him a knock, Jessie. He's coming round the distillery with us today." As Jessie went to wake Bruce, Rab sat and opened his mail.

"No sign of the others then, Rab?" MacNishe asked as he entered the dining room.

"Good God!" Was the reply as Rab brought his fist crashing down on the table, before striding into the hall bellowing, "Bruce".

MacNishe knew better than to enquire further, so helped himself from the now laden sideboard, and began his breakfast.

"Get down here and explain this." Rab waved the letter at him as Bruce, still in his dressing gown, descended the stairs.

"What? What's this about? I can't explain if I've no idea of..."

Rab cut his son off mid-sentence. "Get into the morning room. I've no wish for the entire house to hear my words."

"Rab, what..." MacNishe faltered as his son rounded on him.

"Oh you'll enjoy this, Father. You've never had a high opinion of your grandson and this..." In his fury, Rab flung the letter on the table.

Picking it up MacNishe studied the contents and the colour left his face. "A MacNishe did that?" he queried.

"Look, what is this all about? Someone tell me," Bruce demanded as he sat.

"I'll tell you, and the words are poison in my mouth. This foul letter is an expulsion," his father answered, taking his seat.

"I don't understand. What..." Bruce whined.

"You've shamed us. That's what. Fettes want you out! Gone! Branded you a thief, a gambler, a drunkard and a ..."

"Let me, Rab." MacNishe said stern faced.

"Besides which, Bruce, you're accused of maltreating a young girl."

"Oh that, Grandfather. She was just a trollop, looking for money. You know what servants are like."

"I've never met a servant yet, Bruce, who asked to be beaten. You've blackened our name, poured shame on us. You're not fit to be a Laird. Fisher would make a better job of it."

"Fisher, that lumbering oaf!" Bruce stood, about to say something else, but flinched as he saw his grandfather's face.

"Get out of my sight!" The old man roared. "We've blackguards enough in our history without spawning another. You're not fit to be a Laird. D'y hear?" MacNishe then grabbed his grandson by the collar and thrust him through the door into the hall.

"Go." He pointed to the front door. "See if any of your mother's relations will house you. Not one foot will you put on this estate as long as I'm alive, unless you mend your ways."

"B… b… but I'm a MacNishe." Bruce stammered.

"No longer. From this moment on you're a McPhail and not welcome here." Slamming the door in Bruce's now frightened face, MacNishe turned to his stricken son. "I mean it, Rab. And if you weaken when I'm gone you'll regret it all your life. Damn me he's nearly seventeen and rotten already!"

Bruce made his way to the stables and, with no Gregor in sight, saddled up his grandfather's horse. As he rode he wondered if the old man could actually prevent the succession? No, surely he couldn't. He'd calm down before the day was out. Still, best head to Fort William and his other grandfather for the present. He couldn't go anywhere without money though. He'd better call in at the distillery while the others were still at breakfast, and see what he could find.

Using the back stairs Bruce entered the office, helped himself to the petty cash and a bottle of whisky. One day it would all belong to him anyway. There was no way his grandfather could prevent it. Damn it all, he was the only heir after his father. The thought of being Laird at last, with the wealth and power that would bring, made him feel good. He mounted the stallion and dug his heels into the beast with such ferocity that the animal flung its head back, bared its teeth, and took off. It flew over the moor, unseated Bruce at a ditch, and galloped home to the stables into Gregor's tender care.

Cate lay on the heather, a rare touch of welcome sun bathing her body, glad to be away at last from the arguing and unpleasantness in the house, though she couldn't help remembering what Jessie had told them about the upset at breakfast, and her warning, 'Mark my words: harm will be done this day, so it will.' But with Rory settled at her side, Cate soon closed her eyes, tired with all the extra work the guests made, and slept.

Bruce had been no more than winded by his fall, but now he'd have to find his own way home and get another mount. Rounding a crest of rocks he came to an abrupt halt. Below him he could see the bloody little tinker and the dog. He sank to his knees. Ever since she'd appeared in his life she'd been trouble. He'd tried all his bullying tricks on her, but she'd never cried or screamed. Just looked right through him with those ridiculous green eyes and called him coward. Now here she was, away from the protection of Kevinishe House.

His anger at the loss of the horse was replaced by arousal at the prospect offered below him. Yes, this was an opportunity not to be missed—pleasure and revenge for those childhood scratches! She'd fight, but the odds were very different from that first time on the Kevinishe lawn. The very thought of it was stimulating. As for the dog, he'd have to be careful. It usually gave a low growl when he was around. Thinking of hurting the pair of them made him forget about his fall. Now he'd get his revenge. Better plan this right though. Deal with the dog first, but how to get close enough?

Crouching behind the sheltering rocks, he chose a heavy stone, hefting it as high as he could. The aim would have to be precise. He'd only have one chance. With the dog injured, she'd be too preoccupied to notice his approach. Then he'd have her. Slowly he rose, took careful aim, and dropped the rock. The anguished yelps of pain satisfied him. Risking a glance below, he saw her cradling the stupid animal. Perfect. Moving round he approached from the other direction.

"Well, well if it isn't the filthy little tinker brat, weeping over the useless house dog."

"You cowardly booger." Cate spat. "You couldn't even face up to a wee doggie before you tried to best it."

"Oh, come now, why would I waste my time with the worthless animal? But you, I might find it worth my while to waste some time with." Bruce could see his words caused a flicker of fear in the hated green eyes. Good, the sooner she saw something different about

70

him, now he was grown up, the better. He watched as she raised her hand to her face to wipe the tears away. Never, since she'd first flown at him all those years ago, had she ever cried, no matter how he'd hurt her. She'd always fought him and that was exactly what he wanted now.

"Go away, you big bully. Wait till MacNishe hears that you hurt the dog. He'll soon make you sorry."

"That's where you're wrong. You're nothing but a servant. Who'd believe you, a filthy tinker?" Bruce saw her expression change, the temper and outrage at his words preceding her physical attack, just as he'd expected. He caught her hands as they flew to his face ready to scratch. Then as she tried to kick he tripped her off balance and she fell hard onto the rocks. Undaunted she flew at him again, but he was ready and pushed her to the ground. As she flailed with her arms and kicked out underneath him, he held the arms with one hand and slapped her hard with the other. Something in that movement excited him so much he carried on slapping her face while trapping her body firmly with his own. Still she struggled and fought. Fully aroused now he could wait no longer. Grabbing her shoulders he lifted her head before smacking it to the ground. Taking advantage of the temporary lull in her struggle he pushed her skirts up round her waist before tearing her under-things and opening his breeches. As she began to recover, she fought him again, but nothing could stop him now and he rode her hard while she flailed beneath him.

Looking at the dazed girl as he did himself up, Bruce couldn't believe how good it had been. The boys at school had been right—that's all women were good for. Now, for the first time since she'd flown at him and thwarted his attempt to get rid of his stepbrother, he'd come out on top, literally. Well now, this boring holiday might be saved after all. She'd never tell and he'd have her as often as he liked. Then, remembering he wouldn't be here, he consoled himself with the thought that sooner or later he'd be back.

Much later Cate opened her eyes, but let them slide shut again. Her head felt so bad. It all came tumbling back—Rory was hurt— she struggled to her knees. Cradling the dog, she wept. She'd seen evil in Bruce since they'd been children, but to hurt a pet animal! And what else? Cate tried to clear her thoughts. Slowly now the scene replayed in her head. He'd attacked her. She'd struggled, but he was too strong. Then he'd cracked her head. Pinned her down. Entered her! And still she'd fought. No wonder her body hurt. She'd read of things like that, seen what happened with animals in stables and crofts. But the pain and shock of what had just happened to her—the realization was too much: the feeling of something lost, part of her taken, lost to him of all people.

Now amidst that pain and shock, the childhood dislike of Bruce hardened into a deep anger, a hatred that soaked into her soul. Head bowed she let her bitter tears flow.

Fisher eased his weary muscles as he let the reins go slack. His workload seemed to increase as each year went by and today both MacNishe and Rab hadn't come in—some trouble up at the House—just when he needed them. Somehow he hadn't felt like going home at the end of the day, but now he was on the moors he realised how tired he was. "Sorry, fellah. Home I think." As the horse whinnied in reply Fisher thought he heard another sound. "Stand now." Yes, it was definitely human. Slowly he made his way round the rocks. There she was, cuddling the dog, and herself with blood on her bent head, sobbing. Good God! What had happened here?

By the time he'd heard her story and loaded them both onto the horse, Fisher's rage was such that if he'd come across the boy there and then, he'd have thrashed him, or worse. Instinct warned him Cate could never go back to Kevinishe House, though the dog must, once he'd cleaned the wound. All this would break MacNishe's heart. No, he must save them both. As he rode he began to plan. First he'd take her back to the Cailleach. She would tend the lass's wounds and then he'd arrange to send her away somewhere. Better if those up at the Big House were made to think she'd run off with the tinkers. That way she'd be safe. For his part he'd keep a close watch on young Bruce, see he caused no more harm in the glen.

Part Two

Glasgow

1905

6

Cate knelt at the top of the stairs leading down to the next floor in the tenement block and as she wet the cloth to begin the task of cleaning them, her thoughts turned to Kevinishe. April, the snowdrops would be almost over, though the mountain would still have a white coat of late winter snow. If only she could be back there.

Moving down the steps her thoughts turned to her present home. The only mountains here in the Gorbals of Glasgow were blocks of tenements. Each building was the same: level upon level of cramped accommodation with only one toilet to a floor. Not that those living in them didn't try to keep the place clean. In fact every day both stairs and toilet had to be scrubbed, but because of traffic on the one and use of the other by dozens of people, the smell of urine, dirt and unwashed bodies lingered. It wasn't that everyone didn't do their best—the living conditions were terrible and the inhabitants all scraping a living to merely exist beneath the tyranny of unscrupulous landlords.

A clamour of voices and feet from above made Cate push the bucket to the side of the step she was on and struggle to stand, with her hated swollen stomach. She was just in time as Mrs Petrie, a neighbour, shepherded her large brood down the stairs.

"Aye weel, hen, you'll be near your time. Never you mind, eh. Maggie's the best there is at the lying-in. Albert, will ye stop tormenting that wee beggar and away doon the stairs or I'll fetch you such a clout you're heid'll be on back tae front. Weans! They're a right scunner most o the time, but there we are. You'll soon have yin yoursel."

Cate watched the group as they made their noisy way down. That was another thing: these people spoke as if they'd no time to take breath—the speed of it, and always at shouting pitch. The Glasgow patter they called it. Indeed everything here was loud and busy. People everywhere! Horses, trams, and even motorcars in the posh West End, she'd been told. Not that she'd ever been there. People said it was beautiful, but she didn't care: all she longed for were the sounds of the Highlands. Kneeling, she started the irksome task of wiping all the steps again, thinking, if she hurried, she might finish before another set of dirty footprints appeared.

With the last step dried she stood, bucket in hand, but a searing pain made her drop it. Clutching her stomach, she was unaware of the dirty water flooding the stairwell, and the empty bucket clanging against the wall. Unheeding, she crawled to the top step, her fear strangling her cries for Maggie. She could only batter the door.

Maggie took one look at the frightened girl and stretched out her arms to comfort. "Oh my! It's time lassie. It's time."

The sound of the soft Highland voice and the comforting sight of the matronly figure steadied her. Maggie helped her into the tiny tenement flat that had been Cate's new home for the past eight months. Maggie was Fisher's widowed sister and it was there that the Cailleach and Fisher sent her after the rape on the moor.

"Maggie, it hurts so. I'm fair scared. Make it stop."

"Wheesht now Cate. The bairn's coming, that's all. Come you away inside now and we'll get ready."

Cate tore herself out of Maggie's arms. "No! Never! I'll no have it. You can…" Another pain scorched inside her. As it eased she tried to make for the stairs. "I'll throw myself down there! That'll sort it."

Maggie grabbed Cate, dragged her inside and keeping Cate between her and the door, kicked it shut with her foot. "No more of that now. C'mon, I'll help you and we'll get through this together. You…"

"Maggie—I'm only sixteen. I…" Cate sobbed as the older woman once more enveloped her in a hug and sat her on the wall bed.

"Sit quiet now and I'll get the newspapers laid out next door and the water on. If you can, walk round and round the table there before the next pain. When it comes pant like that dog you used to have, when he'd just run after a rabbit. It'll help. Think of something else, something nice. Think hard as it hits."

Rory lolloping free: she managed a momentary smile at the thought, but then the moors reminded her of Bruce. This was his doing. Well he wasn't going to get the better of her again. She'd get through this labour by remembering what he did and she'd fight him in her mind with every pain until it was over and the bastard he'd thrust upon her was born.

With everything ready for the birth Maggie came back into the kitchen. Cate stopped her walking and together they made for the closet bed, now covered with an old sheet on top of the papers.

"See you and lie there like a good girl—mind what I said— think of other things and breathe right." Maggie had barely finished speaking when she heard the door open and knew Lizzie was home.

"Lizzie," she called out, "away you and see if Mrs. Petrie is home, and mind the bairns if she is, while she comes down here. Cate's baby's coming."

"Oh Mammy, that's Cate screaming…"

"Aye well that's the labour pains, now you away upstairs till it's over."

With Mrs. Petrie downstairs and her four little ones to see to, Lizzie made them some bread and dripping and let her thoughts wander as she watched them eat. She knew herself to be a plain little thing and the arrival of the bright red-haired Cate from the Highlands had been like a bit of magic for her. Suddenly everyone wanted to be with them. When they'd found that Cate's hair, like the bright colours of the wasp warning of the danger of a sting, was indeed an indicator of her temper and that crossing her could very easily turn to fisticuffs, they'd accepted both of them, and Lizzie knew her world to be transformed. Bairns washed and fitted head to toe in the closet bed, she sat in the rocker by the stove and tried not to think about the pain her Cate was going through downstairs.

As a miserable slurried dawn crept through the narrow window, Mrs. Petrie let herself into the room. Waking Lizzie, she put a cup of grey tea into her hands. "It's no great, but it's warm."

"Cate, what about Cate?"

"Ach dinna you fash yersel aboot that yin."

"What—nothing's happened to her?'

"She's had a bairn, that's whit. An you've never seen the like the anger of her. See here, she shot that wee fella oot as though he was the devil's spawn, so she did."

"But she's aright, her an the bairn?"

"She's had a bonny wee boy. An she's worn oot like the rest of us. So away you doon below to your bed for a bit—else you'll no be fit for your work the day."

When Lizzie had peeped at the wee boy in the drawer she joined her mother by the stove. "We'll need to let uncle Fisher know, Mammy."

"That we will. But right now we all need our beds."

Cate was not in fact asleep. She too was thinking of Fisher. They seldom wrote to one another, but she supposed he ought to be told. Could she tell him she wished the infant dead! She'd refused to prepare for the birth, and now she wanted nothing to do with the child. How could she? This thing that Bruce had forced into her! And in all the pain she'd seen no comforting sight of *the red-headed woman*. Had she abandoned her too?

Wishing for what she couldn't have was stupid! Up until two weeks ago she'd done whatever work she could find, and tomorrow she would look again. She mustn't be idle when they needed every penny. After all Lizzie, walked miles to and from work as a kitchen maid and Maggie worked at the Chemicals. They were what made this Glasgow bearable. Their kindness to her, a perfect stranger, had been overwhelming. What little they had they shared and Cate knew she would never forget that, or the way Fisher had rescued her from the moor.

Lizzie was so out of breath she could hardly manage the tenement stairs. "Mammy, Mammy, listen to this now," she gasped as she staggered through the door. "Where's Cate?"

"She's gone looking for work, like she's done every day in the past six weeks, that poor wee bairn strapped to her back. If she doesn't find some soon, she'll have no soles to her shoes."

"That's it! Oh that's it!"

"Lizzie lass, sit down! Get your breath, and start again. What's 'it'? What's all the commotion about?"

"It's Mr. McAlister—he's tellt Cook to get another maid. I spoke up for Cate. She's to come with me the morn. Oh here she is now! Cate! Cate!"

"Calm down, lassie. Let her get through the door!"

As Cate undid her shawl, sat, and put Rhoddy to her breast, she nodded at Lizzie. "What is it Lizzie? You look fair worked up."

Having gone over the facts again Lizzie could hardly contain herself. "What do you think, Cate? You will come won't you? It'll be great."

"Of course I'll come. I need to earn my keep. But what about him?" Cate gestured to the swaddled baby on her knee.

"What aboot Mrs. Petrie, Cate, she'd do it. She's aye willing."

"Do you think so Lizzie? For I'm sick of carrying him around, one glance at my back and the answer is always no, and your lawyer would be the same."

"Cate," Maggie spoke gently. "You mustn't say these things. I couldn't wish for a nicer lass but your way with the bairn is no right. Up immediately after the birth, walking the streets for work, and you no fit. Something'll have to change or that bairn will begin to feel it." Maggie waited, but Cate made no reply. "Look at Lizzie. She cuddles him like one of the dolls her daddy used to bring back from the fishing trips; can you no do the same? An you really must name the bairn. It's bad luck, you know."

"Mammy, what's Uncle Fisher's name?"

"It's Cameron, Lizzie, but he's been called Fisher since he was a boy."

"Why, Mammy?"

"Because he was never out of the boats from as soon as he could walk."

"What about Cameron then, Cate, after Uncle Fisher?"

"No, Lizzie! Fisher's special. This bairn isn't. I'll name him Rhoddy if I have to. Might as well give him the other grandfather's name—him they called evil Red Rhoderick. The bairn was the result of an evil deed, so why not?" After the rape, and now the birth, she knew there would be no bonding with this spawn of Bruce.

Maggie turned to mash the tea. Her mind understanding the girl's reaction, but her heart aching for the bundle now winded and in the dresser. She knew Cate was never rude or unkind, but she'd a defensive wall round her, and only Lizzie was allowed over it. For that Maggie would always be grateful. Her daughter was timid and the world took advantage. She'd blossomed since Cate had come. God knows what she'd do when Cate left, as she surely would. She didn't belong in the tenements—not looking or speaking the way she did. It would only be when, not if. Of that Maggie was certain.

Cate, glad though she was of the job this past two months in the lawyer's house, wiped her hands on the sacking apron and thought that Life had a funny turn to it. First off she'd been that nervous when she'd come for the interview with the cook, Lizzie standing by her side worrying. It had all been fine though—Cook had set her scrubbing as a test, and remembering how she'd near taken the bristles off the brush, she went at it that hard to prove herself, made her smile. Then it had all worked out well with the two of them sharing the cleaning and kitchen chores, but a month after she'd started with her, Lizzie slipped by the bins at the basement door and broke her leg. The Lawyer, Mr. McAlister had sent for the doctor that evening and he'd splinted the leg, but because Lizzie had dragged herself indoors she's made the break worse and now it looked as if it wasn't going to mend well. Because of this it was unlikely that she'd be able to return to work, and now Cate had to manage by herself until a decision was made about Lizzie

For some reason Cate suddenly thought of Nanny. Where in Glasgow was she? Did she hate the tenements too? Probably. Their life in Kevinishe House couldn't have been more different. Mind,

80

Nanny was too old now to expect anything else but Cate had never forgotten MacNishe's words: 'to make something of herself'. She felt she could do that in the future, but knew it wasn't going to be easy now there was the bairn. She'd come, with much urging from Maggie, to take more notice of her son. She did try but whenever she looked at him it was a constant reminder of Bruce and the rape.

Cate heard the front door opening and then the drawing room bell rang. Cook was still in her attic room, so she left the vegetables and went upstairs to answer it.

"Where's Cook?" Caroline Bryant was never quite sure why this latest kitchen maid disturbed her. With her shapeless brown dress, brown mobcap and that ridiculous sacking apron she should have faded into the background like the other nervous wretch had.

"She's having a break before she starts her dinner preparation, Madam." Cate could feel the other woman's dislike and was at a loss to understand it.

"Well that's too bad, cain you rouse her? Aiy require some tea."

"I'll fetch you a tray to the drawing room, Madam. Save disturbing Cook."

"The sheer impertinence of you. As though someone like you could prepare maiy tea tray."

Cate knew the big houses in their wide crescents and terraces in Kelvinside were a world away from the tenements, but the women with their affected way of speaking seemed silly.

"Well, do as you're told, gerl. Don't just stand there. Rouse Cook this instant! Aiy'm not used to waiting. Do you hear?"

"Yes, Madam. Right away, Madam."

Caroline fumed as she waited for cook. Never had she heard someone be so rude while using all the correct words. The girl would have to go. She couldn't bear the thought of the wretch with her polite way of speaking remaining in her father's kitchen for one more minute! Why wasn't she like the other servants, afraid of her? Trembling when she spoke? Where had this girl learned to talk properly anyway? Probably some rich man's doxy thrown out on the street, and that was where she belonged.

Meanwhile upstairs, Cook shuffled her feet into her shoes and winced as her bunions were forced into the sides. Her excellent cooking had piled the pounds on and overlong days standing in the hot steamy kitchen had given her varicose veins that throbbed by the end of the day. Going down she met Cate with her tray.

"What's this, lassie?"

"I was just on my way to get you, Cook. Mrs. Bryant is here ordering tea. I offered to get it for her, but she wanted you, so it's all ready for you to take in."

"You're a good wee maid. But mind yourself with that one."

"Yes, I will Cook."

Pushing the door open with her ample backside Cook forced a smile and greeted the daughter of the house. "We weren't expecting you today, Madam."

"No. I haid hoped maiy Father would be at home."

"Oh, you're much too early for him. He's working late so it'll be some time before he returns. Anyway, here's your tea, Madam. Hasn't young Cate done it well? Laid it all out for me." Cook hid the smile as she set the tray down.

"Well, aiy don't really have time now. So much to do you know? Baiy the waiy, aiy'm having a dinner party next week and aiy'd laike you to prepare one of your rather nice desserts for me. Aiy'll send a cab for it on Thursday." Sniffing as she looked at the tray, she continued. "No I definaitely couldn't touch that."

As she watched the woman sweep out, Cook had a sniff of her own, picked up the tray and made for the kitchen. "Madam doesn't seem to want your tea, Cate, so we'll have it ourselves. Shame to let it go to waste."

"What did she come for, Cook? She knows the master is never here at this time."

"Oh she only comes when she wants something. Ashamed of him she is."

"But he's a legal man with his own office and clerk." She'd only had rare glimpses of her employer but he seemed a nice gentleman, though thin. Cook was always on about not getting enough food into that tall frame.

82

"You have the right of it. He's a real gentleman. Oh, not of your Lords and Ladies type, but a good professional man who's made a tidy bit of money. Now the son and daughter try to mix with their betters and the master will have none of it, so, as I say, they only pay duty visits. The son was never so bad till he married another of those stuck-up Kelvinside girls. It makes me mad. The master doesn't deserve family like that. No wonder his hair is grey that early. It's a wonder he still has some, the trouble they are! An another thing, the grandchildren now."

"Does she no bring them to see him?"

"Oh that one's too posh to have weans—aye supposing she'd let her man—aye well, no, she doesn't have any. Mr. Ian has the two boys, and precious little the master sees of them."

As usual Mrs. Petrie's flat was bedlam, when Cate arrived. She was never sure just how many bairns were Petries, as the mother was always ready to mind others for a few coppers. Looking at the older woman, with her straggly hair and loose figure, the result of many births, wrapped in a pinny that refused to meet in the middle, never mind wrap over, Cate shook her head. "How can you do it, Mrs. Petrie?"

"Do whit, hen? Maisie gie him back his penny whistle. Weel I dinna care whit he did. Gie it back or I'll fair skelp you. Rhoddy, here's your ma."

Cate scooped Rhoddy up. "See you tomorrow then, and thanks."

"Och, he's nae bother. Some of these would wreck anything. Why the park looks like it's had a visit from yon locusts the wee preacher fella is aye talking aboot after they weans have bin there!"

Cate was still giggling as she let herself into the flat. The lino worn thin but sparkling, fire cleaned out, laid and ready for the spill. Everywhere spotless, what a contrast to the room she'd just left! Putting Rhoddy on the floor, she cut the crust of bread she'd saved for him, dipped it in the jug of cold tea and sprinkled some of their precious sugar on it. "Here we are then. Just you suck on that till the others get home. I'll need to get the chores done now." Mrs. Petrie was right—he really was a good bairn, rarely crying except with the teeth. By the time Maggie got home the fire was lit, table laid and the bread and dripping waiting for their tea.

"Did you get it, Maggie?"

"Aye an he's polished it all, needles an everything. I'm that excited for her, Cate."

"Well, we've Mr.McAlister to thank for it. He was that upset when she had her accident. What with doctors and everything, Lizzie's been very lucky. Now the money for the sewing machine."

"A proper gentleman indeed, Cate. And with the money we've cobbled together, an the bit more Fisher's sent this month, she'll be able to buy threads and material and make a start on sewing for her living."

"It'll be better for her this way. She'd never have managed in service again. Pity the leg's no healed so very well. Does she mind now she has the limp, Maggie?"

"Oh she minds, but what's done is done. Wheesht now—here she is. Sit down quick."

Lizzie put her shopping basket on the table. "Not much today, only some shin bones, but I managed some cabbage and an onion at the market and the baker gave me a yesterday's loaf for minding the shop while he had his tea. Oh, and he says I could mebbe do the odd day in the shop." Looking straight at the two women, Lizzie realised they were up to something. "Now then, what are you two grinning for?"

Cate got up from the table and put her hands over Lizzie's eyes.

"Here you! What're you doing? I canna see a thing. I'm too old for Blind Man's Buff!"

Seeing Maggie had the machine uncovered, Cate took her hands away.

"Well, you daft gowk, what was that all aboot? Mammy, what's the matter with…?" Lizzie's eyes alighted on the machine and her mouth hung open in astonishment. "What? Whose? Oh Mammy, what's that?"

"Well it looks like a sewing machine to me and who's the one in this house does all the pretty stitching?"

"It's never lifted?"

"Lizzie Balfour! As though your Mammy would steal anything!"

Rhoddy began to grizzle for his tea and Cate decided it was time for an explanation.

"Mr.McAlister gave us money for it and Maggie, Fisher and I put money aside for threads and things. Now you can bring in sewing and mending and then you won't have to work in service with that poor old leg of yours. We'll help with the finishing and Cook says, now that I'm doing the work of two since your fall, I might get more money."

With the child asleep, the others gathered round as Lizzie began sewing imaginary seams as she worked the treadle with her good leg. Cate drew notices on the back of a paper bag to put up in the market and the baker's. Then she sketched the dress that snooty Mrs. Bryant had worn. Drawing pictures for young Davy when he was alive had always given Cate pleasure and Mr. Wilkins had encouraged her to continue after the boy's death.

When bedtime arrived, Lizzie insisted they leave the machine uncovered so she could fall asleep looking at it. Maggie and Cate washed in the kitchen sink and, with a last look at Rhoddy, they tumbled into bed convinced that better times were coming.

7

Cate could hear the rain continuing to splatter on the basement steps as she peeled the vegetables for the lawyer's dinner. She couldn't believe how wet it had been. Now here was the tradesman's bell jangling again. Who could that be? All the orders were in, and unpacked. Cook's good scones were long digested by the hungry delivery boys, soaked to their skins.

Opening the basement door the wretched figure standing there couldn't have been wetter had he been in the sea. This, plus the cough that racked his body, brought instant sympathy from Cate. "Come in out of the wet." She knew she should have asked who he was, but he looked such a poor soul she was sure he meant her no harm.

"I have...." another fit of coughing interrupted the speaker.

Cate left him to it and sped to the storeroom, returning with an earthenware beaker into which she'd put two good big spoons of honey with a pinch of ginger and some hot milk. "Here, sip this. It'll ease the throat."

While he was drinking the milk and cradling the warm beaker for comfort, Cate studied him. A scrawny fellow whose complexion was not much better than the milk she'd given him. Her time with the Cailleach made her aware that he was really quite ill, possibly consumptive. Still, it could just be the normal physical condition of many of the poor of Glasgow, but probably both.

"What do you want anyway?"

"Thank you for that. I'm indebted to you."

He may be poor, Cate thought, but, like me, he doesn't fit in. Well spoken and eyes, now that they'd stopped streaming, full of intelligence. She found herself liking this bedraggled stranger while waiting to hear his answer.

"Mr.McAlister sent me for some papers. He said to tell you they were on his desk in the big brown envelope."

"You're never a legal man then?"

"No. No. I'm just a clerk. A legal clerk though."

"Well that's something isn't it? You might be a proper legal man one day if you work hard enough."

"No, that's not how it works. You have to do the studying and…."

"But, if it makes you one of them, surely you can study?"

"Well it's the money you see and the time."

Cate saw the eyes dim and the shoulders droop. Well, no wonder he would never get on—he was beaten before he began.

Her thoughts were interrupted by cook's voice.

"Now then, what's going on here? Who's this? Not a gentleman caller, I hope. You know better than to break the rules, Cate."

"Of course I do, Cook. He's the master's clerk." Nodding at the young man. "He's come for an envelope."

"You'd think they'd have such as they in their big office instead of coming out in all weathers for a wee bit of an envelope."

"It's a large brown one on the Master's desk in his study. He's been told to fetch it."

Cate watched the nervous figure take a step back as Cook, hands on hips, faced him. "It's got special papers in it that they need for all that legal work, Cook. So it's important, see. He'll have to have it." Cate could almost feel the thrill of pen and paper as she spoke, and hoped the clerk would back her.

"And how would you know about such things, may I ask?" Cook spoke sharply. "When the Master is out it's my place to deal with strangers. You know that."

"Well I thought it was a delivery boy." Cate knew she should have kept quiet. But it brought back memories of the times in the Kevinishe library, working on the book catalogue, when the Laird's solicitor arrived, all the way from Edinburgh, with important legal papers. Mind, Cook was right: she should know nothing of these things. "The young clerk man told me just now. Shall I show him the study?"

"You'll do no such thing. How do we know who he is?"

"Perhaps if you were to bring the envelope—he says it's the only one left out on the desk."

"What, me disturb the Master's things! Cate, really what can you be thinking about?"

"But don't you see, Cook, if there's only one envelope on the desk he must be the clerk man for the Master or how would he know?" Cate could see that if Cook took the wrong decision, they would all be in trouble. Hired help of any kind were still at the mercy of their masters, and a simple error could easily result in instant dismissal with no 'character'. Then another position would be impossible to find.

'Hurumphing' to herself Cook turned and waddled up the stairs, stopping half way to ease her breathing.

"You did know about such things didn't you?" the clerk said nodding his head.

"Well yes, but not a word now."

"After your kindness with the drink I could do no less. I'm Solly Isaacs, by the way".

"I'm Cate. You should take care of that throat." Before she could say much more, Cook came wheezing back down again.

"Here, take it, and don't keep the Master waiting. Go on, be off with you."

As she returned to her vegetable peeling, Cate wondered about the thin young man. Had he really no hope? Was he very poor? Why did he look so worried all the time? It was almost as though he was just waiting for everything to go wrong for him, in her experience that's just when most things did.

Making his way back to the office, the clerk carried, not only the envelope but also the image of the green-eyed girl, and for once he ignored the jeers of the barrow boys as he made his way through the market.

Whether it was Cook's bunions, her legs or her breathing, Cate was never sure, but somehow that evening she could see the woman was too tired to be running up and down with the master's meal while she, on the other hand, was still working well and with all her jobs nearly done.

"It's a great pity you never had the training for upstairs, Cate. I could do without it tonight. And you with the fresh legs on you."

Cate knew an opportunity when she saw it. "I've watched you and those fancy maids Mrs. Bryant hires in for her dinners. When the guests have gone to the drawing room it's me that clears it all up. Why couldn't I try it for one night?"

"You're quick, true enough, but what about the master?"

"You're always telling me how he'll get indigestion eating so quickly, with his nose in his papers. Perhaps he won't even notice me."

"Well, there is that. Right, let's try it."

Malcolm McAlister was weariness itself as he sat down to his evening meal. He'd spent all day arguing the case of a docker whose legs had been crushed and whose family were now starving. In the end he'd managed to achieve a pittance for the man. When he contrasted that with the wasteful ways of his own offspring, it depressed him unutterably that his children had turned into such vain snobs. It was one of the rare times he was glad Alice was dead—she, who'd always been ready for a good cause, the kindest person he'd ever known. Hadn't she taken pity on him as a lowly clerk and braved her family's wrath by falling in love with him? As he worked his way up the ladder, studying hard and working ever harder, she'd backed him all the way. The thing he missed most since her death was the sense of contented peace that Alice had brought. How unlike her their daughter was! She invaded the still waters of his life; turning them into ruffled waves, calm returning only as she left.

It was the thought of peace that made him look up from his papers. Usually he ate and read to a backdrop of huffing and panting as Cook laboured up and down the stairs. Now he became aware of stillness in the room. The young kitchen maid was working away on the dishes with barely a sound. The dress was too large for her and the cap awry. She looked like a child at a fancy dress party.

Cate felt the change. The papers no longer rustled. The clinking of cutlery on plate was missing. Sneaking a glance before she served the dessert she had just brought up, she found herself looking straight at the Master, who was staring right back. She held her breath.

"If you don't breathe soon I shall have to eat that off the floor when you drop it in your faint."

"Oh sir, I—mean I—I never faint and I wouldn't dream of dropping your afters even if—if I did."

"Well that's very kind of you, but why don't we take the easy way out? You keep on breathing and just put it in front of me."

In her flustered state, the kind humour in McAlister's voice and the gentle smile was lost on Cate.

"No, indeed not, sir! First I have to clear the old plate and…." She was silenced by the wave of his hand. Now both she and Cook were for it and really— well she'd tell him, not just think it. "You see, sir, Cook's veins and her bunions were really bad, and when you put that with her lungs…" Damn, she wasn't making sense. "I mean you can't blame Cook. I said I would do it and if you'd kept on with the papers I would've been done and gone and the clearing finished when you were away in your study." She had to stop, as she was running out of breath. That, and the thought that her taking Cook's place was about to lose them their positions, finally silenced her.

"You take more stopping than a cab that doesn't want a fare! Assuming Cook's bunions and veins have not been transported to her lungs and that she has at least a small use of her legs, will you fetch her, please?"

As a puffing Cook accompanied Cate back to the dining room McAlister waited until the older woman was breathing more freely.

"Do I take it, Cook, that you felt a little unwell and arranged for Cate to perform your upstairs duties for you?

"Aye (gasp) you (gasp)…" She prepared to go on.

"A simple 'yes' or 'no' will do, Cook."

McAlister had grown used to the old woman's ways, she'd been with them since Alice and he'd been married. Perhaps the stairs were now becoming too much for her.

"That's no fair, sir. She takes time to speak after climbing the stairs and anyway it's no her fault. I said I could do it and…."

"Yes, I understand. It's my fault for not keeping my head down."

"Oh no! I mean yes, at least—well everything else was all right. I did serve it all properly." Her anger at the injustice of being dismissed for doing something she'd done well had the words popping out of her mouth. Now she'd done it. But surely not Cook too? "Cook shouldn't go. She couldn't help being in pain and, even if she had done the dining room, I'd have stayed behind and run up and down the stairs for her, so it wouldn't really have been Cook serving it then anyway. I mean that's not honest is it?" Temper and tears overcame her and she fled to the comparative safety of the kitchen, knowing, by speaking before she was spoken to, she'd broken a cardinal rule of service and probably done Cook a great harm. Why, oh why, did she have the red hair and the temper? Now look what she'd done! How could she face Maggie and Lizzie? Without her 'character' how would she get another job in service?

Lizzie held the finished dress in front of her and, nodding her head in satisfaction, laid it carefully on the table and went to the stove to test the flat iron. She was never quite brave enough to spit on her finger and then touch the iron's surface so over the years she'd learnt to hold it near her face 'till the heat felt right'. There was no way she was going to spoil Cate's birthday present by scorching it. This was by far the most difficult piece of sewing (Cate was forever on at her to use the word 'dressmaking') she'd done. Old Ma Hutchins at the market hadn't been able to get rid of the dress and each week Lizzie had watched it, praying the dirtier it got the less Ma would charge for it. Her patience had been rewarded all because of an unexpected downpour, at the end of which the lace dress, unfit for tenement wear anyway, was a sodden rag. True she still had a bit to pay but she could manage that by the end of the month and now, after all the waiting, worrying and hard work, there it was, finished.

Just for a moment Lizzie held it against herself. It was far too long for her. Cate was really quite tall now. Still, the dress felt good. Lizzie wiped a small tear away and with it her dreams. Even with a new dress she would still be the pale moth to Cate's butterfly, and who would want a wife with a limp? Taking comfort from the pleasure her surprise would be, she folded the dress inside a blanket and placed it in the wall bed.

Maggie shook the last drops of rain from her shawl glad to be home. The work in the chemical factory was hard, but it was regular money and allowed the luxury of letting Lizzie work at home. Her sewing work was improving, but it was still bits here and there for people who could barely afford it. Cate was always on about looking for better trade. She talked of Lizzie and her setting up together, maybe even getting a market stall where they could display some of the dresses Cate drew and cut out for Lizzie to sew. Tonight they would celebrate Cate's birthday. There was a meat pie and steamed dumpling with a scatter of raisins.

"Well now, petal, are we right for the birthday girl? You look tired, Lizzie. Is the leg okay? I see you've patched Bert Green's fishing smock."

"Aye, it's finished. It's good that one or two of Daddy's old fishing crew keep in touch and Bert sees to it that any sewing they need comes my way. He's been real good to us since Daddy drowned. Mind, seeing as he's a widow man, and takes you to the park and teashop on your day off—mebbe…"

"That's enough talk like that. What about your leg?"

"It's fine, but I'm real tired with the sewing and everything."

"What's the everything? You've no had too much trouble with the clootie? Only watching the water. Surely you never tried to lift it off the fire? I…."

"No, Rhoddy took a while to go down after I fetched him from Mrs. Petrie, and then I had sewing to do, but it's done now."

Maggie could sense Lizzie was holding back but knew better than to press her. Instead, changing the subject, she opened her bag and the smell of the meat pie circled the tiny room. "That'll make a fine birthday treat won't it? Away you and get me a plate from the dresser and we'll put it in the oven to keep warm."

As Maggie took her coat off and hung it on the back of the door, Lizzie took the two steps necessary to reach the dresser and, scooping the pie onto the plate, took two smaller ones on the other side to reach the stove, which was giving out a welcome heat on this cold autumn day.

"Now then, see we've the two wee sparkly clips. The glue has held on the broken one just fine. And there're two bonny new ribbons as well. You choose, Lizzie. Which ones do you want to give Cate?"

"It's okay, Mammy, I've a secret of my own for Cate." The flare of pride as she said those words felt so good. Her mother and Cate were the strong ones. They made all the decisions, but this time she'd been on her own from start to finish. Mind, she'd almost found it too much and she'd never felt so tired, but she'd done it. Oh, if only Cate would be home soon! Lizzie almost couldn't wait.

"So that's what you've been keeping to yourself, Lizzie, all this time! Well I never did. My but she's late. What's keeping her?"

"Oh it'll be that snooty Mrs. Bryant. She aye has the late suppers—dinners she calls them. Why she eats them at the end of the day, I'll never know."

"Well, I'll lift the dumpling out and the smell will make her feel right fine as she opens the door. Mind, she'll mebbe no think about a birthday, since it's only pretend for her."

"How's that, Mammy?"

"Och, do you no remember how she never had one until that grand Lady Sarah made it the day she went into service at Kevinishe House?"

"Tell us again about the big house. Was it like the McAlister one?"

"Mercy me, lassie, you could put two or three of them into Kevinishe House and still have space left!"

"Why did you leave, Mammy?"

"Your Daddy was working on the boats and he had kin in the village. He was visiting them there and we met at a ceillidh. We liked each other right fine, so, whenever the boat was laid up, he came back to court me and then we married."

"Is it nice being sweet on someone?"

"If you find the right one it's just that, right. Wheesht now! There's her step, and no before time."

They'd eaten well. With full stomachs and toddler fast asleep in the other room, they pulled their chairs round the fire, where Cate delivered her news. She looked at these two friends. Maggie, more of a mother to her than anyone had ever been. And Lizzie, little frightened Lizzie with a giant's heart in her. They were her family now. Both the women were staring at her in amazement as she finished speaking.

"But, but what happened in the kitchen, when Cook came back?" Lizzie asked. "Surely he's never gone and finished you both?"

Maggie said nothing. Cate's wage was essential in their struggle. She'd look for work, turn her hand to anything, but it wasn't the same as a regular job. And what about the scraps that Cook sent home? They'd come to rely on those when money was short.

"Cate!" Lizzie's cry broke the silence.

"Wheesht, you'll wake the bairn!" Maggie silenced her daughter. "Cate, for God's sake, what happened then?"

"I'm to be a parlour maid!" She enjoyed the stunned looks on her friends' faces. Then they were all talking and hugging one another until a miserable cry of 'waater' from the other room put a stop to it.

Settling Rhoddy down again, Cate found it hard to forget how close to losing her position she'd come. Certainly, if there had been a Mrs. McAlister or that horrid daughter of the house had been there, right now she'd be jobless. Her fear, when Cook had collapsed into her rocking chair and wiped her eyes with the dirty apron, had set her heart pounding until it echoed in her head. Then, just as she'd thought she might indeed faint, Cook had looked straight at her and said the Master wanted to see her. Knowing it was the end she'd dragged her unwilling limbs upstairs to the study.

Normally she loved that room, reminding her as it did of the Kevinishe library, but that night it held no comfort. Then he'd smiled and told her, since she was good and quiet, she could do the upstairs service. But one thing he wouldn't stand for was Cook's big clothing. Funny that. When he'd smiled he looked a different man and, sitting down, he'd no looked so long and skinny. Cate smiled as she watched her son, thumb in mouth, fighting the sleep threatening to overtake him. Aye, the two of them would be just fine. She still had a job and, with a new kitchen maid to be employed, mebbe her hours wouldn't be so long. Closing the door she crept quietly back to the fireside.

"He's quiet then?" Maggie said.

"He's fine". Cate studied them both.   She understood that Maggie had been upset at the thought of her losing the job in the Lawyer's house, for with her limp Lizzie could not go back to the long walks and hard work in service. Cate knew she was stronger than Lizzie. Also, there was a determination inside her that had nothing to do with physical strength. Whatever the task, she went at it as though she'd do it better than anyone else ever could. She was sure that, no matter what happened to her now, she'd fight her way through.

"Come on now Cate, after all the excitement, haven't you forgotten something else?"

"I was never meant to get a message, Maggie. Oh I'm that sorry! With everything I just…."

"It's your birthday Cate! The 17th of September, 'Bramble Time', as you call it." Lizzie could wait no longer. Her lids were closing with the warmth and the day had been a long one for her. Going over to the bed she brought the precious blanket parcel and laid it on Cate's lap. "Go on then, open it. It's your present."

Lizzie felt wonderful. These two took such care of her and she was always the one doing the taking. Her pale face, flushed with pleasure as much as from the warmth, had a delicate prettiness about it, but she was unaware of it, having eyes only for Cate.

The gasps, as her work was revealed, fingered, held up and finally tried on, banished all her tiredness. Dazzled by the sight of Cate in the cream dress and sparkly clips, Lizzie was filled with a warm glow of satisfaction. She'd taken her first step to independence.

Cate stood back in the dining room to admire her handiwork. The silver glistened, the crystal shone, and the florist's flowers bathed the room in perfume. Like the rest of the house the furniture was over heavy for her taste, the decoration too dark, but she liked the feel of the deep rugs that covered most of the floor. In a way it reminded her of Kevinishe, though the furniture was smaller. If she ever had a house it would be like Lady Sarah's room, with colours from the sea, gardens and skies, comforting instead of frightening you with the dark gloom of it all.

In the last year she'd served dinner parties before, but this one was special. All the master's family were to be there with some of the legal men of Glasgow and their wives, for he was well liked.

"You can see your face in everything, Cate. I'm almost blinded by all the sparkling. As usual you've done well." McAlister complimented her as he came through the door.

"Thank you, sir. I do want it all to be right for your fiftieth birthday." Cate hoped it would be, though she didn't trust the daughter of the house. Ever since Cate's promotion, Caroline Bryant seemed never to be out of the house. Always criticizing and complaining; dropping things to make a mess; spoiling the displays; a bang here a push there, and all the time nagging the master to sack her. Unpleasant though it was, Cate had to smile. Little did Mrs. Bryant know that the tinker boys and then Bruce had been doing that sort of thing since she'd been very young and she'd coped with it all. Still, she had a feeling about tonight and it wasn't good.

As the meal progressed Caroline Bryant took every opportunity to get in Cate's way during dinner—a fork dropped here, a knock there, hot soup on the girl's hand while she was serving—anything to disrupt the meal. Cate meanwhile delivered course after course, that the useless maid Mrs' Bryant had hired, brought to the dining room, knowing the service had been somewhat ragged because of the interruptions by the daughter of the house. Serving complete she made her way to the kitchen and told Cook all about it.

"I tell you, Cook, it's no right. That woman! I could spill the damn soup over her, never mind me!"

"She never did, Cate? What about the guests?"

"Oh, she's too clever to be seen."

"It's no right. You must tell the master."

"No, I can't say anything. I might lose my position. What makes me madder than anything is she's just trying to show me up. But to do it on the master's special party! It's too much. How could she, Cook?"

"Ach, yon one was aye selfish. Everything had to be hers. Too spoilt for her ain good. If the mistress were still alive she'd die of shame. Ada, yon fancy maid's cleared off, so go you and start clearing, now they're all finished. Here y'are, Cate. There's the coffee for the drawing room. The men'll likely have it there tonight with the ladies, seeing as it's a special occasion."

"I'll serve the coffee. Then, when I can get away, I'll help you in the dining room, Ada. So come on. The sooner we start the sooner we'll get away."

Ada, the new kitchen maid was easily frightened and was never at ease upstairs, but did as she was bid.

Caroline Bryant was furious. She'd tried to trip that hussy up all during dinner, but nothing worked. For some time now she'd seen her father come to depend on the slut, and it wouldn't do. Somehow she had to disgrace her in front of the guests. She'd thought Ian would help, but then her engineer brother could never see anything unless it had nuts and bolts in it! She'd only moments left. Looking round the empty dining room she tried to think of something. Eyes searching the now cluttered table, they alighted on the port carafe. Perfect! Two minutes later she was horror struck as the red runnel dripped onto the Abusson carpet beneath.

The exclamation behind her brought new danger until she saw it was only the stupid kitchen girl. "Look at the mess that parlour maid has made of maiy father's carpet. I must find him at once."

"B b b but it was you—."

"How dare you speak to me? Aiy know she did it and so do you!" She emphasised her words with a sound slap across the terrified girl's face. "Don't you?"

As the wretched girl nodded, the older woman made to pass her only to come face to face with her father in the doorway. "Oh, Father, aiy was just…."

"Leave it now, girl." Waiting until the frightened maid, hand to her face, disappeared, Malcolm McAlister closed the door and faced his daughter. "Why have you deserted your guests, Caroline?"

"Well, Father, I've been unhappy all evening about that girl."

"The kitchen maid?"

"No. No. The other one."

"Ah, you mean Cate? It seems to me there is no pleasing you where Cate is concerned."

"Only because she does seem to be so bad at her job. Sack her and I'll find you a much better one. After all, just look at that mess! And it was Mother's favourite carpet. Whatever will she do next?"

"Probably clear everything up and take the long walk home."

"Oh, you mustn't feel sorry for her, Father. You gave her every chance."

"Actually it's you I feel sorry for."

"Me, Father? It's been no trouble looking out for you. You know aiy like doing it."

"I don't think so. Let's put an end to this farce. You spilt the port. Both the new girl and I saw you, and then you bullied a lie out of her. I'm ashamed of you, Caroline. Why, in God's name, have you taken such a dislike to Cate?"

"She's a trollop and useless."

"Enough. Since that girl has been here my home has been well run and my every need catered for."

"Exactly, Father. She's a slut!"

"So help me, Caroline, I've never struck a woman, but that remark, with its insinuation, deserves it and that thought dishonours only yourself. Let me make this quite clear. This is my house and I make the decisions in it. Cate suits me perfectly, and, if tonight is anything to judge by, this is not the first mischief you've done her. No more. Do you hear? Now away and do your duty as hostess. Your guests will have finished their coffee by now and be perplexed by your absence. I'll follow in a moment or two to avert suspicion of any problems."

So she'd lost and, now her father was aware of the situation, she daren't try anything else. But as she saw Cate leave the drawing room with her loaded tray she stepped back into the recess.

Cate was never really sure what happened. One minute she was carrying a tray of empty coffee cups from the drawing room. The next she was crashing down the kitchen stairs, cups flying, coffee dregs in her eyes, and then blood, before she passed out. Caroline nodded in satisfaction as the girl hurtled downwards. It had been such a very little push.

8

"Oh there y'are, Lizzie, and how's the wee man the day?"

"Ma Mammy didna come home last night, so she didna, Mrs. Petrie."

"Is that right, Rhoddy? Now why would that be, Lizzie? She's never after a fella, is she, hen?"

"Mrs. Petrie, Cate's no like that. No, no. The family had a big party for the Lawyer's birthday and they were likely so late she just bedded doon in the wee box room."

"Would you just listen to that lot in there! Bedlam this early! God help the park the day! C'mon bairns, time we were aff."

With Maggie already gone, Lizzie finished tidying and then, wrapping up well against the chill autumn winds, made her way to the baker's.

"Will youse take care on they stairs! Margie, whit're ye greeting for noo? No, ye canna have a penny chew, so just had your bawlin. Rhoddy, grab Ian's han till we're doon the stairs." Just then she recognised the woman coming up. "Hello there, hen, how're ye doin? I havena seen you since you rented roond the back. You here for a visit then?" Maudie thought her old neighbour certainly wasn't looking well.

"Weel, ma man's bad again. He's never been right since the accident, ye ken. We're finding it a struggle—him with less work like. I'm for the woman up the stairs from you. She's needin new lodgings next week, an I can do wi the cash. Here, is all they bairns yours?"

"No, no, hen, they're no all mine. Mikey, staun still! Are you still bad wi the lungs, hen?"

"Aye, weel, Maudie, if I stopped the fags mebbe it'd be better, but I canna do withoot ma yin pleasure now, can I?"

"S'right, there's nae much else."

"You'll need a bigger hame soon if you've any more bairns."

"There's no the money for that, hen, I can tell you. Jessie, will ye get aff the groon! You're fair black enough."

Solly was nearly knocked over in the crush of small bodies, milling around the top of the stairs. He could barely catch his breath after the steep climb, but the plump woman rescued him.

"Staun still bairns, will youse! Let the man see some space for God's sake." Am right sorry, so I am, Mister. Are you aright there?" Lord, but he was a poor looking fellow, a Jew by the size of his nose. Put the lie to the thought they were all rich. He was shabby as well as being right poorly.

"Could you tell me where Mrs. Maggie is?"

"At the chemicals. Where else at this time o day? Lizzie's at the baker's." Seeing the stiff white envelope in his hand, she hoped to God he wasna from the bailiffs. That kind of notice nearly always meant bad news. "Is that for Maggie then? You're no a bailie man now, are you?"

"No, I'm a clerk from Mr. McAlister. This is a letter about Cate."

"Do you here that, Rhoddy? Your Mammy has a braw big letter from the lawyer."

"Maudie," her neighbour interrupted, "that lawyer, name of McAlister, you say. Was he no the fella that got compensation for yon man? You ken, him that bides roon the close, Donald. The one with baith his legs chopped off wi a girder. In Brown's yard it was."

"Yes, I do believe that we handled that case." Solly had difficulty making himself heard with all the background noise.

Maudie Petrie felt her neighbour had barged in. The letter was none of her business. Turning to the clerk she held out her hand. "See, here now, gie's the letter. Dinna you worry yirsel. I'll see she gets it, Mister."

Solly reluctantly handed the letter over, waded through the jostling group of children and made his way back to the office.

Mrs. Petrie, her importance regained, watched him go, then turned to her friend. "Weel, take care of yersel, hen. Come on noo, bairns, careful doon the stairs. We've the park first, an then the messages. An we'll need tae be back in good time for your Mammy, Jordi, so we will."

Safely in the park, watching the bairns chasing round and round, she couldn't help thinking of the lawyer, wishing there were more like him. Just look at her old neighbour. It was always the same in the yards. Work was there, but you had to be fit. If you didn't work there was no pay. Oh, the unions were trying to get a hold but the owners were defiant. Her man had fallen to his death at the shipyard and the miserable bit of compensation money was soon swallowed up in the expense of the hearse and such like. Well, you couldn't let your man go shabby to his grave. She'd struggled and, yes, she'd had the odd man pay for a favour or two, but you had to live.

By the time she heard Maggie's step on the landing below, the letter in Mrs. Petrie's care had suffered the fate that befalls all things in a day full of unruly children. Stained with bits of food, crumpled by sticky fingers, finally folded and stuck in her pinny pocket for safety, it was a poor looking thing that she held out to her neighbour. "I'm that sorry, Maggie, but you'd need eyes in the back of yir heid with they bairns. It disna look sae braw as when the clerkie fella geid it tae me, but at least it's safe."

Anxious though she was about the contents, Maggie smiled at the big-hearted woman.

"Thank you anyway. I'll away an read it indoors." Ignoring the disappointed look on her neighbour's face, she turned the key in her lock, to put an end to the conversation.

Cate groaned as she turned in her sleep. Then, fully awake, she pushed herself up on the truckle bed, in the box room. There were bruises on various parts of her body and cuts to both her hands, where she'd landed on broken crockery. The left arm and shoulder now tightly bandaged had taken the brunt of the fall as she'd pitched headlong down the stairs, sending the tray and its contents hurtling ahead of her. Now they hurt unbearably.

It was just so strange. She'd been up and down those self same steps with far heavier burdens and never once had she even stumbled. The worst of it was that it had spoiled the Master's birthday, what with all the noise and everything. Two of the gentlemen guests had moved her into the laundry room and laid her on the table, so Ada said. Then, when the doctor arrived, she remembered the pain as he'd strapped her arm up. The next thing she knew it was morning and somehow she was on the bed in the box room. That was yesterday, was it? Cook and Ada had seen to her and the master had been down himself. Now that was kind, worrying about hired help. She was lucky to be working for someone like him. She had to get back on her feet. She'd a job to do, and by now Maggie would be really worried. Struggling upright she was glad to see Ada.

"Oh, Cate, I dinna think you should be oot of bed. What'll Cook say?"

"Wheesht, Ada. Here, give me your arm to steady me." What she would give for a good strong dram of Craeg Dhu right now to ease her aches and pains! Some of the Cailleach's liniment would help matters too. By the time they'd struggled along the corridor to the kitchen, Cate knew she was fit neither for work nor indeed for the journey home.

"There's no way you can work like that, Cate. Sorry as I am for your accident I can't do everything, what with Ada new an all. One day's enough. Try as I might, I can no longer manage."

"Where's ma Mammy, Auntie Maggie?"

"She's working extra, Rhoddy." God forgive her for the lie, but no need to upset the bairn. "She'll mebbe be away for a wee while now, but you'll be fine with Lizzie an me."

"An Mrs. Petrie an bairns?"

"That you will, ma wee pet, just like normal. See, here's Lizzie! Now we'll have our tea." At the question on Lizzie's lips as she came through the door, Maggie shook her head, pointed to the envelope on the table and then gave Rhoddy his broth. With Cate's money stopping, it would be back to bread and dripping for them all.

"Mammy's letter." Rhoddy stuck a stubby finger towards the table.

"That's right, Rhoddy. That's how I know Cate won't be home for a wee while, just like I told you. Isn't that right, Lizzie?"

"Aye, it is. See, we'll look after you just fine, and then your mammy will be back home."

With Rhoddy washed and bedded down, Maggie drew her chair to the stove and read the letter again. Oh, it said all the right things. Cate had had a bad fall and wouldn't be home for a few days. But what sort of fall and who would do her work? Mr. McAlister had been good to Lizzie, but stands to reason he wouldn't keep supporting hired help who couldn't stand on their feet, never mind do their job. That was the puzzling thing. Maggie had never seen any one as nimble as Cate. Even when she was carrying she'd still skipped about. Like the young fawns on the hillside she'd been, until the final weeks of her pregnancy. Ah well, once again the threat of unemployment hung over them.

Coughing over the papers on his office desk, McAlister was interrupted by his clerk

"You'd be the better of being away home, Mr.McAlister, sir. That's a right bad cough you've got."

"You're right, Solly, and you would know with the chest troubles that you and your mother have had all these years. I'm sorry your efforts couldn't save her."

"Well, it was a blessing in the end. She was fair worn out. I'll finish up here for you, sir, and see Bessie out when she's done cleaning. You could stop at home tomorrow, sir, and then you'll have the weekend after that to sort yourself out."

"I'm not for taking days off, but your right, Solly. I certainly don't feel well. I'll see you on Monday then. If anything comes up tomorrow, just slip the necessary papers round to the house on your way home and I'll study them there. Goodnight to you." A solid lad was Solly, hardworking and intelligent but a weak constitution. Malcolm hoped what was ailing him wouldn't spread to the young man.

Hearing the coughing as he came through the door and knowing the Master was early, Cate left the laying of the table to meet him in the hall. "Sir, you'll need to be taking something for that cough before it goes to your chest, you know."

Ill as he felt, it was good to come home to such concern. Remembering the hoo-ha over her fall and his insistence that they must muddle through till she was on her feet again had certainly been the right decision. Typically, her injuries hadn't stopped her coming to work before she recovered completely.

"Sir, are you...?

"I'm sorry, Cate, I was thinking. Yes, I'll have one of your magic potions. You've half the neighbourhood at my doorstep for those."

"Well, I'm sorry for that, sir, but most of them are too poor to pay for salves and such and I enjoy doing it. I've been told I've healing hands. I used to rub the horses in my old place and folks' aches and pains are more or less the same. I get my own ingredients for the mixes where I can. I'm not taking them from you. Well, a few bits of goose grease and things that would only be thrown out."

"And welcome to them you are. Now, a tray to my room with something light and whatever I'm to take from you for the cough."

"Are you to have a bath first, sir?"

"No. No. To tell the truth I'm bone weary and...." A fierce coughing fit put an end to his speech. He waved his arm upwards and made for the stairs.

Later, knocking quietly, Cate pushed the door open. Right enough, he'd drifted off to sleep. Removing the tray, she shook her head. He'd barely touched the meal, a light consommé and a nice piece of chicken breast to follow. Cook had the right of it. Even when well he simply didn't eat enough. Strange that. Here he was, a fine gentleman no bothered about all the food he was given, and there were those in the tenements near starving. He looked fevered, mind, and she felt uneasy. She knew enough to know this was no ordinary cough and cold. She'd keep the kettles filled on the stove and make a poultice ready. He could be in trouble in the night.

How many days had it been now? In the sleepless nights that had seen the master slide quickly from his bad cough to the pneumonia, Cate had been forced to remember those other days and nights she'd laboured long and hard to save a patient. The memory of wee

David's death was always upsetting for her. She'd read stories of girls' first loves but those were of girls on the eve of womanhood. She'd found her first love as a child, and given him her all. His death still hurt now. She'd no love, but gratitude for the kindness from Lady Sarah and affection for the old Laird. Yes, and respect. He'd introduced her to many new things and urged her to better herself. Mind, when it came to it, they stuck to their own. No word when she'd left from any of them. It was as if she'd never existed.

Of course there was Fisher, who'd been so kind to her then. She never even thought in words about what had happened. It was a sore place deep inside her. What she did think of was what she'd do to Bruce some day. Oh yes, she'd work and scrub and—but that would never get her where she needed to be! No. Somehow she'd have to find another way. What was it that MacNishe used to say? 'Use your intelligence'.

The learning, that's what she'd have to keep on with. Oh, she'd mastered the parlour maiding and even the cooking when Cook was ill, but it still wasn't enough. She'd need to take time to go back to her reading. Would the master let her borrow a book from the study? She could stop a while after hours and read there in the kitchen where it was warm. Maybe when he was better—ah, but would he get better? Mrs. Bryant would soon get rid of her if he didn't. That was definite. Then she'd be sliding down the ladder to the bottom again. Mind, she still had the drawing of the dresses, but even that was no good without the money behind it. A hoarse whisper from the bed brought her back to the present.

"What time is it?"

"Never you mind what time it is, sir. More like what day is it! Oh sir, you've been really bad. Doctor's been every day and we've been that upset for you." More than could be said for his own family when they finally got around to coming, 'Aih couldn't possibly come closer, the germs, you know, and mai position.' That's all the sympathy the daughter of the house could give, but quick enough to check with the doctor as to how ill the poor master really was and whether he would last. The son only wanted to know if he should make arrangements to see to his father's business. The doctor, an old friend of the master's, was so put out he'd muttered under his breath and slammed the front door as he left.

"A drink, Cate, if you…."

"Right here, sir. See I'll slip my hands under your shoulders and hoik you up. Slowly now while I sort the pillows. There, that's better. Now here's the medicine we've been given by the doctor, so another wee spoon and wash it down with this hot elderberry. I've sweetened it well with sugar to build up your strength. The juice from the berries will help with the sweating and ease the bronchials."

"Mmmm. That smells and tastes good. What time did you say it was?"

The gurgle of her soft laugh washed over him and he could almost have been back with Alice. On that thought he drifted off again.

Very gently Cate tucked the bedclothes round him and took the glass downstairs to the kitchen where Cook and Ada looked up as she came in.

"Whit's he like the day, Cate?"

"Och, Ada, I think he's going to be alright."

"Praise the Lord."

"More like praise Cate." Cook interrupted. "An would you look at her now! Come on, my girl, you need your bed. Couched in a chair night and day, you'll be the next one. Damn! There's the front doorbell! No, you stay where you are, Cate. Come on then, Ada, go and answer it."

"I couldna, Cook. I dinna know how."

"Ada Furniss you come in through a door every day of the week. You just open the blessed thing! True enough you're no the bonniest sight to be greeting anyone, but that canna be helped. It's most likely the doctor any road. So get on with it. Merciful heavens, who's battering the basement door now? You sit still, Cate, till I get some food into you. I'll get that."

Cate waited until Cook was out of sight and then made her way upstairs again, passing Ada scurrying back to the familiar safety of the kitchen. She caught the doctor at the bedroom door.

"You, young woman, should be in bed. You're done in."

108

"I'll be alright, Doctor. Someone must look to the Master."

"Indeed, but it shouldn't all have been left to you, lass."

Checking his sleeping patient the doctor knew the crisis was over, but his patient would need a lengthy convalescence. The young woman standing discreetly behind him would see to that. It had been her mustard poultice and drinks that had eased the patient before he'd even been called. When questioned, she'd told him she'd helped the old woman from her Highland village to use these things for the poor. They were making great progress with medicine, but only a fool would decry the healing of centuries.

"He's a bit easier now, Doctor, isn't he?" Cate enquired of the silent doctor.

"Indeed he is, and mainly thanks to you, lass. But now if you're to continue to care for him, the first thing you need is food and sleep. No, no arguments. The crisis is over and he should sleep now. Get that frightened wee soul who opened the door for me, to sit with him. She can wake you when you're needed. Do you hear now?" Accepting Cate's reluctant nod, he continued. "He'll need time at home and you'll have to keep him occupied or he'll be out of that bed and back to the office before the chest is mended. I'll call in a few days. If you're worried, send the girl for me. Time, the right food and good care—that's what he needs now."

Letting the doctor out, Cate made her way to the kitchen. True enough she did feel tired, and really she must make the effort to get home, though they knew she would stay till the master was better. But Ada would never do to sit with him. Lizzie now—she could, and maybe earn a penny or two for doing so. At least she'd get well fed for a couple of days and Cook might even spare a few bites for Lizzie to take home. The thought made her hurry down the stairs to see if Cook would agree.

"Well, what's the use me telling the clerk here you're dying on your feet with the lack of sleep and you come running down the stairs?"

"I'm that sleepy alright. The doctor's said Ada was to keep watch an...."

"No, no I couldna! No up the stairs an in his bedroom!" Overcome the girl hid her face in her apron and wept.

"Shsht now, Ada. I thought that, but if Cook agrees I have another idea— hello." It was the clerk again. He'd been round more times than the family. He was looking after his job right enough, but he did seem really worried about the master.

Solly smiled at her, while thinking she really did look ill.

"What's this idea then, Cate? Most likely it'll be a good one. You're a great one for the ideas. How you think them up goodness knows."

"I knew Ada wouldn't like it, Cook, but what about Lizzie? We know her and she knows the house. We could send Ada for her and…."

"If it would help I could go. Remember I've delivered a letter there," Solly would do anything to help her.

"Right you are," Cook answered for Cate. "Away you and find Lizzie, and there'll be a meal waiting for you both when you get here. Cate, back up there with you and have a wee snooze in the chair till they come and then food and bed for you, my girl. You've still a wheen of nursing to be done, if I'm not mistaken. Ada, you get to your scullery and wade into those vegetables. We've all sat around too long. Let's get this kitchen back to normal." Clapping her hands Cook urged them on. "Well, away with the lot of you. I've work to be done."

Warmly ensconced in his fireside chair, blanket wrapped round him by Cate, Malcolm McAlister studied the letter carefully and wondered if it might be worth considering. Certainly his illness had shown him the weakness of his position. A partner might not be a bad thing at that. They'd need another clerk, and then Solly could be trained to handle more work and get a larger wage. He was a good man was Solly. He must remember, next time he looked over his own will, to put something in it for his clerk. Now what had brought wills and dying to mind? Thinking of partners and his illness probably. Well, why not another young man given a lift up the ladder? He'd liked the look of him at the party and he'd heard Hardy was ambitious. Certainly well qualified and, if he was a bit sharp, he would always be there to keep him in hand. He'd think about it once he was back in the office. At the moment Solly brought the papers here to his study and they worked there with Cate on hand to see he didn't tire himself.

Sitting here, surrounded by his books and with the study fire practically sending him to sleep, he felt no real urge to return to full time work. That was the trouble with being made so comfortable at home. The only stressful moments were when the family deigned to call. Oh, Ian was not so bad, but they'd nothing in common. He'd once hoped the boy would follow him to the law, but he'd never shown any interest. Always the engineering that had fascinated him, and he'd a good job with Browns at the Clyde. He'd go far one day, literally. He was forever talking about America. Refused to buy a house despite his father's advice to do so. Apparently he wanted no ties to keep him here. Just up and away when he was ready. His wife, now, was too much like Caroline, his sister. Funny that. Alice, his own wife, who'd come from a rich background, had never had any side to her, while those two were forever trying on the fancy accents and sidling up to the great of Glasgow. The servants in his own house seemed to have more worth than his own offspring. A sad thought that, but one he had to admit was the truth.

Master fully recovered after weeks at home, Cate had returned to the tenements. As she made her way home this particular evening she thought over the various ways she could deliver her startling news. It had been obvious for some time now that Cook's health problems were worsening and today the poor woman had finally admitted she could no longer cope. Sad as she was for her, Cate was thrilled with the Master's suggestion to solve the vacancy problem, but now she had a problem of her own. How could she explain it? Letting herself in she could see Maggie and Lizzie sat round the stove, supper on the table, waiting for her.

When they'd finished washing up, Maggie turned to Cate. "You're over quiet the night, lass. No sickening for anything are you?"

"No, I'm fine, Maggie, just thoughtful."

"What was work like the day, Cate? How's Ada doing?"

"Ada's fine, Lizzie, but poor Cook has to finish work." There, it was out.

"Cook's never finishing? What are you saying, Cate? Is it the varicose?"

"That and the bunions, Lizzie, but mostly it's her lungs, she's huffing and puffing like one of they steamers on the Clyde. Give her half an hour on her feet and she's wheezing fit to drop, supposing her legs would hold her anyway." Cate knew the rest of this conversation was going to be very difficult. She'd no real choice. For once she was finding her way forward, but it meant a battle between heart and mind. They were the only real family she'd ever known but now they and their feelings would have to give way to her determination to 'get on'.

"Come on, Cate, tell us. What'll happen now? Will you mebbe get Cook's job? You've been doing most of it anyway this last year. What did the Master say?" Lizzie's excitement for the girl who'd become the sister she'd never had seemed to blind her to the obvious. Maggie, sitting quietly mending could see only hurt ahead for her beloved daughter. She'd always known it would happen, but had hoped the two girls could advance together somehow. Sadly dreams were for the rich, not for them.

"No, I've no got Cook's job."

"AAh, Cate, that's no fair. You do all the work." Lizzie was ready to do battle for her heroine.

"It's alright, Lizzie, don't get so worked up." Feeling Maggie's gaze, Cate knew she understood, but the next words were hard. "It's all going to change now. Mr. McAlister is tired of hiring in help he doesn't know, so I'm to be a housekeeper and when he's finished looking at the new cooks who apply I'm to choose from his choices." There. It was out. But the pleasure was largely spoilt at the sight of Maggie's knowing eyes. "I'm sorry, Maggie."

"It's okay, Cate, I'm glad for you. You've done really well for yourself and I know it'll mean big changes."

"Mammy, it's so exciting! Fancy our Cate a housekeeper! She'll be right posh."

Despite her disappointment, Maggie knew she had to keep the smile on her face. "Oh yes, very posh, but no too posh to come and see us now and again, eh Cate?"

"Don't be so daft, Mammy, she bides here."

Then the awful truth hit Lizzie. Housekeepers were just that. They kept house. Saw to everything from setting it going in the morning to checking everything last thing at night. They slept there.

Maggie and Cate kept their feelings hidden as the weakest of the trio worked out that her world was about to be shattered into fragments that might never be reassembled. Her lips trembled and she turned eyes so full of pain towards her friend that for a brief moment Cate faltered. Then, forcing herself to continue, she turned to Maggie.

"I hope you know me better than that, Maggie. You were the ones that gave me help when others had used me and thrown me out like unwanted rubbish. How could I ever be too posh to forget that? Besides, you're the only family I've ever really had. I don't know much about how families go on, but I do know I care for you both, so never forget that, for I never shall I..." Voice broken, Cate had a moment to wonder why it had never occurred to her that 'getting on' would mean hurting those she loved while giving her the ability to get even with those she hated.

"You'll be biding there. You'll leave us. Oh, Cate, I dinna want that and..." It was too much for Lizzie. All the dreams of going forward with this 'sister' of hers came tumbling down and smothered her with a blanket of hopelessness. She hid her face and the sobs swept through her small body, while the others could only watch as her pain made their unshed tears the harder to bear. They would have done anything to spare her, but knew there was nothing they could do.

Cate was the first to respond. "Hey. Come on now, Lizzie. Dry your tears." Taking the weeping girl in her arms she forced her head up till their eyes met. "Lizzie Balfour, wherever I go somehow you're coming with me, just as soon as I can manage it. Listen. Remember my bonnie dress? I love it. I bet you worked on it for weeks before it was ready for me?"

Still sobbing, Lizzie nodded.

"Well then, this will be just like that."

"Wh....what?"

"Well, it was no use for me when you bought it from the market was it"

"No....oo." The sobs quietened and a puzzled frown took their place.

"That's what it's going to be like. Just now what I have to do is very little use to you because I have to go away, but I'll be back, Lizzie, and then, wherever I am, you'll be there too. We'll fit just like the dress did in the end. Do you see?"

Sensing Maggie's unease, Cate released Lizzie and stood before them. "Look at me, both of you. I know you don't believe me, Maggie, but I mean every word. You know I have to do this. Someone once told me I had it in myself to be anything I wanted. Right now I don't know what that will be, so I must take any kind of advancement that's offered. Better jobs mean more money. That means I can be more in control of what happens to me and therefore to you. Don't you see?"

Cate knew she must make them understand, and was glad of an interruption from Rhoddy. Having settled him she came back to the kitchen her words ready for the other two. "Think of it like this. Now, I'm to be a housekeeper. Since I can't take Rhoddy with me I can pay good money to you, Lizzie, if you want to look after him, and for his food and lodgings to you, Maggie. So you see, as I move up you're coming with me. Remember what I've said. You're no forgotten. You're coming on this journey with me. Do you hear? You have my promise. See: cross my heart and hope to die!" The childish oath brought a smile to their faces and it was only Rhoddy's plaintive cry that sent Cate to tend to him again.

The other two sat in silence, awed by her passion and sincerity. Lizzie lost in wonder at the hope offered to her; Maggie sensing the strength, drive, and shaft of ruthlessness that flowed through the girl. There was no doubting at this moment Cate meant every heartfelt word, but just where would the road lead, and would the declaration be forgotten or perhaps just too inconvenient to remember?

Cate could not keep track of the months as they sped past. It had all happened as the Master wished. He'd chosen three cooks from his list of references and she'd been with him as he spoke to them. Her decision had been easy. The one from the country house had reminded her of Kevinishe and here was an assistant cook looking to better herself. A woman who knew the ways of a large establishment, a source of information and learning that Cate knew would benefit herself. So she'd chosen Mrs. Fraser—the Mrs. a polite title for any unmarried Cook, a trim, fresh-faced woman in her thirties, and they'd bedded down well together, each admiring the other's qualities.

Weekly payments to Lizzie, Maggie, and Mrs. Petrie, all three sharing the responsibility of Rhoddy, and the complete mastery of the housekeeping position had all fallen into place. Now another winter loomed and the annual turn around of light to heavy curtains, bedding, furniture protectors, and fuel orders upheaval was upon them.

"Cook, can you spare Ada for a bit this morning? I want to turn out the Master's bedroom."

"Right enough, Cate, when her vegetables are done and the floors scrubbed. Surely it's no long since it's been thoroughed?"

"I know but I'd like to start a proper clean now, before we get the winter things out. Ada, the linen will have to be boiled once it's stripped. Be as quick as you can. I'll get started straight away. I want it finished for the master coming home." Enjoying the thrill of organized working, Cate went upstairs to begin.

Cook watched her go before turning to Ada. "I've never seen the like of that one."

"How's that, Cook?"

"Well now, you know I like things done just right, but if the floor's clean there's no call for extra scrubbing. Now is there?"

"Noo-oh. But—but Cate disna do the scrubbing now she's made up to a housekeeper."

"Oh, away you an get stuck into the turnips and tatties, it would take too long to explain."

As she set about her bread, Cook let her thoughts dwell on the young woman cleaning upstairs. Cate had been quite frank when she'd been chosen for the cook's job. Said she'd only just been made up to housekeeper, so they'd both be starting together, in a way. She'd the speaking and the ways of the housekeeper now though. Sharp she was if things weren't right with the meals, but just let that high and mighty Mrs. Bryant order special dishes and Cate was the first to help out in the kitchen. She wasn't above doing the daily cooking when needed. Come to that, when necessary, Cate would even scrub. Still, there was surely no need to keep on at things when they were right enough as they were. A mouse would be safer crossing Sauchiehall Street than running across a floor in this house! And she couldn't say it's the Master who's looking for it. When did men ever notice if the floor was scrubbed?

No, it was something within the lass driving her on. It wouldn't be a restful life for her unless she let up now an again. She'd wear herself out if she wasn't careful, and the Master never noticed anything but his legal papers. Mind, she'd read in the Herald he'd got a load of silver for a fitter who'd been crushed. Made the yard bosses pay up, he did. Quite right too, with the sovereigns pouring into the gentry's pockets from all the ships they sent out of the Clyde. Ah well, she'd put the meals on the table and let the rest sort themselves out. There could be worse faults than being over eager to get everything right. And there were some housekeepers that were right bitches. Cate was certainly better than most, young as she was.

9

Cate came into the dining room to finish clearing the dirty dishes. A discreet cough attracted her employer's attention. "I've put your coffee in the study, sir, and stirred the fire. It's colder now the nights are setting in."

"Yes, Cate, winter will soon be on us and we'll all be spluttering with coughs and colds. At least we'll be saved poor old Mrs. Jamieson's wheezing this winter."

"Mrs. Jamieson, sir?"

"Our old Cook."

"Is that what her name was? I never knew."

"If you remember it all started with the 'bronchials', the 'varicose', the 'bunions' and most of the remainder of the medical books."

"That's right, sir, and I was so afraid you were going to finish me. And Cook was near to choking trying to speak up. Then there was her uniform. I fair drowned in it." Cate laughed at the picture they must have made for the Master.

It made him smile too. How nice to share an amusing memory with this young girl. Her laughter made him feel less careworn at the end of the day. "Yes indeed. I was sorry to hear of her death, though it was not unexpected after her illness."

Cate's gasp and saddened expression moved him.

" I'm sorry. Did you not know? Come now, don't let it distress you so. I ensured she was taken care of when she left us, after all she'd served me well for years. I only had news of her death this week and naturally I went to the funeral. I meant to tell you but it slipped my mind." What a warm heart the girl had, unlike his daughter Caroline! She would barely have spared a thought for the woman who'd provided all those clever dishes for the Kelvinside household. "I'm sure you wouldn't have liked her to suffer all that ill health just to prolong her life." He suddenly found a great need to wipe the sadness from her face. "I see you've another book on the side there. You do enjoy reading, then?"

"Yes sir. It's 'Oliver Twist' this time. Sad it was and downright cruel."

"Indeed, but happy at the end. That no doubt pleased you. Will you read some more?"

"Oh yes, sir. I was going to change it when I took the coffee in, but by the time I'd done the fire and...."

"Well, let's do that now. Perhaps you'll let me make some suggestions. Leave Ada to clear for once. I may be a selfish man but I do notice what goes on. There is no need for you to see to every task yourself. The others will never learn if you don't let them, and you will wear yourself out. I can't have that on my account!"

"But, sir, I'm so glad to have the position and I must do my best."

"Your best certainly, my dear, but the impossible is not really necessary. I've watched you: up before dawn, at it all day and never asleep until late. Working and learning are worthwhile, but not if you wear yourself out. And what of Lizzie? I trust you've not forgotten her in your care of me?" Speaking of the timid young Lizzie had been a mere ruse to wrench her thoughts from Cook's death.

Never forgotten, Cate thought, but neglected certainly. She meant to go more often, but there was so much to do here, especially with the reading. Anyway, Rhoddy barely spoke when she saw him. He was always full of Lizzie this and Mrs. Petrie that. Understandably so, as they were now more in his world than she was. Maggie she barely saw, as evening times she had to be here. Sometimes it was just easier to send Ada with the money for Rhoddy's keep. At least the kitchen maid enjoyed the outing and by all accounts had become quite friendly with Lizzie. Always full of it she was the next day, though never a word to anyone here in the house about the boy. After all, only respectable girls were given better positions. She turned her attention back to her employer.

"No sir."

Damn it all! Malcolm saw, by her silence, he'd just replaced the sadness over Cook, with worry. Obviously she'd been too busy to see her friend. He must put that right. "I thought so. Don't neglect your own need for company."

As they entered the study he gestured at the fire. "Look. Your poker has done us proud. A roaring fire! Why don't you choose your book and sit quietly with it while I attend to some paperwork?"

"Sir, the very idea! I couldna."

"I see you're truly shocked. Your fine accent has slipped just a little." Really, he mustn't tease her. She wasn't Alice. "Come now, I wasn't complaining There's no need to look so surprised. But it does seem ridiculous that you creep up to your cold attic room when all this warmth is being lavished on me. I certainly don't mind, so why on earth should you?"

"We…ell sir."

"Fine, the offer's there if you want it. I must to my work." Settling himself behind the desk, he leafed through the paperwork while glancing sideways at the young woman in her dilemma. He'd sensed quite early on that she appreciated fine things. The loving way she handled the leather-bound books, the care with which she shone his silver, the way she arranged his food on the serving dishes, all pointed to someone who craved quality. Now he could see the temptation that the warm study held for her. Where better to curl up and read a good book? Finally, she lowered herself onto one of the smaller chairs, perching uneasily on the edge, and opened her book. Somehow the work on his desk was then completed more easily. That silent figure engrossed in a grim Dickensian world had indeed lightened his own.

Cate caught the tram just as it was leaving. It was again some weeks since she'd visited the tenements and she really didn't have time today, but spending coppers on the tram would certainly speed it up. Alighting at her stop she hurried towards the close. Cate knew she wasn't being fair. It wasn't their fault they were so far away, and they definitely couldn't be blamed for the way she used her time trying to make everything just right for the master so that he wouldn't be able to do without her. Surely they could see the importance of that? Thrusting aside the possibility that they did see it, and thought the less of her, she called out, "Lizzie, it's me," as she approached the door.

"Well now, it's a while since you've been, Cate. What a pity Rhoddy's away tae the park with the other bairns."

"It can't be helped, Lizzie. Look what I've brought." Putting the basket on the table, Cate tried to hide the fact that she wasn't too upset at Rhoddy's absence. "He'd no want to miss playing now, would he? How's the leg, Lizzie?"

Lately this had been the pattern. More often than not the first few words between the two girls were almost those of strangers. Once tea was made and the sewing brought out, the old warmth returned, but each visit the awkwardness at the beginning stretched a little further.

"The cold makes it ache, but never mind. Oh Cate! Look at all that food! Mammy says…."

"What, Lizzie? What does Maggie say?"

A shake of the head was the only reply.

"Come on, Lizzie. It's me, Cate. There's nothing you can't tell me."

Lizzie turned to the stove and poked an already glowing fire.

"Lizzie, what's troubling you and Maggie? If it's something you need I'll get it for you." Cate tried again.

"No. No. You bring more than we need. No it's just—it's just we miss you Cate. Somehow it's no the same anymore. I dinna want you to change, Cate." She couldn't help it as tears rolled down her cheeks.

Cate was horrified. Lizzie crying!

"My dear, dear Lizzie, I'm so sorry. I will try to come more often. I treasure your friendship. You must believe that. It's just— oh, I get so into seeing everything is as good as it could possibly be in the house so as I don't lose my position. Then there's the reading. I'm learning so much, Lizzie, I feel my head will burst with it all! In the evenings sometimes in the study we, the Master and I, talk about his work and the ships and a million other things. Oh, Lizzie, it's all so wonderful and exciting and I want to know and do it all. I'm sorry, truly I am. But it's all there for the taking—this is my chance to get on. Don't you see, Lizzie?"

"I think so." She wasn't so very sure. This whirlwind of a girl was speaking of things that shouldn't be. Surely she could see that? Servants didn't talk to masters except to answer when spoken to. Studies were holy places where great works of the mind went on. Heavens, she'd be going to the legal office next! No wonder they were awkward with one another! Cate meant well, but she didn't belong in the tenements any longer, even to visit. And yet, behind all the talk, she was certain that deep down, Cate, her Cate, was still there. Maybe it was only half right.

"Yes I do see, Cate. But we're here too, Mammy, Rhoddy and me. You must mind him, Cate. You're his Mammy. I know it was hard about Bruce and everything, but none of it was the bairn's fault. Mind whit the preacher says aboot the sins of the fathers no fir the bairns. It's no right, Cate."

"One day, Lizzie Balfour, you'll find out just how good and brave a person you are. You're certainly far, far nicer than I'll ever be. I will try harder to come more often, for all your sakes. Come on, give's a hug. Put the kettle on and get the sewing out

As Malcolm put his pen down and stood up to stretch, he studied the bent head with the crown of red hair in front of the study fire. "Your head's never out of a book is it, Cate?" He smiled as he watched her drag herself out of the make-believe world of words back to reality.

"Oh it's great, the reading. Thank you, sir, for letting me borrow them and sit here in comfort of an evening. I'm sure it's not the done thing. You must just say if you change your mind. I can sit in my room, but I would fair miss the books. I need to learn, you see. I can be that ignorant about things, but it's because I don't know about them. I never had the chance."

"Well, you've certainly learned as far as housekeeping is concerned. I've rarely been as comfortable in my own home as I am now."

"I'm glad, sir. It was brave of you to let me tackle the job. I know others didn't agree with it at all."

"Ah, others! You must understand, Cate, that different people are driven by different emotions."

"Surely we're all the same really?" As soon as she said it Cate knew it was foolishness. Take that gentle soul Lizzie, her heart full, caring for someone else's bairn, her limp accepted with humility. No ranting and raving for sweet Lizzie, and how easily hurt she could be.

"We may start out the same, Cate, with all the same emotions, but each and every one of us develops those basics as we grow. Of course, we are also shaped by our worlds."

"You mean where we live and what happens to us, sir? Surely we can change things though? Supposing you weren't content with what you had and were?" Cate challenged him.

"My, you look fierce all of a sudden! Was it something I said?"

"In a way. I've always wanted to better myself. Do people like me get to change more than people like you, sir? I mean can you start really low and work up? Would just working do it?"

"Yes it would. I worked my way up. But do you mean becoming wealthy Cate?"

"Oh yes, sir. Surely, if you'd money, then you'd make yourself somebody? I mean, you could then do as you wanted."

"Now that depends. Money is certainly the key to advancement, in that you can then buy things and therefore improve your life, but it's certainly not the answer to everything."

"No, you must be wrong there, sir? You would want for nothing, supposing you had the money to buy everything."

"Certainly it would be great to go out and get everything you felt you ever wanted, but what then, Cate? What of true happiness? I know many wealthy people who have what is necessary for a good life, but they either still want more or they're unable to get what they really crave. With great wealth comes power and that too can bring its own unhappiness."

"I don't understand." That must be wrong? When she 'made something of herself' she would have money and with that she would be able to work out a way of getting her revenge on Bruce. Then there were the others at Kevinishe House. She'd worked hard for them and thought they liked her, but Bruce had been welcomed back and she'd been thrown out. Not a word. The permanent knot of rage she carried deep inside her tightened as she thought of it. Fair enough, she'd never expected them to throw Bruce out. He was the only heir after all. But to just wipe her from the picture! The old Laird, who'd saved her from the jail and always been kind to her—you'd have thought he at least would have sent word or maybe helped in some way. Surely Lady Sarah could have done something for her? Look at how she'd protected Davy from Bruce. What about protecting her from Bruce, or at least taking care of her afterwards? There was no point in all this looking back. They were all the same: they just ignored the poor. No wonder they were all lairds and the like! That's why she tried never to think of any of them—except Bruce. Oh, him she'd never forget! How could anyone forget what he'd done to her? Never mind the childish bullying. By his brutal assault and rape he'd left her with an illegitimate child! No. She would neither forget nor forgive Bruce MacNishe.

Now her clever master was telling her she'd never get even, no matter how much money she saved. Well, he was wrong. If she couldn't do it with money she'd get even with Bruce somehow. She'd just have to find a way!

She'd also have to balance her revenge and ambition with her determination to accommodate the other three across town. Lizzie had made her see, as the older, wiser Maggie had already guessed, that she was drifting away from them.

"Come, those frowns will leave dreadful lines. I'm not saying money won't buy you things. For instance I have a good business, and can afford servants to look after me. Money is no problem, but I would willingly have given most of this up to save my dear Alice from the grave. No, Cate, happiness does not come from money alone, and the power it gives has to be used wisely."

"I'm right sorry, sir, about your wife. I knew someone who died once and the sorrow stays with you." Afraid she'd said too much, Cate rose to go. She really enjoyed these evenings. In the beginning, serving his coffee in the study once the meal was cleared, she'd choose a book and take it to her room. Then he'd invited her to sit in the study reading, and that had led to the talking. There was no way she wanted to upset the Master and perhaps lose those treasured discussions. But it made it difficult to leave enough time for her 'family' in the tenements. It really was wearisome sometimes, trying to balance the two.

"I'll see to your cocoa and then lock up." Cate said as she left the study.

She certainly wasn't going to think overmuch about it all just now, and especially of young David and his early death. It still hurt too much and somehow, without really understanding why, she knew that that kind of 'soft' feeling was not what she needed to arm her for the future. Despite what her kind gentleman said, she would succeed. Quite how was as yet unclear, but she'd made a start. Better jobs, more money and finally the ability to control what happened to her and those she cared about was her main aim. Everything else had no room in her life, now or ever.

There now, yet another winter and the Master poorly again. Each time he'd had a bout she'd thought he'd never make it. Cate knew her job depended on him and his weak chest worried her. Despite paying Lizzie, Maggie and Mrs. Petrie, her pile of silver was increasing along with her learning, now she rarely lapsed into the speech of her childhood years or used the tenement words. She'd worked hard at her reading, studying the papers. Then there were visits to the museums, listening to the bands in the parks and observing people wherever she went. She drew the dresses the fine ladies wore, studied the way they walked, their speech, and their mannerisms. She'd read until her head ached sometimes, always learning, absorbing facts, figures, squirreling away anything and everything she could into the recesses of her brain, understanding that, somehow, somewhere she would use all of it.

As she climbed the stairs to check on him her thoughts were on the tenements. She tried hard to visit regularly, to play with Rhoddy, but it was obvious he preferred Lizzie. Why wouldn't he? Lizzie saw him as the child he was, whereas she saw her son as an extension of the father. That seemed an impossible hurdle to clear. But what use would any of the work, the learning and the caring be, if her employer died and she lost her position? She must take such good care of him he wouldn't. That had to be her immediate concern.

It wasn't only the position and the money. Oh, it was just fine to buy what she needed, which was little enough, but it was the money for the other three and all she'd saved that pleased her most. No, the Master was right. There was something other than being well fed and housed. It was like MacNishe all over again. She was happy seeing to her work, but it was the evenings and when he came home from the kirk on the Sabbath that she relished most. The kirk, however, was a delicate subject between them. All God-fearing people went to the kirk on the Sabbath. Trouble was she was far too angry with God to fear him. In fact she wasn't even sure he was there anyway. Most of this she kept to herself, knowing others felt it wrong. She didn't care what they thought, but it was a shame he was saddened by it. Apart from that, those times when it was just the two of them were like another kind of life, as if she were a completely different sort of person. He was definitely the best, kindest person alive. How those two children of his could look down on him and grieve him the way they did she'd never know. Knocking on the door she entered and was glad to see him awake.

"Here we are now. Have a wee gargle with this and then sip it slowly."

Raising himself on his elbow, Malcolm managed a brief smile. "Now what weird and wonderful stuff have we here today?"

"It's for your poor throat. All that coughing through the night—it'll be red raw. Right, swill it round and spit the first bit here." Holding the bowl close, Cate felt that, despite his bad night, he did look a little stronger.

"What in God's name is it, girl?"

"An infusion of sage, mint and chamomile, sir. It'll help ease your throat and chest"

"Well, if you say so, but, by the time the poultices are on and you've got me breathing heaven knows what over a bowl with my head wrapped in towels, I hardly feel human. Here, take it! I'm done with it."

"We have to give the body every help we can, sir, and you can aid it by sleeping. Precious little you had of that last night."

She watched contentedly as her patient slid under the blankets and closed his lids. Taking her place in the fireside chair she pondered on how their relationship had slowly changed in the last two years. Smiling, she remembered Ada too frightened to come and sit with him. She'd had to do so much more than that. Sponging his body when he was delirious, averting her eyes where possible, but in the long run this man held the key to her future and no modesty was going to get in the way of that. Had he guessed what she'd had to do, he'd have been mortified. Still, she'd helped him recover before, and that was the important thing, and she was well on the way to doing it again. A good sleep would see him turn the corner. He was a really good person. She liked older gentlemen and she was growing fond of him, just as she'd been fond of the old Laird.

Malcolm McAlister was uneasy as he drifted in and out of sleep. Although his partner could no longer be called 'new', having been with the firm for some time, James Hardy had not turned out to be the blessing he ought to have been. He seemed to court the more influential clients, and there were times when his judgement was contrary to the firm's principles. Take the eviction case he'd just handled. Malcolm had wanted to get more time for the family, but on his return from one of his many business trips he discovered that his firm had in fact been operating for the landlord as well. It was all smoothed over and apologies had been made, but it worried him. The man was getting a good reputation for being effective and the business was definitely thriving, but did he want to go down that road? Sharp practice and silver-tongued lawyers seemed to go hand in hand these days, and it was a trend he wanted no part of. Then there was Solly, a loyal clerk, whom his partner despised. 'Damn Jew boy', he'd called him.

The trouble was that he was spending less time in the office, his recurring bouts of illness requiring him to do more of his work at home. Or was it just his preference? That was the other source of uneasiness—Cate! Since Alice died he'd never much cared about who took care of the home or himself. The children were up and gone, so it was of minor importance with only him to consider, but all that changed with the advent of Cate. Now his home was really the only place he wanted to be and her company was like one of her soothing herbal medicines— it made him feel so much better.

Then there was Cate herself. He knew she was ambitious and she certainly worked hard enough to succeed. Yet her position was tenuous. Should anything happen to him, she would need to find new employment, and he was only too aware that Caroline would do all in her power to make it difficult for her. Ridiculous! He was a lawyer—all he needed to do was to provide for her should illness finally finish him. Nothing too elaborate, so as not to arouse ill feeling from his heirs, but enough to tide her over together with sealed references, so Caroline couldn't get her hands on them. After all, other than Alice, he cared more...!

What an old fool he was! No wonder he felt uneasy when she tended him in his bouts of illness. It wasn't just the embarrassment of her youth. He didn't want to be her patient. He much preferred the intimacy of the study fireside, watching the animation of her face as they spoke of her reading, basking in the sorrow she showed when discussing some of the poor wretches he fought for at work. Of course he cared more! Simply stated, she'd become an integral part of his life.

Even back at his office desk, his chest quiet for the time being, McAlister couldn't seem to get Cate out of his thoughts. Admitting this made him realise that she, on the other hand, though regarding him kindly, thought of him as just an employer, meaning she was free to go should she get a better offer. Probably a good thing he entertained infrequently since Alice's death. Only a few people knew of Cate's existence so the likelihood of her being enticed away was remote at present. Replacing her would be relatively easy— inconvenient, but easy. Trouble was he simply couldn't contemplate it. Her housekeeping skills were exemplary but it was the warm welcome that lured him home these days. He didn't want a housekeeper free to move when she wished.

He wanted her to be his companion as well. He thought now of the many evenings in the gloaming, the way she made him feel better even when he could barely breathe, the spring in his step as he neared home at the end of the day, the joy of their meals together (his suggestion), the way she made him laugh, and the peace and contentment her easy running of the house provided. He needed her. She was no longer someone he could do without. Companionship was what she gave him, with her ready laughter, her intelligence, and all the other things he enjoyed about her: the way those stray curls of flaming red would not be contained, however many hairpins she stuck savagely into them, and how her lithe body moved so quickly but never gave the feeling of unrest to her surroundings. When had he become so aware of her body? Old fool that he was! Surely he was beyond all that? And yet he'd missed it in the intervening years. He'd replaced that side of things with an increased workload, giving more time to his passion for righting the wrongs of those in power

By God, how good it was to feel the blood flowing again! Perhaps the man he once was could after all be resurrected? No. What kind of foolishness was that? Yet he'd been a happy man lately. He'd only now come to realize just how much Cate meant to him. Not as a housekeeper, but as a person. Why not make her a better offer? He'd raise her wages. Make it legal, a written contract. That's what he'd do. What if she refused? Would she refuse? Surely not! What better way could she find of 'getting on'? Oh it might not be the most exciting future, but they had an existing warm affection between them and could build on that. Yes, he'd do that. Then they could carry on as normal, though she'd be bound to him legally. But would she accept? She might well refuse. She was striking, young and unattached. She'd have no wish to remain in service for a long time. Would she want to leave and get married? And yet he knew she'd lost someone dear. Was her heart broken forever? It did happen. Why shouldn't the two of them live in quiet companionship for many years?

He could sit in the office no longer. A good walk would help him to present his case. Present his case indeed! What was he thinking about? It was a domestic arrangement he was going to make. Ah well, he was ever the lawyer. Yet, it was the man in him that sent him jauntily out of the office and it was the man in him who would fret till he knew her answer.

10

The scene was set. They'd enjoyed a lively meal discussing the rights of women, or the lack of them as Cate saw it. Both agreed with Glaswegian Helen Crawfurd's stand on votes for women, sympathising with her frustration because the press seemed to have lost interest in the subject in the last few years. Here they were in 1909, and women no nearer to getting the vote. Now they were settled in their respective armchairs with the newspapers strewn between them as they each looked for another article worth discussing. Should he bring her future employment up now? Why was he suddenly uneasy about it?

Studying her as she leafed through the pages of the Herald, she looked so completely at ease. She'd blossomed from a pretty girl into a lovely woman who'd grown into her position. She looked more like the mistress of the house than the housekeeper. The thoughts shifting uneasily at the back of his mind were so outrageous, so unlike him, that he feared bringing them forward. They did, however, make him pause to reflect on the employment contract. Somehow that seemed ill advised now.

Malcolm couldn't believe the difficulty he'd been having for weeks, be it at home or work. Good heavens, even in court today listening to evidence, her face had appeared in front of him. For years work had been his entire world. He'd paid little attention to his home comforts, entertaining, socialising—without Alice nothing but his legal calling had seemed worthwhile. Now Cate had gradually drawn him back into the everyday world of the living. She even appeared to be with him at work.

In the past, when he'd come upon any major problem, Alice always seemed to have the answer. Now he was turning more and more to Cate. Was he now beyond the companionship stage? The thought had been lurking there at the back of his mind for some time. He knew he had to address it before he'd find any kind of peace. He'd go and talk it over with Alice. The peace of the graveyard might help.

He'd waited another week since his visit to Alice's grave. He simply couldn't wait any longer. Seated in the study, sipping their coffee, he spoke. "Cate, I want to ask you something."

"What, sir?" She put down the Herald she'd been combing for an interesting topic for the night's discussion and waited.

"Will you marry me, Cate?" There he'd said it.

"Marriage? No! It would never do! It wouldna be right, sir!"

What had he expected when he proposed? No wonder she thought it wouldn't be right, a man twice her age! "You're right of course, Cate. Forgive me for being so foolish. I just thought— anyway dismiss it from your mind."

Cate watched as he got up from his chair and left the study. In her bewilderment she sensed she'd hurt him, but his proposition was just plain silly. He knew nothing of her. Dear Lord, she was but a tinker girl, and even the tinkers didn't think much of her. An important legal man married to her? Never! Staring at the red embers of the fire she tried to steady herself. 'I want to ask you something' he'd said. She'd expected some sort of household query, or maybe even what she thought of the day's newspaper she'd been reading, but marriage!

Looking round the study, her favourite room, she let her mind consider the pleasure of being there by rights. No. He was a good man, loyal and kind and always fighting for the rights of others. How could she be less than truthful with him? Across the city Rhoddy was asleep, a son never acknowledged in public, the begetting of him too shameful to be told. How could she ever be a professional man's wife with a hidden background like that, never mind the uncertainty of her own birth? And what about his family and friends, even the servants, Cook and Ada? They'd all find it wrong. He would be damaged by it. How well she understood what society did to those who broke the rules!

Yet she had grown quite fond of him, but not in the way couples in the books seemed. After Bruce how could she ever feel like that? His brutal assault had spoiled that sort of thing ever being for her. Still, if love were not for her, wouldn't this be better than ending up like Nanny, old and alone with a crabby sister? How could she even think like that? She would just be using him to get what she wanted. Her innate honesty knew it was wrong, however convenient it might be. She couldn't do that to the man who'd housed, fed and kept her and her 'family' these past four years.

"I see you've set only one place for dinner tonight, Cate. What's this? I know you have no wish to be my wife."

"Sir, it's not that, but...."

"Does that mean I may hope?"

"Mr. McAlister, sir, you know it could never happen."

"I know nothing of the sort. Come now, set your place, serve our meal as usual and we'll discuss the issue." Would you listen to him! Discuss the issue indeed. No wonder the girl wouldn't hear of it. What had happened to the man who'd so jauntily left the office the other day, his heart on his sleeve? It had shot straight back inside the crusty lawyer's body, that's what! Now here he was hiding behind that professional persona. It wouldn't do. Neither would this silent fiasco of a meal. "Shall we have coffee in the study as usual, now we have finished a somewhat silent meal? Then perhaps we can continue this conversation?"

Ada clanked down the kitchen stairs, plates wobbling in their haphazard stacking. "Cook they're no right, those two up there the night."

"What makes you say that, Ada. I thought you were getting on nicely with bringing the dishes down and such."

"I am, Cook. Cate said the other day she were right pleased wi me, an how I was speakin proper an all, remembering my 'have you finished now's and 'excuse me's, an everything'. No, it's them. One at each end o that table."

"Away, Ada, where's your eyes? They've been eating together for a while since."

"I know that! But they aye spoke aboot all sorts, and now—well nothing."

"Ada, it's been a long day and I'm ready for my bed. Just what are you blethering on about?"

"I'm telling you they're no speaking. No a bloomin word!"

"Never! They're always that friendly. Good for the Master, Cate is. Cheers him up after spending all day in the jails with criminals, drunks and the like, or sorting out all that money the big families squabble over when the head dies."

"Is there no enough tae go roond, then?"

"Enough of what, Ada?"

"The money."

"Whose money, the Master's? Of course he's enough, and anyway it's none of Cate's business, the Master's money. Here now, did you hear him say he'd money troubles? I thought they werrna speaking. If he has we'll all be looking for work. That's what's wrong with them. Away you back up and finish clearing and—shsst, she's coming for the coffee tray. Not a word now."

"We're finished now, Ada. You can clear the rest."

"I'm doing well with the clearing and all, am't I, Cate?"

"Yes, yes of course you are, Ada. I thought I'd told you how pleased I was with you. In fact I'd been thinking I'd get you a new uniform and we could start you on the serving but…." Perhaps she wouldn't be here. Could they really carry on as if nothing had happened? "But there may be some changes. We'll see. Off you go and finish the clearing and then you can get away home. There's a good girl. I'll take the coffee now, Cook, and thank you—the fish was lovely."

Watching Cate leave, Ada picked up her tray, brow furrowed. "We niver had fish, did we Cook? What's the matter wi' Cate? 'Changes'. Whit did she mean?"

"We're done for, Ada my girl. Done for. I should have listened to you when you started on about them no speaking. She's that worried she doesna even know what she's eating. He's gone and given all his money to those criminals and the poor he keeps speaking up for, and there's none now for the likes of us. He'll be for selling up and going to live with hoity toity Mrs. Bryant, and we'll be out, all of us. Just you wait and see. Now away and clear, we're in enough trouble withoot you no doing your job."

Now they were back in the study, Malcolm tried again. "Cate, listen to me. Let me....what on earth is that row, coming from the dining room?'

"I'll go and see." Grateful for an excuse to leave, Cate investigated

"Ada, whatever's the matter. Why on earth are you sobbing?

"Oh, Cate, I'dve liked a uniform (sniff) an everything an Cook's says (sniff) we're doomed an those criminals don't deserve the master's money and he'll no like livin' with Mrs. Bryant...."

"Ada stop!" The silly girl was raving mad. Yet servants knew what was going on in a house. Perhaps—no this was ridiculous! In fact everything in the past few weeks had been a bit like that. She might not marry him, but she must hold onto her job. Was he trying to get rid of her by proposing to her, knowing she would have to go if she refused? She could never go to Mrs. Bryant's.

Hearing the raised voices, Malcolm went towards the dining room, only to run into Cook at the top of the kitchen stairs.

"Sorry, sir, but I heard Ada crying. She's such a silly girl—good girl but definitely silly, so I...."

"Indeed, exactly so. Shall we investigate?" His first thought on entering the room was that it could have been a scene from one of the popular farces at the Empire Theatre. Ada distraught, Cate ashen-faced and Cook, sensing the drama, hand to mouth moaning softly. After the stresses of the day it was too much for him and he gave way to laughter. This at least stopped the racket and focused their attention on him.

"Good. I'm sorry, but if you could only see yourselves." For some reason the puzzled but indignant stares set him off again, and slowly Cate's mouth began to tremble until she joined him. Before long the room was full of it, and none of them could have said exactly what they were laughing about.

Piecing together the individual accounts of the garbled tale, he realised that, though it made little sense, it did reflect the uneasy atmosphere in the house of late. One consoling thought was if Cate couldn't remember what she'd eaten, at least his proposal had not left her unaffected. "I think this requires a glass of whisky, if you please, Cate."

"Thank you." Taking the glass he continued. "Well I really didn't feel like talking tonight, Ada. It was that simple. Now be off home with you. It's late. Be assured the house and all of us will still be here tomorrow and indeed for a long time in the future." Muddled though she undoubtedly became at times, young Ada had certainly spotted the atmosphere in the dining room. "Right then, I think we've all had enough drama, so I'll say goodnight to you. Selling up indeed!"

The Petrie kitchen was bursting with children, some crawling on the floor, others playing hopping games round the table, and two infants asleep on a threadbare blanket under the table. Rhoddy sucked his thumb and pulled at Mrs. Petrie's apron.

"I dinna like ma Mammy, Mrs. Petrie."

"Rhoddy! Whit a thing to say! Dinna speak aboot your Mammy like that."

"Weel it's true, so it is. Mind I like Lizzie and Maggie and yirsel."

Shaking her head she shooed Rhoddy off to join the hopping game, as the door opened.

"Oh, see, here's Maggie tae fetch you the day, Rhoddy. I didna hear yir knock wi a the noise. You're early surely, hen? No sickening for something are you?"

"No, nothing like that, Mrs. Petrie." Maggie felt there would be time enough for Maudie Petrie to find out about the shorter hours the factory bosses seemed to be planning. After all if the men stopped agitating for unions coming in, it might come to nothing.

"Come on then, Rhoddy, say ta-ta to Mrs. Petrie and we'll away tae the bakers to meet Lizzie."

"I'm fond of the wee fella. It's a shame Cate doesna visit often. Poor bairn. He's no long finished saying he doesna miss his Mammy overmuch. Funny whit bairns say, Maggie".

"You know Cate must work long hours to get her wage. We're all grateful for the help she gives us. She's like the rest of us—we needs do what we must."

"Aye, your right there, hen. None of us can choose whit's visited on us. That we canna." Mrs. Petrie watched till they were out of sight but she wasn't convinced by Maggie's answer.

When they'd collected Lizzie, with Rhoddy intent on chewing a stale bun from the bakery, Maggie couldn't help bringing up the subject. "Really, Lizzie, I'll have to speak to Cate."

"Whit aboot?"

"She's never here. Cate's been sending Ada with the money for nearly a month now and it's no right. No good for Rhoddy." Maggie knew she was being sharp but she was truly worried. Her conscience told her that she ought to take issue with Cate if others were talking about her neglect of her son. They were right, but supposing she did speak to her? Would Cate take the boy and foster him elsewhere? Truth was, that with those damn men causing trouble at the works, holding meetings, calling for unions to be allowed, they might all lose their jobs, never mind just getting shorter hours. Without Cate's money they couldn't manage then.

"But that'll upset Cate, won't it? You'll no fall oot wi her, now will you, Mammy?"

"Well, perhaps we'll leave it for a bit. Mebbe she's just too busy. Come on now, time we were all home." Dear Lizzie! She'd given her an excuse, at least for the present, but Maggie knew only too well that it was a trouble stored and the keeping of it would only make it grow. Lizzie might very well sleep at night. Maggie was quite sure she wouldn't.

Malcolm McAlister never made his mind up in a hurry, but he'd let his offer of marriage to Cate hang over them for two months and she just avoided the subject, as if by doing so it would disappear.

Her resistance made him more determined than ever. Here they were, yet another evening in the study and still no progress. He knew he should let the subject lie: give her more time to get used to the idea, but something made him press on with his suit.

"I simply can't understand." Puzzled, Malcolm sought her eyes. "Surely I'm not such an ogre as to make the whole idea impossible for you?"

"No one could ask for a better gentleman than you, sir."

Malcolm thought it was like trying to wade against an implacable tide. What had happened to their comfortable relationship? His proposal seemed to be in danger of robbing him of the very happiness he'd hoped it would achieve. Surely she could see how miserable her refusal was making them both? "Well then, what is it? You haven't got a young man tucked away in the tenements have you?" God forbid.

"Sir, how could you think that of me? It's nothing like that. It's just no right."

"Cate, you are one of the most obdurate females I've ever come across. Until you present me with a logical reason for your refusal I shall keep on asking. You understand that?" Speaking sharply was hardly likely to further his cause, but he couldn't help it. Despite years of practice, he was finding he could no longer contain his emotions and it showed in his frustration. Somehow her steadfast refusal to explain her reasons, or to become upset, or even to argue, made him want to shake her and then, being that close, kiss her. Looking at the set expression of her face, he knew he was beaten for that evening at least. He was away for the rest of the week so perhaps that might be no bad thing. Give her more time to consider.

Already the week nearly gone and she'd thought and thought but could find no easy solution. That wonderful homely atmosphere, the affection between them, everything about their relationship— even the rest of the household seemed to be affected.

In the strained silence in the dining room, they'd no appetite, and that angered Cook, while poor Ada had taken to dropping things. That caused ructions in the kitchen. She couldn't stand it a moment longer. He would have to be told—about Rhoddy, Bruce and the mystery of her own birth. She didn't even have a surname! That would clear the atmosphere, but it would be the end of her housekeeping job. It needn't be, though. She could accept him. Although it would be a poor bargain for the Master because she'd be accepting for all the wrong reasons. She couldn't bring shame to the man she'd grown to admire. No he'd have to be told, and that would be the end of everything!

Certainly she wanted a fine house, respectability, and security, but she would get all of those things somehow, somewhere, by herself. Then they would be truly hers. She would not cheat him for her own gain. She was too fond of him for that.

The whole housekeeping thing had gone wrong. Had it been her fault? She'd tried so hard and thought it was all working well. Now this. She could take no more. Never one to dither, she'd do it as soon as he returned. Then it would be finished. Used to solving her own problems, it never occurred to her to discuss it with the others or ask Maggie's opinion.

She heard him come through the front door, then the thump of his suitcase as he deposited it in the hall. She waited until he came into the dining room.

"Ah, there you are Cate. How good it is to be home. I trust Cook has a hot meal waiting and the study fire is well stoked. I'm weary after my journey, yet I've papers I must see to before tomorrow."

So this wasn't the right time to speak to him. It would have to be after the meal. Cate couldn't believe how long it took them to get through it. They toyed with their food and conversation was stilted. Finally, when they'd finished, she rose to get the coffee.

As she entered the study Cate had had enough. She couldn't go on like this. Tired though he was, she must have her say. He had to be made to understand that what he was suggesting, was for so many reasons, impossible. He'd made this ridiculous proposal with no real thought to it and now the situation was unbearable—the closeness and easy affection between them gone. Someone had to put a stop to it and, even though she knew she was throwing everything away she had to speak. "Here's the coffee, sir, and I've put another log on the fire. I'd—I'd like to speak to you."

Malcolm looked up from his desk. "Cate my dear, I have to finish this report tonight so I can mail it tomorrow. Besides, I'm exhausted after my long journey, surely it can wait till the morning, or preferably tomorrow evening when we'll have an opportunity to discuss whatever you want. I simply haven't the time to spare right now."

Well, what did she expect? Fine when he wanted answers or something doing. Oh yes, always time for that. Hadn't he been on at her for weeks? 'Give me an answer.' Now, when the time didn't suit him, just dismissed it. Well, she'd an answer to finish the whole stupid thing. She'd thought and worried and tried to work out how she could save her job, not upset him, and get back to where they'd been. It was making her sick. There was no way she could make it work. She couldn't stand the upset and the worry any longer. She'd simply have to tell him the full story and that would be the end of the matter. Back she'd slide to the bottom again. He wouldn't even give her a reference once he knew the facts, but she had to finish it.

"Well we'll have to make time because I can't go on like this and it's no fair. It's my turn to speak and you'll just have to listen. You won't have it, me saying no to your proposal, and I'm surprised at you. You've no sense, never mind you being a clever lawyer. I've told you and told you it wouldn't do, but you won't take no for an answer. Why should you? Employers are always right. Well you're not and I'll make you see it."

Seeing he was about to stop her, she cut him off. "No, let me speak. I'm only a woman, a servant, and you think you can do what you like, but I'll not stand for it. You'll listen and I'll make you see sense. I thought I could spare us both, but it's no use! You'll not be sensible and see the obvious reasons, but there're other things you need to know as well. I'm no better than they cheap women who walk the streets at night, and you know what they're offering. And I've a wee boy, hidden away in the tenements, so there! I'm a tinker by birth as well. I don't even know who my parents are, or were. For all I know I might be a bastard too. Fine wife I'd make—a tinker bastard with her own bastard child! Believe me, I know there'll be no marriage here, not ever, and no even a job for me anymore." Vainly trying to keep the sobs from escaping, she wiped her nose while her employer sat stunned into silence.

"I'll leave now, right this minute." Cate hurtled on. "I canna abide it anymore. I never thought you'd make me say all this. I tried my very best to please you and give you a comfortable home, but of course you're right. Doesn't matter how hard I try—the likes of you'll make sure that I'll never get on." Her anger by now consuming her, she strode to the desk, thumped it with her fist and spat her words. "You and all the others just wait! I won't be blamed for deeds that were not my own. I'll better myself with no help from anyone—an certainly no a man!" Finally giving way to tears that were a mixture of sorrow and anger, Cate fled, out into the dark night, running from yet another dream in tatters and into an uncertain future.

Climbing the tenement stairs Ada banged on Maggie's door until it opened. "I've come for Cate. She's needed back at the hoose."

Maggie and Lizzie looked at her as though she'd gone mad. "Surely that's where she is, Ada."

"No. No. She's run aff."

Maggie gripped the table and tried to keep calm. However much the fear in her chest frightened her, she had to keep these two young things from collapse.

"Come now, Ada. Stop crying and tell us why you think Cate would be here at this time of night."

"Weel, where else wid she be?"

"At the house doing her job surely?"

"Mammy, nothing's happened to her, has it, no to our Cate? Surely not."

"Shsst, Lizzie. Ada, are you sure Cate's not in the house somewhere?"

Ada's renewed burst of tears as she shook her head, confirmed Maggie's fears. Had she gone for a walk or—something? Stupid thoughts. Cate worked so hard she could barely stand at the end of her day, so why would she be anywhere but in her bed?

"Ada, what's happened tonight?"

"I brought up the food an…."

"Never mind all that, Ada. Why is Cate not there?" She'd choke it out of the girl if she didn't make sense soon. She knew she was being sharp, but she simply had to get some answers.

"That's whit I'm trying to tell you, Mrs. Maggie. She's run aff, an the Master's oot lookin for her, an I'm here, an Cook's fair demented, saying it's no safe for wimin oot alone in the dark. She'll no be killed, will she? Cate was right pleased with me an my speakin an everything, an now I'll niver get a uniform 'cos she'll be deid!"

Meanwhile, on the other side of town, Malcolm's search had been fruitless. All the neighbouring streets had been combed. Cook was right. She'd have made her way to her friends or relatives. Which were they? What else didn't he know? Might as well go back to the house. She'd come back with Ada surely. Shrugging his coat off in the hall, he met Cook's worried gaze. "No luck, Cook. There's no sign of her."

"Oh sir. Oh sir."

"Yes I know, but I'm certain she'll come back with Ada."

"But she's no been herself for months now an this last few weeks I dinna think more than a morsel has passed her lips. The good food I've had to throw away—an all they poor people starving."

"Now, now, Cook, forget all that. You go and make yourself a nice cup of tea in the kitchen. Or would you like a glass of sherry?"

"Sir. The very idea! My old Cook, her I trained under, warned me at the very beginning the sherry was for cooking and only for cooking, less you'd never know what might happen. 'The slippery slope' she called it. And to this day never a drop has passed my lips. I'll just have a fresh cup o tea."

"And very wise too. You do that and then go on up. I'll wait for their return."

"I'll stay in the kitchen, sir. I couldna sleep a wink, so I couldna."

Seated by the study fire, whisky glass in hand, Malcolm finally had time to dwell on what she'd said before her abrupt exit. It had so startled him that he'd remained seated long enough for her to disappear. So the dream was over!

He wished he wasn't so tired. His brain couldn't handle all this. Closing his eyes for a moment he drifted off, only to wake with a start as he heard voices in the hall. Thank God she'd come home! He leapt to his feet and opened the study door. His disappointment must have been etched on his face as a strange woman shook her head at him and waited. Cook broke the silence.

"She's no there, sir. This here's Mrs. Maggie, from where Cate bides. Ada brought her."

"Thank you, Cook. Take Ada to the kitchen please. You are Lizzie's mother?"

"Yes, Mr. McAlister, I am. First I must thank you for all your kindness to both her and Cate. I worry about them both. What happened here, to Cate, if you don't mind my asking, sir?"

"Not at all. Come into the study, where it's warm. Please take a seat and I will try to explain." As briefly as possible Malcolm covered the events of the last few weeks, leading up to his proposal.

"Dear Lord, you did no such thing surely, sir? Could you no see it would never do. No. No. Never do!"

"That's what Cate said, but I didn't agree with her and continued to plead my case. I now believe I know what her real reason was."

"Employers don't marry paid domestics, sir. Never have and never will. It's the rule sir. Your society wouldn't have it."

"I believe there have always been exceptions to rules. Granted not many in this case, so there must have been other reasons, and I found those out tonight."

"She's never told you, sir?"

"Yes, I'm afraid she has. Not that she'd be the first young girl to fall into prostitution, but I admit it saddened me and—are you alright?" The woman's face had turned waxen and he thought she was about to faint. A strange woman collapsing on his study hearth he could certainly do without. "Come now, surely you knew of this? After all she lived with you and since her profession was one of the night…"

"My Lizzie couldn't speak highly enough of you, Mr. McAlister, and I believed her. But what sort of man could think that of a poor helpless girl?" Maggie was shocked. "How could you think that of Cate?"

"I am not standing in judgement on her. She probably did what she had to do. I'm sure she had her reasons."

"Rape is no reason—you have no choice. Or are you defending the boy?"

Malcolm sank to his chair. His voice, when he could speak, came out in a hoarse whisper. "Rape?"

"Well, what else would you call it when he'd near killed the pet dog and, when she was crying over it, took her by force? With such force it took them weeks to mend her, and she was left with the bastard seed in her. Do you know what was the worst? He was an arrogant bully of a boy. A boy, I tell you, but the Laird's grandson, the heir. So that was all right you see. After all she was only a wee tinker girl. What's the matter with the world when this could happen?"

"But she told me herself. In this very room."

"About the rape and everything? It doesna seem like it. Or are you just pretending for my sake?"

"Now you misjudge me, Maggie. May I call you that? She implied she'd been a 'woman of the night.' "

"A harlot! Our Cate! Never!"

"Then why would she say that?"

"She'd have been too ashamed to tell you in so many words, sir. Whatever she said, you've no understood the rights of it. That I do know. Didn't my brother send her to me from the Highlands with a letter telling me all about the evil deed. "

"What a mess! Now what do we do?" Why was he asking this woman? Why should she know the answer? Surely it was because he was out of his depth here. Deep down he knew the night's revelations changed the situation, but all he could feel was an urgent desire to find Cate and right the wrongs done to her, to wipe away the hurt that he had inflicted on her by forcing her, not only to confront her painful past, but also to shame herself in his presence.

Cate had run and run, as though by doing so she could forget the scene in the study and its consequences. She'd been that distracted she now found herself lost. Once again her temper had overcome her, and look at the mess she was in! Not that she'd any wish to go

142

back to Mr. McAlister—yet that was nonsense. She couldn't deceive herself. Sitting in the lady's chair on the opposite side of the study fire chatting away to him, was exactly where she'd like to be right now. How had it all gone wrong?

Anyway, now she'd told him about her background, and Rhoddy in particular, there was no way he would want her back. Why in God's name had she not had the sense to get her coat and some money, before she ran? Childish, that's what she'd been. A sensible adult would have said what had to be said, gone to her room, packed her things and left in the daylight. Temper and impulse had ruled once more, and now here she was, hopelessly lost. Why hadn't she just run straight to Maggie's? More importantly, how was she to find her way there in the dark and penniless?

James Hardy caught just a flash of red in his lights before it dawned on him that the figure, or at least the hair, was familiar. Just what was McAlister's prim but pretty housekeeper doing in this part of town? Had she been visiting someone she'd have been in an outdoor coat and most probably been accompanied. This was not the sort of area young women walked alone in, half dressed, unless they were looking for business. Now here was an interesting turn of events. Throughout his short legal career, he'd made a number of beneficial moves by keeping his eyes and ears open for interesting snippets, and they'd usually paid off handsomely. This particular piece of information could have a rather pleasant outcome. Kicked out earlier by his mistress, his evening might not be wasted after all.

Waiting until she caught up with him, he called out. "Are you lost? It is Cate is it not?"

Cate peered at the figure in the automobile, but it was so dark she was uncertain about the identity. "How do you know my name? Who are you?"

"Come now, surely you remember me? We met at Mr. McAlister's."

"I see. Well I'm afraid I've taken a wrong turning somewhere and now I've lost myself."

Was it true? Even so, there was a good chance she didn't even know him. He'd only seen her the once at the house. Ordinarily he wouldn't have paid a servant girl any attention, but unless his gut instinct had been wrong, he was sure McAlister was more than just an employer to her, and so he'd had a good look at the girl.

"I think you'd better let me give you a lift back then."

"I'm not going there tonight. I'm heading for my lodgings in the Gorbals." Lost as she was, a helping hand to get to Maggie's would be welcome and he did seem to know her.

Still convinced she was working the streets, Hardy was delighted. Lucky for him he'd been on the same kind of errand.

"That's no problem. Get in and you can direct me once we're in the area. You're certainly well lost, if that's the direction you're heading in."

They'd been driving for sometime and Cate hadn't recognised any of the areas they'd driven through. Suddenly she saw the sign to the Gardens. Of course, Mrs. Petrie's favourite children's playground. "I think I can find my way from here. It's been really kind of you to help me. Thank you so much. I'm sorry I don't actually recognise you. It must have been at his birthday dinner. I was busy, and then, of course, I fell. That's it. You probably helped to carry me to the table before the doctor came. No wonder I don't remember you."

"I'll just turn in down here and let you out then. Delighted to be of some help." If his memory was accurate this lane ran parallel to the railings and they would be completely hidden from view. Piece of luck her not remembering him, and who would believe her story anyway?

"I'll be fine now, and thank you again."

Switching off the engine, Hardy faced her. "I don't think you truly appreciate the help I've given you. Goodness knows what might have happened to you, a young woman lurking alone in the dark night. Surely you can do better than a plain thank you?"

"Well, I'm really grateful, of course I am, and I'm sure Mr. McAlister would offer his thanks too for…."

"Yes, I'm sure he would, but supposing you gave me a little of his medicine? That would seem to be appropriate." It was quite interesting, her display of naiveté. Was that how she encouraged her customers? An interesting ploy, but it was time to get down to business.

"I'm sorry, I didn't know you were ill. You don't look it." Cate suddenly began to feel uneasy. Ordinarily she'd never even have spoken to a stranger, never mind accepted a lift, but he'd known her name and must have been at the birthday party. No, this was silly. She'd just say goodnight and get out. "Goodnight then and thank you again."

"We've wasted enough time, young woman. Come here and let's cut the pretence. You were quite prepared to take anyone on and I'll be a much better bet than the sort of person you'd find from the streets." Pulling her roughly towards him, his lips sought hers, while his hands ran greedily over her slim figure.

It had all happened so fast. Cate was trapped before she knew it. However hard she struggled, the man's grip was firm and soon he'd torn her dress and was fondling one of her breasts. Her mind flashed back to Bruce, and suddenly she went limp. Struggling was not the answer.

"That's more like it. Come on now. Show me your tricks. Look what I've got waiting for you. Be nice to him now."

Cate let him guide her right hand and squirmed to face him. The tortoiseshell hairpin she always wore was almost within reach of her left one. She turned her body a fraction more, just as he laid her hand on his swollen member. The disgusting move gave her courage and she yanked the pin out and stuck it hard into his thigh. As he yelped in pain and put both hands to the wound, Cate had the door open and went flying back the way they'd come, to the safety of the lights and Maggie.

11

By the time Maggie arrived home, McAlister having called a cab, the other two were fast asleep. Closing their door so as not to disturb them, she made a pot of tea. She didn't bother going to bed—she'd never sleep. What in the world had the stupid girl gone running into the night for? More puzzling was why hadn't she come to them? True, there had been a bit of cooling between herself and Cate, but surely that wouldn't have stopped her coming back to the only other home she had in Glasgow? Mind you, with the temper and the fierce pride of her, would she admit failure to anyone? Whatever she'd done, it was madness to be out at this time of night.

"Can you no sleep either, Mammy?" Lizzie asked as she came into the kitchen.

"Not a wink for worrying. There's tea in the pot, Lizzie. Rhoddy's no awake is he?"

"No, he's fine. Whit'll we tell him in the morning?"

"We canna tell him anything till we know something ourselves, and mind, not a word to Mrs. Petrie, or it'll be all over Glasgow by dinner time."

"What do you think Mr. McAlister will do, Mammy?"

"What do you mean? There's nothing he can do unless she comes back."

"I wonder what it was all aboot. I canna see Cate making a mess of her job, can you?"

"No, Lizzie, it was nothing to do with her job." Should she tell her or would it be better to leave her guessing?

"Whit was it then? Why'd she run away?"

"Believe it or not, Lizzie, the lawyer wants her to be his wife."

"Our Cate a legal man's wife! Surely no? Mind you, she could do it an all. She told me they used to sit of an evening an talk aboot all sorts of things, his legal work an everything. She's right clever is Cate."

"Mebbe so, but she refused him anyway."

"Did he put her oot for refusing then?"

"No, she told him about Rhoddy and then ran. I think, even knowing all that, he might still want her, at least to keep house, if not as his wife. He seems over fond of her and looked fair sick at the thought of her being out on her own. He was so sure she'd have come to us."

"Why didn't she, Mammy?"

"If I knew that, I might have got some sleep tonight. Well we can do nothing till morning. It's late enough as it is. Away to your bed and I'll do—dear God, who's that hammering at this time o' night?"

"Will we go to the door, Mammy?"

"Wheesht you! Go on off to your bed with Rhoddy. I'll see to it." Picking up the poker, Maggie spoke through the door. "Who's there?"

"Mag, Mag!"

"My God! Cate!" Maggie unlocked the door and saw no one. "Cate, Cate?" The sob came from the floor. Maggie looked down, saw the crumpled figure clutching the torn dress and thought, dear God, not again, please God not again!

Huddled in a blanket, tea in hand, Cate didn't know where to begin. Maggie saved her the bother.

"Where in God's name have you been? Ada was here looking for you hours ago."

"Cate! I thought I heard you. Oh, look at you! Whit's happened?"

"Sssht, Lizzie, come through an sit doon. Let her speak."

"Why was Ada here, Maggie?"

"Why do you think, Cate, you daft lump? They're all out of their minds at the house. The lawyer was beside himself. He must think a great deal of you to get in such a state. By my way of thinking, you're more than just a housekeeper in his eyes." She'd keep her talk with the lawyer to herself for the moment.

"Well he'll no want me back now!"

148

"Why Cate? You're a good housekeeper."

"Lizzie, I told him about Rhoddy. You know the rules about domestics."

"Mebbe so, Cate, but that man knew all about everything and he was still out looking for you, so what do you say to that?"

"Maggie, he was never on the street looking for me?"

"He was so, even knowing all about Bruce and Rhoddy. Now just what happened out there? We need to know, Cate."

"There was a man. I was a fool."

"Aye well, we're all that at times, but just how much of a fool were you?"

"It's okay, Maggie, No real harm done, I got away from him with just a bruised breast and the loss of a precious tortoiseshell hatpin."

"No the bonnie one you wore in your hair?"

"That's the one, Lizzie. The Cailleach gave it to me when I left Kevinishe. It was like a good luck charm for me and it certainly worked tonight when I stuck it in his thigh!" Indeed, without it Cate knew it would have been Bruce all over again. Was she never to be free of men and their needs?

"Cate, where were your wits when you went out in the streets at that time of night alone?"

"Muddled by losing my temper, Maggie. Mind, roaming the streets, even though I was just lost, in some ways he canna be blamed for thinking I was a whore."

"Cate, what a word!"

"Maggie, that's what he thought."

"That's as may be, but to get in the state you were in! What happened?"

"As I said, I was a fool. A man called me by name and offered me a lift in his automobile."

"Did you ride in it?"

"Wheesht Lizzie, let her tell her story."

"Some story, Maggie. He knew my name so I thought he must have been to Mr. McAlister's party—you know the birthday one. Then he offered to take me back there but I said I was coming here. It was by the Park, down the side, he tried—well I got away, but only just!"

"At least you can tell Mr. McAlister that— an he'll soon sort him for hurting you."

"She canna, Lizzie."

"Why, Mammy?"

"I don't know his name, Lizzie. He was just a man who knew my name."

"That's how it must stay, Cate." Maggie spoke firmly. "Even if you did know him, do you really think they'd take your word against his, a rich man in an automobile? No my girl, you must never tell a soul. I wouldn't involve the lawyer anyway. The less he knows the better. We'll say you ran in a temper, got lost, wandered the streets till dawn and then made your way here. I think it's best if you have a bit of a chill for a few days and then we'll see what the lawyer has to say."

"But that's dishonest, Maggie. And the man should pay surely? Why should I always be the one to suffer? It makes me mad even to think about it."

"Now you listen to me, Cate. Remember what happened in Kevinishe. Do you think Fisher would have sent you to me if he'd thought them at the big house would welcome you and your bastard child?"

"Mammy, you're swearing!"

"Aye well, the pair of you just take heed. Women, be they rich or poor, who get taken advantage of, or indeed just let themselves give way to their feelings, always suffer. Disgrace, thrown out and ruin. That's it. No matter the situation, the woman is always in the wrong and, believe me, she pays the price. So a chill it'll be and the lawyer none the wiser."

"Maggie, what if he, you know the man, what if he…."

"The man, nothing, Cate. Believe me. If he's one of the lawyer's cronies, he'll keep quiet. He'll have no wish to let his friends know he was trawling the streets. Like as not he's married anyway. C'mon now, to bed the lot of us. I'll let them know at the house on my way to work in the morning. You two stay indoors tomorrow, and not a word to Maudie Petrie, except Cate's home with a chill."

Maybe she had grown away from them of late, but the lass still needed their protection. Damn world! Thank God Lizzie was not a 'looker', though she'd keep an eagle eye on her anyway. As for Cate, looking as she did, the lass seemed destined for man trouble, so she'd just have to learn how to handle it. Though, with that passionate nature of hers, God help her if she ever felt strongly about a man.

The next morning, Cook opened the basement door and was glad to see Maggie standing there.

"I hope you've news. He's no been to bed an looks like he's ready for his own funeral."

"I have that, Cook. She turned up at dawn this morning."

"Dear Lord! Whatever was she doing all the night then?"

"She ran out of here in such a state she'd no idea where she was going. By the time she'd collected herself, and the temper had cooled, she was lost."

"Bye, but she was lucky to come through unharmed then. It's no safe to walk the streets at night."

"Well, she's no exactly unharmed. No, no, don't fret yourself. She's no damaged as such. Just a nasty chill with being out all night and no coat like."

"Mrs. Maggie, I'm thinking they must have had some words for her to run like that. Come now, what about some tea? The kettle's on the hob."

"Cook, I'm that sorry but I must away or I'll be late for work. In these uncertain times, I wouldna want to let them have any excuse to finish me."

"Ah well, another time perhaps. How long before she's back?"

"A few days perhaps. Now could you let Mr.McAlister know I'm here? I need a word."

As she waited for Cook to find her Master, Maggie was glad that she'd work to go to. Tea would have meant satisfying the woman's curiosity. Now she hoped to God the lawyer would believe her story. If Cate wouldn't look out for herself, then she would do it for her.

"You're to go through. He's in the study. Tell Cate we're looking forward to her coming back. She is coming back?"

"That'll depend on himself. I'll away through." Not sure what she would say, Maggie hoped he'd start the conversation. She didn't like lying, but truth would serve no purpose here.

"Maggie, I'm extremely grateful to you for coming round. She is all right? It's nothing more than exposure is it?"

"No, she'll be over the chill in a few days, but as to your disagreement, I'm no so sure."

"You don't think she'll agree to my proposal?"

"Sir, we see the trouble it could cause with your family, your friends and even your business people. They'd none of them approve."

"I realize there would be dissent, but that's my problem. Interestingly, you don't voice your disapproval."

"Well now, I'm older than Cate. I've seen more of the world. If you'll pardon me for saying so, sir, she needs looking after. A young woman with her looks and ability will always be at risk from people like you, because of her lowly station."

"I hope you…."

"Hear me out please, sir. I don't include you among them. You've shown yourself to be a true gentleman."

"I'm grateful for that at least."

"I need to know if what I told you the other night has changed your feelings towards Cate. I mean do you want her back—either as your housekeeper or your wife?"

"Your revelations, indeed Cate's words, which seemed to put her in a worse light, only made me wish to erase all that hurt. Oh, I do realize that it would be a slightly unusual situation, but I want her for my wife and I'd like your support in that— and any other advice you can give."

"Well I'll tell you, she'll no come easily. She sees it as damaging to you and there's the shame of it for her—you knowing all about it now. If it were up to me, I'd have her back as she was, to the housekeeping, and then go slowly towards the other. I canna say if it'll work, but I'm for you."

"Excellent advice, and I'll count on your continued help. Get her back here as soon as you can and no mention will be made of her outburst. No one else knows the real reason do they?"

152

"Not a word to anyone outside, though I've told Lizzie, mind that's no difficult for her to take in. She fair worships the girl. Thinks she'd make you a grand wife."

Taking her leave of a much happier McAlister, Maggie could only hope that she was doing the right thing. It was also to be hoped the other rotten one, whoever he was, would keep quiet for all their sakes.

Closing the door behind him, as he set off to work, Cate sighed as she watched her employer go. In the past three months she'd settled back into her old routine at the house once she'd recovered from her ordeal. Having had plenty time to think since then, she'd had to take a good look at herself and it hadn't been particularly comfortable. Going now to tidy the linen cupboard, she dwelt on the struggle within her as she sorted the laundry. Honesty made her admit she wouldn't have changed any of her actions since coming to Glasgow. The opportunity had been grasped as a means of hauling herself upwards, but now she did realize that somehow the others had failed to understand that her aim to be someone, do something with her life, simply couldn't be altered. If this required her to put her friends second then that's what she'd do, but it didn't mean she'd forget them.

Then there was the Master. She'd not appreciated what a truly good man he was. To have found out all about her and not sent her packing: that was difficult to understand. Maggie kept telling her, that a man of his age was experienced enough to know his own mind and, if he wanted her for his wife, despite the difference in their age and stations, she should be honoured by the proposal and think seriously about it. He hadn't said anymore about that, but she realised he wasn't deterred. She'd have to sort her life, so that those who were dear to her had more of her time, and she'd have to think carefully about his proposal. She'd hate to think he felt she was using him to better herself. Oh, she wanted to get on, but by her own efforts, not using such a wonderful man as him. He deserved better than that.

'McAlister'—that was another thing. They'd had a right old fuss about his name, once she'd come back. Call him Malcolm indeed!

Well he would not have 'sir' or 'Master', and she'd refused to use his Christian name. The old Laird had saved her. If 'MacNishe' was fit for a laird, then 'McAlister' would do for her master and that was as far as she'd been prepared to go. Other than that, they'd slipped back into their familiar roles and the house was a haven for all of them once more. She loved the house, her work and the life they led. Yet she couldn't take that final step. Was it because she was unable to love? She had confusing emotions where Rhoddy was concerned and yet she'd loved young David. Even the dog, Rory, had melted her heart.

Cate knew she was happier getting on with things rather than sitting around thinking about them, but look at the mess her lack of thought had nearly landed her in this last time. Now it was the opposite she couldn't make up her mind. Behaving like Mr. Shakespeare's Hamlet, she was—not making decisions.

Another meal finished, they made their way to the study, where Cate settled with her book and McAlister opened his briefcase and began working on his papers. Ada, proud in her new uniform, performed her usual circus trick of bobbing a curtsy, lowering the coffee tray to the table by the fire, smiling at Cate and glancing nervously at her employer, more or less all at the same time, before scuttling from the room.

Waiting for the sound of her receding steps to fade, they looked at one another and laughed. "It's no good, Cate, you'll have to tell her!" Wiping his eyes, Malcolm shook his head. "One of these days she'll have either the tray or herself, or possibly both, on the floor."

"I know, but she's trying so hard. She's even been practising 'the coffee's here'. Yesterday she was in the pantry with an empty tray, muttering away, so we're in for an extra treat one of these days."

"God forbid if she adds speech to all those actions! Yet she does make me laugh, though I shouldn't. Did I tell you about my briefcase?"

"You've not lost it?"

"No, no. It was Ada. I left it in the hall the other morning, and she came running after me crying out for all Glasgow to hear." Malcolm cleared his throat and, in not a bad imitation of Ada,

154

delivered. 'Sir, your baggie! You forgot your posh baggie! Your wee legal baggie, sir!' This with her skirts tucked up, pelting after me. She sent many a soul on the street off to work with a smile."

"You have to admit she's got a good wee heart."

"True enough. Now, the evening's comedy act over, I must to my papers."

Later, having finished his work, Malcolm let his gaze fall on Cate, engrossed in her current book. Since her return they'd let the question of his marriage proposal lie uneasily between them. He was adamant in his own mind he would have her for his wife. Only when she was missing had he really understood his true feelings. They'd nothing to do with his home or his comfort and everything to do with his heart. He now knew just how much he loved and wanted her. This uneasy truce was stretching his patience to the limit and yet he was reluctant to press her, bearing Maggie's advice in mind, less she ran again, Next time he might not find her. That was too upsetting a thought to contemplate.

As a shivering Cate entered her old home in the tenements she found Lizzie mashing the tea. "A hot drink is just what I need. It's freezing out there."

"Aye, I've the stove banked up ready for Mammy. She'll be frozen too, so she will."

In low tones so as not to waken Rhoddy, in bed with a bad chest, they set the table with the goodies that Cate had brought, finishing just as Maggie appeared.

"Well, and how's yourself then, Cate? All well across the way?"

"Ada seems to have the same chest as Rhoddy an I'm hoping she hasna given it to McAlister"

Maggie could see Cate was making an attempt to sound like them, trying to bridge the growing social gap. Wondering whether she would have the head bitten off her, she sat at the table and, and while helping herself, asked the question anyway. "How're things at the house Cate? Are you and him agreeing now?"

"Mmmm, most of the time."

"An the proposal?"

"Please don't bring that up, Maggie. I still feel it wouldna be right. Surely you agree with that?"

Not expecting any further discussion, Cate bit into a piece of Cook's pork pie she'd brought with her.

Seizing her chance, Maggie said. "You know he was right bad when you ran off. No. Let me say my piece while you finish your bite. The man's over fond of you and I got to thinking. This just might be the way up, Cate. I mean you like him don't you?"

"Of course I like him." Cate mumbled through the crumbs. " He's been kind to all of us, me especially, but that's no reason to wed him. It wouldn't be right."

"Oh but, Cate, if you ken he'd be good to you, no belt you an the like, that must be something."

"Lizzie, what are you saying? I should wed the man? I thought you were both against it." Cate wondered what on earth had come over these two. Wasn't it bad enough, creeping round the house waiting for McAlister to raise the matter again, without this?

"Well, we know you're determined to improve yourself, Cate, an there could be worse ways of doing it." Maggie felt they'd gone far enough and went to see to Rhoddy.

"I widna mind if you did wed, Cate, s'long as you didna forget us."

"Lizzieee, how many times must I say I'll no do that?"

"Weel, I'm torn. I think it'd be great if you were a posh lady an all, but I—here, mebbe I could be your maid! Dress you in the mornings and such like? Whit aboot that, Cate?"

"Whit're you saying, Lizzie?" Her mother asked as she came into the room.

"She was speaking rubbish, Maggie. Be my maid, ssst!"

Maggie refilled the teapot and brought it back to the table, choosing her words carefully she spoke. " Cate, orphan that you are, it's no wonder you don't take to the idea of loving, an the two men you've had truck with so far could easily put you off for good. But the lawyer's a gentleman no like them. Think of that."

Cate realised they were in deadly earnest. She felt as if she'd been plunged back into the sea at Kevinishe with the tide pulling her back faster than she could gain the shore. Surely they weren't serious? But they were. Could she be wrong then? She didn't really know. And there was the bed business. No. No. There was no way she could do that. If only they could stay as they were.

Putting more logs on the study fire Ada was startled as her employer came into the room.

"Where's Cate, Ada?"

"She's awa tae Lizzie and Maggie's. Young Rhoddy's got a chest on him again." Ada prepared to sidle out of the study.

Freely translated, Malcolm presumed Rhoddy was ill. Oh why wouldn't the stubborn girl see sense and marry him, all this silly business of her here and the boy there could be taken care of.

"Oh, sir, whit did I say wrong? Dinna glower at me—oh sir." And with that Ada left him to seek the safety of the kitchen.

"Cook, he's mad at me an' I dinna ken why. Should I no have telt him where Cate was? Mind, he did ask. I'm no for doing yon coffee the night. Should he rage at me I'd drop it, so I wid. I canna, Cook, I canna."

"What on earth is the matter, Ada?" Cate, coming into the kitchen, took her coat off and waited.

"No use asking me," Cook answered Cate's questioning look. "God only knows what goes on in her head. For our Ada here doesn't, right enough."

"I'll just go to the study and find out, Cook."

As Cate entered the room the lawyer looked up, glad of her return.

"Ah, Cate, you're back. We seem to have a small problem with Ada."

"I know. I've heard all about it. Why were you angry with her?"

"With Ada? My dear Cate, at times Ada seems to be racing me to the asylum! I promise you, I simply asked her where you were tonight and the next moment chaos."

"But she said, to quote her, 'he fair glowered at me, he wis that mad, an I dinna ken whit for.' So why the angry face?"

"Because of you, my dear."

"But, I wasn't even here!"

"Precisely. This is ridiculous, Cate—you here, the boy over there and everybody else running off the rails when you're not around. Surely you can see that? We all need you—me most of all."

"You're saying that by me being wed to you everybody would be happy? You speak of going mad. I feel as if I'm the one doing that! Before, the whole thing was quite clear. Maggie, Lizzie, even Cook and Ada, knew this marriage would break all the rules. Now everyone seems to be all for it."

Malcolm could see she'd been shaken by something that had been said during her visit to the tenement and obviously the kitchen incident had endorsed that. It could be just the right time. He couldn't wait any longer!

"Cate." Crossing the room he took both her hands in a firm grip. This time he determined she would listen to him. "Look at me, Cate. Surprising though it may seem, I find I can't live without you. Don't look so shocked! Did you really think I just wanted to make sure you didn't leave me short of a housekeeper? I don't know why, but you seem to have no idea what an attractive woman you are. Quite frankly, my dear, I love you and want to spend my remaining years with you. Oh, I'm older than you, but—you make me feel young again. Please, Cate, marry me."

"But, but…."

"No, Cate, this time I'll not take no for an answer. Come on, lass, I know you don't love me, as you might a younger man, but you do at least care for me a little. See the practical side. You would have Rhoddy here with us and I'll put nothing in your way to stop you seeing Lizzie and her mother. Why should I? They've been a true pair of friends. After all, without young Lizzie I'd never have met you."

"Please, McAlister, let me go up now and I'll speak to you in the morning. I still need time. Oh I know I've had time, but now things seem to have changed. Mebbe I've changed. I canna think right now, I'm that tired." Seeing the droop of his shoulders, Cate knew she was being unfair. "Look, I'll no run away again and I'll think this all out if I can—having Rhoddy an the like, I never thought about that you see. When we've had dinner tomorrow evening, I'll give you your answer. Goodnight then."

As the slow tread of her footsteps on the stairs faded, Malcolm lit his pipe with trembling hands. It was going to be all right. He could tell. The slipping into the vernacular; no shocked telling him it was impossible; the final sign her weary steps on the stairs. Never had Cate done anything at less than a furious pace and here she was dragging herself up the stairs. She'd even forgotten his cocoa. What about a good night's sleep? Would that revive her opposition? God only knew why, but he didn't think so. Nevertheless he was about to undergo a most anxious twenty-four hours.

"You're looking peaky this morning, Cate. You're no sickening are you?"

"Nothing like that, Cook, I haven't slept well and...."

"You've no really been right since, well since, you know...."

Cate knew she was referring to 'the running away' but was not prepared to discuss it. "I've just got some difficult decisions to make."

"Pardon me for speaking out of turn, but you and him might as well be wed for the way you both are. I've seen couples no nearly as friendly as you two, and them wed for years. Now the pair of you circling one another like a couple of stray toms! What's happened to you?"

"Not you too, Cook? Come on. Let's get down to work. What's for lunch and dinner today?"

It was too much. Surely they couldn't all be wrong, and yet what about her own feeling? She enjoyed his company. She liked the house and took an enormous pride in running it. But she didn't love him in the way she should. It wouldn't be right. And his family would never stand for it, even though they seemed to care little for him. However long this day was, she felt it would be too short to let her decide. Yet, she'd given her word. An answer he must have this very night.

Scrubbing away at her pans Ada frowned before deciding to say anything. "Cook, I'm sure Cate's no well."

"I said the very same to her, only this morning."

"Whit di you think it is? Surely she's no picked up my bad chest. I used them cloths Cate gave me for my nose. An I remembered to cover my mooth wi ma han when I wis coughin an all."

"More like a disease of the heart, I would say, young Ada."

"Niver! Our Cate's too young for heart trouble. It's the auld yins whit die o that. Here now, you dinna think she'll die, Cook?"

"No I don't, Ada. Away you and take this basket to them in the tenements, afore you get your facts all muddled. Cate'll be just fine. Ssht now, that's her coming down the stairs."

"Is that my basket, Cook?" Any excuse to get out of the house would be welcome.

"It is that, Cate. Ada was just off with it."

"That's alright. I need a walk. I'll take it this time. I've some thinking to do and perhaps the fresh air will help. I'll have something to eat with Lizzie, but I'll be back in plenty of time for dinner. I'll be off then."

Ada waited 'till the door closed, and Cate had gone.

"Weel, at least Cate's no doin extra scrubbin' an polishin' the day. We've to be thankful for that, Cook."

"True, Ada, but if my thinking's right, there'll be plenty extra work coming up."

"Why's that now, Cook?"

"Never you mind, young Ada. Away and scrub those tatties for our dinner. I've that nice piece of lamb left over from last night an I dare say you'd no say no to a bit of apple pie, now would you?"

Two weeks since she'd answered him, and still she'd told no one. Maybe because she could hardly believe herself that the decision had at last been taken. Well, if anyone was to be told, it was Maggie and Lizzie. What better time than now? Climbing the tenement stairs she paused on the step where her labour with Rhoddy had begun. What a long time ago that seemed! Sometimes she could hardly credit the changes in herself. No longer the young ignorant girl, but a grown woman of twenty-one.

"Anybody home? Lizzie, It's me." Each time she came back here, the rooms seemed smaller, but they would always hold a special place in her heart.

"Whit are you smiling aboot, Cate?"

"I was remembering my first months here with you and Maggie. Will she be home soon?"

"Aye, she's on early the day. She'll be back afore long. Cate, I canna seem to get this bit right. Whit's the matter wi it?" Lizzie handed the garment to Cate.

Taking the jacket from Lizzie, she unpicked some of the stitches and freed the lining. They had just completed the mending when Maggie arrived.

"Well now, it's grand to see the pair of you with your heads in the sewing. Did Mr. McAlister catch Ada's cold, Cate?"

"No, Maggie, he's fine." In fact he was more than that. She couldn't believe the change in him. "He's something to be fine about now. I've said 'yes' to him." There, it was out and, hearing the words out loud like that Cate began to believe it.

"Well, and no before time. Yon puir man has been hanging on your word for months, Cate."

"You're to be a lady, Cate, a proper lady!"

"I'll just be the same, Lizzie, only I'll be wed."

"There'll be changes though, Cate."

"Whit kind o changes, Mammy?"

"There's Rhoddy for one."

"Rhoddy's no getting wed!"

"Quite right, Lizzie, and I'm not sure what I'll do about him. It all depends on Mr. McAlister, you see."

"When's the wedding, Cate?"

"I've no idea, Maggie. I just said yes to his proposal. That's all I know." She felt she'd much rather leave it all to McAlister. He'd see to it, wouldn't he?

That evening, settled in the study, coffee safely delivered by Ada, Malcolm put his cup down and crossed to Cate's chair. "You darling girl. You do know you've made me the happiest man alive?" Kissing her gently on the cheek—he knew he had to go carefully. She'd already told him of her fears when she'd accepted him. All except one of them he had no qualms about. Her very true fear of 'the bed thing' could be a major obstacle and he would do all in his power to reassure her and prove that manhood and the act of love should never be judged by the likes of that young swine from the Highlands.

"Now then, what about the wedding? Personally, I'd like to get everything underway as soon as possible. Your wedding day must be very special. You can have the whole of Glasgow to see you in your finery if you wish."

"No, no, nothing like that. Could we not just have a wee 'do' here?"

"Prepare your own wedding breakfast? I think not my dear! Absolutely not! I want to spoil you. I'm quite content to have a small family…."

"They'll not come, McAlister."

"And that will be their loss. We'll book a function room and get caterers to do the meal. How about we have just Solly, Maggie and Lizzie with Rhoddy, and Cook with Ada of course. They'll enjoy being waited on for a change. Oh God, what sort of havoc do you think Ada could bring to a wedding?" At least that had brought a smile to her face. He'd get the whole thing over as fast as possible and then they could all settle down to their changed future.

12

On hearing the front door, Cate frowned. He was home too early. Surely he wasn't sickening again? Leaving the flowers, she made her way to the hall, quite unprepared for the appearance of a raging Caroline Bryant.

"You slut! Aiy knew you were trouble from the first moment aiy set eyes on you. What is the meaning of this ridiculous thing?" Caroline waved the card in the air, then tore it to pieces and flung them on the floor

"There now, that's what aiy think of it!'

Meanwhile a puzzled Cate just had time to realize that McAlister must have sent out the wedding invitations, before Caroline began again.

"Marry my father! Don't even think of it! Aiy want your bags packed and out of here this minute.

" Caroline won't...."

"Don't you Caroline me, you slut."

"Since we're going to be family it hardly seems reasonable...."

"Family, Family! How dare you even think you'll get away with that! Aiy'll blacken your name throughout Glasgow. You'll be accepted nowhere."

"You'd do that, even if it harmed him? You might stop to think...."

"I'll tell you what I think. The marriage will never happen. I won't let it."

"But your father…."

"You may have fooled him but aiy've always seen through you, scheming hussy that you are. All you want is his money."

I think you'd better leave Mrs. Bryant, before one or the other of us says too much. I'll tell McAlister of your concerns and you can then take it up with him."

Cate made to move toward the still open door as Caroline fumbled in her bag.

"Don't you dare talk to me like an equal. You're going to leave right now. Take this." She waved the bag of money she'd taken from her handbag. "It's more than your worth, but your sort can always be bought of. Take it and get back to the slums where you belong."

Facing the raging woman Cate had difficulty controlling her rising temper. Meanwhile Caroline continued raging

"Go on then, you filthy tinker. Oh yes! Aiy know the whole sordid tale. Aiy've made it my business to find out about you. One of a band of thieving tinkers—the worst possible kind of people, no morals, illegitimate children spread everywhere, criminals all of them. Don't you worry, maiy father will hear about your disgusting past and then he'll kick you out, so take this and go!"

Flinging the bag of sovereigns on the floor, Caroline stood in anticipated triumph. Unfortunately, she'd been so incensed with the situation and so sure she would prevail that she'd not paid enough attention to Cate's face, which was now contorted with rage.

"You would do that, wouldn't you? Ruin, not only a good man but your own father. You don't care about him. I don't think you ever have. He's the kindest man I know and you treat him—well, like your own husband. Aha, that got you! You see I've been told a few tales as well. Married him for his money you did and now treat him like a servant!"

"How dare you! You little guttersnipe! I'll make you go. I should have pushed harder when I sent you flying, you little tart. Oh yes, that was me—and why not? You should never have been allowed out of the scullery. Even that was too good for you. Your sort should be in prison. Filthy little tinker! Now get out of my sight!"

Caroline lunged at Cate grabbing a handful of her hair, so that the remainder spilled around her shoulders, and began to drag her through the open door.

"Out with you, slut, filthy tinker! Vermin, that's what you are, not fit to live with decent people, never mind marry them!"

Later Cate could never tell whether it was the attack on her person or the echo of Bruce's words but she reacted instinctively. This was the sort of behaviour she knew about. Launching herself at the older woman, Cate unbalanced her, and the pair fell to the floor, arms flailing.

"I may be lowly born but I have better standards than you, Mrs. hoity toity Bryant. Just what makes you so special?"

Cate spat the words at her as they rolled over, each one trying for a better hold.

"You take, take, take, be it from your father, husband, cook or anyone else. You were born selfish, and I bet your father's glad your mother didn't live to see it." With that Cate straddled her opponent and tried to secure her arms.

This was too much for Caroline Bryant who brought her knees up to unseat Cate, while restoring her hold on the other's hair. Moments passed as the two women traded scratches, before Caroline Bryant managed to free herself long enough to continue the verbal battle.

"Don't you soil my mother's name, even by mentioning it! I'll see my father hears of your attack on me. I'll see you in the jail you whore!"

Her words loosened Cate's frail control of her temper. Such was her fury that Caroline was once again pinned under her, but this time the older woman was held firm while Cate shook her with such force her head made contact with the Victorian floor tiles. That was, alerted by the loud voices, how a frightened Ada found them.

"Cook! Cook! It's Cate! Cate! Cook!" Ada screamed for help before trying to attract Cate's attention.

"Whit are you daein Cate? You'll kill her, so you will. Oh Cate! Cook! Cook!"

Ada, feet stuck to the floor, simply watched as Cate continued her struggle with Caroline Bryant.

Cook, hearing Ada's frantic cries, rushed to the scene.

"God almighty, Ada! Don't just stand there— pull them apart! Here, out of my way. Cate, lass, stop it! Stop it now! Ada, grab her other arm! Come on, girl, before murder's done this day."

With Cate upright and imprisoned, all three stared at the dishevelled woman on the floor. Cate, the first to recover, freed her arms and pushed Cook forward.

"Get her up and out of here. She came looking for trouble, and that's what she got."

As Cook helped her up, Caroline struggled to her feet, hair down over her face, clothes awry, her hat, now a poor mangled thing languishing on the tiles.

"Prostitute! Dirty Slut! Dregs of the earth, that's what you are! One day I'll see you pay for this, and so will my father, silly fool that he is. Just remember that! I'll be waiting for the first opportunity, and you'll be sorry you ever crossed my path, believe me! Whatever I have to do to get even, I'll do it. I'll inflict pain on you that will cause you misery for the rest of your life. Oh yes, you'll rue this day, filthy slut that you are!" Grabbing her bag and trying to rearrange her hair, Caroline Bryant went.

The silent women she left behind, closed the door and retired to the kitchen, where Cook settled the kettle on the hob before bathing the scratches on Cate's face, while shocked Ada sniffed into her apron, as the enormity of what had happened and the consequences of it concerned all three.

The sound of the front door opening and closing endorsed their fears. He was home. Just how do you tell your employer that his future wife and his daughter had had a cat-fight? In silence they tracked his progress from hall, to study, to dining room and then his inevitable steps down the stairs into the kitchen as he searched for at least one member of his household to provide his tea.

"Well now, and why no welcome and…?" Suddenly he became aware of the atmosphere in the room. "What? Cate, you're not ill? Has somebody died? For God's sake, one of you, answer me!"

"McAlister, I….it's Mrs. Bryant. She came and she…."

"The invitation had arrived then?"

"Yes and she came to…."

166

"Make trouble? Yes that would be Caroline's way. How did you handle it?"

"Sir. Sir. She beat the livin daylights oot o' her, Sir, that she did an all. You should hiv….hiv…." The scandalized faces around her tore Ada's words away.

"Thank you, Ada. Most graphically described. Is this true, Cate?"

"Yes, it's true, and if it hadn't been for Ada and Cook, I might well have done your daughter serious harm."

"I take it then that Caroline was unusually offensive."

"McAlister, that woman's no heart. Now I know it's wrong to say this to you, her father, but it's true. I could have borne her trying to discredit me, but when she said she'd ruin you to get rid of me, I simply couldn't stand it. "

"Thank you for your sturdy defence of me. Not the wisest thing to have done perhaps, but I'm impressed. Now surely a man deserves a cup of tea when he gets home, and maybe something sweet, Cook? Let's talk about this in the study, Cate."

Once settled in their chairs and the details of the event gone over, he smiled at the wild young woman soon to be his bride. "You should know by now that you can do no wrong in my eyes—wait now, hear me out. Your defence of me was justified, though perhaps a mite on the forceful side, but then Caroline was never the most intelligent of women. You must see that her dislike of you stems from nothing less than pure jealousy. She puts no effort into anything other than her own gratification. Did you really think I was unaware of her faults? Did you also know she tried every rotten trick to discredit you in the early days? Even I fear, to pushing you down the stairs. Oh, I have no proof, but I suspect it."

"I didn't know until she admitted it to me today. She'll never agree to the wedding. Not now, after today."

"Of course she won't, my dear, but we'll have it anyway. I'm afraid some of the others will do likewise. Then we'll see who our true friends are."

"But what of your work? You'll lose clients surely?"

"Oh I'll not lose many. The high and mighty will use my partner or go elsewhere. I can cope with that."

"You would do all that to marry me? Lose friends and business, when by leaving me as your housekeeper you'd lose nothing?"

"Ah but I would, Cate. I would lose the right to share the remainder of my life with you and that is worth any losses. Don't fret about Caroline. I stopped being hurt by her lack of affection a long time ago. She will always be my daughter and I will leave her well provided for, but that's all. Perhaps, as far as your involvement with her is concerned, I do think it might be wise another time not to try to—again now, how did Ada put it?"

"You're laughing at me! You're laughing about it."

"Indeed I am. I'd have given anything to witness Cook and young Ada prising you apart."

Cate had to laugh at that and they were both smiling when Ada arrived with the tea.

The wedding morning, a month later, found the three women in the tenement flat dressed in their finery. Cate wore a simple cream suit with a cream cloche hat and veil. Maggie and Lizzie clothed in their new green and blue belted coats with matching Tam o' Shanters on their heads.

Lizzzie gazed at Cate in wonderment. "Oh, you do look lovely, Cate."

"Thanks to your sewing, Lizzie. You made everything up beautifully."

"You drew them for me though."

"Designed, my dear Lizzie! If we're going to be in business one day, we must use the right words."

"Will it be right though, to be in business I mean, now you're to be Mrs. McAlister."

"Lizzie, I can still think up dresses and you can still sew."

"We-ell, but it'll no be the same as having you here."

"I haven't been here for some time now, so what difference is it going to make?"

Even as she said it, Cate wondered whether this wedding would make a difference. Take today, for instance. She'd insisted on leaving for the ceremony from the tenements—she owed Maggie and Lizzie that much. McAlister had agreed somewhat reluctantly. It

168

was almost as though he didn't want to let her out of his sight. After the way she'd behaved, just disappearing into the night, who could blame him? Well, she, Maggie and Lizzie were ready and the car would be here soon. First a parade for Mrs. Petrie and Rhoddy, who'd refused to come to the ceremony, preferring to stay and play with his friends, and then she'd be on her way to her wedding.

The ceremony in the town hall seemed to pass in a blur. At the reception Cate ate little, shook hands with strangers, spoke to those she knew and spent time with her friends. When it was over they said their goodbyes, had rice thrown over them, and made for the hired car. As it negotiated unfamiliar streets, Cate questioned her new husband.

"This isn't the way home?"

"No, my dearest Cate, my wife at last, we're not going home. We're going to the station and then to Perth." She really was his Cate now. He could barely believe it. They'd both been nervous exchanging their vows and he'd felt the reception would never be over, even with the few friends and family. At least Ian and his wife had come and, surprisingly, Bryant had turned up—minus Caroline of course!

"Perth, but why?"

"Because, my dear, the first days of any marriage should never be spent with familiar eyes watching. We'll be alone, apart from the housekeeper, who doesn't know us and will only be there for our meals. Time to get accustomed to our new roles. I don't mind telling you, I'm a trifle nervous. It's been a long time since I've been a husband."

"You're nervous? At least you've done this before! I'm beginning to wonder if I should be doing this at all!"

"I'm reliably informed that all brides feel that way. Have no fear, Cate we're lucky—some couples marry as complete strangers. You and I know we can live happily together. Dammit it all we've done it for years!"

"That's true but—well, not as man and wife."

"Oh, my dear girl it will be nothing like that other horrid experience. I'm a mature man and I'll be patient. Rest assured, it'll be fine. Here we are at the station. Now for our compartment to Perth, then a short cab journey and I know you'll approve of my choice.

Deposited at the picket gate, McAlister took Cate's arm and pointed to the low-slung cottage in front of them. She gulped a lung full of fresh country air, as she looked around. Tucked into the hillside, the little house seemed so sheltered and welcoming. The garden ran down to a river and there were horses grazing in the fields either side of it.

"I see it's the outside that's taken your interest. You've missed the space and freedom of the countryside?

"Oh yes. I'd forgotten just how much. I love the outdoors—the space, the air, the sky!"

"We do have air and sky in Glasgow you know."

"I know, I'm being rude about your birthplace, but it never felt like this—to me anyway."

"It does feel very pleasant, I must admit."

Seeing her so in tune with these new surroundings, McAlister thought it might be an idea to see whether he could take a long lease on the cottage, so that they could spend some weekends here on their own.

"Look, I think Mrs. Muir, the housekeeper, is calling us. Come along, my dear Mrs. McAlister."

"Delighted to, McAlister. And, before you ask, I'd like to keep using that. At first I was too nervous to call you anything else, but now I like it too much to change. Is that alright?"

"Dear girl, call me anything you want. Come, give me your arm and we'll see what Mrs. Muir has in store for us. No Ada to make us laugh though!"

"Well she did make me laugh this afternoon at the reception when she was all tearful and had no apron to hide her face in. Did you see her? She almost picked up her skirt instead!"

"She thought better of it once she'd realized what she was about to do. She was so proud that you and Lizzie had gone to such trouble making hers and Cook's outfits. In fact you seemed to take more trouble over everyone else's clothes than your own. One of the many things I adore about you."

The new dawn was sidling over the horizon as Cate slipped out of the big double bed, watched her husband murmur in his sleep, and turn over. Yesterday they'd had a lovely evening and when bedtime came they'd continued to chat, just like old times in the study, and then he'd wished her goodnight and gone to sleep. She'd understood he was waiting for her to feel ready and she could have cried at this thoughtful gesture on his part. He was such a kind man and would surely be easy to love. After all he'd only gained a wife, whereas she'd gained a husband, a name, a home for herself and Rhoddy, and best of all, security. She knew gratitude was not what he sought, though he'd have hers, and she'd be the best wife there could be, for he certainly deserved that. In fact she'd go to him as his true wife that very night. Not giving herself time to think about it, she threw on her robe and, barefooted, romped across the dewy lawn to the river.

Once breakfasted, they began a glorious first day as man and wife. They explored the tiny village, walked the fields bathed in beautiful spring weather, consumed Mrs. Muir's excellent meals, and spent quiet time seated in the gloaming by the water. Now Cate was upstairs and Malcolm content by the fire, happier now than he'd been for years. Pouring a last drop of port he swilled it round the glass as he watched the dying fire, passing the time before going up. Giving the new bride time to fall asleep.

Upstairs, Cate shivered as she sat on the window seat. What was keeping him? The morning's decision made she didn't need this time to reconsider. It made her even more nervous and troubled. She rose and paced the floor—how long had it been now? Where was he? She'd been up here for ages. Dammit why didn't he come? Her throat was so dry she wouldn't be able to speak, never mind anything else. How to let him know? Would he think her too forward? Should she be in the bed? What would she say? How should it all start? Would she be okay? Could it be like it was in books? No, she didn't suppose so. Fiction it was—how could that act ever be nice? Suddenly her worrying about it seemed to overwhelm her. Trying to steady herself, she took comfort from the fact that at least he'd not knock her out like Bruce! In her nervous state, the thought of McAlister, the kindest of men, suddenly becoming violent was so unlikely it was almost funny. She began to giggle and then couldn't stop.

As the bedroom door opened, revealing his familiar figure, the sight and her nerves increased the giggles. By the time she'd haltingly explained to her greatly puzzled husband about her decision, the long wait and the rest of her nervous thoughts, she was laughing so much that he began to laugh with her. When he explained that he'd stayed downstairs for so long in order to let her fall asleep only to find she was upstairs waiting for him, wondering why he didn't come, it set them off again. Soon they were tucked up in bed. With the laughter still between them he held her gently and lovingly led her into her new life as a wife.

As her wedding anniversary approached, Cate knew her happiness was complete. She'd only been married for three months when much to their delight she found she was pregnant. Now here she was, after a relatively simple pregnancy and easy labour, with a newborn baby daughter. Her thoughts were interrupted as the nurse entered the room with a sullen Rhoddy. Cate knew this was going to be difficult, as she watched her son trying to wriggle out of the nurse's firm grip. Smiling at him Cate lifted her hand and beckoned him into the room.

"Come in, Rhoddy and see your new baby sister."

"Dinna want to see her."

"Of course you do."

Rhoddy, finally managing to escape from his captor, ran out of the room.

"Rhoddy, you come back here." Oh, why did she always end up shouting at him?

"Now, now, Mrs. McAlister, no upsetting yourself! We don't want trouble with your milk, now do we? After all, boys aren't interested in babies. It's women's work. Males just clutter up this important event."

Where in God's name had McAlister found this awful woman? Whatever the nurse was used to, it wasn't the life that Cate knew. It was all very well employing a nurse for her and the baby, but she felt cut off from everyone up here. Even her husband was allowed only a few moments at a time with them, and, as for Lizzie or Maggie, the old gorgon wouldn't hear of it. 'Madam had to save her strength'. A bubble of laughter fought its way to the surface. What would her keeper have thought of her traipsing the streets with Rhoddy on her back in a shawl, only two days old!

Letting her thoughts run on, Cate had to admit her son had hated leaving the tenements and his beloved Lizzie. He'd wanted to stay there, but McAlister had been adamant: Rhoddy was her son and should be with his mother. That was all fine and well, but it hadn't worked out. It was McAlister who now had the easy relationship with her son. Apparently any one but his mother suited the five-year-old. Yet you couldn't blame the child. After all she'd hardly been with him in his early years. Other than the friction with her son, the marriage had turned out well. She grew fonder of McAlister by the day, though they had some right old arguments. Mostly they were solved by one or the other of them collapsing in laughter. Occasionally he couldn't be moved, as in the case of the housekeeper he'd hired, and what an error that was proving to be. Now the gorgon nurse was another.

She'd seen little of Lizzie and Maggie since her pregnancy. Somehow they were reluctant to visit, what with the new housekeeper —Cate hadn't been too happy about that appointment, but McAlister had insisted as soon as he knew she was pregnant. It had not worked out. Their peaceful existence had suddenly become hedged with all the old formalities, while being idle hadn't improved her temper. She visited the tenement as often as she could, but, with Rhoddy beginning school and both women now working, it was difficult. Even reminiscing didn't put her in a quieter frame of mind, so she rose and put the baby in the bassinette.

Pulling on a dressing gown, she made up her mind things would have to change. McAlister would find she could be just as determined as him, though maybe a show of strength was not the way to go about it. For a mild man he was thrawn when he set his mind to it, and yet he'd made her happier than she'd thought possible. She'd send the two women packing while he was away and deal with the fallout on his return. He'd had his way, his daughter was safely here, and now his wife was going to have her say about their future.

McAlister was disturbed to find that while he'd been in London seeing a client both housekeeper and nurse had packed their bags and gone. Love her as he did, he was not prepared for this. So he went in search of his wife and found her in the study.

"Cate, Cook tells me you've removed the extra help I'd hired to make things easier for you. I really must protest. You can't have thought this through."

"McAlister, I've thought of nothing else these last weeks. I've barely seen you. Our precious daughter I'm allowed to feed and that's all. I feel like some prize cow rather than a new mother. I miss you. I miss you both. Rhoddy's running wild downstairs. I could hear his tantrums from up there and—"

"Alright! How on earth you'll cope with it all I don't know." This was all too much. The joy of being a new father at this late stage in his life was being swept aside in a maelstrom of domestic unrest. The serenity of his life with Cate seemed to have gradually disappeared over these last few months and it was wearying. He'd hired the housekeeper to save Cate, but this seemed to have turned her into a mass of frustration instead.

"I'm sorry. I don't mean to cross you. Shouting at you is unfair. I know you've done it all for my benefit."

Taking his hand she led him to his chair and knelt before him. "McAlister, I'm young and healthy. I've sat about like a lady for months now waiting for our child. I'm not used to that. This birth was easy and I'm fine. Please don't be cross with me. I know it was all done for my benefit and I'm truly grateful, but I want our home back. You'll see it will be better for all of us. Poor Ada has nearly had a nervous breakdown in the meantime. She's forgotten everything I've taught her and that woman wants her sacked. Cook's fine. She just ignores 'the Prune'."

Seeing his puzzled expression, Cate smiled. "Come on, didn't you ever look at those lips all pursed up so her whole face was as wrinkled as a prune?" She watched as he struggled to keep a straight face and then failed. This was the way it should be. They'd soon get back to normal, enjoy their baby and bring some laughter into the house again.

"You're a wicked woman, Cate McAlister, but at least we're laughing again! We'll try it your way, but you must have help with baby Sarah. Why that name, by the way?"

"I know it'll seem strange naming her after Lady Sarah."

"I do find it odd considering the way she treated you."

"It's silly really, but if it had been a boy I'd have liked to call him David, so somehow his mother's name is the closest I can get. Anyway, she was very kind to me in the beginning, and she did set me on the road to improving myself."

"And I imagine she didn't fight with the housekeeper, now did she?"

"No, but then I'm no lady. Perhaps our beautiful daughter might be. Sit there and I'll bring her to you. The benefit of the gorgon nurse having gone is we can give her cuddles whenever we like— don't try and tell me that won't please you, because you know it will."

It would all be too much for her, he was sure, but somehow he was too tired to argue tonight. He'd had indigestion again last night and all this upset was making him anxious. Still, if he knew his Cate, she would make it all work. He could see it would be for the best.

As she went to fetch her daughter, Cate was certain that her rebellion in sending both nurse and housekeeper through the door while he'd been absent, would not only sort their home lives out but would close the gap with her other 'family'. Lizzie could be the new nursemaid and live in, which Rhoddy would love. Once she was in place, Maggie would no doubt get over her scruples about visiting and of course they could all visit the tenements on Maggie's day off on the Sabbath. Having Lizzie staying would surely improve Rhoddy's temper and his relationship with herself.

She'd wait though before arranging it. Her way was to get on with anything new, but slowly she'd learnt that her husband liked to study the problem from all angles and then go back and study it all over again. She'd won her victory today. She'd cope until he brought the subject up again. Then he'd probably agree.

As she climbed the stairs, her feet skipped along for the first time in many months. She could just be getting the two halves of her life joining much earlier than she'd expected. At last she could keep her word to those two dear women and lighten their load. Yes, she had 'got on' and soon they could go forward together. Now for her precious daughter and sharing her with her father. Then they'd have the proper family home that both she and McAlister desired.

"Now then, my little girl, just where do you think you're going?" Malcolm scooped his daughter into his arms as she squirmed on the mat. Cate, having put Rhoddy to bed, would be down in a minute, and they'd enjoy Sarah's last feed in the study before putting her down in the nursery for the night. As her chubby fingers tried to catch his cheek he chuckled and gently pulled them away.

"Your mother is a very clever woman. Did you know that, young lady?"

He let his thoughts roam over the past months and freely admitted that Cate had been right. Cook and Ada had settled down again, Rhoddy was beginning to be more responsive with his mother, and his new daughter was a delight. As she wriggled against his chest he felt a sharp pain. For a moment breathing was difficult and then it passed as it had done before. Cook's good food and his own increased appetite proving too much for his stomach again no doubt. Cate's entry interrupted his thoughts.

"Well now, look at you all comfy there! Room for another one beside you?" Cate sat on the rug and, taking her in her arms, prepared to feed Sarah.

McAlister, meanwhile, stroked the crown of his wife's head, wishing he could loosen all those damned pins and let that glorious red hair fall down her back.

"I've just been thinking how right you were to end those two appointments, even though they'd been made with the best of intentions."

"Don't worry, McAlister. I know that. I never wanted to blame you, it's just that they were wrong for all of us."

"Indeed, my dear, though it hasn't escaped my notice that your promise to have additional help of your own choosing hasn't happened yet. A bargain is a bargain, Cate, and I feel it's time for you to do your part. I'm selfish. I want more of my wife. I want to take things easier."

"You're not unwell again, McAlister?"

"No, no my dear. It's just that the days pass so quickly and I see so little of you. I want to go to the cottage with you again."

"It may not be there anymore. I mean perhaps the owners won't rent it any longer."

"You'd like to go, though?"

"You know I would. Here, wind her for me." Watching him with Sarah, Cate felt overwhelmed by affection for this man who'd become her husband. It may not have been the great romance of the novels, but they were both content and she could barely believe now that she'd ever had doubts about marrying him.

"Well then, there's no problem, as the owners will very definitely let us have it again!"

"You've already checked, haven't you? Always the perfect lawyer with all the facts to hand."

"Well, I have to keep ahead of my clever wife."

Cate was unaware that her husband had bought the cottage in her name and planned to give her the deeds on her birthday.

"Now, if we're to get away to the cottage, I want extra help in the house, and soon please."

"Yes sir, I'll see to it by the end of the week, sir!" She made a mocking curtsy in front of him.

"You, Madam, I will deal with later. First remove this delightful but soggy bundle and let me finish up my papers."

As she put Sarah down in the nursery, Cate was already visualizing her visit on Sunday to Maggie and Lizzie. How thrilled they'd be for Lizzie to have a paying job that wouldn't be too arduous. Maggie would miss her, but she'd understand that it would be right for Lizzie, and Cate couldn't wait to see Lizzie's face when she asked her. Finally she'd be able to keep her promise to her 'family'. Life was indeed good and she couldn't wait to go to the cottage again. She loved that little place. Oh, the Glasgow house was fine, but somehow that little nest on the banks of the river was special to her, as were her husband and baby daughter. Yes, at last everything was coming right for them all.

Part Three

Travelling

1910

13

As she opened the front door, Cate was surprised to see Solly there. Normally he came to the basement door, but she was glad to see him. He'd become a good friend and was now included in her other 'family' as he'd also made friends with Lizzie.

"Hello. Don't tell me it's another brown envelope you're after." There was no answering smile from him at the shared memory. "Solly?" When he didn't reply Cate knew something was wrong.

"My husband. He's not bad again, is he? Why hasn't he come home? "

Solly tried to speak but the words wouldn't come. It had been so quick in the courthouse. He was still in shock.

"Solly! What?" Cate, frightened now, shook the silent clerk. "Tell me, Solly. What's happened?"

"The hospital. Mr.McAlister. They've taken—I'm so sorry. His heart—he's gone!" Solly saw the colour leave her face at his words.

"He—he's not dead. He—no, no he can't be. You're mistaken. Solly, you're wrong! You must be!" Just looking at the silent clerk, her shock mirrored in his eyes, Cate knew it was true.

Next day Ian arrived, as Cate knew he would, and she showed him into the study where, after exchanging condolences, he began going through the desk. It hurt Cate to see him with McAlister's things, but it was to be expected. He was now head of the McAlister family and as such would deal with all the arrangements for his father's funeral and affairs. Shocked as she was by McAlister's death, she needed that respite before tackling her now uncertain future.

Later, pushing the last of the files to the side, Ian rose, back cramped. No food or refreshment had appeared so he made his way to the kitchen in search of some. The three remaining members of the household sat in silence, but Cook rose as he entered.

"Oh sir, the poor master. It doesn't seem possible."

"It's been a great shock to us all, but then he'd been ill several times these last few years. Now, something to eat and a glass of wine in the study, for me please. There's a lot of work to be done before the funeral."

A familiar shout from the hallway above forced him, with some relief, to leave the mourning trio, and hurry upstairs to waylay his sister. He knew all about the trouble between the wife and Caroline, but they could wait till after the funeral to settle their differences. He'd have no family squabbles aired in public until his father was buried. Coming face to face with her he could see she was in determined mood.

"Ian, where is she? We have to get her out of here."

"You could show a little grief, Caroline. It is expected."

When his sister began to edge past him, Ian stopped her. "I know how you feel, but we have to do this right. Throw her out and there'll be a scandal. Frankly, as long as she doesn't snaffle all the old man's wealth, I don't care and neither should you."

"Oh but I do. That slut deserves nothing. She took advantage of my poor father and I was the only one to see it. I suppose she's there with the other servants planning how she's going to spend our inheritance."

"Actually, Caroline, they all look too shocked for that. For once take my advice. Leave it to me."

"Ian, I won't let her get a penny. Right now I'm going down there and I'll drag her out the basement door onto the street where she belongs."

"And just what sort of unwelcome publicity would that bring? We've a funeral to arrange, Caroline, an obituary to write, a eulogy to prepare, catering arrangements to see to, and whatever needs to be done to settle the law practice. We can't do all that while you're brawling in the street."

"I don't see…"

"Leave this to me. You need neither see her nor speak to her before the funeral. After that I don't care."

"But I do. Think what she might do to rob us of what's rightly ours."

"I don't believe she'll do anything."

"You could never see what's under your nose, Ian."

"Perhaps not, but go home, Caroline. Leave the arrangements to me. Turn up, suitably grief-stricken, at the funeral, and then we'll see."

"We have to do something, or she'll take everything."

"Caroline, let's get some facts, hear the will read, before we start assuming what she'll do. Now go home, think about the catering side, and leave the rest to me."

"I'll go, but as soon as the funeral is over I'll get her out of here and on the road—penniless if I have anything to do with it."

Three days later, with most of the arrangements completed, Ian closed the study door and went into the drawing room. Helping himself to a drink, his thoughts turned to the woman he'd left in the study. She'd been no trouble. Spent most of the time with the sullen boy and the baby in the nursery. The cook at least, fed them lunch and dinner, though the woman ate little and spoke only when asked a direct question. Stretching his legs out in front of the fire, he went over the details for the next day. The partner, Hardy, had been a splendid chap about the will, giving him the basic ideas in advance. That had surprised him—breaking with tradition. The fellow was not in the least the sort of partner he'd imagined his father would have.

Caroline, on the other hand, had been delighted with him: the man agreed with her unusual insistence that only the baby was a McAlister, and treated as such. His sister had never shown any motherly instincts before now. Rarely visited his own sons, so this desire that the child should be considered was out of character. She refused to let the servants look after the child while they were at the funeral. Produced an agency nurse to do so, and he'd told the widow it was his idea—anything to avoid more trouble between the two women. Still, he was uneasy about it, and he wasn't keen on Caroline's choice of venue for the wake. She'd always been a snob and the choice of the expensive Country House Hotel on the outskirts of Glasgow was typical of her.

Cate stood, wreathed in black, holding a squirming Rhoddy tightly by the hand, as the preacher droned on amidst the crowd of black clothed strangers, her mind on McAlister and the times she'd nursed him back to health. She could have saved him, weak heart or not! But she hadn't even had time to try. Dead, and she'd not even said goodbye. She hadn't loved him in the beginning, though that had been growing, but they'd been content with one another. He'd been a good man, and every day she'd spent with him had increased her fondness. He'd had the peace at home he required—up until the baby anyway. Thankfully they'd resumed their peaceful existence at the end. She couldn't have borne for him to go troubled to his grave; though she wished she'd expressed more of her true feelings to the man she was learning to love. Now it was too late. Please God he'd understood. Perhaps he had, but it would have been so much better had he heard it from her lips.

She watched the last of the line of mourners leave the open grave, until they'd all gone, then she moved to the side of the yawning hole and stood staring at the earth splattered coffin. Taking the white lily she'd pinned to her black coat she dropped it and her precious black bag, his first ever gift to her, into the space and closed her eyes. Motionless, she remained until Rhoddy, tired of waiting, approached her, pulling at the arms folded across her body to keep the world away.

Eventually she turned and followed him to the church door only to find that the next funeral was underway. How quick it had all been. Seems the dead had no need of lengthy departures, and as she left she saw the gravediggers hefting away, completing the blanket of soil that now swaddled the earthly remains of Malcolm McAlister. Once more it was her son who penetrated her grief.

"Mammy, I'm cold an they're all gone, so they are."

Reluctantly, Cate took Rhoddy's hand and they made their way to the street outside.

"It's no here. The horses—they're no here! Where are they, Mammy? How're we to get back?"

Rhoddy's plaintive cry made her aware that the road outside the cemetery had other carriages, but no familiar ones. She couldn't understand it. Ian had said they'd wait. She'd no idea where the wake was, he'd done all the arrangements and she'd never asked—all she'd thought of was getting home to her baby. Home, that's where they'd be, and it was there that they'd tell her when she'd have to leave. That problem would have to wait till she got there. She couldn't miss her husband's wake. Fine story Caroline would make of that!

At last, dragging a tired and dusty Rhoddy, they came in sight of their front door. There were no carriages waiting, so they must have been dismissed. She couldn't see into the house as the black mourning blinds were securely down. At least they were here. Hopefully she hadn't been missed. The door seemed to be stuck. Trying the handle again, Cate had the first vague sense of unease. Again she tried and still it wouldn't turn. Why? Every morning in life Ada unlocked the door and cleaned the brass knob until she could see her face in it. The door was never locked again until she herself turned the great big iron key in it at night. How could it be locked now? Panic lent her strength, she rattled the knob fit to pull it from the door. Her baby was inside with the nursemaid. But where were all the mourners, if not here? Why had the girl locked herself in? Oh my good God, where was her beloved Sarah?

"C'mon Rhoddy, we'll try the Assembly Rooms. They're bound to be there." Pulling the protesting boy along the road, Cate tried desperately to think where the others could be. It had to be the Assembly Rooms. Where else—his office perhaps? No—too small. One of the tearooms in Sauchiehall street? No too public. Or could it be the Co-op reception hall? No, that wouldn't be grand enough for snooty Caroline. She'd just have to try all three. The neighbouring houses had all been quiet, presumably because they were all at the wake, so there'd been no help there.

The summer evening shadows were closing in by the time she'd tried every venue she could think of, and some unlikely ones that kindly people had suggested. The whole affair would be over by the time she got there. Worse still, Rhoddy was now tearful and she felt faint. She'd eaten little and slept less in the previous week and that compounded with the sudden rush of anxiety made her unsteady.

"Rhoddy, I'll have to find a seat for a minute. I'll sit here on these steps, just to…Rhoddy I'm…." The darkness overwhelmed her and she felt herself falling.

"Mammy! Mammy! My Mammy's dead too!" Rhoddy wailed as he stood over his mother's unconscious body, staring at the trickle of blood.

A harassed doctor and nursing sister stood at the foot of the bed, studying the silent woman, having seen to the dressing of her head wound.

"What about the boy? Is he no help, Sister?"

"None at all, I'm afraid. Calls out 'Lizzie' in his sleep. Do you think they can be brother and sister, Doctor?"

"Possibly, more likely mother and son, though there's no resemblance. Might not be related at all. Anyway, with the boy either unwilling or unable to furnish us with any facts, the woman in some kind of shock, probably concussed as well, we're unlikely to get any quick answers. Thing is, what do we do with him?"

"What do you mean, Doctor?"

"Well, we can hardly keep him here in the infirmary. After all, he's not ill. The woman is injured, so she may stay, but the boy will have to go."

"If we don't know who he is, how can we find his home? Oh no, Doctor! Not the orphanage! It's not his fault the woman is ill and can't look after him. I mean he's hardly in rags. Someone, somewhere, must be desperately looking for them both."

"You would have thought so, but they've been here—how long now?"

"Admitted three days ago. The policeman, who called for the ambulance, said the woman was unconscious and the child crying on the steps of that new office building in Sauchiehall Street. Looked as though she'd tripped and fallen on the steps."

"Well, I'll leave it for another couple of days, but then we'll have to think of something. Perhaps by then she'll have come back to us."

As she washed the boy and tucked him up for the night, Sister Mary Anne had an idea. Whether it would work or not, she couldn't tell, but anything would be better than the orphanage for the poor little lad.

The Convent looked so stern from the outside, but the grey sombre walls hid a world of kindness. She should know. As an orphan it had been her only home for as long as she could remember. The sisters had made an exception in her case and kept her there. She'd worked at simple tasks in the beginning. Later, when she went to school, she'd helped with the sick little ones, done housework, and anything else that needed doing. It was Sister Assumpta who'd first set her feet on the nursing ladder, getting her taken on at the infirmary, where Mary Anne had worked her way up from ward maid to sister, and now, at twenty-five, was one of the youngest. The convent was still a haven to run to even now: a good gossip, friendly advice and emotional warmth that her lodgings and her adult world didn't always provide. Would Sister Assumpta now help another poor soul? She'd take him round after her shift.

"And who's this you've brought with you, Mary Anne? Hello lad, what's your name?"

"He won't speak. Seems he was found with a woman who'd collapsed in Sauchiehall Street. Mind, with all those shops, he could belong to anyone, even someone from outside Glasgow."

"Where's the woman then? Surely she could give you some information."

"That's just it. They were both admitted to the infirmary. She's concussed and makes little sense, and not a word from the boy."

"I see, so once again we're to come to the rescue. This convent does have other reasons to exist, you know. We're not here simply to pick up the infirmary's woes."

"I know, but the doctor won't let him stay. What with the woman making no sense and the lad no injured... well, an orphanage or, even worse, the workhouse, is not for the likes of him. Look how he's dressed. No, someone will be searching for him, and you know fine well, as soon as that workhouse door closes, he's lost."

"Well, I suppose we could put him in with the orphan lad with the bad leg. This one's what—six, or so? An older child for company might just do them both a bit of good. It can't be for long, mind. We'll settle them in, then I'll have all your news."

A rich bit of gossip was a prize to brighten an impoverished life, so Bessie hurried round to her old friend Maudie Petrie, hoping the other woman hadn't heard the news. She caught her on the stairs and wasted no time in preliminaries.

"Maudie, you remember yon lawyer's letter for Maggie."

At Maudie's puzzled nod, Bessie stood taller and imparted her news. "Dropped like a stane, the butcher said, an him no that long new married and with a wee bairn. Mind, he was too auld for they kind of goings on. Men! Do they niver tire of that nonsense? Bet you they soon wid if they had to hae the weans!"

"Aye, your right there, Bessie. But men niver think the thing through."

"That's 'cos they think wi what's in their troosers, Maudie!"

"Mind, Bessie, I think yon lawyer was the one whit married Maggie's Cate."

"Niver! Was her lass wed to a legal man then, Maudie?"

"No, no. It wisna Maggie's ain lass, it wis the one frae the North—her brither's lass I think. Any·road I'll need tae awa an tell them. They'll be upset, I can tell you."

"Aye, death's there for us all, but it's still that terrible when it comes, Maudie. Though the butcher says it was a grand burial. Feathered horses an loads of carriages, an the wake in some posh hotel in the country. Strange it was, Maggie no being invited. Or mebbe she just forgot tae mention it." Bessie was more than pleased at the thought of her nosy neighbour missing out on a bit of gossip. It didn't happen very often.

"No, she wouldna dae that. She canna hiv known. Seems they've no seen ower much of young Cate since she went to live in the big hoose. No, I'll awa an let her know just in case. Away bairns! We've bad news to tell. Come on now, or there'll be no jelly pieces when we get back."

Like her friend, Maudie Petrie made her way downstairs savouring the importance of her news, but wasting no time in case someone, anyone, got there first and deprived her of this vital piece of drama. Her strident knock brought Maggie to the door.

"I'm that sorry, Maggie, tae be the one tae tell you." Maudie began as she imparted her news

Maggie's reaction had been all that her neighbour could have wished, though some of the success of her mission faded when the woman in front of her looked as though it had been one of hers that death had claimed.

" Anyways, I'll awa an leave you be wi yir grief."

Maudie Petrie climbed the stairs less elated than when she'd descended, and was soon immersed in the bedlam that was home.

Closing the door, Maggie tried to collect her wits before her daughter returned. As expected, when Lizzie came home, she greeted the news with tears.

"Come on now, Lizzie, he's been poorly for a while, with that chest of his. And it seems he went that quick it would've been easy on him. Dry your eyes."

"But why would Cate no tell us, Mammy? I'd have liked to stand by the road for him. It would only have been right for me to show respect, working for him, an all he'd done for me. He was that kind to both Cate and me. A good man."

Why indeed? Maggie thought. She'd seen it coming. First the housekeeping job, then the marriage, and the removal of Rhoddy. Now that had truly upset Lizzie. Right enough, Cate wanted to continue the money to help them. It wouldn't have been right though, taking money when they no longer looked after Rhoddy— charity, it would have been. Ever since her man's death she'd managed without that and she wasn't going to start now. They'd had words about it, and they'd been cool ever since. Cate wouldn't understand why the financial help was unwelcome when they could do with it. After all, they were her family, she said. But that was the problem. They weren't. Truth to tell, she'd felt a split then would be better in the long run for Lizzie's sake. The new baby daughter's arrival in the McAlister household had also changed the picture, completing a proper middle class family: a new world for the ambitious Cate. She'd always known it would happen.

"Mammy, you're no listening. I'm saying we should go and pay our respects. If it's in the paper it must have been a while ago. What must Cate be thinking of us?"

Considering Lizzie's words, Maggie felt, that if they did go, perhaps Cate would be too busy to see them, and finally Lizzie would understand that all her friend's brave words were just that—words. It would be cruel, but better to put an end to it now than have the dreams lingering any longer. "Alright, Lizzie, we'll go tomorrow, see'n as it's the Sabbath an we've no work."

As they stood in front of the deserted house neither woman could believe what they saw, though it was clear enough. Lizzie was the first to break the silence.

"Mammy, whit's all this? There's—where are they all? Where's Cate?"

"I'm no sure, Lizzie. Shssst. Let me think."

The shuttered house screamed the truth. It had been closed up and all life had fled. Silently answering Lizzie's forlorn plea—'she's gone, that's why!' Maggie swallowed such a sob of despair, as she'd not felt since her husband's untimely death. So it was over. Oh, she'd known it would be hard, but not this hard.

She turned to comfort Lizzie and found she'd moved up the road, speaking to a woman dressed in Sunday best, home from the kirk most likely. As Lizzie turned to come back, Maggie could see by her face, that the news was unwelcome, as she knew it would be. Her distraught daughter sobbed over the facts that were even now splintering her dream world. Maggie couldn't bear it, so she gathered her fractured daughter in her arms and led her home.

Safely there, still sobbing, Lizzie was beyond comfort. Maggie, on the other hand, was burning with rage. How could she? Not even a chance for Rhoddy to say goodbye to them? After all, they'd been more family to him than Cate'd ever been. No note telling of her plans or a promise to write! That would at least have softened the blow. And no word for Fisher, after all he'd done! What kind of return was that?

This was what she'd always feared. Sold up and away, the whole family were, to start a new life in America, the neighbour had told

Lizzie. Sailing on one of the brand new steamers of the Anchor Line on the Clyde.

Her rage subsiding, Maggie felt a heavy sorrow descending and realised that, despite preparing herself for this kind of outcome, she too was bitterly disappointed. Truth was she'd never really believed that Cate would forget them. Oh, her head had made it quite clear and she'd thought she was prepared, but deep down she too had thought they might just be carried along the road the tinker girl had been so certain she would forge for them all. Well she'd found the way, but had sailed without them, choosing to go with the rest of the McAlister family, despite having said time and again how much she despised them. Aye, that one would always do what she had to. Wasn't she always talking about 'getting on'?

At last Lizzie was asleep. Sipping her tea, Maggie wondered if now was the time to think about Bert Green again. For years now he'd been keeping Lizzie busy with mending, for himself and any of the others in the boat who needed it. He'd been a good friend—more really. He was always hinting, in their various outings, at marriage, but somehow the time had never seemed right. Supposing she said 'yes' now, it would mean a shift to Dunoon. There'd be no memory of Cate there. Mind made up, Maggie rinsed her cup and left it on the draining board. Tomorrow she and her gentle Lizzie would begin again. No more wild dreams. They'd settle for Bert. Maggie had no doubt he would be good for them both.

14

Before his morning rounds the doctor checked her notes and hoped that when the sister arrived she'd have some news. He put the notes down as he saw her coming.

"Any luck with the enquiries, Sister?"

"Not a bit of it, Doctor. I've tried all the births registered in the past year and I've found them all but one, and that one is away with the parents on a boat to America."

"So there goes our breakthrough! It was bright of you to spot she was crying for her baby. Since there's no infant, that would explain her trauma. I should think it's the same old story. Disgraced daughter or servant out on the street, child dead or taken away from her."

"The puzzling thing is though, Doctor, where the boy comes into it? "

"That I couldn't say. Will they keep him for a bit in the convent? She could come to her senses any time. I just don't know when."

"Mebbe a while longer. They say he's no trouble. He plays with the lads, but just doesn't speak."

"Well, we're doing all we can. It'll be a case of wait and see. Let's hope for the pair of them that it's sooner rather than later. That way we might be able to reunite them, otherwise I'm lost for solutions. Right, let's have a look at her and then get on. It's my half day today, and Rangers are playing."

"Aye, but no very well—they haven't won the cup since 1902."

"True, but we live in hope. Who knows, this might be their year!"

"Sister—oh excuse me, Doctor, but…."

"What is it, Nurse?"

"Sister, it's the woman—she's getting out of bed."

"Now that is good news! Come along, Sister. Our problem looks like solving itself."

As she followed him to the end of the ward, Sister Mary Anne wasn't quite so sure. The woman, holding on as she tried to stand, didn't look fit to go anywhere.

"I've got to get out of here! Rhoddy, Sarah, where are they?" Cate balanced unsteadily at the edge of the bed as she spoke to the pair.

"Not quite yet." The doctor replied. "Let's start at the beginning. You were brought in three weeks ago, unconscious. You'd had a nasty blow on the head. Do you remember how that happened? Anyway I'm delighted to see you're recovering".

"I was at the graveyard." Cate tried to remember.

"Were you now? You were found in Sauchiehall Street, so that doesn't make any sense. Do you know your name?"

"Of course I do. It's Cate. You must find them."

"Cate, we can't find anyone till we know more about you. When you were brought in you had no identification on you, not even a purse—though that could have been stolen as you lay there."

"I've told you. Doctor, I'm Cate McAlister, and now I'm looking for my bairns. I must go and find them."

"I agree we must get you up, but slowly. You've been abed for some time now."

"Some time? Some time? They'll have gone by now. They'll be lost."

"Now, now, we mustn't get excited." The doctor tried to forestall the hysteria. "That'll do your head no good at all. You've had some kind of trauma as well as the physical blow to the head, though that's healing nicely now, so we have to be careful. Can you tell us why no one has been looking for you? You must understand our difficulty here. It would appear that you've no friends or family in Glasgow." He couldn't quite make up his mind whether she was truly suffering from amnesia, or whether she was a good actress or just a consummate liar.

"Of course I've friends and family."

"Their names?"

"Maggie and Lizzie Balfour from the Gorbals."

This was rubbish, the doctor knew, the accent, the clothes—nothing about her was from the Gorbals. None of it made sense and never had. His first instinct had been correct. She was lying, but he'd go along with it. She was almost ready to be discharged anyway.

"You're sure I could release you to their care?"

"Of course you can, Doctor." Cate slumped back onto the bed.

"Good, then we'll just check you over, and if you seem physically able, we'll let you go. Not for a few days yet. You need to be up and steady on your feet first."

Cate watched as they made their way out of the ward. She, who'd always been so fit and healthy, could barely hold her head up. Could hardly stand. She was so tired. Where were Sarah, Rhoddy? Had Maggie got them? Why hadn't they been to see her?

She searched for her wits—McAlister? Of course the graveyard, he was dead. The blackness threatened again, but she forced her mind to confront it. Dead, dead, dead, that's it! He'd gone. Her lovely man had gone. What was it about her? Each time she found someone to love they died, or somewhere to live she lost it. Was she cursed? Where were the bairns? It was all too difficult. She was so tired and she wanted Maggie. She needed Lizzie, who never lost faith in her. She wanted them both. With no McAlister, they were all she had—the bairns and them. The avalanche of tears that had frozen inside her since that day on the doorstep with Solly, cracked, rolled out and engulfed her.

Days later, still grieving, but with a better grasp of reality, Cate was released from the Infirmary and, with the few coppers kind Sister Mary Anne had given her, she made for the tram. Some details were still blurred. Whether she'd been hit or fallen and cracked her head, she'd no memory. At least Rhoddy was safe. The good Sister had told her to find her friends first and then bring them to the hospital and she would take them all to get Rhoddy. Funny that, it was as if Sister Mary Anne understood, but the doctor didn't believe anything she said. Well, Maggie would put that right. She'd soon speak up for her. Had she told them about McAlister? She must have done. Had they been at the funeral? Dammit, why didn't she know? Well she was here at last. Just climbing the interminable stairs, remembering all that long-ago scrubbing, made her feel better. She knew her firm knock on the door would bring Lizzie and everything would be fine then.

Cate stared at the strange woman who answered the door. Who was she? Where was Lizzie?

The fog, that had so recently engulfed her in the hospital, threatened anew.

"I, I don't understand. Gone! What'd you mean they've gone? Where? When will they be back?" Cate knew they must be here. They lived here. This was their home.

"Weel now, I canna say, Missus. They flitted afore I came."

"But they can't have done! I need them here." Cate leant against the wall to steady herself.

"See you now, Missus, you're no listening. They're no biding here anymore. Whit, are you daft or something? They've gone, weeks since. Away you and leave me in peace."

"No, no please. I'm sorry. I was just upset. Thank you. I'll go upstairs and ask Mrs. Petrie where they've gone. She'll know."

"Well that's as may be, but you'll no find her upstairs. She's awa tae bide with her friend Bessie, an before you ask, I dinna ken where." A firm slam of the door ended the woman's conversation.

Cate stared at the closed door, her mind fighting the facts. The woman must be wrong. People didn't just disappear. Where would Maggie go? Knocking on Mrs. Petrie's door, Cate could feel the knot of fear in her stomach building. No noise. Never had the stairwell seemed so deserted. Oh God, for the clamour of that unruly group!

As a door opened across the landing, Cate could feel, as she listened to yet another unknown woman, the life she'd known here evaporating and herself descending into a murk of madness. She clutched at the unknown woman's words, willing them to bring her some sanity.

"I keep telling yi. She's no in, Missus. At work at Singer's and God only knows when her an her man'll be back."

"Mrs. Petrie is working? She has a man?"

"No her, hen. Can yi no listen? She's been away for a while now. Moved in wi a widowed woman. Roond the back some place. The bailiffs kicked her oot."

"Poor Mrs Petrie."

"Aye weel, wir a in the same boat. Coppers are hard tae come by when the yards are laying off."

"Maggie from downstairs—did you know her?" She clawed at the edges of reality, a sliver of hope keeping her afloat.

"A smile given here an there. Dinna know her as such, Missus, she wasna from Glasgow though. Whit aboot her?"

"Do you happen to know where she went?"

"No me, Missus. She flitted a week ago. Couple of big brawny lads shifted her, fishermen by the smell o' them. Sorry I canna say more than that. There's ma kettle whistling, I'll need tae get on. Good day tae yi."

Cate had reached the close before her next problem overwhelmed her. My God, Sister Mary Anne, the Doctor—they wouldn't believe her now! Cook and Ada—where did they live? She'd no idea? Were the people in the infirmary right? Had the blow on her head made her lose her senses? It was as if her time in Glasgow had never happened—a part of her life wiped clean as the beach on Kevinishe after a strong tide. Only Rhoddy and herself remained in what she'd built here, and they were homeless and destitute!

Resolutely searching for some backbone, Cate tried to stand taller, unspoken words stiffening a feeble search of her mind for her deserted wits. She was neither homeless nor destitute, but a respectable widow with a house in a good neighbourhood. Or she had been. Now it would go to Ian and Caroline. Unspoken wails of despair ravaged her: McAlister, why did you leave me? What's going to happen to us? Where's Sarah?

How could she find Caroline or Ian? Kelvinside, that's where Caroline lived, but where? Anyway, she'd be the last person to offer any help. Ian she'd never really known, and where he lived she'd no idea. Somehow she'd have to find him. Perhaps if she went to the office she'd get help. Of course, the office! Solly would know. He'd help. How stupid she'd been!

Solly would come to the hospital. He'd know what to do. He'd tell those at the Infirmary. He'd be able to find out where Ian McAlister lived and take her there. That's where they'd all be, not wanting to stay in their father's house now the funeral was over. Tomorrow she'd find out where the office was and see Solly and McAlister's partner. What an idiot she'd been. They'd know all the answers and make sense of this nightmare. Perhaps they could even trace Maggie and Lizzie. Exhausted, she struggled back to the Infirmary.

Finding the doctor she began to explain this new problem. However his expression only confirmed her feeling that he hadn't believed her before and was even less likely to do so now. She had to change his mind.

"But you must see, we simply can't keep you any longer." The doctor realised his first impressions had been right. No doubt the blow on her head had been courtesy of some man. This woman had neither friends nor home and was evidently used to telling a tall tale. Her pleading words didn't move him.

"Only another day, please, Doctor. I've nowhere else to go. Tomorrow I'll see the lawyer, I promise. It'll be fine, you'll see." He must allow her to stay. She couldn't sleep on the street.

"I'm afraid it won't. You keep changing your story, and frankly I've never believed any of it. As a patient, it was my duty to treat you. I've done that, and you've been discharged. I'm sorry there is nothing more I can do for you. Good day."

Cate watched the figure disappear and her newfound hope crumbled. She needed this shelter for one more night. Perhaps Sister Mary Anne would help? She searched the wards with no success. Finally she found a nurse who knew where the missing sister was.

"Off duty dear, and won't be back for two days. Sorry." The unknown nurse bustled down the corridor and Cate could think of nothing else to do but leave. Where could she go? She trudged out through the gates and let her feet choose a direction. She no longer had the strength to think. All she could do was find somewhere to rest until the morning and then surely all would be solved?

Having spent the night walking about, resting wherever she could, Cate was thankful it was summer. She may have been warm enough but her clothes were crumpled and dirty. She tried to tidy herself before setting out for the office. She'd never been there before, but thought she could find it. After a couple of wrong turns a kindly road sweeper walked her there. The first blow was no Solly.

"Look, I've told you—he left in a hurry. I'm new here, and not likely to stay long either, if I let someone in without an appointment. He'd kick me out for something like that."

"That's not right. My husband would always have listened to anyone. His partner will surely see me. Just tell him I'm here."

"Missus, I'm telling you…."

With no sleep and still weak, Cate knew she had to get in before she collapsed. "Out of my way. This is my late husband's office and I've every right." Faint though she was, her temper lent her strength and for a few moments the two of them pushed and pulled till Cate succeeded in slipping past him.

"You come back here! He'll no see you, I tell you. Come back!"

She'd almost reached the next door, when it was flung open by an angry man.

"Just what is going on here? You fool, I said I'd see no one, so what…." His eyes now focused on the intruder. Well! Well! The clothes were rumpled, the face somewhat grubby and the red hair had lost its lustre, but it was her! He was certain it was. Damn. He'd hoped to be away by now. Two more days and he'd have left Glasgow behind him. This could be dangerous—or perhaps not! Just maybe he could turn this to his advantage. Memory of the painful hatpin wound he'd had to explain to a suspicious wife had been tricky. Yes, this could be quite pleasurable. The slut had got away from him then. Now perhaps he could ease any problem arising from the McAlister business and save both himself and the family trouble. Oh yes, and he'd enjoy causing this bitch some real problems at the same time.

"Mr. Hardy, isn't it? You were my late husband's partner? I'm in need of help—a great deal of help." Cate was so relieved she'd actually found him. Realising that the clerk was listening, Hardy spoke. "I haven't the slightest idea what you're talking about, woman. I'm afraid you've come to the wrong office. I don't deal with people like you. Show this woman out, boy, and be quick about it or you'll be following her!"

He was sure she wouldn't go quietly, if their last meeting had been anything to go by. A rumpus was just what he wanted—the noisier the better, and with a witness to back him up. Thank God he'd booted the Jew boy out before the McAlisters' affairs had been settled. That one would have made life difficult for them all. The current one knew nothing, and he'd be out on the street within the next day or so anyway.

By now Cate was in no mood to be turned away at yet another door.

"No! No! You'll not get rid of me that easily. I know something's wrong. I'm coming into that office and I won't leave until you've explained what's been happening here." Somehow she'd find the strength to make him listen, however rude he was.

"You most certainly are not. Now out of my way. Here you! Take her other arm and get her out of here!"

As the partner pulled at her arm something in his action seemed familiar to Cate but she couldn't quite think what it was. Knowing her strength was limited, Cate tried to free her arms, screaming at the two men while she did so.

"Right, lad, outside and find a policeman! Be quick about it."

As he watched the back of the departing boy, Hardy knew exactly what he was going to do now: discredit her, so that any queries would be scoffed at, and at the same time taunt her with the truth, both about himself and the McAlisters. That would serve her right. His next words would be for her ears only, and a bit of violent handling would compensate for their last meeting.

"Now then, you red-headed doxy, this will teach you to assault your betters." The first blow rocked her head. "I'll have that one as payment for the last time we met—remember—you ran out on me then." He saw realization dawn and prepared for the attack. Now he'd get his own back!

"You! But you were his partner! What if I'd told him? Oh you...." She knew words were useless, so she went for him. This evil man had worked alongside her wonderful husband. Her scratches this time were for McAlister, and she was glad to see the blood welling up on the partner's cheek, though his cruel expression told her she was in for more blows, but she didn't care.

Blows exchanged, Hardy stood over her as she sagged against the office wall. Physically beaten he would now destroy the slut mentally. Lighting a cigar he settled at his desk, enjoying the prospect of the news he was about to give her.

"Well now let's hear what brought you here?"

Cate mouthed the word, "Solly."

"Hah! The Jew boy's long gone. Friendly with him too were you? Spread your favours did you?"

She would have gone for him again, but she didn't have the strength.

"The McAlisters, the bairns...", was all she could manage.

"Ah, the missing family. 'Fraid they've deserted you. And I made it possible. All of it."

"All, of —what are you saying? Please, please tell me."

"That's better, bitch, on your knees and begging. I like it."

"For God's sake..."

He cut her short, enjoying the thrill of dragging the details out, but he'd better get on with it before the boy returned with the Law. Making his way across the room again, he stood over her and watched her crumble as he destroyed her world by telling her what Caroline McAlister and he, for a very large fee, had done.

"So there you have it. Your husband's family never had any intention of leaving you with a McAlister baby, so she's spirited it away across an ocean where you'll never find it, and now you're left with nothing. The man you'd thought you'd hooked left you nothing. Not a penny."

Hearing footsteps, Hardy stepped back and began mopping his cheek as the boy and policeman appeared, satisfied that the act of committing her to jail for trespass and an assault on himself would inflict the final blow.

"Now then, sir, looks as if you've had trouble here. The lad never said anything about any violence. Just a bit o bother wi a woman. What's gone on, sir?"

"I'm glad to see you, Constable. I thought you'd never get here. She just flew at me and then she stumbled, hitting her face on the wall."

The constable glanced at the woman but turned to the lawyer.

"I can see she damaged your face, sir. You should get yourself to the Infirmary. God knows where the likes of her have been. You get off, sir. I'll whistle for some help and we'll take her in. We'll get your statement later."

"Look here, Officer, heaven knows what the wretch really wanted. I'll clean up all right. The thing is, I'm leaving the city in a day or so and won't be back. Could you just lock her up for a night or two, in case she tries again, then let her go? The office will be empty, so not worth her trying to beg or make more trouble. After all, I don't want to be hard on her, and I certainly don't want to come back to Glasgow to give evidence. What do you say?"

As he watched her being dragged onto the street, Hardy knew that the money he'd slipped the policeman would suffice for his wishes to be carried out. Now just the boy. Two more days and a handsome sum with a few veiled threats should keep him quiet for long enough for all this to die down, and they'd get away with it. After all, the others were mid-ocean by now and the extra money he'd received could never be traced—he'd seen to that. All that would be left would be a bedraggled woman who'd been in prison, known as a troublemaker. What could have been very tricky, if not downright dangerous, had turned out very well indeed. He'd enjoyed beating her. With no resources of any kind, working the streets would be all that was left for the bitch. A good day's work done.

Two days later the same policeman opened the door onto the street.

"Out with you, and, whoever you are, next time we'll see you in the workhouse." He was glad to see her go. She bothered him. Quite what it was he couldn't work out, but, when she did speak through her swollen lips, it wasn't with words that belonged to the poor and homeless. Then there was that frightened lad at the office. He'd said nothing about her being injured—just a woman claiming to know the lawyer and having an argy bargy with him. Yet when he'd got there—true the lawyer fellow was bleeding, but something was—ah well, he'd silver to jingle in his pocket from the lawyer and his old woman knew nothing about it. A good time he'd have at the pub, forgetting the whole thing. Still, he was glad she was out and back on the street. That way no blame could come to him. He'd taken her in after a fight. No charges had been brought and, due to her injuries, he'd kept her for a day longer than he should have. Pity, that was all it was. They could do no more than tell him he shouldn't be so soft.

15

Having come to plead for more time, Mary Anne was not surprised by the reply to her request.

"The end of this week, and that's it, my girl." Sister Assumpta knew it was wrong, but what could she do? The convent was overflowing and those who could walk just had to make room for those from the streets who couldn't. Their space for the sick and injured was limited. They did what they could.

"It's just that she's disappeared. I gave her money...."

"Now that was foolish of you, Mary Anne. No wonder she's gone! Will you never learn?"

"Only a few coppers for the tram, Sister. She was too weak to walk to her friends."

"Well now, if it's friends she has, why in the name of the Holy Father were we looking after the boy?"

"We didn't know about them in the beginning, Sister. Then we arranged for her to go to the friends and bring them to the hospital and on here to pick the boy up."

"And?"

"She never came back. I was off duty, and when I returned she still hadn't come back."

"Well now, that's the last we'll be seeing of her, if I'm not mistaken. So it'll be the workhouse for the boy. Don't be looking at me like that, Mary Anne. What else can I do?"

"If I managed a few shillings, Sister...."

"My dear sweet girl, it'll only delay the inevitable. Keep your money. Leave it till the Sabbath and, if she's not appeared by the

Monday, the boy goes. I can do no more. Big as your heart is, neither can you."

Making her way back to the infirmary, Mary Anne knew she was beaten. She ought to let the matter go. What was it about the woman and the silent boy that bothered her so? The names did for a start, the boy calling for Lizzie when he did speak, but the woman was Cate, and seemed so certain of her own identity. She spoke well and her clothes, though soiled by her fall, were of good quality, not the sort the poor wore. However, it was the way the woman had looked her right in the eye when explaining about her friends. Somehow, no matter what Sister Assumpta said, Mary Anne felt she was telling the truth. Well, here was the infirmary and she'd work to do, she'd better put the whole thing out of her mind and concentrate on her patients, or Matron would have something to say about it.

"Mary Anne you're late! You'll never guess what's happened. Come on. I'll tell you on the way. You knew that woman had disappeared."

Mary Anne nodded.

"Well, she's back, and what a sight. Looks like she's been sleeping rough, and someone's given her a beating."

"Is she still here?"

"In the day room."

"What happened to her?"

"Who knows? Gave no explanation, Mary Anne. Just asked if she could wait to see you."

"That'll be to take her to the boy, I suppose. Will they let her stay there till I'm free?"

"Don't think so. Matron wants to see you for a start—as soon as you came in, she said. And you're late."

"I know I'm sorry! Here's hoping I'm not in too much trouble." As fast as she could, Mary Anne made for Matron's office, her nerves perceptible in her timid knock at the door.

"So, Sister, you've deigned to report for duty eventually, I see."

"Sorry, Matron, I...."

"Never mind that now. I thought you'd arranged for that woman to bring her friends and collect her boy? "

206

"Well I did, Matron...."

"You most certainly did not. She left, you went off duty, and her notes were not completed. Now the woman has returned, having obviously been in some sort of nasty business. This is a medical infirmary, Sister, not a port of call for these types of people."

"No, Matron. I understand."

"Good. I've arranged cover for you. I wish you to collect that woman, reunite her with the wretched boy, and never let me see either of them again. Her case is closed. Is that understood?"

"Yes, Matron." Obeying the brisk wave of the hand that accompanied Matron's words, Mary Anne made her escape. Approaching the day room, she couldn't help wondering just what she would find.

"By all that's holy, what happened to you?" The woman looked even worse than when she'd come in after her accident. At least this time she was conscious.

"I met a rather nasty man, Sister." Cate answered.

"Now look here, you were never —you know...?"

"Certainly not, Sister. I know I'm in a sorry state, but never, ever, have I been reduced to walking the streets. Though what's to become of me now, I've no idea."

Cate knew her only immediate hope was this kind Irish sister.

"Well, you certainly can't go walking about the street like that."

"Rhoddy's safe Sister?"

"Only till Sunday. Tis the best I could do. As to yourself, I could squeeze you in at my lodgings till Sunday but what I have is a tiny room and really only fit for one. So it'll have to be the chair or the floor for you. Still, it would give you a few days for some of the worst bruises to fade a little."

"You would do that for me, a total stranger, Sister?"

"Well now, you don't feel like a stranger. If you're to be sleeping on my floor, it had better be plain 'Mary Anne'."

"Mary Anne it is—you know my name already. But aren't you afraid, like the others at the hospital, that I might rob you or something? After all, that's what they think of me—a woman of the streets, likely to take advantage of you."

"Sister Assumpta says I'd have every waif and stray off the streets if I could. Most of the time I've chosen right, though some at the hospital have never believed you. Still, you mustn't condemn them. They've notes to keep, beds to find and healing to do, and neither money nor time to do everything."

"I have a friend like you, Mary Anne. The one I was telling you about. Lizzie. She's a bad limp, where she broke her leg and it didn't mend properly, but she bears it all and she'd give whatever she had to someone who needed it. Like you, she sees only the best in others. Me, I'm more conscious of the bad!" The words made Cate truly aware of how much she would miss Lizzie in her life and how stupid and selfish she'd been not making more time to go and see her.

"You miss her badly, don't you, Cate?"

"Worse than I can say."

"Right then, Matron's given me time to settle you, so let's get on the tram and away home."

"I'll walk, Mary Anne, if you tell me the way. I've no coppers, you see."

"You can't walk, Cate. You've not the strength. We'll try and think of some way for you to earn a little money. Mebbe by Sunday the Holy Father will provide."

As they made their way to the tram stop, Cate kept quiet over her feelings about God. By her way of thinking, her own two hands and initiative would find a solution before anybody's God. If only she felt stronger and her face wasn't such a mess!

When she woke, Mary Anne having gone on duty, Cate felt as though she'd walked all the way back to the Highlands with a load of peats on her back. She'd been bone weary before, but never like this. It wasn't just the beating, or even the loss of Maggie and Lizzie. With words as painful as his blows, Hardy had destroyed her hope. Sarah was now as lost to her as McAlister. Her baby daughter might as well be dead as spirited away across an ocean. He'd enjoyed telling her what Caroline Bryant had done. He'd gloated at the despair in her cries, begging him to say his words were false. She'd staggered to the shipping office on her release from jail but they wouldn't even let her in. When she'd tried to explain that her daughter had been stolen and was sailing to America, they'd laughed in her face, taunting her, asking if the baby was travelling first class in a cabin of her own.

Alone in Mary Anne's small room, never had she felt so low as at that moment. She'd been poor, homeless, ignorant, but she'd at least been able to make people understand her. Now, no matter how she explained, or pleaded, no one believed her. It was too much. She'd lost everything dear to her. How could she bear it? Tears trickled down her face and she could feel what little fight was left in her slipping away. But then there was Rhoddy. Dislike her as he may, she was all he had. She couldn't give up. The boy couldn't be left alone. She had to care for him. It was her duty as his mother. The tears would have to stop.

Entering the church, Mary Anne was taken aback at the sight before her. "I can't believe you're sweeping the church yourself, Father O'Brien. Here, let me do it for you."

"Mary Anne! The Holy Father himself has sent you. Haven't I been eating cold oatmeal and milk and making me own bed these past two days, never mind the sweeping here?"

"But why? Where's Mrs. O' Flaherty?"

"Well now, it's a wonder you've not seen her in that grand Infirmary of yours. Sure and hasn't she just had the breaking of her arms while hanging new curtains. What did the house need new curtains for any road? Did I ever ask for them? God love us, did I ever even look at them?"

"Father O'Brien!" Mary Anne couldn't keep the smile from her face.

"Don't be laughing at my predicament now. Out saving the souls of my flock I should be, instead of wielding a brush. So here you are. Sure and those capable hands will do a fine job, so they will." Thrusting the broom into the young woman's hand, he hesitated. "Was it confession you came for or just a quiet word with the Holy Father? You're never rushing away back on duty, with no time for the sweeping?"

"No, Father. I'll do your sweeping, if you'll take a seat and listen to my story." Mary Anne began to sweep. "Poor Mrs. O' Flaherty I'll need to look for her when I'm next on duty. But Father, I might just have the answer to your domestic problem. Mind, I'm not sure. It would mean stretching out a hand to a poor soul whose been badly done by"

"Mary Anne, you'd have every Catholic unfortunate in the parish helped if you had your way. You must learn there are some who simply will not be saved from themselves."

"Well now, that's the first stumbling block. She's not of the Faith, Father."

"I've a feeling I'm not going to like your sorry tale, Mary Anne."

She knew she'd taken far longer with the sweeping than was necessary, telling him about Cate's predicament, but she needed to make him understand that this was one woman who deserved help. And wouldn't it be the solving of his domestic problem? Mary Anne leant the broom against the pew and turned a beseeching look on the priest, while crossing her fingers behind her back.

"That's some story, Mary Anne. Just why would I, a good Catholic priest, take pity on a woman not of my faith and who seems to have come from a very shady background? Give me one good reason now, Mary Anne—and, in the name of all the saints, make it brief! These pews are hard for the good reason they're to keep you and other sinners awake while I'm saying mass, meaning they're little use to give comfort to my old bones. A good and short reason, Mary Anne, before I'm crippled indeed."

"Cold oatmeal and milk?"

"Well now, why in all that list of woes, did you not think to mention that this poor needy body could cook?"

Mary Anne sped down the road wondering if fate would trip her up. Could Cate cook? She certainly hoped so. On her knees in the church she'd asked The Holy Father to look kindly on Cate in her troubles. Listening to Cate in her delirium in the Infirmary, Mary Anne had a good idea what the other woman thought of God, whatever her religion. Fingering her rosary, as she made her way home, Mary Anne murmured the story again, adding an earnest plea for assistance from the Saints, together with a quick postscript on

210

her own behalf, that, whatever Cate could or could not do, she'd be able to cook! Upon that skill everything depended.

Seven weeks later the presbytery gardener watched the good Father as he made his way to the church.

"My, Father, but you're no looking so sprightly, indeed you're not."

"Well now, Seamus, it's yourself I see. Come for a bit of digging so?"

"Indeed that I am, and it would be the lie out of me if I was to say that I'd not be looking forward to the widow's scones with my tea."

"Welcome to them you are then, and God forgive me my thoughts on the scones of dear old Mrs. O'Flaherty, for it's the wrong widow with the scones this day."

"She's mended then, the auld woman? And the other one, with the hair?"

"If it's the fiery hair of Mrs. McAlister you're after, it's a great disappointment you'll be having. Her time has come to go."

"True enough Father. Two widow women in the house would never be agreeing. But back to those scones, Father...."

"Sure, Seamus, and didn't we have the O'Flaherty scones for years before?"

"Tis the right of it you have, Father, but they were fit only for the filling of the stone walls, hard, so they were. Has she gone then, the other one?"

"Saying her goodbyes to the living and the dead this day and on the road tomorrow."

"You'll be missing more than the scones, Father, by my way of thinking. Inside the presbytery was never as fine, with all the flowers and the polishing fit to see your face that that one did. Sure and didn't she do some stitching for myself, and not a word of a lie now, they were like cobwebs, that dainty, on the old trousers."

"Well, The Lord Giveth and The Lord Taketh away. We must abide by his wishes, Seamus. Now get you to the digging. I have to have a word with Himself. You know where I am if I'm needed."

"So you'll forego the O'Flaherty scones then, Father?"

Pretending he'd not heard Seamus, Father O'Brien made for the sanctity of the church, the precious remaining scones from yesterday safely secreted in his habit.

The head was erect rather than bowed in prayer, but the sight of it stopped him in the doorway. Was this to be one of the Holy Father's wondrous miracles? Was the widow seeking comfort?

Hearing the door open, Cate turned and smiled at the dear man, reading his mind, knowing of his hopes. "I'm afraid not, Father. Though, however lacking in faith I am, the beautiful windows drew me to the outside and my curiosity bade me take a look inside. Is that forbidden for one not of your faith?"

"Well, we would like your soul as well as your eyes to be engaged, but I'll not send you away with my nagging in your ear. We've both had our say and we must respect one another's views. Though I'm sure your burdens would be easier if...."

"Father, the rules! We agreed."

"Now you can't blame me for having one more try. It's my God-given job never to give up."

Cate had no idea that a church could be so beautiful. The spires and the stonework outside were splendid, but the inside was breathtaking. The flowers looked enchanting in their setting beneath windows of such beauty, that one could almost believe heaven was there. All the tapestries and the gold decorations were so unlike the grisly grey of the Wee Free Church.

"It's beautiful, both inside and out, Father."

"We believe the beauty of the church is necessary to show our adulation of the Redeemer himself, Cate."

"Well, Father, this unbeliever will carry today's picture with her always. After all that's happened in my life lately, somehow this beauty almost makes me believe—no, Father, I'm sorry, not in The Faith—but that in some spot somewhere you could recreate this kind of atmosphere to ease your mind at the end of a hard day. I have seen so little beauty in my life recently, and I hunger for it. That's why I must make my way back to my mountain."

"Come then, to the vestry and we'll have a last cup of tea and one of your delightful scones."

"I left some for Seamus. Did he get them?"

212

"Well no. Didn't I just forget and bring them back here with me. We mustn't have the spoiling of the man, you know."

"Father!" She'd grown fond of him in the time it had taken his housekeeper's arms to mend and would never forget the lifeline he'd given her or the look of horror when he saw the bruised woman, complete with silent boy, that Mary Anne was preparing to install as his temporary housekeeper. Many's an amusing meal they'd had together, and the Irishness of himself and Seamus had made her homesick for Kevinishe with their similar ways. She'd miss the two men and Mary Anne, good people that they were, and all three had been wonderful to Rhoddy. Then earlier today, at the graveside, she'd said goodbye to McAlister, the best of men, who'd encouraged and taught her such a lot, as much by example as instruction.

She would leave Glasgow a grown woman, shaped in many ways by her sojourn there, though with the heaviest of hearts. The loss of those dear friends, Maggie, Lizzie and Solly would stay with her always. Sarah's abduction was as a death. She just had to believe that the McAlisters would recognize their blood in her baby and treat her as one of them, not as a reminder of herself. For that reason alone she was glad her daughter had not inherited her red hair. To preserve her sanity she had to believe that her child was being well cared for and loved, otherwise she couldn't bear the burden of her loss.

The journey from Glasgow northwards reminded Cate of her tinker days. True this was a motorised lorry, but the cab had room for only two and she'd insisted on the young priests having that. Rhoddy and herself made do in the back, with its old tarpaulin hood. The diocese in Glasgow used it to ferry supplies to the smaller churches and settlements, where mass was held whenever it was needed. Father O'Brien had arranged for Cate and Rhoddy to travel north by way of Tarbet, Crianlarich, and Bridge of Orchy. That was as far as the lorry went. Cate was grateful for the lift, as it saved her using her hoarded wages for a good part of the way back to Kevinishe. It also meant they could sleep in the vehicle overnight, and meals were provided whenever they stopped.

She was indeed sorry to wave goodbye to the two young men as they began their return journey. They waved until the ramshackle vehicle had coughed its way round the last corner out of sight. Now they were truly on their own, and Cate was determined to use only what money was absolutely necessary to get them there. Who knew what awaited them in Kevinishe? So she'd have to hoard the silver they had. After all, hadn't she walked miles in a day as a tinker child? Though she'd have to make allowances for Rhoddy.

Looking at him as he stood at the side of the road, Cate realised that this was the first time they'd ever been truly alone together. Since his birth there had always been others to ease the relationship. She couldn't say she was looking forward to either the onward journey or the life in Kevinishe with this youngster, who seemed to have a determined dislike of his mother and only spoke when forced to. Though, after what he'd been through, who could blame him? And she wouldn't.

Picking up their bags she set off, her mind still revolving round the problem that was Rhoddy. She still found it hard to connect with him, but then that was nothing knew. Oh, she'd take care of Rhoddy, see no harm came to him, but it was unlikely ever to be a close relationship. That was as clear as the road in front of them. Turning, she urged him on.

"Come on, Rhoddy. We've done well to be carried this far. Now we must make our own way. See now, you'll soon get used to the walking and there's the ferry to look forward to. You'll like the ferry, won't you?"

Cate knew the answer to her own query. Rhoddy wouldn't like anything she did. All she'd ever done was take him away from people he liked. He didn't want her. It was Lizzie, Maudie Petrie and his playmates he wanted. She could hear his resentment each time he scuffed his boots along the road as he trailed behind her.

As Rhoddy dragged his feet more and more, Cate knew they'd have to stop. The next sign said Balvourie, but entering it, the village was barely worth a title. It did have a quarry, so there might be a resting place and perhaps some casual work.

"Look, Rhoddy, there seems to be a lot of noise coming from over there. Maybe there's a fair on." There was no sign of a fair, but a gaggle of women screeching and raging at something in the village pond, so Cate pushed forward and, as she reached the front of the crowd, stared in shocked silence.

In the middle of the dirty water was a slim young girl, naked and bald. The missing hair scattered at the water's edge. Several of the women began throwing stones and Cate simply couldn't bear it.

"Stop that. It's inhuman! Dear God, she's but a lassie! What kind of women are you?" With that, Cate waded out into the pond and screened the girl from the crowd.

"You'd have done the same if it was your man she'd lain with!" A single voice answered Cate, and then other women echoed the cry, though the stone throwing stopped. A stranger seeing this changed things. It was a village matter.

"Well, she must have been busy if she'd the lot of them is all I can say! She's a poor wee thing. Look at her. What's her side of the story?"

"Here you!" An old crone elbowed her way to the edge and pointed with her stick. "They say she'd men in the house all at once. They were seen leaving. Doing themselves up an all."

"Is this true, lassie?" Cate glanced over her shoulder while keeping her body square to the crowd.

The shivering figure simply bent her head and wept, the tears rolling unheeded while she tried to cover her body.

"Come on then. Let's get you out of here." Cate walked forward pulling the girl behind her until they were face to face with the women. "Let the girl speak. Any crime deserves a defence."

The women backed away, leaving the crone standing alone at the edge of the pond.

"Her Father died no long since and she was in the cottage by herself." She volunteered.

Without turning to face the victim, Cate said, "Here's your chance, lassie. What have you to say?" Still hearing nothing, she turned, only to see the girl sway and slump into the water. There was no worrying about anything now but dragging the limp body out of the pond. While she and the crone struggled, the village women melted away. Aye, thought Cate, rough justice they'd administer without a qualm, but drowning they'd want no part of.

Back at the girl's home, once they'd settled her in bed, the crone introduced herself as Jeannie, 'Old Jeannie' the villagers called her, and Cate introduced herself and Rhoddy. Over a dish of tea the old woman set out the picture of the village.

"Her Father was the tallyman at the quarry till he died. He'd a good wage and I know the rent's paid to quarter day, so she's no need to move yet. A good man he was, fair, never cheated the men in their piecework. The quarry was a happy place while he was there." Taking a long draught of tea, Jeannie pointed to the other room and continued her story. "Shy she was and like no other village girl. Jealous they were of her, the village women and lasses. She worked as a seamstress for the Lady Jemima. Kept to herself she did, and had little to do with the rest of the village. She was either up there or doing her learning here. Could read, write and learned the figuring from her father. All that and her sewing at the Big House made the others envious. She wasn't one of them—that's what all this is about."

"But what? Surely jealousy was not enough for this?" Cate pointed to the hair she'd had Rhoddy collect from the pond edge, while they'd more or less dragged the semi-conscious girl back to her house.

"Well, I do think there just might be something in what the woman were saying. The men were seen leaving the house late at night."

"Had they gone there from knocking-off time?" Cate couldn't believe sober men would have attempted something like that.

"No. No. It was Saturday, payday. The alehouse first on their half day and then, with nothing better than home to an angry wife, I suppose, they didn't need much persuading to follow the ringleader."

'With ale in them, a scolding and a cold supper the only thing waiting, could it just have been a bit of mischief perhaps? A prank that went wrong, Jeannie?"

"More like Grubber Machie."

"Who's he?"

"Nasty piece of work. Married one of the village girls, way back. Had to. He's never been exactly careful where he spreads his seed."

"And you think…?"

"Has his mark all over it, girl. Mind, the rest, befuddled with ale, probably thought it would just be a joke. Still, we none of us like to watch others having a better time than us—an easier living if you like. Envy is a powerful motive, and yon lass would have none of the village boys, and Grubber has never been one to take no for an answer."

"Hmm. Who's this Lady Jemima then? And where's 'up there'?"

"Dowager at the Big House. When her husband was alive the village was just right, but now a nephew has inherited and he's no from here—lives down south somewhere. Funny that is, Cate. Owns a big estate of his own and now has this one. Whole village belongs to him. Doesn't seem right somehow. Can you wonder at their mood? With the tallyman gone, seems there's no one to look out for the village, speak up for us like. She'll want to know about Bella." Feeling she'd said all that was required, Jeannie studied the newcomer with the bright red hair.

"Who's Bella, Jeannie?"

"Her in there. She'll no be fit for work now. Lady Jemima'll no take kindly to that."

"No I suppose not. Employers never like their routines upset, no matter what troubles their servants may have. Still, with Bella's father dead, she'll need work. Had he anything put by that would tide her over? She'll no be fit for some time, I doubt."

"I don't know, lassie, but this'll have to be put to rights by someone, and none of the villagers will do it. To my way of thinking it'll have to be you."

"Not me. I'm just passing through. A few days' work and rest for the boy, and I'll be on the road."

"I doubt that. You'd have passed the pond by, if that were your way. No, you're the sort who'll never let trouble lie. You would aye need to sort it. Take the side of the weak. I could see it in your eyes by the way you stood up to the women. No, I think you'll rest here. If you were to go up to the Big House and offer for the sewing, it would stop the lass getting in trouble and pay your way for a while. You can sew?"

"Yes I can sew. But I see you've decided, whether I can or not. So what if I refuse?"

"Someone has to let them up there know what's going on. None of the villagers can speak for fear of losing their livelihood. Now, you're well spoken—not the usual cut of a woman on the roads, though that's no my business. You could sort all this out: the girl, the men and the unfair doings at the quarry. Then you'll move on, having rested and earned some money. My days are numbered, but I'd not like to meet my Maker having left the village, where I was born and lived all my life, in the mess it's in."

"Mmmn. We'll see. For now let's see if there's anything in the house to eat. We'll get her story when she wakes. I must feed and bed the boy down."

16

As Cate made her way to see the Dowager, she was undaunted by the long rhododendron drive and the cream-coloured house with its aprons of lawn and manicured flowerbeds. Just like Kevinishe, except this house was a hundred times more beautiful.

"Aye, aye, it's a bonnie sight is it no?" The unseen gardener studied her carefully.

"It's truly beautiful. Your gardens could be paintings."

"No, there're real right enough. Are you for the big house?"

"To see the Lady of the house."

"Round the back then and speak up. She's a bit hard of hearing nowadays."

"Thank you." As she made for the back door, Cate wondered why she was doing this. Once again she was acting from instinct. Would she never learn? Yet she needed money. Then there was Bella. Two days now and she simply lay there, still crying occasionally. Neither food nor drink would she have and not a word uttered since the incident. She'd been badly used and Cate knew all about that. Probably that was why she was doing this, together with the need to rest the boy.

Pulling herself away from these thoughts, Cate marched swiftly up to the house. She just had to convince this Lady that she could fill Bella's place and, for the help Jeannie had been giving, she would see what else she could do. After all, the old woman was sitting with Rhoddy and Bella.

The scullery maid opened the door and then led her to the butler's pantry, where he was not pleased to be interrupted.

"What do you want and how did you get in?"

"I've come to see Her Ladyship."

"She won't see you and that's that. The stupid maid had no right to let such as you into the house!"

"Why?" Cate felt her temper rising. Once more she was being dismissed without a hearing.

"A ragged thing like you. Not likely! Certainly not while I'm butler here."

"Shouldn't you let her Ladyship decide that?"

"Decide what, Guthrie?" An elderly woman stood in the doorway, her question and manner establishing her as the Dowager, though her dress was somewhat bizarre.

"Oh, My Lady, this ragged person...." He hadn't heard her coming.

"Which person, Guthrie? Speak up, man."

"He means me, My Lady." Pushing in front of the butler, Cate showed a brief curtsy and smiled at the formidable figure.

"Ragged she may be, but she speaks better and a great deal louder, than you do, Guthrie. Now, why do you wish to see me? I presume you do wish to see me?"

"It's about Bella." Seeing the frown on the older woman's face, Cate spoke up. "She's very ill, My Lady."

"Ill? Why wasn't I told? Guthrie, what's the matter with you these days? Why am I not better informed? What's the matter with the girl? Told her father time and again she needed feeding. Wait till I see him. Strange though—he was always a considerate man. I can't understand why he hasn't let me know."

"He's dead, My Lady." Cate felt there was no point trying to answer all the other questions the woman had fired at them.

"Dead as in buried, you mean?"

"Yes, My Lady."

"Guthrie, fetch a tray of tea to my sitting room and a brandy. Now, man! You, girl, come with me. I've a feeling you're going to interest me."

Seated in the Dowager's sitting room, Cate could only stare. Here there was none of the calm of Lady Sarah's room with its peaceful pale greens and greys and a few carefully positioned beautiful pieces of matching furniture. This room gave out the same frenzied message as the Dowager's appearance. It was like a painting where the artist had gone mad and jumbled every hue with a mass of objects until it hurt the eyes even too look at it. When she returned her gaze to the owner, Cate saw she was smiling.

"Hideous, isn't it?"

"Well yes, but if you don't like it, why?"

"Can't be bothered. Was never one for staying indoors. Horses, hounds, estate more my thing, you know." She nodded at the massive portrait of a man over the fire. "Since he went, lost the will for most things. Enough of that! Tea?"

"Let me, My Lady. I used to look after a Lady like you."

"Good. Get on with it then. Now where did they put the brandy?"

"I believe Guthrie has forgotten it."

"Tea it is then. Now, what's all this about?"

Cate, having relayed Bella's story, watched the Dowager and waited. Everything depended on this woman's character. Was she just allowing things to go downhill or did she not know about it?

"So, any other recent changes?"

"I really couldn't say, My Lady, but old Jeannie…"

"Good Lord! Is she still alive? Heavens, she's older than me!"

"She may be getting on, but she has all her wits about her."

"And I haven't. You tell it like it is, girl. I thought you said you needed Bella's sewing."

"I do, My Lady, but I cannot alter facts. If you do not know what is going on at the quarry, then perhaps you have not been…."

"Obviously!"

In the silence, Cate wondered if she's been too blunt. Rising quietly, she made to go.

"Sit down, girl! How can one think if you're bobbing about?" Tugging the bell rope she stood under her husband's portrait and waited. "Ah, Guthrie."

"You rang, My Lady?"

"Of course I rang, you dolt of a man! Where's my brandy? Don't play games with me, Guthrie. When I've a mind to, I can easily outthink you, as well you know. I've been asleep this last year and it won't do! You understand me I presume."

"Oh yes, My Lady."

"Good. Get—what the devil's that racquet?" As a rotund young man entered the room, Lady Jemima shook her head. "Ah, Bertie, I see. Thank you for informing me of your arrival."

"Sorry, Aunt Jemima. It sort of slipped my mind." Changing the subject quickly before she flayed him with her tongue, he blustered on. "Can't find Guthrie anywhere Aunt Jemima. Do you…." Catching sight of the butler at the back of the room, the young Lord was now on safe territory. " Ah, my coat, Guthrie."

"My Lord."

Guthrie divested his Master of coat, hat and gloves and removed himself from the imminent battle.

"Have you any idea what's going on at the quarry, Bertie?"

"None whatsoever, Aunt Jemima—quarrying I should think."

"Damn it all, man, how can you keep two estates going if you ignore them? You're a great fool, Bertie."

"Aunt Jemina, I don't. Never have done. London's much more my kind of thing. Derwent does the estate business."

"Why Algie ever left this estate to you, I'll never know. Now your brother Derwent would have revelled in it."

"Oh, I say, old girl—first born and all that. I mean it's the done thing, don't you know."

"That may be so, but it would be the ruin of you without Derwent."

"Now come on, old thing, it's not all bad. Got an excellent fellow to take over the quarry from that wizened old chap."

"You mean old Charlie the foreman's gone? No wonder the place is a shambles. What do you know about the new man?"

"Not a blessed thing, Aunt."

"What about the tallyman?"

"The tallyman?"

"Bertie, you're an utter fool, and I'm a worse one for not remembering that.

What are you doing here anyway? Running away again?"

"Filly trouble! This one has a very large determined Mama. Bit like yourself, Aunt."

"You haven't even got the common sense to know when you're being rude. This chit of a girl has more sense in a strand of that extraordinary hair than you have in that overfed body of yours."

"I say! That's a bit over the top! Put a bit extra on, I must admit, but…"

"Bertie! Shut up and go away. I need to think."

"Oh, very well, but not a great welcome for a chap…." The expression on his aunt's face reminded him of his terrifying childhood visits, so he left in search of Guthrie and a bracing brandy.

"So what else had Jeannie to tell you?" Lady Jemima continued as though the interruption had never happened.

Cate relayed what Jeannie had told her, while the other woman paced up and down, miraculously avoiding the myriad of objects.

"Can you really sew, or is it just that some benign providence sent you here to bring me to my wits?"

"I can sew. As I told you earlier, I was in service for three years. First in the nursery, where Nanny taught me to sew, and then with Lady Sarah as her personal maid."

"What you doing here then, girl? Why leave a good position?"

"I have a son."

"Ah, the old story. I've often thought if the males in the big houses stopped spreading their seed with such gay abandon perhaps the rightful heirs wouldn't turn out to be such sops. Damned silly of you, girl, to give way to that sort of thing."

"It's rather difficult to object when you're unconscious. I gave way to no one. I fought till I was overcome, and then I was raped." Cate spat the words into the silence.

Studying the eyes that flashed at the recollection, Lady Jemima felt the shafts of hatred that seemed to shoot out of them. This chit of a girl would surely do some damage one day! Of that there was no doubt. Damn it, what a fine daughter she would have made! Checking her thoughts she spoke.

"Right then, sewing first, so upstairs with you. Dressing room second right, silly bits and pieces are all laid out. God knows why we wear frilly lacy things. Damned clothes are always coming undone. Used to wear my brother's things when I could get away with it. He died, you know— stupid African War. Ungrateful chit of a girl refused him and he ran off. Never saw him again. Such a waste! He was ten times the man Bertie will ever be. Mmmph. Go on, off with you then. You've brought me to my senses, and I'll see to things. Same time tomorrow and bring the tea up with you."

Upstairs, Cate gasped as she opened the door. The room was a mass of strewn clothing. Surely no lady's maid would leave it like this? It took her a long time to bring some sort of order to the chaos. Finally with a large pile of mending she set too.

As the autumn light began to fade Cate tidied the completed garments away and made for the back stairs and the kitchen, on her way out.

"You're to take this here for young Bella and the child. Though whose child I don't know."

"It's mine and the basket will be welcome, Cook."

"I hear you outsmarted that rogue Guthrie. About time someone did. The Master would be turning in his grave, so he would, if he knew about all the goings on."

"I think her Ladyship might just be about to change all that."

"Glory be! If she is, and you'd anything to do with it, I'll no grudge you the basket."

"Well thank you, but I only said what the old woman, Jeannie, told me. Can you tell me why the Lady has no personal maid? Her clothes are terrible."

"She's never been one for the dressing, just rummages about and then flings any old thing on. She made more effort when he was alive, but since then she's gone downhill. She sent the maid packing. Likes Bella though. She can work with her, Bella can."

"Well, until Bella's better, I'll be doing the sewing. Thank you again for the food. I'm certainly ready for it, and the others will be equally grateful."

"I'm having a bite myself before her dinner. Have something with me now, and then there'll be more in the basket for them at home. I miss my chats with young Bella. Alright is she?"

Recounting the previous day's events while they ate, Cate was glad to see that the cook was as horrified as she herself had been at the incident.

Having finished her food Cate made her way out through the garden. There wasn't much to be seen in the twilight but the smell of bonfire smoke teased Cate's nostrils and the occasional whinnying of the horses from the stables brought back all that had been good about Kevinishe House. For the first time on the journey she felt a glimmer of hope.

Finally they'd managed to rouse Bella, and now, as she watched the girl sip the broth from the big house, Cate's thoughts turned to her own future. She enjoyed her daily walks up the hill and often went early so she could talk to the gardener and wander round the stables. Somehow, after the chaos of the last few months and the brutality of the village women, there was a sense of healing in those stolen moments.

"Cate, will you stay here?"

"Funny you should ask, Bella, I was just thinking of that myself."

"Will you, then?"

"I don't know. I've never got as far as making a decision. Silly really. I was just thinking how lovely the big house was in the early mornings."

"If you like it that much, why don't you stay? If we both worked we could maybe stay on here, and Jeannie'd look out for Rhoddy while you were up at the big house?"

"First we have to get you out of bed and up on your feet. See here, I've made a wee bonnet for you till the hair grows back again. Now then, I want you to try to be up tomorrow before Jeanie gets here. We've to get you about before we can make any plans for the future." Seeing the reluctance on the girl's face, Cate gave her a firm pat on the shoulders and went to bed down with Rhoddy. There she tried to think of the future but found her herself mentally re-arranging the chaos that was the big house.

"Well, girl, two months gone and I do believe you haven't a stitch left to sew! So what are you going to do now? Haven't thought that far ahead, have you? Should have made the sewing last longer. Always been this quick with your hands and on your feet?"

"I think so, My Lady. It just seems to be the way I am."

"Right then, tea first. How's Bella?"

"She's been up and about for a while now, but only in the house. The next thing will be to get her to go outside."

"Tricky that, my girl. What's the mood in the village?"

"Jeannie's been telling them Bella's side of the story but it'll be difficult. Oh I think they see the truth in it—that the Machie fellow was the ringleader and only one or two others were involved. But the men won't say, and Bella doesn't know. No doubt the others were as bad—they did nothing to stop it. I can't see her being able to stay in the village. The house is tied to the quarry, so she'll not have many weeks left with the rent paid, and then what?"

"And you? What are you running from? The boy's father?"

"No. I've done that running."

"You're still hiding something though."

"My husband died."

"Good Lord! Since when have you had a husband? What about the other one, the father?"

"My husband died of a heart attack some months back. More tea, My Lady?"

"I see—closed doors is it? Never does any good bottling it all up inside, you know. Look at me. Let the place go to pot. Mourned for too long, you see. That's what you did for me—forced me out of it. New man in charge of the quarry now, and I've threatened Bertie if he doesn't mend his ways I'll have his brother Derwent out from under his nose and up here seeing to things. Bertie can't afford to let his own estate, The Marches, go, so he'll do as he's told."

"I'm pleased that things are working out for you and the village, though I worry about Bella."

"No need. I'll see to the girl. Right then, about you? What are you not telling me?"

"I don't know my plans yet."

226

"Nor will you till you settle your past. Come on, girl, out with it. After all, one good turn and all that."

'I had a child...."

"I know that."

"No, I mean another child."

"Good God! You planning to repopulate single-handedly?"

As she listened to Cate's story, of her flight to the tenements, Rhoddy's birth and her ups and downs in McAlister's household, Lady Jemina was intrigued. What a fighter this one was! So the lawyer too had recognised the girl's quality, but a brave man indeed to go against convention and marry her. Aware of a sudden silence, she prompted, "And then?"

"He went to the office and never came back. Died in the hospital."

"But why were you on the road? Ah, the family kicked you out?"

"No, they simply disappeared to America."

"So good riddance to them."

Watching Cate, the older woman saw the misery in her eyes and pulled the bell rope.

"What else is there? There's more you're not saying."

"No, I cannot say more." Cate rose and made for the window. Perhaps the sight of the beautiful garden would help ease her pain. She could not, would not, open the wound that was the missing Sarah. She wasn't strong enough for this. The sound of the door opening made her brace her shoulders and, nails biting into her hand, she steadied herself.

"Thank you, Guthrie. That'll be all." Waiting till the door closed, the Dowager addressed the forlorn figure at the window. "Here, I've ordered a brandy for you, girl. Drink it and then finish your story— it'll help in the long run. Pain like that is better out than in."

Gulping the fiery liquid, Cate made a face, "Whisky's better than this."

"Whisky? Where did you develop a taste for whisky?"

"That's easy." Cate closed her eyes, and with no conscious thought, told her Highland story in the natural soft accent. By the time she'd finished she could almost smell the sea lapping on the village shore.

"I understand that connection. It's how I've always felt about this estate. Good times and bad, the land makes everything worthwhile. Now what happened at the end in Glasgow? It's not just idle curiosity, although I admit I'm intrigued. I think you need to make sense of it yourself."

"I still can't make myself believe it."

"Until you do, you won't find the way forward."

"His death was so sudden. Ian, his son, came and made all the arrangements. The daughter hated me, said I'd killed her father. Mind, I told you, she'd hated me before that. Tried to get me the sack at every turn."

"And the lawyer had angered her further by marrying you?"

"Yes, but, before he did, she came to the house and offered me money to leave. Said she'd disgrace me by telling her father everything she'd found out about me."

"Did she?"

"No. Anyway, it wouldn't have mattered, as I'd already told him. Well I couldn't marry him under false pretences, now could I?"

"There's some that would—anything to get their talons into a good man. Seen it often enough. So what happened with the daughter? You obviously didn't go."

"I'm ashamed to tell you."

"That does intrigue me, girl. Come on. Out with it."

"I, I'm afraid I damn near throttled her! Went back to my tinker ways, My Lady."

"Where do tinkers come into the picture? Oh never mind. Let's get back to what you're running away from. With all this, I've nearly lost the heart of the matter. Won't do, girl. Won't do at all. Let's hear the rest of it."

"Well, there was the funeral. I didn't seem to understand that it was McAlister they were dropping in the grave. I waited, looking at that hole, willing him to come back. Then I had some kind of accident."

"Don't you know about it? Surely the family didn't go for you?"

"No, apparently I was wandering the streets and fell, knocking myself out."

"How do you know that?"

228

"They told me at the Infirmary."

"Another brandy, I think, before you complete your amazing story."

Pacing up and down, she recounted the events from regaining consciousness in the Infirmary to the shipping clerk's mocking words, and her own realization that no one would believe her.

"That's inhuman. How could any woman stoop to that? Now you know what she meant by getting even with you."

"That's the way I see it too. Right from the beginning she seemed to dislike me. Then after the fight she said she'd get even one day. She'd no bairns of her own. And the husband was a poor henpecked creature. Hadn't quite turned out the way she wanted. She'd be well rid of him. Though I think the feeling would be mutual. She couldn't have been an easy woman to live with. I do know Ian had always hankered for America. I think Caroline took the chance of using her maiden name, solving all her problems, getting her revenge on me being the most important one. She knew McAlister and I doted on that wee girl."

"Was he a good lawyer, your husband?"

"He was that. Stood up for the poor and won compensation for many of them."

"Probably not too well off, then?"

"Well, he also had wealthy clients, and never seemed to be without silver. He'd his own practice and big house as well."

"Was there a will?"

"A will?"

"Don't be a parrot, girl. When the man died he must have left a will. No self-respecting lawyer would have left something like that to chance."

"I don't know. What does it matter now anyway?"

"It matters, my dear girl, because you probably would have been mentioned in it."

"I don't think so. I do know he would have cared for the family. They didn't like each other very much, but he'd always intended to see them right. So I suppose that's what he did. Left everything to them. Like your husband."

"He most certainly left a will."

"It never stopped him from signing your home and property away, though."

"You've a point there, girl, but that's the way of the world. We women are not considered fit to own anything other than dresses. I don't suppose you've read Josephine Butler's book about 'The Education and Employment Of Women'?"

"No, but McAlister and I often discussed Glasgow's Helen Crawfurd and her support for women. I read that she greatly admired the Butler woman's stand on women's rights, though Crawfurd thought that we'd never be seen right until women had the vote. So there's you're answer. It'll all have gone to Ian and he's cleared off to America with it. Since then only Rhoddy's existence kept me from going mad." Cate fixed her stare on the older woman and shook her head.

"Strange that. I've never been right with him, you know. I'd never see harm come to him, but I cannot feel for Rhoddy, as I should. Yet, because of him, I had to carry on. Not just give up."

"And you didn't give up?"

"No, my Lady. All this is not his fault. Why should he suffer? It's just him and me—we're two souls bound by a bad memory, with nothing in common but our blood and the fact that we're together at the bottom of the heap once more."

"You left Glasgow, though?"

"The Convent Sisters couldn't keep Rhoddy once I was on my feet again, and we'd no place to stay. Then that kindly sister from the infirmary let me stay with her and later fixed me up with the Catholic Father."

"Ah, one of the Pope's own?"

"Not me, my Lady. I'll have none of any of them. God's done little enough for me, so he can do without my praising him."

"Probably not wise, girl, but I can appreciate your reasons. Had a bit of a falling out with the Almighty myself over my brother's death. Wavered again when he took my Algie. Still, need to know we're all going to end up together again. Comforting that."

"If Bruce, Caroline and that lawyer Hardy are there, I'll do without it, if you don't mind!"

"I take your point, girl. Now the remainder of the story, if you please."

"I'd to leave the presbytery when his housekeeper's was mended. He was so good to the both of us—gave us shelter, food and a good wage for three months. Then he set me on the road with a lift all the way to Bridge of Orchy."

"How did you happen here then?"

The story had been so long and involved, Lady Jemima felt her old bones stiffening and rose to stretch them while the tale ended.

" After Bridge of Orchy I made for the road and took what work I could find. Bedded down in the hedgerows at night and bought food at cottage doors.

I came through the village looking for work and somewhere to rest the boy for a bit. He's not used to walking."

"I think we've earned ourselves another strong drink after that tale of woe. Then you must return to the cottage, while I give all this some thought. After all, you gave me counsel when it was sorely needed and we must make sure your next move is the right one."

Back at the cottage, the two women stood in the kitchen arguing.
"Bella, you must go out."
"I can't, Cate. I just can't."
"How are you going to continue sewing then?"
"I've thought it all out. I hope you'll get the lady's maid job with Lady Jemima and you can bring the sewing back for me.

"And the house? You have to leave, you know. They need a new tallyman and this will be his house."

"I don't know, Cate. I wish you'd not nursed me so well." Crying now, she turned on Cate. "I'd be better dead."

"Bella, Bella, don't start upsetting yourself again. We must think of a way. It won't just happen on its own. I'll do all that I can, though I'm not sure I can stay here."

"I can't face the village alone and homeless. I can't!" Running from the room in tears, Bella set Rhoddy crying too.

"Enough, Rhoddy. I can't think with all these tears. I'll sort something out for us all. Now come and eat."

"No. Won't. You made Bella cry. I hate you." Then he too ran from the room.

Cate was surprised that he'd actually spoken directly to her, but not at what he said. The problems between them were now deeper than they'd ever been, and there seemed no way to solve them. Whether it be Lizzie, Maggie, Maudie Petrie, McAlister or now Bella and Jeannie, with anyone other than herself, Rhoddy was an almost model child. Knowing the problem was largely of her making did not mean it was any easier to bear. Somehow she had to find a way to secure their future and Bella's. At present she had none of the answers. Like Rhoddy, her appetite had gone, so she unpacked the basket and tidied the food away for the morning. Then, shoulders slumped, she made her way to lie beside the stiff form of her son. Her final thoughts, before sleep eventually came, were just how much she hated Bruce MacNishe, who had started all this with his rape.

Next morning Cate found her mistress in a foul mood, the desk in her sitting room awash with papers and the floor around masked by those that had fallen.

"Don't start your 'shall I pick these up, My Lady'. I can't be doing with your neat and tidy ways. I can't seem to make sense of these damned papers. I don't suppose, among all your other talents, you can figure as well?"

"I did work in the distillery doing the daily journals, and sometimes in the evenings Bella has shown me the figure work her father taught her. I don't know much of it just yet but I'm beginning to understand more. I did do ordinary house accounts for McAlister when I was his housekeeper and then I managed the money he gave me when we were married. I like the feeling of working with figures."

"Right. What do we do with this?" She swept some more dockets to the floor in disgust. "Blasted housekeeper has let it all get beyond her and merchants want paying."

"First, My Lady, we must put them in the correct order."

"Heavens, girl, that'll take forever. I've never seen such a muddle."

"Why don't you take the dogs out, My Lady, and I'll make a start."

"Splendid idea. Talking of ideas—no, you'd better tackle this job. We'll have tea and chat later."   As she walked, Lady Jemima wondered if she should keep the girl on. Apparently she could turn her hands to most things and would certainly make a huge difference to the house. Yet she knew it wouldn't work. The girl would eventually remove all the familiar clutter. Wouldn't be able to help herself and then they'd be at odds. It wouldn't do for either of them. No she'd have to guide her in a different direction. And there had to be something shady about that lawyer, the partner. That ought to be investigated. Mmmm. Much work to be done, but first get the dogs walked—a much more pleasurable task than bills.

By the end of the day Cate had all the bills in place, with a separate sheet showing the correct sums, in dated order, written neatly and totalled below. She'd been so engrossed with her task that the day had flown. Sweet memories of her days in the distillery office, and the pride and satisfaction she'd gained from them, had made the current task an absolute delight. She also recognised the benefit of her evenings with Bella. Was there a possibility of staying here? There were many things that she could do, but what of Rhoddy? Children never lived in and he was too young to employ.

Refreshed by her walk and afternoon tea, Lady Jemima sought the girl out in the study.

"Ah, I see you've finished. Leave them—I'll see that Bertie attends to it on his next visit. Now, while you've been beavering away, I've not been idle. Ring for tea in the drawing room. I've no wish to catch sight of those dratted things anymore today. Come on now, jump to it!"

Following her employer downstairs, Cate wondered why the aristocracy never seemed to feel the need to say 'thank you'. Fair enough if you were just doing the job you were paid for, but helping out in other ways was just seen as 'why not? I employ them'.

Seated in the drawing room, Lady Jemima continued. "Now then, as she won't venture out into the village, it seems Bella had better live in from now on. She'll be safe enough here and, unlike you, she will always need sheltering."

"So there's to be no shelter for me, My Lady?" Well, what had she expected? Once again Rhoddy seemed to be the reason for stopping her 'getting on'.

"No need to look like that, my girl! Wouldn't suit you, stuck away here. Oh, you'd be fine while you cleared everything up, with timetables for this and that. But you'd shake us all out of our comfortable ways and you and I would soon have a falling-out. Yes, you'd hold your tongue for as long as you could, but the red hair would tell in the end. No, no—you're destined for better things than here."

"How can that be, My Lady?"

"I haven't quite figured that out yet. A new tallyman and competent quarry foreman are coming, but it will be a month or so before Derwent can spare them, so we have some time. Right now, let's have our tea. You continue with Bella. She should begin to recover when she knows she's coming to me."

Cate knew she should be pleased for Bella, and indeed she was, but any mild hope of her having a permanent position had now gone. What would be the next step for herself and Rhoddy?"

Another month and the smell of the well-rotted horse manure adorning the pristine flowerbeds, all cut back, roots safely mulched, reminded Cate that winter was well on the way. One day she hoped to have a garden of her own. She loved the rhythmic orderliness of it. Like the figure work, the sewing, the keeping house, the cooking, they were all patterns, which if you followed them in the correct order, were successful and easier. No wonder she felt adrift all the time. Nothing in her life had been organized lately, certainly not on any permanent basis, since the funeral. The feeling of being as driftwood, abandoned or casually wave-tossed, was not what she wanted. Control, but how to get it? There had to be a way.

Entering the house, Cate encountered her Ladyship, who noticed the younger woman's lethargy.

"Now then, where's the sense of urgency this morning? Getting tired of us, aren't you?"

234

"Of course not, My Lady."

"But?"

"I feel unsettled. Winter's coming and time is…"

"Running out. Yes, girl, decisions must be made. Tea, and I'll make some."

"Am I to have no say, then, My Lady?" Well what else did she expect? When was anything ever different, Cate wondered? Was she always to be powerless?

"Aha, I'm right, you see. You're getting prickly. Much better. Time you started regarding your own feelings."

"People like us have no time for feelings, My Lady."

"Now you're feeling sorry for yourself. I should know—been there. Look at the mess I made of things. Nearly as bad as Bertie! No, my girl, you do better when you're using that battling spirit that saw you fighting your Highland monster and rescuing Bella."

"That was because my mind knew what to do. Now I have to take to the road and then what?"

"Cross are you? Not getting a position here. Think I'm wrong, girl?"

"It would have been easier, My Lady."

"I like that about you. Believe in saying what you think. Somewhere in your background there's breeding my dear. You can always tell. Why don't you know anything about your origins?"

"As a child you accept what you know. If you're parentless with no permanent home, and no one is willing to provide facts, you just believe there are none to be told. Anyway, being on your own takes all your effort. You're pulled and pushed—do this, do that, powerless, that's what you are. No time or desire to worry about your position in life. Too busy just surviving and keeping out of trouble."

"Ah, deep down, you see, there's bitterness there. I can hear it in your words. It's those 'closed doors' again. Well, some day, my dear, you'll simply be forced to open them. Of that I'm certain. Now, however, the immediate future is the thing."

"Yours is easy, My Lady. It's here."

"The callousness of youth! Listen to you. Your life is still before you. Mine is nearing the end—not yet, but it's waiting for me. As you say, it's definitely here on my beloved estate, even if its mine no longer—though I still feel I own it."

"That's what I mean. Despite its being inherited by someone else, you're still here. You've always been here, secure."

"There are parts of you still incredibly naïve, despite your obvious intelligence."

"What do you mean, My Lady?"

"Granted my family have owned this land for generations. As a child it was my own personal paradise. I never thought of leaving it. Then, first my brother died and then my mother. Suddenly there was only my father left in direct line. He did the obvious thing, married me off to a suitable groom. Suitable for him that was. Luckily he chose well for me, and after some initial problems, it worked. But, unlike yours, my children didn't survive. Then, when it was too late for more, my husband died. Do you think I had any choice? Of course I didn't. After all, I'm only a woman. How could I manage the estate? The fact that I'd lived all my life here, knew everything about it and loved every bit of it, counted for nothing Distant Cousin though he may be, Bertie is from a different country, younger generation. He cares nothing for this estate, while I love it, so where's the fairness in that? You see we're not as different as you think."

"That's so unfair. Why must we always be the ones to give way to men?"

"My generation had no say in it, but yours is beginning to question all that. You may well have the chance to make a difference."

"Where could I make a difference?"

"Start with something or somewhere you feel strongly about, girl. What or who is your idea of perfection? Something you'd fight to save from harm?"

"Once it was an invalid boy who gave me his heart. He's never been replaced, so now it would be something I know—Beinn Nishe, my mountain."

"Capital. There you are then. You must go back to it. Start from there. Begin again."

236

"I was set on going, but I'm beginning to think I could never go back. Think why I left."

"Poppycock. Have you no idea of the changes in you?"

"I don't bother much with mirrors and the like, My Lady."

"I know. And I find it very refreshing. That's why you and I deal well with one another. We both lack vanity. What I meant was you're no longer the frightened tinker girl."

"I was never truly frightened."

"Well said. So what's there to be frightened about now? You're well armed—a grown woman who's known violence, danger, hunger, birth, and death. The list goes on. Go back, make a place for yourself and, in doing so, I'll wager you'll help others."

By shutting her eyes Cate could see, almost hear, the roar of the waterfall, sense the security of her cave, and believe in the bounty of the countryside. She'd saved herself from starving as a child—why not try again? What other choice did she have?

Within the week Cate had settled Bella in the Big House, said her goodbyes and accepted the train fares as well as her wages from Lady Jemima. Stevie, from the stables, took them to Balvourie station and, with a sad handshake; Cate boarded the train with Rhoddy. Once more she was heading for an uncertain new chapter in her life.

Part Four

Kevinishe

1911

17

Through the early morning mist, Cate had her first glimpse of Kevinishe as a grown woman. The iron-grey sheet of sea still stretched to the horizon, though the foreshore looked smaller, the machair shrunken, the road more pitted, and the cottages tiny. Only the mountain, away to the left, seemed the same.

News from the Highlands had been fragmented during her Glasgow years. Truth was she'd wanted no part of Kevinishe. Basically the two worlds were so far apart, not only in distance, but also in their way of life, that little held them together. Now, looking at the village, she wondered if the Cailleach was still alive. She'd try the Black House first and then the cave, if need be.

The Cailleach had seemed old to Cate as a child, but now seeing the aged woman anew, she did look truly bent and frail. She accepted this return just as she'd always done in the past. "You're back then." A breakfast, of broth and soda bread, was laid on the old shed door with its 'legs' of peat, and when the meal was over, Cate talked, Rhoddy was silent, and the old woman listened. An occasional nod and the intervening years were dealt with. When young, Cate believed the Cailleach had little English, as she normally spoke Gaelic. What she didn't do was speak unless it was absolutely necessary. Cate understood this, but Rhoddy seemed afraid of the old woman's silence and their new surroundings. The first day ended with fried herring and soda bread and an early night on the newly made heather beds on the floor, though the Cailleach's box bed squeezed against the wall, left little room for them.

Cate woke, and in the darkness was lost. Then the old familiar smell of peat smoke told her she was back in the Black House. The rough stone walls blackened by peat smoke; the turf roof with it's army of beasties shuffling about; the crooked shelves lining the walls with their salves and potions that healed the villagers; herbs hanging to dry from the roof: nothing had changed. The old woman must have stirred the fire before going outside and Cate now rose and made her way to the adjoining shed that some grateful villager had built. It housed a toilet pail, another for washing, a tin bath, a stack of peat, hay for the house cow, and a barrel of salt herrings to tide them over the winter.

Settling into her childhood ways, Cate took on as many chores as she could for the frail old woman. Today she'd set out to collect fuel for their fire. Unfortunately the remnants of the previous night's storm were visible in the bounding waves. The sea had reclaimed the piles of driftwood and seaweed she'd gathered the day before. Why hadn't she carried them all up to the house then? Today there was but a thin strip of grassy dune in front of her, the foreshore gone. She noticed the movement of figures in the distance, but, having no wish to meet them, made her way empty- handed to the Black House.

The two village women watched the retreating figure.

"There she is again, Morag, off back to the Black House and the Cailleach. Is she from the towns, do you think?"

"She's looking more like one of us than them, Kirsty. See she has the shawl wrapped round her and the creel on her back. I never heard of the Cailleach having a relative from the towns?"

"Well, whoever she is she's as fed up with the shore the day as we are. I'll away an try to catch her."

"If she's anything to do with the old witch you'd better be careful. She might turn you into a sea creature or such like."

"Away with you. Yon old woman's no witch. Mind she's clever with the moor flowers. Just put some dead leaves in a cup of water, swirled them round and round, strained them through muslin and poured the liquid down the throat of Donald Uig, and the terrible coughing stopped."

"What for did she put it through the muslin then?"

"So's he wouldn't be choking on the bits, I suppose. Och, now look—she's too far away! I've missed my chance of a craic. Well, well, Morag, we might as well be gone ourselves. There's no harvest to be had on the shore today, so there's not."

Although she enjoyed the luxury of their milk, Cate couldn't help wondering if it was worth all this trouble. The house cow, like the shed, was a new addition to the Cailleach's household. In the past black tea had been their staple drink. Milk had only been brought at the whim of the villagers. Now, with a resident house cow, it was obvious to Cate that she should take on the milking. Come the summer the beast would be allowed to forage for her own food and milked where she could be found. In these winter months the cow had to be brought home, milked and fed. Today the stupid animal was missing. Wandered deep into the moor, no doubt. The whole system was ridiculous. Over the years the majority of the villagers had fenced their patches of ground to contain their beasts and somehow that's what she'd have to do here if she stayed. The sound of hooves interrupted her search, and as they approached, she recognised Fisher. She knew she should have made the effort to see him sooner, but she'd avoided it. Now she'd have to face him with her guilt.

"I'm sorry, Fisher, I...."

"Well, well it's yourself." He knew and understood why she was embarrassed. What didn't make sense was why she was here instead of oceans away. No doubt he'd find out soon enough.

"Fisher, you haven't seen the Cailleach's cow, have you?" The question a ruse to avoid the conversation she didn't want to have.

"She's high up on the moor, there to the left."

Dismounting, he took time to study this grown woman, or what he could see of her, bundled up in the traditional black shawl, covering head, shoulders and most of her body. The eyes had not changed and today they shone with embarrassment.

"Fisher, I don't know how to...."

"Don't then. You're steering clear of everyone, I see. You should know better than to think you can hide, especially here. Young

Kirsty has the whole village alerted to the fact that the Cailleach has a relative with her, supposedly brought here to follow the old woman in her curing. If it's hiding you're looking for, this is no the place for it, even if you did creep in on the dawn."

So he had seen her. Despite her shame, Cate felt a warmth inside her as she studied the man. Her first memory of him was the business of the pram and him bringing her back to Kevinishe House to be put in jail. Then she'd grown to like him later as she visited the distillery, but it was his actions after Bruce's assault on her that had consolidated that liking. Now, just being there in front of her, this big man, with his solid frame, quiet clipped speech and underlying strength made her feel better—how good it was after all the previous turmoil, to see him unchanged in any way. "I'm so sorry. I just didn't want to see him, Fisher."

"Aye well, you should have stayed in America then."

"America?"

"Oh, we may be out of touch, Cate, but that doesn't mean we don't get news of everyone now and again. To America you ran this time, so I'm told."

"I don't know where that came from. I've been no further than Glasgow, where you sent me, and now I'm back."

"And what of those you ran from? You'd a husband."

"Dead, this past year."

"Well and I'd heard that, but it was said you'd gone to America with his family."

"Fisher, I would go neither to heaven nor hell with that lot. God dammit, they've stolen my baby!" She turned to hide the threatening tears.

He waited till she'd control of herself. There was no doubt there'd been mistakes made and he felt a huge surge of relief. Somehow, running from everyone had never sat neatly with the girl he'd known. It was to be expected that she'd shun the villagers, and she'd have no wish to run into anyone from Kevinishe House, but to avoid him? That had hurt.

With an effort, Cate continued. "What happened to Maggie and Lizzie? I couldn't believe they would have left their home without telling me, Fisher. We'd become family!"

244

"But it was yourself who'd gone, Cate. They went to the lawyer's house and it was all shut up, ready to be sold, the neighbour said, and the family gone with you and the bairns to America."

"No. No. I never left Glasgow!"

"So you tell me, but now I'll need the whole story before we can set this right." Leaving the horse to graze, they perched on an outcrop and he listened carefully as she filled in the details and, as she finished, he shook his head. "Seems as though you're never to have an easy road, lass. But the others were fair broken at your leaving. Maggie married that Bert Green, by the way. You'll have heard of him no doubt."

"A friend of her late husband—a fisherman, wasn't he?"

"Aye, you have the right of it. She thought it best to get Lizzie and herself away from Glasgow after you left. They're in Dunoon now."

"Fisher, I still can't believe how everyone just disappeared."

"Well, they haven't disappeared—they're in Dunoon. But who else has gone missing?"

"Cook and Ada from the house."

"They'd have been told the same story most like. See here, lass, folks who've done well by you can be scunnered to find you'd just up and away, leaving them thrown out so to speak. Do you no know where they lived?"

"Cook lived in the house, and I never knew where Ada lived, nor Solly."

"Solly? Who's he?"

"He was my husband's legal clerk. When I went to the office it was closed. Another friend lost."

"Sad to say, they'll all be thinking the same then, that you just upped and left without a thought for them. The boy, he's here?"

"That's another sad tale." As she spoke to Fisher of her troubled relationship with Rhoddy, somehow Cate knew he was the one person who'd understand. Their shared knowledge of Bruce would be explanation enough.

Having rounded up the cow, Fisher rode slowly behind them as they made their way home. By the time Cate had milked the animal, Fisher and the Cailleach were deep in Gaelic conversation, black tea, no doubt with a dram in it, in front of them, and Rhoddy glowering at them from the three-legged stool in the corner of the room.

As they stood by the door in the early gloom of the winter evening, Fisher told her the news from Kevinishe House.

"Master Rab dead? How Fisher? He was still young. Never a sign of sickness."

"Aye well, a frightened horse doesn't stop to consider the rider's age, or his health, however good it might be. He bolts no matter who's on his back. Thrown, Master Rab was, and the neck of him broken by the fall. According to Callumn. He'd have had no time for any hurt."

"Lady Sarah?"

"Away back to England to nurse her pain. There was nothing to hold her here."

"Oh, Fisher, MacNishe—what a blow for him!"

"A broken-hearted man whose days seem overlong for him now, with Rab gone and only...."

"Bruce...." Cate understood the Laird's unhappiness.

"Exactly so. The next Laird of Kevinishe, may God help us all!"

They stood engrossed, each with their own horrifying picture of what that would mean to them.

"An another thing, Cate, the tinkers are no longer in the long field."

"Surely they were no sent away? MacNishe seemed to have an agreement with them."

"Aye, that he had, but the old tinker woman died, an the young ones had no real connection once she'd gone. We've no seen them since. Now it's only the Cailleach and MacNishe himself who are the remaining strands of that particular story."

"But there's you too. You've always been here."

"Oh, I'm no party to all the skeletons in that strange family cupboard. I've a thought or two, but that's all. You'll be missing them, Cate?"

"I—I'm not sure. The old tinker woman was kind to me when she could be. I would like to have said goodbye to her, and to Master Rab for that matter—though he was for jailing me! I just always wondered why she took me on the road every summer. Neither she nor the Calliach ever answered my questions."

"Well, the two of them started you on life's road. By making you stand on your own as a child, it's been a good beginning that's seen you through your hard times. Just be thankful for that. No doubt the real story will be told in time. Now, I'll need to be on my way, Cate. See here, the Cailleach is to come to the house tomorrow to see if she can ease MacNishe's rheumatics. You'll come with her?"

"That I'll not. I never want to have any doings with them up there, Fisher."

"He was aye good to you."

"Good to me! Good to me!" Cate spat the words at him. "Good to me indeed! Threw me out and never a word or a helping hand! How good was that?"

"But they'd no idea."

"What! Fisher, surely you told them what happened!"

"Now, Cate, how could I be breaking the heart of MacNishe by telling of the boy's black deed. Wrong though it was of the boy, he was still a future Laird. They couldn't put him out. We did what we thought best, the Cailleach and myself. Told him you'd gone with the tinkers and then stayed in Glasgow. Sad he was too at your leaving, but better that than knowing of Bruce's evil. He's had a few more years of peace you see. That's all changed now."

"Why's that? Oh, Bruce is as bad as ever then? MacNishe has found that out?"

"I think he's always known, Cate, but hoped for a change as the boy grew. That hope's dead now. They hardly ever see one another. MacNishe here, the boy in Edinburgh, going the same way as old Red Rhoddy his other grandfather, black hearted soul that he was."

"He's dead too then?" Cate thought it was a pity he'd not taken his grandson with him. "But all these years, Fisher, I've thought they just didn't care. Cursed them, I have."

"Well, that's understandable, and mebbe we should have done otherwise. We just did what we thought best. Hid you here to mend and then, with the bairn coming, we thought Maggie would be the answer. You couldn't run around here with his bairn at your heels, now could you?"

"Don't you see? That's exactly what I'm doing!"

"No. Cate. You're a respectable widow woman now with a young son. No one need ever know different. Saves heartache all round, it does."

As she watched Fisher ride away her thoughts were of all the changes in Kevinishe. It was Glasgow all over again. Here too everything was shifting. It was like the driftwood on the shore. There one day, gone the next.

Donald Uig was surprised to see his fiancé making her way to the west of the village. Putting down his load of peat, he shouted after her. "Where are you away to Kirsty? Are you no waiting for Morag?"

"No. I have a wee job I want to do by myself."

"Well now, that's a change of tune for you, mo ghoile."

"Can't I be doing anything on my own without all this questioning? I'm no married to you yet, Donald Uig, so I'm not. Nor likely to be if you're to be at me all the time with the questions."

Kirsty, head down, carried on walking and was away before her intended had time to stop her. There had been no sign of the other woman on the shore lately, and curiosity had Kirsty taking the initiative. Though she appeared wary now she was up on the moor alone. Her timid knock brought Cate to the door.

"Yes. What can I do for you?" Cate recognized the younger girl from the shore. Dark hair wound on top of her head and a pleasant face, roughened by the outdoor life.

"Well it's just…." Now Kirsty could think of nothing to say.

"Are you not well? Is it the Cailleach you want to see?"

"God, no!"

"It's okay. She'd never harm you. The stories about her are just that— stories."

"Well I'm sure, but she does look a bit frightening. The villagers say she 'sees' things. I mean what if she 'saw' things I shouldn't have done?"

"I very much doubt she would be interested in that. As I understand it, she has no control over what she does or does not 'see'. Anyway, just now she's no too well herself. Can I get something for you?"

"No. I was just—I mean there's no so many young folk in the village and—well, you know, mebbe you'd come from the towns and could tell us what the women were wearing, an that sort of thing."

"Where's your friend today? I saw you together the day of the storm." Cate understood. Curiosity had to be satisfied. She had to start somewhere and why not here? "Let me check the Cailleach and get my shawl. We'll have a walk to the shore."

By the time introductions had been made and Cate had revealed a carefully edited version of her past history, several other women had come to their doors, washing lines, or even to the shore. Brief nods of acknowledgement and then they busied themselves while keeping an eye on the pair.

"If you have some spare paper, bring it to the shore in the morning and I'll draw you some of the dresses the women wear, if you like."

"Can you really do that? I'd never get the material, never mind I can't sew anyway!"

"Perhaps we could work something out? It's been grand talking to you, Kirsty, but I must be getting back. The old woman really is unwell. Perhaps I'll see you in the morning. Don't worry if I'm not there. It'll just mean I can't get away."

Hurrying back to the village, Kirsty went in search of Morag. The women, still outdoors, called to her to come and have a craic. Head down, she ignored them. The news carried straight to her friend.

Making her way home, Cate was smiling. Young Kirsty was the perfect broadcaster. First to the friend Morag, then the pair of them would take her story home and by the end of the day at least twenty versions, both English and Gaelic, would be circulating in the village. Well, if was to stay, her story had to be told. This way only those events that she deemed necessary would be broadcast and by the time all the versions were heard no one would be really sure of the facts.

The Cailleach was no better when she got back, and Cate settled down to some serious nursing. The big house would have to wait for both of them, though Fisher would most probably come along to see why they hadn't been.

Tomorrow would be the start of a new year, 1912, and Cate knew that the Cailleach would see little of it. She was fading. These past few weeks there'd been no spare moments for Rhoddy or Kirsty or anything other than tending to the Cailleach in the Black House. Stiff, Cate stretched her cramped body and made for the door.

Huddled into her shawl, she walked across the machair to the shore. Although the snow crunched underfoot, the sea was quiet. Just a gentle murmuring as it caressed the shore and a simple sigh as it withdrew in the moonlit night. The contrast to the peat-fumed house on the moors with the old woman's harsh coughing amid muddled mutterings of Gaelic, English, and delirium was not lost on Cate.

Another day and her patient seemed weaker. Between the long silences there were still periods of delirium, mostly in the Gaelic. Even if she could have understood all that was said, the various hints and scraps of history that she did decipher somehow made Cate uneasy. It was almost as though the old woman, as she clawed the air for breath, was turning into the creature the villagers feared.

As the day wore on the air seemed to grow heavier and Cate was wary.

She put the bowl of gruel down and wiped her patient's mouth. She was fond of the Cailliach, had enjoyed these last months learning more of her herbalist secrets, but there was something in her dying presence that was unnerving. The cracked whisper and the outstretched hand broke into Cate's thoughts.

"Mo ghoile? My hand."

As she took the shrivelled hand, Cate asked, "Are you thirsty?" Getting no answer, she wiped the damp brow and studied the weathered old face with its white hair bound up in a bun atop her head. Without the ever-present black shawl almost covering her face it was easy to see the Cailleach might have been pretty as a young woman.

"You'll see now." The words were dragged out of the frail body on the bed, and yet her hand gripped Cate's like a clamp.

Was this the end? The Cailleach's eyes were open but sightless. The grip on Cate's hand slackened and she felt a strange warmth flow through fingers, almost stripped of flesh, into her own and up along her arm. Then the peat smoke faded—*Through wreaths of swirling mist came the noise of battle. Red-coated soldiers battled with ragged Highlanders. Men lay wounded amid the heather and in the distance a red-headed woman struggled to support the weight of a plaid clad figure before merging into the mist.*

Then, Cate became aware she was still holding the Cailleach's hand, although now it was cold and the old woman asleep. The sound of hooves on the moor and a call from outside the house gave her no time to dwell on what had happened. Shivering she pulled her shawl tighter round her body as if to shield herself from the unknown. She opened the door and relief swamped her as she made out the stalwart figure of Fisher.

"Come you away in, Fisher. She's sleeping." Cate watched the big man as he studied the old woman.

"Aye, an it'll no be long before she has the long sleep. You can see she's going. I'll need to away to the big house to tell MacNishe."

"Fisher, he'll know soon enough when she goes. This village is better than the wireless broadcasts."

"No matter. I'll away. Sick or no, he'll come to see her."

"He's not fit. Why don't you just tell him she's going?"

"No. No. They go back too far for that. I'll away and see to it."

Not wanting to go back inside, Cate watched Fisher leave till he was out of sight, then strode up and down outside the house still uneasy over the afternoon's experience. Oh it linked in with her imaginary childhood friend and the old story the Laird had told her, but it still smacked of witchery and she wanted none of it.

Cow fed and milked Cate collected peats from the stack and made for the house, when the sound of a pony and trap coming along the shore road, hurried her inside to leave the peats by the fire, before she went out to greet the men she knew would be there.

As Fisher tethered the pony, Cate waited for the Laird to speak.

"So you've come back to us then." MacNishe said as he climbed down from the trap and stood in front of her.

She was shocked to see how he'd aged. All those years ago he'd seemed such a large important man, so full of life. Now he was bent and his hair as white as the Cailleach's. Gathering her wits she faced him in the gloom, meeting the eyes that had once looked so kindly on her, and let her shame show. "I thought, with wee Davy's death and me not really needed, well, it seemed…."

"Just so, Cate, but it was unkind, and we were hurt."

"I was but a child." Not for anything now would she tell this old man what his grandson had done. "I'm a widow now."

"Aye, so Fisher here says, and with a fine young son."

At that moment the Cailleach cried out. The Laird entered the Black House, drew up the stool and spoke in the Gaelic to her. Fisher motioned Cate away from the door towards the pony and trap.

"That was well done. No need to cause him pain now. You understand that he would never have let the matter go. Though he would have found it hard to bear the true facts."

"I feel so ashamed for thinking all these years that he'd simply thrown me over. I knew he couldn't disown Bruce but I thought some help could have come, if not from him, from Lady Sarah. I never thought he'd age like that. Rab's loss has been too much for him to bear, I couldn't add to that."

"Indeed not and with her going," Fisher nodded towards the house, " he'll feel the time is right for himself."

"Were they that close, Fisher?"

"He's always had a soft spot for her. Though they do say it was his father—oh, who knows what's between them? But her death will grieve him."

"I've had enough of mysteries these past few days. After all, it's only gossip and hearsay, and what's it got to do with us anyway?" Cate had a nasty suspicion that somehow or other it did concern her in some way. One thing she was certain of was that she'd do her damnedest to avoid whatever it was. From now on she wanted to be deciding for herself. Creating circumstances where she was in a position to take charge of her own life.

18

Looking round the bedroom to see they'd left nothing behind them, Cate turned to Rhoddy. Understanding his pleasure during their short stay here, but knowing he had to face the truth, she tackled it immediately. "Come now, Rhoddy, we can't stay here. This is Fisher's house. We've to go back to the Black House."

"Don't want to. It's nasty horrid there."

"Well it won't be like that now."

"Why not?"

"Rhoddy, I told you. As the old lady has passed away we were staying with Fisher while the Laird's men made the old place into a proper village house, like Kirsty's. Let's go and take a look at it. You'll see it's all been changed. Come on now." Cate couldn't help thinking she seemed to have spent most of Rhoddy's childhood pulling him unwillingly from one place to the other, and the boy couldn't help being suspicious, as most of the moves they'd made had been unhappy for him.

Since the Cailleach's death, things had changed a great deal. MacNishe lingered on, and she spent long hours reading to him, just as she'd done as a young girl. It had been his decision to rebuild the old woman's house. Fisher believed he'd have done it years ago if the Cailleach had let him. The Laird wanted Cate and Rhoddy to move into Kevinishe House, but she'd been adamant. She'd never do that, even though Bruce rarely came back to the Highlands these days.

Crossing the moor to the Black House, Cate took Rhoddy's hand as she opened the door.

"See, I told you it would be different. Have a look over there—a wee room all for your own."

"Where did all the stuff come from? It's no ours?"

"Oh but it is, Rhoddy. The Laird let me rummage in his attics and I furnished the whole place. We'll have to make do with the old bedding and things till I can make others."

"How can you make others, Mammy? We've no cloth."

"Oh, but we have. See, on the dresser here, all these curtains and material. They're from Kevinishe House, but they're all too big just now. I'll make them fit, though it'll take time. Will you away to look for the cow while I get started here."

"Aye, I will."

"Fine, I'll get to work."

Cate inspected the four small rooms, touching here, looking there. Apparently, MacNishe's father had in fact given the Black House to the Cailleach, and now it was Cate's. The Laird had sent the distillery workers in to upgrade and expand it. The dresser, table, chairs and settle, made by the distillery coopers, were a gift from the Laird. Could Rhoddy and she settle down and begin again? Have a proper mother and son relationship? There was still the small matter of earning a living in this small community where only the men were paid workers, and the women worked the crofts.

In the following weeks she cut, pinned, and sewed, till the black House soft furnishings were completed. The sewing had now become a daily chore. She was sitting for long hours over the old treadle machine these days. That had been another treasure salvaged from the Kevinishe nursery. Kirsty had started it all. She'd never forgotten the dress drawings and, when she'd first seen Cate's smart new curtains, cushions and bedcovers, she'd begged her to make some for Donald Uig's house before their wedding. Slowly, month by month, requests had come in and now she worked all hours to make sure she kept everyone happy. Today her back hurt and she had just stood up to stretch it, when she was interrupted.

"Hello the house!"

Damn! Just when she wanted a walk to stretch her stiff bones! Forcing a smile she opened the door to, she thought one of Fisher's second cousins.

"Janet, isn't it? Come in now. Will you take a strupach?"

"If it's yourself is having one, a cup would be welcome. My, but the old house is smart now. Though the Cailleach's shelves with all their herb baskets are just so on the wall, though straighter than they were."

"Yes, I'm glad the men were able to use them, black as they are." Cate could see that yet another version of her newly furnished room would now be circulated in the village.

"Well, and she'll have had them in the beginning from the shore no doubt. A breaking boat probably, for I'm sure under the smoke-blackened layer you'd find tar. Mebbe you should have had the coopers do some new ones."

"No, I asked them to use hers if they could. Those and her remedies are all I have of her, you see, Janet."

"Well that's only right, and you related an all." Janet waited for the answer.

Cate smiled. There it was again—always a sly query to satisfy the gossips. She put the teapot on the table. "Here, try my bannocks, and there's some crowdie to go with them."

"It's yourself is doing well with the crofter ways, seeing as you were never brought up to it. I mind you as a scrawny tinker bairn. Always on the moors or mountain, wild like the Laird's deer, you were, till you disappeared.

"I've had to learn. I must feed myself and the boy." Cate ignored the rest of the speech.

"I see he's at the school now. He doesn't have the red hair. He'll be like the Father, I suppose?"

At least she could answer this one honestly. "Yes, I think he is, but bairns change as they grow, so we'll see. Now was it just a visit or can I get you anything?"

"Now that you mention it, Cate, I hear you do the sewing."

"You mean, sew for others?" Why, couldn't she just ask straight out?

"Well yes. See here, my waist is no what it was this twenty years past and my funeral dress is no fitting. Stretched till it can stretch no more, God love it."

"Have you the new material, Janet?"

"Well now I wasn't thinking of making new, mo ghoile. No, no. My mother's good black dress has been in the under bed kist these long years past, so with hers and mine we could surely make do. After all, the dead'll no worry about a few seams patched here and there, I'm sure you'll be agreeing."

"Why don't you bring them to me then, and I'll see what I can do?"

"Now then, how lucky is it that I just happen to have them at your own door and himself has dropped off a bittie barrel of good salt herring for the winter."

"That's too kind. I'll have a look at the dress when we've had our tea." Herring was food, but oh to have someone produce some money for her work! At present they lived on what she could garner from nature, the house cow and the sparse vegetable plot she'd fixed up round the house. Everyone paid her in kind and they certainly weren't starving, but it was a meagre existence. The truth was that she wasn't the needlewoman that Lizzie had been. Drawing the styles, making the patterns, she enjoyed, but she didn't have the patience to run up seam after endless seam. The sewing had its uses though. Gradually she was becoming less of a novelty for the villagers.

With Janet gone, Cate went to gather some peats. As she raised the creel to her back it slipped, spilling the contents onto the ground. She'd learnt how to cut and leave them drying, but the loading and unloading were skills still to be mastered. She knew her problem was that she filled the creel too full. That was typical of her. Get the job done quickly. Trouble was, crofting life ran at a snail's pace, every job done 'in The Lord's good time'.

"You'll have filled that too full." Fisher, coming upon her struggling, looked at the scattered peats as he dismounted, trying to hide his smile.

"Don't you dare laugh! I know I filled it too full, but I haven't the time to go back and forth all day."

"No, nor the inclination, I'll be thinking."

"I am trying, Fisher. It's just—a very little return."

"I'll grant you the crofting life is hard."

"It's not that I'm afraid of work."

"Anyone can see that, though I'm thinking you're no over fond of this kind."

"It's just, it's so, so wasteful."

"I don't see that at all now, Cate."

"Think about the seaweed gathering or the peat, each of us picking up a little. It would make more sense if we all gathered together and had someone carting."

"Wouldn't there be squabbles enough if that was the case? They've always done it the old way. Oh, sometimes a neighbour will help with the hay, or even the peat, but not as a whole village thing. Mind they'll no let you starve, Cate if you're sick."

"I know. Someone will milk the cow and things will be dropped off at the door. It's all so disorganized though. They've no sense of time, Fisher."

"It's the city life you'll be after then? That'll be fast enough, I'll warrant."

"No, I hated the city. There's no space. I love the Highlands. I'm young! I can do more than this, but what?"

"Well now, mebbe this letter I'm bringing will cheer you up."

"A letter for me? Are you sure? Who would be writing to me?'

"Wouldn't the best way for the answers to be reading it? I'll away then. Just leave these, I'll gather them tomorrow after work."

"Fisher, you've done more than enough for me. I'm sorry. I'm out of sorts, today. I'll learn how to do it properly. You'll see, I promise."

"I've no doubt of that, lass."

Back in the Black House, Cate studied the envelope. She'd neither written nor received a letter since she'd been back. Why hadn't she thought to write to Maggie and Lizzie, now she knew where they were? As usual she'd been too busy, trying to make a new life in the village and they seemed so far away now. Somehow it was always the future that beckoned.

With Rhoddy settled for the night, Cate drew her chair close to the new stove and gazed into the fire. The salt in the sticks she'd gathered from the shore spat and sparked at her. Although a peat fire lasted longer, she much preferred the bright dancing flames of the sticks. Her letter spread out on her knees, she picked the pages up one by one, reading and rereading them. Lady Jemima's writing was hard to make out, but the meaning was clear enough.

How had she made such a champion out of the older woman? Why should a great lady concern herself with a tinker girl? Cate felt overwhelmed. She'd never been one for tears, but they were close now. To go to all that trouble! What would it all mean? She'd have to see Fisher in the morning.

Next morning in the distillery, Cate watched in silence as Fisher read the letter.

What do you think Fisher?"

"Well now, it seems right enough. So you'll need to be away again?"

"Yes, but what do you think she means, Fisher, by 'righted the wrongs'? Can she mean Sarah?"

"America is a fair bit away now, so I wouldn't set your hopes too high. More than likely it'll be about Glasgow affairs."

"Since they're all long gone to America, there's nothing left in Glasgow for me. Oh no! There's Solly. Mebbe she's found Solly?"

"Well then, why don't you leave Rhoddy with me and get on the morning post bus—always supposing Wullie gets himself up in time. Have you the fare?"

"Yes, I have some money left. Are you sure about Rhoddy? Kirsty would mind him otherwise."

"No, at eight, it's time he had a man around him. We don't want him turning out like his father now, do we?"

"Thank you, Fisher. You always appear when I most need you. Believe me, I'm truly grateful."

In the morning, having been deposited at the station by Wullie, she'd caught the mail train. As it approached her destination, Cate tried to steady the fluttering in her stomach. She'd need the long walk to Balvourie to quieten her nerves. As the train drew in she was one of the first out. It seemed a long time since Lady Jemima had sent her back to Kevinishe from this very station.

"Cate?"

Hearing her name she turned to see the groom from Balvourie. "Stevie! What a surprise! You're still with her Ladyship's horses, then? Surely you're no here for me?"

"I am that—been meeting the train these last few days. As to the horses, they'd no do without me, my pretty beasts. Her Ladyship was certain you'd come and I've the trap outside. You're to come to the house and stay with Bella. The Lady Jemima's orders."

"I can't wait to see Bella again. Is she well?"

"She's fine now, Cate, but timid if she ventures out."

"The past takes a long time to put behind you, Stevie. Especially after…."

"Well and it's no surprising—though we never mention it. She's fine living in the house."

As they trotted into the drive, once again Cate was reminded how beautiful the approach to the house was. "I see the gardens are as fine as ever."

"She's always had more interest with the outside of the house, Cate. Likes that and the stables to be just so."

"I remember." As she looked around and drank in the beauty, Cate determined that one day, somehow, she'd have a home like this. She was thankful to have the renovated Black House, but something inside her wanted more. The gardens and the house would be like the outside of Balvourie, and inside she'd recreate Lady Sarah's sitting room. That would be just right. It might be foolishness to dream like this, but it kept her mind fixed on the future.

As she entered the house, Cate wondered what she'd find out from Her Ladyship. Seated in the drawing room, Lady Jemima studied the young woman as she entered. "You're too thin, girl. Not enough to eat in the God-forsaken Highlands?"

"My Lady, that's unkind."

"Which, your figure or your homeland? Does nothing but rain up there!"

"Yes, I suppose it does. The diet is somewhat restricted and the life is physical, but I'm alive and well."

"That's the spirit. So, tea and business and then Bella's waiting for you."

Cate felt she'd never been away. Tea poured, she listened carefully to the older woman's words.

"So, there we are. You're to go to the lawyer in question on Monday and he'll give you all the details, but the gist of it all is McAlister's wretched children and their shady lawyer did you out of what was rightfully yours."

"What'll it mean? Will there be some money?"

"Yes, there'll be money! I know we women are always hard done by but apparently your late husband had indeed made provision for you. His family perverted the course of justice. I made it my business to sort it out. One of the perks of being the gentry—people listen and family lawyers never like to be threatened."

"My Lady, you didn't?"

"Dammit all, girl, do you think things get done by being gentle? Told him Sir Albert would remove estate business to England. Soon became co-operative after that."

"But would he, I mean his Lordship? He doesn't even know me."

"Course he doesn't and wouldn't give a damn about you either. No, no, Bertie knew nothing about it."

"Then…."

"Thought you used to be a bright young thing? Left your wits in the sodden moors have you? Of course Bertie threatened no such thing—I did! I may be an old woman, but I can still pull a verbal punch or two when necessary. Names, my dear, always help. Just you remember to use mine occasionally in conversation. You'll be amazed at what you can get done then."

"It doesn't seem—well honest."

"Mmmph, bend a little, my girl, otherwise you'll stay poor. My threat was completely harmless. I knew that, but the lawyer didn't. Bluffed my way, you see. He might have faced me down, but he couldn't be sure, so he played safe. Bridge, you see—best game out to sharpen the wits and teach you to keep your emotions out of your face."

"I believe you enjoyed all that, My Lady."

"Course I did. Have always disliked stuffiness and these legal men are so pompous, acting as though we didn't have a brain in our head. Then there was the moral issue. Can't stand to see unnecessary wrongs, not when it can be avoided or if one knows about it. Heavens, all this talk has made me dry. More tea, then get yourself away up to Bella. The child is mending slowly. She and I do well together. Never fear, she'll be cared for."

"Thank you, My Lady."

"Come now, one good turn and all that. I just harangued a stuffy old lawyer. You stood against a raging crowd, and you shamed an old woman into action. Now get away with you, I've dogs to walk."

The next day, Cate couldn't help smiling as she caught sight of her reflection in the Glasgow shop windows. The outfit may have been years old but Bella and she had cut and sewn into the night until the skirt hung straight and the jacket nipped in at her waist and flared over the hips. The green velvet almost matched the hat they'd found and her Ladyship had been delighted with the transformation of her old clothes. Well, here she was, with no idea—into the office first and then what?

The receptionist took her name and told her to take a seat. The door in front of her opened and a young man spoke to her.

"Mrs. McAlister, please come in and take a seat."

Now she was here, Cate was nervous.

Now then Mrs. McAlister, you're here to get some good news, thanks to the efforts of the lawyer acting for Lady Jemima, although my father already knew of the case."

"Your Father?"

"Mr. James Wiseman, my Father, is the senior partner here."

"I see. Her Ladyship seemed to think I'm to be provided for."

"You most certainly are, Mrs. McAlister, and not before time. Ah, here's my father now." Waiting till the older man had closed the door, the son made the introductions.

"So, how far have you got with Mrs. McAlister?"

"Just beginning really, sir, I'll leave you to it if you like."

"Not at all, my boy. I won't be around forever and young Mrs McAlister here is going to need advice for many years." Turning to the young woman he addressed her. "Always deal with someone you know and can trust, Mrs. McAlister. Never forget that, now you're a woman of some wealth."

Cate stared at the two men, but her mind just kept hearing the words over and over again. 'Woman of some wealth', 'woman of some wealth!' How could that be? From tinker girl to—no it couldn't be! "A woman of some wealth? Surely that can't be right sir? Not me?"

Seeing how shaken she looked, the lawyer allowed her a few moments before he continued. "Indeed it is. On the death of your late husband you were to keep your marital home and that came provided with an annuity, so that you and your children would be secure. McAlister's children by his first marriage were granted the disposal of his law practice and any personal mementoes from the family home, with your approval, together with a substantial sum of money apiece."

"But I thought the house would be theirs, sir."

"Ordinarily, that's what would have happened. I believe Mr. McAlister knew that neither the son nor the daughter liked the house and so he made cash arrangements instead. You see, his partner— you did know his partner, did you not?"

"I knew of him." That's all she was prepared to admit for now. "Did he deal with the legal matters after my husband died?" Cate knew he had—he and Caroline conniving to outwit her and steal her daughter. Just how much did this lawyer know, and would he be any better than the hateful Hardy?

"Yes and no. Mr. Ian McAlister dealt with the practice, which was wound up very quickly, on account of his desire to emigrate. The partner expedited the will for that same reason. The trouble was that you'd disappeared. No one knew whether you were dead or alive so everything couldn't be settled till your whereabouts, or if necessary your death, could be proved. I only heard of the confusion when I employed a young clerk who knew you and used to work for your husband up until his death. Unfortunately, on Mr. McAlister's death the young man in question was dismissed. Apparently the partner had never liked him."

"You don't mean Solly, do you, sir? He works for you? I thought I'd lost him too." Cate couldn't believe all this. It was all just too good. Was she really going to be as lucky as this, all because Lady Jemima had given her a helping hand? It was hard to believe. "Does he work for you? Is he here? Can I see him? I thought I'd lost touch with him."

"What a lot of questions! He does work here, but I'm afraid he's out at the moment delivering papers to the court."

"Oh. But you do know where he lives? I could go and see him?"

"Mrs. McAlister, let me give you some advice. You're now a woman of independent means, but should you marry again, your possessions would automatically become your husband's, and that could lead to a reversal of fortune for you. Now Solly's a good clerk, a conscientious worker, but you can't be too careful, so I would advise...."

"Oh would you? Well let me tell you that poor lad would no more cause me nor any other body a jot of harm. Shame on you for thinking that!" These people were all the same. If you were poor you were dishonest, not to be trusted. As if you didn't know better. How dare they!

"Come now, Mrs. McAlister, you misjudge me." This new client of his was intriguing.

"I'd not meant to be rude sir, but you'll find no one more trustworthy than Solly. My husband always spoke highly of him."

"No offence taken, my dear, but, if you'd let me finish, I was going to say but others are not always so. You have, in fact, your friend Solly, to thank for my own interest in the case."

"Why's that, sir?"

Although your husband obviously kept the original will in his own office. I believe he'd reservations, both about his family and his partner. I take it that you didn't get on too well with the family."

"Indeed I did not, sir, through no fault of my own."

"Of that I'm sure." The lad had said as much. "The thing was, that when Solly made enquiries about you, he was told the entire family had emigrated to America and the house was to be kept in case they returned."

"But I hadn't."

"We know that now. Let me put the situation clearly to you. On your disappearance, having been assured you'd left, Solly was troubled. You see, your late husband had entrusted him with an envelope and the instruction that should your husband predecease you, and you had any trouble with the family, he was to give the envelope to yourself or another lawyer, not the partner." Rising, he perched on the edge of his desk and continued. "Solly was adamant in his belief that you would not have left your friends without saying goodbye. Unfortunately, when he tried to contact…"

"Lizzie and Maggie? But they weren't there either."

"Exactly."

"So how did you know, then? About me, I mean, Mr. Wiseman?"

"Pure coincidence, Mrs. McAlister. Some time later Solly came to me looking for a position. I employed him and he settled into the practice. One day he asked my advice about the envelope and explained the circumstances. I thought nothing of it, assuring him that if you were indeed in America, you would presumably return one day, and so I put it in the office safe. I let it rest there until Lady Jemima's lawyer came looking for Solly and explained that you were not only not in America but also in straitened circumstances. That was when we opened the envelope."

"So the house has not been sold?"

"That's correct. I imagine the plan was for the house and your legacy to be left dormant. They had no immediate need of it and, after the correct length of time, you would be presumed dead and your estate would revert to them. Of course they did hold an ace."

"An ace, sir?"

"Your daughter. Should they be pursued, I believe their defence would be that you'd abandoned your daughter and, as the next of kin, they'd undertaken her welfare. The injustice as far as your inheritance went was one of omission."

"You mean they didn't actually steal it from me. Just forgot to give it to me?"

"Exactly so. It was all arranged very neatly, and you made life easy for them by disappearing."

"So what do I do now?"

"I've arranged for you to stay in a discreet boarding house near by. Go away and think about what I've told you and about your future."

"My future?"

"Yes. It is best to have some ideas as to what you will do now your circumstances have changed. Think about it overnight. Come and see me the same time tomorrow, and Solly will be here, so you may wish to lunch with him and catch up with all his doings. I hope you'll be pleasantly surprised. Good day, Mrs McAlister."

Having finished her pleasant meal Cate left the dining room of her lodgings, meeting the lady of the house as she did so.

"I do hope everything was to your taste, Madam. We like to take particular care of Mr. Wiseman's clients."

"Yes, it was delicious. Thank you."

"Breakfast at nine then, Madam. Would you like a morning call?"

"That is kind of you, but I'm a naturally early riser, thank you."

'Madam' this and 'Madam' that—the whole thing was just so unreal for someone who, forty-eight hours ago, was hauling peat in an overstuffed creel. Madam might not be quite up to standard, though, when she appeared in her one and only outfit for a second day running. As she made her way to the bedroom, Cate tried to put the facts she'd learned earlier in some kind of order. She now had Malcolm's house to do with as she wished and some money. She hadn't quite liked to ask just how much. It seemed so grasping, somehow, but hopefully it would be enough to pay for her night's lodgings.

As she entered the office the next morning, there was Solly, writing away at a desk. As he heard her come in he jumped up. "Cate! I mean Mrs. McAlister. I thought you were dead!"

"Solly, dear Solly! Oh. Oh, Solly, I thought I'd lost you too."

"Me? Never—I'll always be in some lawyer's office."

Coming out to greet her, the lawyer surveyed the scene. So that's how things stood between them—the boy smitten and she just revelling in finding a lost friend. No, the fascinating widow would have no trouble with the timid clerk. Her instinct had been much truer than his. Solly was no threat. No threat whatsoever.

"Good morning, Mrs. McAlister. I trust you were comfortable last night."

"They looked after me well, thank you, but what about their payment?"

"For the lodgings, you mean? No need to worry about that. It will all be added to your account and will be settled when you've made some decisions."

"I haven't made any yet."

"Probably for the best not to decide too hastily over anything. Perhaps you should confer with Her Ladyship."

"I don't think so, she's done more than enough for me and I know just what she'd say."

"Do you now?"

Cate smiled and for a moment became her Ladyship. "Good God, girl, you've got your independence. Now use it! Damned silly to sit around and waste it, don't you know." Cate's mimicry had surprised her audience and for a moment she wondered if she'd gone too far. "She really does sound like that and I didn't mean to be rude or anything."

"Of course you didn't. It was just that, for a moment there, you did sound as I imagine her Ladyship would. Quite a talent that, very amusing! Do come through. You can catch up with this young man later." Once they were seated he continued. "The most pressing thing is the house. Do you think you'd like to live there again?"

"No. That's the first decision I'll make. However there are some pieces of furniture I would like but it's difficult."

"Difficult?"

"Yes, furniture without a house is a bit silly, isn't it?"

"I see what you mean. Suppose you take Solly, and go over the house this morning and put a chalk mark on the pieces you want. Then I'll arrange storage for them and the rest can be sold with the house."

"That would be kind of you, sir."

"Come now, you'll have to get used to knowing you can ask for a great many things to be done for you. I suggest you stay here for a few more days and we'll gradually go over all the details before you finally leave."

When they'd finished in the office, Solly led the way to the house. As they walked, Cate blurted out the first thing she could think of. "Solly, I've an address for Maggie and Lizzie. Could you take me there?"

"Where is it?"

"In Dunoon. Is that difficult?"

"It is a little. It's quite a long way and I'd need time off work. He's already given me the rest of today off."

"Oh, Solly, please. Ask Mr, Wiseman for me when you go back and see what he says, will you?"

"Yes, but first we have to see to the furniture. Here we are now."

Cate shivered as she looked round the damp and musty hallway. It seemed so odd without her family, Cook and Ada. She'd no wish to be here without McAlister and her precious baby daughter. No. She must leave immediately. Her last horrid memories of it must remain buried so they never clouded the happy ones she'd had with McAlister.

"You know, Solly, I don't want this house, but I think I'd like to have all the contents from the study. Maybe one day I'll have a bigger house and then his things will be there for me. I'll see what Mr. Wiseman says tomorrow." Thinking of the lawyer, Cate turned to her friend. "Do you trust him, Solly? Like you did my husband?"

"He's the old school kind of lawyer, just like Mr.McAlister. You know, worrying about the poorer people getting their rights. Honest and true. Not like that Mr. Hardy."

"That's alright then. I'll leave the decisions for a bit, if I can trust him. Mind, you could keep an eye out for me, even though you're not studying to be...."

"But I am, Cate, I mean Mrs...."

"'Cate' will do fine. You really are doing the book learning then?"

"Yes. Mr. McAlister left me an allowance so's I could go to night school. Mr. Wiseman has arranged it. I get some time off in the day and I'll do the rest at night."

"Solly, I'm so pleased. Seems like we're all indebted to McAlister in some way or another. Right, now for our lunch and then we'll see about Dunoon."

19

Cate leant over the rail and watched the excited passengers board the paddle steamer: a human wave surging up the gangway, men struggling with baggage, women desperately trying to keep the family in one group, children, heedless of their parents, unable to temper their enthusiasm, darting all over the place. This was the annual summer exodus from the everyday drudgery of work and school. The one holiday of the year! Like them, Cate could barely hide her pleasure. She was actually going sailing down the Clyde. Many times in Glasgow she'd heard people speak of going 'doon the waater', and here she was doing just that. It was grand that Mr. Wiseman had let Solly come with her. Even better was the fact that Maggie and Lizzie would be at the other end.

"Are you enjoying it, Cate?" Reunited with her, he was ecstatic.

"Solly, so much has happened since I came down that it's like a dream. Truly it is, and I'm fair enjoying it all. Though part of me thinks, like all dreams, it'll disappear and it'll be back to the shore gathering seaweed."

"Why gather seaweed?"

"It's a harvest. You can eat it, make face cream out of it and long ago it was burnt and the ashes used in the making of china…."

"Cate, surely not. Seaweed?"

"Of course. I grant you it doesn't taste like our lunch yesterday, but if you're hungry—well, it's better than starving.

"I don't like the sound of that! Surely you won't need to eat seaweed now?"

"I suppose not." Cate took a moment to think how the changes would affect her. Good news though it was, it could make village life difficult.

"You don't seem very sure."

"It's going to be difficult, I think, Solly."

"Cate, you'll have enough money to choose what you want to eat."

"I understand that. I've just thought—well—you see I've spent months trying to make a home for Rhoddy and myself in a small poor community. I'm beginning to be accepted in the village. They won't take kindly to me abandoning the crofter ways. Getting too grand for them."

"Perhaps you should stay in Glasgow then, Cate." He brightened at the thought.

"No, Solly, I'm quite sure. Whatever it is I do now, it won't be here. I want to make a fresh start. Oh look! Are we there?"

"Yes. We get off here." His shoulders slumped.

"Come on, Solly. Don't look so sad. We still have to sail back again. I didn't know you liked boats so much. Mind you, the fresh air is good for those poor lungs of yours—though they do sound better now."

"That's because I've moved to better lodgings, and I suppose I take more care now I don't have Mother to look after." Sometimes Cate didn't really see him at all.

As they made their way to the town, Cate began to feel anxious. Taking Solly's arm for comfort, she missed the nervous trembling and the happy look on his face. "Solly, suddenly I'm so nervous."

"I can't believe that of you."

"Well I am. They think I ran off and left them. I'll not be very welcome."

"But you thought we'd all abandoned you, didn't you?"

"Yes. I was pretty mad at the lot of you and yet somehow I should have known better. I thought the same of some other folk, back in Kevinishe, that I had an affection for, and I was wrong there too."

"Mistakes are made with people all the time, Cate. It was hardly your fault."

"Perhaps, but somehow I think Maggie never really trusted me, while Lizzie trusted me too much. They were hurt and now they might not want to know me."

"We'll just have to hope they don't send us straight back to the boat then. Do you want to get them anything, a present perhaps?"

"I thought about that. Have we money?"

"Yes, Mr. Wiseman has given me expenses for the day."

"No. Perhaps we'd better not get anything. I don't want to buy my way back into their lives."

"I'll just ask for directions in the shop over there Cate. Have you the address?"

Waiting for Solly's return, her nerves increased. This was so important to her, and it could easily go wrong. Armed with the directions, they made their way to the house. "You knock, Solly. My hand's shaking."

The man who answered the door was huge, intimidating.

"Oh. Is Maggie or Lizzie here?"

"Who's wantin' them?" He asked.

Before Cate could answer, a voice called out.

"Who is it Bert? What do they want?" Maggie's questions reached them before she did.

"Maggie, it's me, Cate." The silence that followed seemed endless and Cate felt it said all the things she'd feared.

"What are you doing here? What do you want?"

"Oh Maggie, it's so good to see you again! And before you say it, I never left you behind and I never went to America."

"But we were told you'd taken the bairns and gone with them. Never even let Lizzie say goodbye to Rhoddy!"

"How could you believe that, Maggie? You knew they hated me."

"Well it wasn't the first time you'd run without coming to us."

"CATE! CATE!" The cries exploded down the street.

Lizzie hurried towards them, face alight, hope flooding through it. Maggie stood defeated. Bert took control.

"You'd better come in off the street. The noise Lizzie's making would waken those at the bottom of the sea, never mind the neighbours. I'm Maggie's husband, Bert Green."

With the two girls hugging, talking, giggling all at once, and Bert in conversation with Solly, Maggie made the tea. She could not doubt the true affection the two girls had for one another but her motherly instincts could not be smothered.

"Now then, find seats where you can. It'll no be what you're used to, I daresay." She couldn't keep the frostiness out of her voice, despite Bert's puzzled look.

"Maggie this is a palace compared to the way I've lived this past year or so!"

"Tell us about it, Cate. You aye told a fine story." Lizzie was hungry for all the details.

Her story told, right up to her reason for being in Glasgow, Cate fell silent while the others digested her words. Maggie was the first to speak.

"Aye well, you'll be set for the grand life in Glasgow now."

Looking at the older woman, Cate sensed that she was not prepared to allow her back into their lives. "You still don't believe me, Maggie, do you? In fact you've never really understood just how connected to you both I am." Cate knew the reason for Maggie's defensive attitude. Truth to tell, it had always been there, just under the surface.

"Well you ran, Cate, not us."

"But you did too, Maggie! I've just told you. The new woman— small, black hair, young baby— said your place came up very quickly and she was lucky to get it."

"How do you know that?"

"Because I came to you for help."

"You did not! We heard he was dead and went to you, but the house was all locked up."

Bert understood little, but he'd had enough of the wrangling.

"Woman, have you no been listening'? She's just told us she passed out and was in the Infirmary. Did you look for her there? So you canna blame her for that now! I ken fine you're for protecting your bairn here."

"Bert, I'm full grown an well you know it," Lizzie remonstrated.

"Aye, aye, Lizzie, but to your mammy you'll always be her bairn. Thing is, Maggie, you're trying to protect Lizzie here, but that one's bairn was taken away. Think about that before you put blame her way."

"Bert you don't understand...."

As the others bickered, Cate knew why Maggie was so defensive. After all they were settled here. But then she didn't want to upset anyone. She just still thought of the two women as family. The only one she'd ever really had. She couldn't be in Glasgow and not come to find them, once she knew where they were! She broke into the ongoing argument.

"Maggie since I'm not welcome, I'll leave. But it saddens me, for I'll miss you in my life. Solly, are you ready?" She had to get out of the house before tears overcame her. Somehow she made it to the door, Solly and Lizzie with her.

"Maggie," Bert shook his wife's shoulders. "Listen now. Be quick. You've but minutes to decide. Let her walk away, an Lizzie will never forgive you. Put your thoughts aside and be brave, but do it now or it'll be too late. Yon red-headed lass'll no come again."

"I canna do it, Bert, I just canna."

"You're wrong, Maggie. I tell you you're as wrong as can be, and you'll end up losing Lizzie. I can see it now."

At the door, Cate tried to comfort the weeping girl. "Lizzie, don't cry. Please don't cry. Maggie's angry, that's all. It was a shock me turning up, and it's you she's thinking of."

"But to have you here and then lose you. I canna bear it."

"Silly thing. You don't have to. See, I have your address here and, though I'm no letter writer, I'll try. You will write, won't you Lizzie?"

"Aye I'll write, but it'll no be the same as seeing you."

"So who says you won't see me? You've an uncle lives close by me. Come and see him."

"I couldna do that. Mammy'd never let me, Cate."

"Perhaps. But I always said we'd be together and I meant it. You truly are my family and I need you as much as you need me."

"But, my Mammy...."

"Leave it for now, Lizzie. She's angry. I'm angry with her for not trusting me, but I can see it's your welfare she's thinking about. Don't cross her, Lizzie. I'll not lose you again."

"There's the hooter from the boat, Cate. If we want to catch this one, we must go. Lizzie, would Maggie let me come down to see you?"

"I don't see why not, Solly. She's no angry with you."

"Well there you are then. We'll all keep in touch with one another somehow. Friends for keeps, here's our hands on it." Cheered by their hand clasping they waved goodbye to Lizzie.

Maggie would have liked to know just what was being said at the door, but her pride made her wait for Lizzie's return. "You were gone a while. I was worried about you, Lizzie."

"Why, Mammy? Did you think I'd run off with them? Well, if they'd asked me I would've. Cate says she understands you and we mustn't upset you. Fine, but whit aboot what I want, whit aboot upsetting me? You never even asked if I wanted to see her again? She was the best thing that ever happened to me. She's my only friend and you've just shut her out of my life. She may understand you, but I dinna." With that Lizzie left to seek the shelter of her room.

"Bert! Oh Bert! She's never spoken to me like that, ever."

"I warned you, Maggie. You werna fair to that other lass. Your bairn has just told you off and gone to bed without her supper, but you'll see her in the morning. Think what that Cate must still be going through. Like as not she'll never, ever see her wee lass again. Is it any wonder she was off her head at that funeral? Ach—I'm away to the allotment. I could do with some better air, just now."

"Bert...?" Maggie couldn't believe the two people closest to her had just abandoned her. She'd had to protect Lizzie. Didn't they see that? Well, Cate was gone. Lizzie would come round and, more than likely, they'd not see Cate again. But had she been right?

Wullie the Post was loading mailbags, seed potatoes, and a crate with two hens into the post bus as Cate got off the train.

"You'll have grand company on the journey, Cate."

"At least they're caged. No like Johnnie's ram on the way here. Are you actually allowed to do that?"

"Do what now?"

"I see—I imagined the ram, did I?"

"A postman has to keep his looks smart. Surely you know that?"

"I'm not at all sure where this conversation's going."

"It's going to be an explanation. Johnnie cuts the hair of the village. No ram to market, no hair cut. Sure and what the post doesna see never hurts them. And didn't I clean the bus out real well after? Now then, are we right?"

"As right as we'll ever be, I suspect, Wullie."

Despite the squawking of the hens, Cate slept fitfully, drained by all that had happened in Dunoon. She jolted awake as Wullie applied the brakes with undue force.

"Here's Fisher waiting for you. You'll be walking the last wee bit home then?"

"Thank you, Wullie. Who're the hens for?"

"Morag's mother. They've eaten theirs as they're no laying."

Fisher waited till he'd heard all about Maggie, Lizzie, and Solly. Cate would be upset at his news, angry at not being in Kevinishe when it happened. Now she'd finished her tales; he told her about MacNishe's death.

"Fisher, but Wullie never said! So that's why you came to meet the bus. Not MacNishe! I wronged him in my thoughts for so long, and there's no time left now to make amends. Now he too is gone.

"It comes to us all Cate."

"I should've been here, Fisher. I needed to say so much to make up for the hurt I caused him. I've only been away a week."

"Well and didn't it take him five minutes to go. Supposing you'd been in the Black House, you'd still not have been up there."

"But I—well, I would—after all MacNishe had done for me."

MacNishe understood. He said the Cailleach had told him everything. Set the whole story straight and told me to tell you how ashamed he was of Bruce's behaviour, and to look after his grandson.

"You and I would never have told him."

"True enough. Now get you to your bed. Rhoddy's with Kirsty, for I've things to see to. I've laid himself out in the gun-room, so I'll go with you early in the morning to make your peace with him. The funeral is later and the wake to be in the distillery barn as usual."

"I can go by myself if you've things to do, Fisher."

"That you won't. He's back."

"Who's back? Not? No! Not Bruce, I can't, Fisher, I just can't!"

"You will, Cate. It had to be sometime."

"How will I manage it? Tell me that."

"Like you always did before. Get the better of him."

"But I didn't, Fisher! Have you forgotten Rhoddy?"

"There's no forgetting Rhoddy. Just remember Bruce had to surprise and overcome you to do what he did. You're a grown woman now, respectable widow at that. There'll be no more knocking you out or raising a hand to you. I'll see to that. Deal with him and then it'll be over."

As she made her way home, every step she took reminded her of those two old people—The Calliach and MacNishe. Then there was Bruce! Settling into the Black House again, it was all she could think of. What an exchange, the old Laird for the new! As Fisher said, it had to happen. She'd known that, but to have him near again! It was too much, on top of the old man's death. Tired though she was, there would be precious little sleep for her. A walk on the shore might help. Wrapping herself in her old shawl, Cate caught sight of the green Glasgow outfit now hanging proudly on the wall. Somehow the shawl she was now wearing and the fashionable outfit were a problem—very different lifestyles that somehow had to be welded into a whole, to make a future that Bruce would not be able to shatter.

Fisher was waiting for her on the doorstep of Kevinishe House next morning.

"Is he abroad then?"

"No him, Cate. He's the drink taken and still abed."

"So he hasn't changed?"

278

"The changes will be here, Cate, in the village and the distillery, no in him. That one will always be black-hearted, with his drinking, bullying, gambling and cruelty to women."

"The village, the distillery—he'll not do right by them, will he, Fisher?"

"Not him. The only thing he's ever bothered about is himself. Never came near the place unless he was in debt. How many times did I telegraph him the Laird was fading? He just sat in Edinburgh and waited for the black-banded telegram."

"It's the third death in the big house."

"Aye, the villagers have it on their lips. We've had our just ration of three. There'll be a few ailing village souls feeling the better for knowing they're no next in line for the hereafter any more. Now, come you in. He's in the gunroom. I'll wait here."

As she stood by the side of the coffin, all she could think of was the day long ago when he'd had the heart attack there, in that very room, and she'd run for help. How much she'd learnt from him since that day—her riding, reading, figuring, history, pride in herself and the joy of companionship. How could she ever have doubted him? How sorry she was now that Bruce's evil deed and her abrupt departure had saddened MacNishe. It was a wrong she'd have to right somehow, although sadly he'd never know it. But right it she would, and pay Bruce back for the misery he'd caused. A knock reminded her she needed to leave.

"I hear him stirring. You'd best face up to him outside." They'd barely cleared the front door when they heard his footsteps.

"Well, well, well, if it isn't the little tinker brat all grown up. Come to pay your respects to the new Laird have you?" Bruce smiled at his wit.

"My condolences on your grandfather's death. He was a good Laird and a kind and faithful friend. He'll be sorely missed. Thank you for letting me see him, Fisher. I'm sorry I was unable to bid him farewell before he died. Good day to you both." Cate resisted the urge to run. She would not give him the satisfaction of knowing how the sight of him upset her.

"Fisher, what the hell has made her so smart all of a sudden? Didn't even wait to let me speak. What's she doing back here anyway? Squatting with you is she?"

Fisher made no comment and followed Cate, leaving Bruce on the doorstep.

No Laird could hold a community together, knowing little of it and always being absent.

Later, at the funeral, sitting well away from Bruce and the other dignitaries, Fisher wondered how long the visiting preacher was going to babble on. The man knew little of MacNishe, and his words were worthless. Bruce's obligatory praise had been brief and palpably insincere when it had been his turn to speak. It wouldn't do. Not for such as MacNishe. When the old fool of a preacher drew to a close, Fisher stood up amid the congregation. He knew it would infuriate Bruce, but it had to be done, and as Bruce didn't have the Gaelic, the eulogy could include not only praise for MacNishe, but also a veiled warning of change in the future.

Although she understood little of the speech, Cate was moved by the sincerity of Fisher's speech, and aware of the affection for him that flowed through the audience. This man had risen to the occasion and given the people what they really needed, and what MacNishe deserved.

Once the wake was over, the village would soon find out what Bruce had in store for them. Cate had told no one of her good fortune, because the less Bruce knew the better. He'd never been overly bright and so she must now outthink him, even outsmart him. Her time had come. 'The filthy tinker brat' had money at her disposal and powerful and loyal friends. He would not get the opportunity to destroy her life again.

"Well, well, Cate did you ever see such a turnout? Just look at all those kilted men. They've come from all over for MacNishe. Mind I heard there were words between Fisher and the new Laird, for the wake being here, in the distillery barn, what with the number of important people and all that. They say they'll just stay for a bit and then away to the Big House."

"Since he wasn't here to see to the arrangements, it's a good job Fisher did, Kirsty. Shhht. Our new Laird is going to say something."

"I must thank you all for coming. My grandfather would have appreciated that. Now, before I take the important guests to Kevinishe House."

"See there now, that's put us in our place, Cate."

"Shhht, Kirsty."

"As the new Laird of Kevinishe I am now responsible for the running of the estate."

"May the good Lord help us then Murdo!" Donald Uig whispered.

"It is therefore my responsibility to make sure it pays its way. I'm happy to say the old days are over. I shall review all existing housing and work details and I shall implement any decisions quickly. Fisher will, of course, continue running the distillery."

"Well he couldna bloody run it without him now could he Donald Uig?" Murdo snorted.

"No talking at the back there! This is important, so please listen carefully. My grandfather and father saw to the day-to-day running of the estate. In the vacuum that has existed since first my father's sudden death and subsequently my grandfather's ill health and death last week, Fisher has overseen the estate and the distillery. This will no longer be the case. I have already appointed a factor for the estate. He'll be joining us shortly. It is important that you all understand that from now on his word will be law."

"Excuse me, sir? Will he be a Highland man then?" Murdo asked.

"No. He's English."

"Dear Lord, Murdo, has he no sense?" Donald Uig whispered, amid the shuffling that the word 'English' had caused.

"To continue. All the workers and villagers are to remain here for their wake. Myself, the important guests and the lawyers will toast my grandfather at the house, as is customary, before the will is read. Shall we go, gentlemen?"

"Excuse me, sir." The lawyer knew things were going to be difficult when he informed this bumptious young man of his grandfather's wishes. "My instructions are to conduct all the business here, in the old barn."

" 'MacNishe', is the correct address for the Laird. Furthermore, you're quite mistaken about the will."

"I don't think you quite understand." The lawyer replied firmly.

"I understand you're here to read the will and that will be done in Kevinishe House, just as my father's was."

"Granted that has been the normal procedure in past generations, but I am instructed by your late grandfather to assemble the population of the estate in its entirety so they may hear the will."

"Don't be ridiculous. As if I want these people knowing my most intimate affairs! Out of the question."

"Then, sir, you only have one alternative."

"How dare you presume to give me, the Laird of Kevinishe, an alternative."

The Lawyer squared his shoulders and continued. "You give me no choice, sir. Should you not wish to stay here, you may proceed to the House and wait there until I have read the will here first."

"How dare you! I choose what I want. I'm MacNishe now. This all belongs to me. What I say goes! To the House immediately and then, when you've read the will, you are dismissed. Your presumptuous behaviour is intolerable!"

"We're only obeying our client's orders. You may stay or go, sir, but I must read the late MacNishe's will in front of these people. He also requested I have my companion here, from an independent firm, to verify what I am about to read. I'll take the floor if I may. Can someone find two seats and a small table? Thank you." Moving to the front of the room, the legal men began to arrange their papers, leaving Bruce no option but to resume his seat.

"Look, behind Cate. Fisher doesn't look overly pleased at all the commotion. I don't blame him. It's no seemly. No with the old man just underground."

" Quiet now, Kirsty. We need to know what all the fuss is about." Somehow Cate knew it was bad news. Then the cold was there and a vision held her. *Through a grey mist she saw Bruce, screaming and shouting, threatening Fisher. Blows were struck and she knew Fisher was in danger. Then the mist hid them and the cold receded.* Cate turned hurriedly to check. He was there though, Fisher, safe at the back of the room as Kirsty had said. Bruce was still on the platform with the lawyers. She needed to think about this, but she had to hear what was being said. The lawyer had begun to speak.

"Before I begin the legal duties I would like to tell you that MacNishe was one of the most honourable men I have ever had the good fortune to serve. You have lost a truly noble man in the correct sense of the word and I share your sorrow at his death. The words I am about to read, I want you to imagine that he is speaking. He was most insistent on that point. 'They're my people and they served me well. Now I must do the same for them, although what I have to do pains me.' Those were his words. Remember that as I read his last will and testament."

Picking the sheaf of papers up, the lawyer began reading.

'I, Robert William Donald Craig MacNishe, Laird of Kevinishe, state that this is my last will and testament and hereby authorise the law firm of Scott, Bennett and Scott to see that my wishes herein are carried out. I will be succeeded at Kevinishe House by my grandson, Bruce Robert Rhoderick MacNishe, who will become Laird of Kevinishe and receive my personal wealth and estate, with the exception of Kevinishe Distillery and it's contents, these including whiskies laid down and in production.'

"This is nonsense!" Bruce jumped to his feet. "How can my estate run without the distillery? You're mistaken, or the old fool was demented. I'll challenge this."

"If I may continue, sir—'along with the houses tied to the estate which are required for distillery workers.' "

"But that's the majority of them, you numbskull!" Bruce shouted.

"Name-calling will get us nowhere, sir. Please allow me to carry on." He waited for Bruce to take his seat again. There are several small bequests, some added at a later date, and I have had letters printed for the recipients."

"What are they, Cate? We're surely no getting recipes for cakes here?"

"Kirsty, please, it means they're for the people who're getting a wee something from the old Laird. Shhhst now. Keep her quiet, Morag."

A few snorts of amusement were heard from those close to Kirsty, but they were silenced by a long look from the lawyer, before he continued.

"This next paragraph was of vital importance to MacNishe. He felt a great wrong had been done and wished to go to his grave having righted it. These are his words. 'Throughout my life I have shared most of it in close companionship with Cameron Donald Macrae. He has been my companion, my stillman, my soul mate indeed, and it is time the truth be told.' "

"Who's he blethering about now, Cate?"

"Kirsty!"

The lawyer once again waited for silence before speaking.

"Cameron Donald Macrae, known since boyhood as 'Fisher', is my half-brother and I now leave the distillery and its environs to the rightful heir. He more than anyone is the person to continue the work we both began all those years ago and I leave it in the best pair of hands a man has ever known. God bless you, Fisher, and I'll be waiting on the other side for you when your work is done.' "

The lawyer waited until the excited whispering subsided before he resumed. "That ladies and gentlemen is the will of the late said MacNishe. All that remains is for me to ask my colleague to confirm the legality of the will."

At this the other man rose and spoke. "Ladies and gentlemen, after the death of his only son, I was called to a meeting with the late MacNishe and his lawyers, one of whom stands before you. Although unusual, MacNishe was most anxious that the will and his own sanity be verified, as he expected the contents would prove unpopular. I have here a signed affidavit from his doctor and two mental health specialists stating that when he made this will, the said MacNishe was in perfect health and sound of mind. The veracity of the will should therefore not be doubted. As a member of the MacNishe family, Mr. Macrae is fully entitled to his bequest and MacNishe stated that the said Mr. Macrae was the only valid option for the success of the distillery and his village."

"It bloody well isn't the only option," Bruce screamed, waving his fist at Fisher. "You'll never have Kevinishe Distillery, Fisher, never! As for the rest of you, your houses are all mine! Mine, do you hear? I'll do what I want with them. And you two," Bruce turned on the lawyers, "don't try to bamboozle me with your legal garbage. Oh yes, I assure you, we'll meet in court. I'll make you penniless for dereliction of duty, aiding and abetting a stupid, spiteful old man who'd lived too long."

The assembled crowd parted as their new Laird, puce in face, stormed out of the barn. The important guests following, relishing the thought that, after the wining and dining, they could hurry back to their various homes to spread the startling news. The legal men approached Fisher, shook him by the hand, delivered the letters they'd mentioned to him and took their leave. For a moment there was not a sound from those remaining in the barn. Then a whisper was heard and soon the whispers grew and grew until the noise was deafening. Cate saw Fisher slip away and quickly followed him, guessing he'd make for the distillery.

She found him in the office. "Did you know before, Fisher?"

"About the will? Not a word, believe me, Cate."

"And the other?"

"Yes and no. Oh, there was the house, given to my mother. There was my education with MacNishe and Callumn. I just never thought about it really. When his father died MacNishe moved into Kevinishe House and, as we needed to work all hours, he made me move into the distillery house he and Margaret had shared. I thought it would be tied like all the rest."

"Can you do it, Fisher? Will Bruce let you?"

"If I know anything about MacNishe, the will should stand. His own father was feckless and a drunk. Nearly ruined us all. After what we went through trying to save everything, MacNishe would have wished a repeat of that on no one. Och, he knew fine Bruce was useless. Now if Rab had lived…."

"I can see that."

"There are a couple of problems though, Cate."

"Bruce?"

"Aye, he's a big enough one. No, it's no that.

"What is it then?"

"Well the first one is who's to do the figuring. The Laird or Rab always handled that side of things. I know everything about running the place. Truth is I've been doing it for years, but I'm a distillery man, no an accountant."

"And the second one?"

"I'm no rightly sure just how profitable the distillery is. Things have been let slide these past few years with Rab's death and then MacNishe losing interest through ill health. I don't have the resources the Laird had."

"I see that, but why don't you try the lawyers? They seemed friendly and they weren't overly impressed with Bruce. I'm sure they'd help."

"Well, we'll soon see, Cate. Bruce has laid down his intentions. He'll take every penny he can out of the estate and put no effort in, you'll see. It's a black day for Kevinishe today and all those in it. That, by the way includes you. Still, he can't put you out of the Black House, though he doesn't know that yet."

"Yes, but it'll make him mad when he finds out."

The thought was not a pleasant one for either of them to have to consider.

"I'll have to away and get Rhoddy. We've all a lot of thinking to do about this day and most of it'll not be very comforting."

"Aye, you've the right of it. Before you go one of these is for you." Sifting through the lawyer's letters he handed Cate the one with her name on it. I'll away to see the wake through with the village and hand out these. Then I'm for a ride on the moors to see if I can clear my head of Bruce."

As she made her way home, Rhoddy scuffing his feet behind her, Cate's mind was racing. Fisher's problems were real enough and he'd need all the help he could gather, because Bruce would try to regain the distillery. Of that she was quite certain. How could she help? If the distillery needed funds, would she have enough to help Fisher? Would he accept her help? If only MacNishe hadn't died!

Having cleared their supper away and seen Rhoddy to bed, Cate sat by the fire and wondered. If they could get an accountant for the distillery, would Fisher let her work with him? Would she be capable enough to do the daily paperwork? If Fisher accepted her help, what would the men think? Women were not allowed in the distillery. No wonder those women in Manchester and London were tying themselves to railings and going to prison for women's rights. They'd moved on from peaceable means. Now they were trying more strident action because the authorities, all men of course, had taken no notice of their claims for women's rights. Women right's indeed! They'd none! Mind, in the big cities some women worked in offices. Why couldn't she? Because this was Kevinishe, that's why. In the north west of Scotland women were still kept firmly in the home and, in a closed village like Kevinishe, this was definitely the accepted practice. MacNishe had taken her to the distillery as a girl—why couldn't she go there as a woman? Because she no longer had the backing of MacNishe, that's why. Thinking of MacNishe reminded her she'd left the letter on the dresser. In the glow of the oil lamp she began to read.

Riding hard across the moor, Fisher felt the utter loneliness of losing his best friend. True he now owned the distillery, and his pride increased by knowing for certain he was a true member of the ancient MacNishe family, but he'd give all that back just to have MacNishe riding with him. The old man had forgotten no one. All his long-term workers had had their loyalty rewarded. Thinking of the letters, he wondered about Cate's. She'd no doubt tell him all about it the next time they met. Come to that, apart from news of Maggie, Lizzie and the clerk, Solly, she'd told him nothing about the Glasgow visit. Why not? Had something happened there? Would she be going back? He hoped not. Somehow, with Calumn gone, Rab, MacNishe and the Cailleach dead, Cate's presence in Kevinishe seemed necessary. Like him she'd been connected to the others. Still, it was none of his business and, there was nothing he could do about it anyway.

Cate woke, sent Rhoddy off to school and then sat, teacup in hand, staring at the Cailleach's shelves. She'd hardly slept, the spidery handwriting on MacNishe's letter, seemingly stamped on her eyes, preventing her from closing them. Even now she found it hard to believe. Her grandmother! Why had she never said? How nice it would have been to know that the old tinker woman and the Cailleach were her grandmothers, that she was neither alone, nor unloved. What a difference that would have made! Taking MacNishe's letter out of her pocket she read it again. However often she read it she couldn't quite believe all that it said. She'd take it to Fisher. He'd surely know whether the rest was possible or not. If it were true, it changed everything. She'd see Fisher tomorrow and put it to him. She could tell him about Glasgow then, and the money as well, if necessary. What if she didn't have enough money? What if he wouldn't have her near the distillery? What about the men? No, she'd better away back to Glasgow and see the lawyers first, before speaking to Fisher. No sense in making offers until she knew she could back them.

If she could, what better way to remember the Cailleach, the tinker woman, MacNishe, McAlister, and Lady Jemima? It was as if they'd all known that their help would prepare her for this. She now truly felt she belonged here and she'd save, not only her own life from Bruce's destruction, but also that of the village and distillery. After all these years she just might have found her destiny—at last, a true direction and purpose in her life.

Part   Five

The Distillery

1912

20

Only a moment seemed to have gone by since Cate had first made her way into Weir, Wiseman and Wiseman's law office on her previous visit, and yet so much had happened. Would they think she was mad? Did she have enough funds? Would the distillery, and indeed Fisher, accept her ideas? Well there would be no answers unless she went through the door. Taking a deep breath she made her way up the steps and into reception.

Cate smiled at the receptionist. Did she need an appointment? Would he see her, and more importantly would he agree to her wishes? She'd have to get used to what she could and couldn't do in situations like this. "I'd like to speak to the lawyers."

"Is it young Mr. Wiseman you'll be wanting to see?"

"Well, I'm not sure, perhaps the father because—I mean he's older and wiser. If that's not rude."

"No, no. Like a father he is. I'll check if he can see you."

After a short wait, Cate was delighted to see Solly coming towards her. He looked so different these days: shoulders straight, walk firmer, eyes hopeful. He most definitely looked a lawyer in the making.

"Cate, I never thought you'd be back so soon. How are you?" I see you're in mourning. It's not your son is it?"

"No, Solly, we've had two deaths in the village. Both people who were important to me, so it's the least I can do to show them respect."

"Of course. Mr. Wiseman Senior will see you now. Go right through."

"My dear, this is a pleasant surprise."

Once seated, Cate began. "You did say I could come and talk things over with you before I made any decisions."

"Of course, that's what we're here for. Now I hope you've thought carefully about this."

"Actually, it all happened in a moment."

"Mmmm. That doesn't sound very safe, my dear. Would you like to tell me about it?"

Cate rattled through the events in Kevinishe, trying to explain how everything had seemed to fall into place, but wondered if she was making sense to the man on the other side of the desk.

"I see." Her plans appeared too impetuous for James Wiseman.

"Do you really, sir? The village will go if the distillery goes." She must make him see that.

"And you think you can save it? Are you equipped to do that? It'll take more than capital, my dear."

"Why not, sir? I can hire the necessary help. What better way to use my husband's money? He was forever trying to help the poor in trouble, now wasn't he?"

"Yes, but he was prizing money out of rich owners, not using his own."

"I know he never charged those poorer clients for his services, so in a way it was his money."

"What you must understand, Mrs. McAlister is that simply putting money into a business doesn't automatically save it. We do not know how well the distillery was run previously. What are the books like, for instance?"

"You mean the figuring ones, sir? I've no idea. I've never seen them."

"Exactly, Mrs. McAlister. That really does worry me. "What about this man, Fisher? Surely he'd realize you'd need to see those first?"

"Well, he doesn't know what I plan to do yet."

The lawyer gave an imperceptible shake of the head.

"Mrs. McAlister, this is hardly the right way to go about things. Look here, my dear, you want to invest in a business you know nothing about and you have no idea whether your approach would even be welcome."

"It would be welcome if it saved the distillery."

"What if it's not worth saving, this distillery, Mrs. McAlister?"

"If this office was yours, sir, but you'd no money to run it, would you just let it go then?"

"Certainly not. I'd find a way somehow. After all, the firm has been in my family for generations. How could I possibly let it go? The distillery, on the other hand, is not yours, nor ever likely to be. And, even if it was, a woman simply couldn't run it. You must reconsider."

"Mr. Wiseman!" There it was again, the assumption that a woman had no place, no ability to be part of the masculine business world. Taking a deep breath, Cate forced her mouth into a sweet smile.

"Mr. Wiseman, you'd be amazed at what I can do when I set my mind to it. I'm not as simple as you seem to think."

"Now I never said…."

"No, you didn't, but I daresay you thought it. The reason I said nothing to Fisher was because I did not have all the facts to hand. Has the house been sold? How much money do I have at my disposal for immediate use, and what annual income will I continue to have?"

"I see." Opening the file on his desk he extracted a letter and passed it over to her. "That came yesterday and I suggest you accept the offer."

Glancing at it, Cate was amazed at the sum, but returned it and continued. "Then do so, Mr. Wiseman. And another thing I meant to say is that I've not told anybody I've come into some money, so, if you're thinking I'm being taken advantage of, you're wrong."

"Now that does surprise me, Mrs. McAlister. Though I did wonder when you didn't approach me for funds."

"Well, I'm approaching you now, sir. By the way, I'd like you to look after my money. Solly trusts you, so that's good enough for me.

He'd never wish harm on me, and him being in your office—I mean he could—well, you'll understand I'm sure."

James Wiseman couldn't help chuckling to himself. "Oh yes, I understand. Solly's words about me are to be trusted and he could always keep an eye on me, in case I turned crooked in my old age!"

"I didn't mean—well, right enough, he could, couldn't he!"

Cate's smiling acceptance of his little joke pleased him. He liked her openness. "So, now we understand one another clearly, what exactly do you wish me to do?"

"Would you please arrange a regular six-monthly payment for my living expenses. I'll get the distillery books for you to look at, and you can advise me on using the money from the house in the distillery. Advice mind, about amounts, legal details, that sort of thing, but the decision is already taken."

"As you wish, my dear, but I must say it does all seem a little one-sided."

"Mr. Wiseman, I see you've not really understood. I want to save the distillery and the village, but I also want to actually be involved in the business. Old MacNishe once told me I had to use my intelligence. That's exactly what I'm going to do." She appreciated his easy smile at her mocking tone. "Don't worry, I'm not going to be taken advantage of. I intend to look after my share in the distillery very carefully. They don't know it yet, but I'll be the one doing the figures. Oh yes, I'll see where my money's going alright, and I'll make it grow."

The Lawyer remained silent, overwhelmed by her enthusiasm, yet knowing that the cautious and pertinent arguments he'd produced were necessary.

She could see, by his silence, that he didn't agree. "If you're thinking of ways to say 'no', sir, I'll be sorry. I like you and I appreciate what you've done for me."

"But if I don't agree?"

"I would say I'd go elsewhere if I had to." She liked this old man. Downright ungrateful it would be to go.

"It looks, Mrs. McAlister, as if I've no choice then. You're a valued client."

"Well I'd like to be someone you believed in as well as one of those. Another thing—could you just use my name—Cate?"

"That seems a trifle informal for the office." He couldn't help smiling.

"We could always have our wee chats in the park then." She noted his smile and knew that she could work with this man. He reminded her of McAlister. Solly was right. This was a man who would look out for her.

"In the end the lawyer must always follow the client's wishes, so, Cate, let's get down to business."

This Glasgow wasn't so bad after all. Never had she seen so many crisp notes as Mr. Wiseman had taken out of his safe. He'd laughed at her fear that he kept all her funds in there, and shown her the accounts he'd set up in her name with the annuity money. The sums seemed staggering to her. Yet some inner caution made her applaud the lawyer's hesitancy and his insistence that she approach Fisher as a proper business partner in name at least. That could be tricky, mind. Men never thought of women as partners. Wives, daughters, mothers, yes, but decision-makers, never. Yet McAlister's Alice had stood by his side and helped him get on. MacNishe's Margaret had done the same. Well, she was nobody's Cate, but help Fisher and Kevinishe with the beating of Bruce she'd do anyway.

As she waited for Wullie the post, Cate's mind raced. Her next move in Kevinishe would have to be carefully done. So, it would be Fisher first then. As Wully appeared she was grateful that today's mailbags appeared to be his only delivery. This tubby man, with his ever-present grin and jovial disregard of his employers' vehicle and wishes, considered the bus was provided for the benefit of the people he served, and, if the rules didn't fit that purpose, they were ignored. Mind, he was like one of those great encyclopaedias that sat in Kevinishe House. He knew most details of the villages he served, and what he didn't know, he made it his business to find out.

"It's yourself again then, Cate. The Post could do worse than have you fetching and carrying for them, you're up and down to Glasgow that regular."

"Hardly, Wully. Only now and again."

"And isn't that what I'm after saying. Most of Kevinishe have never seen the smoke of Inverary never mind the great city itself. Visiting was it?"

"Yes, I met a great friend and made another."

"Aye, and with the looks of you and the new dress, it's no surprise. Now then, changes there've been since you've been gone, Cate."

She decided to ignore his hidden question. "What's happened now, Wully?" Since today she was the only passenger she might as well encourage him. Better to know about things, as it could make a difference to her plans. Anyway, the postman obviously intended to tell her. Gossip was like breath to Wully, essential for life.

"It's the Englishman that's arrived. A poor looking soul he is too. Speaks as though he'd got a few wee stones from the shore in his mouth and looks as though he's just stood in one of Murdo's dung heaps."

"Wullie, really!"

"It's right, Cate—the nose of him is that turned up while he looks at you. Telling me exactly how to post his letters. Me, that's been the post bus ever since it started!"

So Bruce's factor had arrived and done exactly what the villagers had expected. Treated them as he would have done those from wherever he'd come. The whole thing was just such a mistake. Like driving the bull away from a cow that was ready, it would never work.

"And the rules and regulations, Cate, you've never heard the like of it. He's for telling them how they're to go on day by day. 'Mondays we'll do this;' 'two days you'll take for that.' How can a body be working like that? Doesn't the wee fool know it rains every bloody Monday?"

"It'll take him time to get accustomed."

"Time! He'll have half the village drowned with our weather the way he's going on. And that's not all."

"He's done nothing worse surely, in this short time?"

"No him—the new Laird. He's served notices on some of the old ones. Says he needs the houses for younger workers. And where will he be getting them I wonder?"

"But he can't do that!"

"Well, Cate, he's going about it clever like. The old ones have always lived out their lives on their bittie crofts, having worked for the MacNishe as long as they were able. That young upstart's no evicting them as such."

"What exactly is he doing then?" Why couldn't the villagers just state the facts? It always had to be in this meandering fashion. She'd give the new factor only a few months before he'd be driven mad by it. Work to a timetable? Not a hope of that!

"Clever he's been. 'Not that I'm telling you to go,' he says, all polite, 'but you must see I need more workers and they'll need houses. A few grizzled old things, they've barely baccy for their pipes. Now where would they be getting money to be buying houses, I ask you?'"

So Bruce had started already. She knew, without borrowing the distillery workers when they were needed, such as harvest time, he'd be short of labour, but evicting was what it was. Bruce knew as well as anyone that money was not an option for the old and infirm. He'd vowed to get even with them all. Well, he'd begun doing exactly that. Just what had MacNishe left them with? His plan for saving the distillery and his beloved village was going wrong already. Bruce had certainly wasted no time.

As the bus cleared the final hill Cate delighted in the pretty view of the mountain, distillery and village, with a gentle sea today. Only as they coasted downward did the ragged state of the houses become apparent. The shore road showing the pockmarked ruts where the rough seas had worn it away, reflecting the reality of life in the village. On the surface all seemed as it had always been, but she was sure there was worse to come.

She should have picked up Rhoddy, but somehow she felt she needed the quiet of the evening to assemble her jumbled thoughts. Having eaten, she decided to try a walk on the moor and mountain, less likely to be seen by others than on the shore, and just as magical.

Climbing to a favourite rock, she spread her shawl, shut her eyes, and was comforted by the solitude. Her dilemma was obvious. She'd no wish to tell others of her good fortune, but unless she did, how was she to help Fisher? Obviously she must discuss it with him, and yet the village would never accept her in the distillery unless they knew why she was there. The estate cottages at risk were another problem. How much did a tied cottage cost anyway? She certainly couldn't go around buying cottages as well as helping the distillery to keep working. As Mr. Wiseman would say, 'money isn't elastic'. Hers would only stretch so far. Then there was the letter. Would MacNishe's words influence Fisher? Should she tell him? The mewling cry of an eagle, as it swooped and soared, quartering the moor, interrupted her thoughts. She watched, lost in wonder, simply glad to be back where she now knew she really belonged.

The next day, with Rhoddy playing behind the school, Cate made her way to the distillery. Using the old stone stairs outside the building to get to the office.

"So you remembered the back door then?" Fisher wondered where she'd gone this time. She was never very forthcoming about her doings away from the village. Come to that she kept most of her life to herself. Not a word about the letter from MacNishe. Was there a man in Glasgow? After all she'd grown into a comely woman.

"You're asking other questions without saying anything, Fisher?"

"How did you know?" She was sharp, no doubt about it. That's exactly what he'd been doing.

"I could see it in your eyes. I never meant not to explain, Fisher. It's just that when I came back it was all about MacNishe, the funeral and then Bruce. Far too much and too important for simple news."

"So what did the great Lady want with you?"

"Just to tell me what she'd been doing for my benefit. It was the lawyer I went to see in Glasgow who told me the proper news."

"Good news was it?" Watching her carefully he could see she was struggling with something. Was she away to the city for good? "I rather thought you might stay with us this time, Cate."

"I am staying, Fisher. After MacNishe did the house up and all, how could I not?"

"Well you seem to be here and then gone, just like the tide."

"Listen, Fisher, I went back to Glasgow to get some more information. Answers I didn't know. I want to help you."

"Help me? What do I need doing? I've all the help I need. Come to that, the last thing I need is another woman fussing over me. Haven't I too many women in my home more often than not?"

"I didn't mean at home, but here, in the distillery."

"Now what could you be doing here? Not a cobweb would we want moving! The Cailleach may have worked her magic on the moors, but we have some of our own magic here in the making of Craeg Dhu. Each ingredient, every piece of equipment, every action, even the surroundings, add a special something to the golden stuff. Change any one of those an it'll no be our own special brew, an those who drink it will notice."

"Well now, I wasn't exactly thinking of scrubbing in the distillery. I helped here when I was young. Remember I did the journal entries."

"Aye, but that was just a fancy of MacNishe's and you never set foot in the still itself. He was careful of that."

"After the funeral Fisher, you said you'd no capital."

"Well now, I said no such thing. I manage my life fine. I said the distillery would need the Laird's money. What I have, though plentiful for my own needs, would be but a drop in the sea for a business such as this."

"Fisher, I can help. My late husband left me a house and some money." There she'd said it.

So that was it! Well with a fine house in Glasgow she certainly wouldn't be staying on, especially if she had the silver to run it.

"Well, say something, Fisher."

"I'm glad for you. You've had your share of bad luck."

"Dammit, man, you don't understand. The house has been sold and I want to use the money to help keep the distillery working."

"Now why would you want to give the money away? Watching her as she prowled around, he wondered what was in her mind. "Have you no an answer then, Cate?" Mind, how tempting was that. A fine house must have sold for a tidy sum. What couldn't be achieved with money like that? But he couldn't do it. "I've never heard the like. You could as well throw the silver in the sea." He said with a smile

"Don't you dare laugh at me! I know it's not sensible just to give money, and you would have none of it anyway. Fisher, look at me. I've a child to keep and a house to run."

"Aye, and the money to do it now, and pay someone else to do the croft work. You were never that keen on it anyway, Cate."

"That's true enough. What I'm trying to say is I want something more out of life than that."

"Well now, are you never satisfied? Is it a husband you want? A woman with money should have no trouble in finding one."

"What in the name of God would I want one of those for, Fisher? I want—I need to work. Make something of my life. I don't intend to give the money away. I want to work with you. Do the figuring. Use my legacy for something worthwhile, for myself, for the distillery and the village. To get the better of Bruce and to keep faith with MacNishe, so think about that before you mock me. I'm away now an I'll wait for your answer." Slamming the door she made for the stairs wiping her angry tears. Would men never listen to her?

21

Cate watched as Rhoddy took the turn on the moor path and disappeared towards the village. With him at school, her time was her own. Trouble was she couldn't settle to her domestics. She also had some sewing to finish, but it was as if her past village life had lost whatever little interest she'd had in it. Truth was she was longing to start on the business opportunity that McAlister's money had provided. A week had gone by and still there was no word from Fisher.

Bruce's factor had been back to the cottages looking for answers, according to Kirsty, but of course the old folk, bewildered by it all, had none. The remainder of the village was quietly fuming over this and the new rules that had been introduced. She could take no action there till she'd heard from Fisher. There was no gossip of him and the distillery. Why would there be? Their jobs were not affected and they were unaware of the cash problem. Obviously he'd decided to refuse her offer, so now what? Try Glasgow and find a business opening there? If she couldn't convince Fisher, her chances of being accepted by strangers were hopeless. Wasn't that what Mr. Wiseman, the lawyer had thought of her scheme anyway?

The spring day stretched out in front of her and for once in her life she felt no urge to be doing something. It had seemed to fit so neatly and she'd been truly alive with the business idea. Now it just felt like a waste of time and energy. Even with her inheritance the future looked empty. Company was the last thing she needed and the mountain was the only place she'd be undisturbed. Glad of some kind of action, she grabbed her shawl and ran, out the door, along the twisting moor path until it petered out, squelching through the peat bogs till she reached the first rocky outcrops.

Breathless, but less miserable, she continued upwards till she came to the first of the mountain ledges. Here she settled, determined to forget her problems, and drank from the wildness around her.

Dinwoodie, the Iron Man, convalescing back in Laggan House, after his serious illness, negotiated the pools so beloved by the midges and wondered why he'd decided to walk instead of taking his usual morning ride. From being a man who considered everything most carefully, since the death of his wife he'd made some impulsive decisions and it would appear he was continuing to do so. Of course the influenza hadn't helped. He'd recovered but had lost his wife and only son within a day of one another. His daughter, Vicky, now Lady Abermarle, was his only close relative left. She'd wanted him to join them in England, but, as he couldn't stand the Lord, that had been out of the question. Somehow his other homes hadn't been right without his family, and he'd been forbidden the foundries, until his overall health improved.

Foreign parts for the sun or the Highlands for the bracing air, was the choice his doctor had insisted he make. A return to Laggan House seemed the least trouble. Not that he'd been impressed with his last visit years ago, but at least this time he'd been spared the foppish English Lord.

His feet were wet now, so he might as well continue and make for the viewpoint he'd found previously. The summer day could rival the foreign parts for sun. Bereft of rain, the blue of the sky seemed mirrored in the calm sea. The slight breeze up here would hamper the midges and the warm sun might dry his feet. If only all the days were like this, Scotland could become a tourist paradise. Regrettably, with all the mountains, wind and rain were the norm in these parts.

He'd not seen the figure as he approached and now he couldn't really turn without at least saying something.

"I do apologise for disturbing your peace. Ridiculous isn't it. A whole mountain to choose from and we both select this ledge."

"It's the best viewpoint other than the full climb."

"Ah, I fear that is beyond me. Not exactly what the doctor ordered."

"You've been ill?"

"A while back. I'm quite over it though. Still, I don't think the legs are fit for more climbing, so I'll leave you to your view." Turning to go down he was startled by her sharp words.

"Don't move."

"I beg your pardon."

"Shhht. Sit down very slowly."

"Really, I find this…"

"Over there. Fix your eye on that rounded stone to the left. Now look at the narrow ledge above. Do you see it?"

He followed her outstretched arm, but for the life of him he felt the old woman must be mad. Then he saw it"

"What is it?"

"A golden eagle. Isn't it beautiful?"

"It's certainly quite a sight, but—oh it's going."

"Yes. You didn't speak quietly enough." Turning towards him now that the eagle had flown, Cate realised her words had offended him. "I'm sorry. He was probably finished sunning himself anyway. Not your fault."

"I think you're just being polite. Which reminds me—I should have introduced myself."

"We don't stick closely to the society rules up here. They have little or no importance for the villagers. Now hospitality or lack of it would be very serious."

"I'm excused the hospitality rule as I'm still in mourning. As you would appear to be."

"Me?"

"Yes, you're wearing black too."

"Indeed not. Look." She removed the capacious shawl, revealing her blue pinafore over the grey dress, and her red hair that had fallen free with the removal of the shawl. "All the village women, young and old, use these. Only on special occasions are the best frocks brought out. Even then, if it's wet, windy or just plain cold, the shawl will be wrapped round on top of the good coat. It's mostly black that's worn, particularly by the old women."

"You're most certainly not old. Your hair—the colour reminds me…."

"It's the bane of my life."

"It's beautiful."

"Not if you were surrounded by boys as a child. They tormented the life out of me. Nearly all the village lassies have lovely shining black hair. I'd have that any day."

"Still, yours is striking. I have to admit I've only ever seen quite that colour once before—of course. It was here!" He remembered the young girl from Kevinishe.

"What was?"

"The hair. Please let me introduce myself. Daniel Dinwoodie."

"I remember you, Mr. Dinwoodie. You had the letting of Laggan House. I had an accident there when I was young. Well not there, but on the moors and your people took me back to Laggan House."

"The nursemaid. Of course, that's who you are."

"Yes, I was then."

"And now?"

"It's a long story."

"The sun is shining and I'm a good listener."

Fisher knew he ought to see Cate. It had been a week since they'd spoken. She deserved an answer, unwelcome though it would be. The whole thing was impossible. Not necessary anyway. He'd had a letter from MacNishe's lawyers. There was a good bit of money in the accounts, though Bruce had tried to draw that straight away. Good job those lawyers knew what they were about and been ready for that. Truth was he'd be no match for Bruce on his own. They both knew it. He'd trip him up somehow, and then what would happen to the glen? Now the working of the distillery was different. He'd always been the clever one there. MacNishe on the figuring and selling, with himself on the distillery floor, what a team they'd been! Still would be if only Rab had been spared. Like his father he'd been an office man through and through.

That was the trouble—a woman in the office? They'd never stand for it. Distillery men were as superstitious as seamen. Half of them were fishermen anyway in their spare time. Mad about boats, just like him. Fed their families from the sea and searched the shore for its bounty. No, a woman would never do. Who was he to get then? Mebbe he'd better get himself off to Edinburgh to talk to the lawyers, but it was here he was needed.

How much time did Fisher need to make up his mind? What was he thinking? Well, whatever it was, Cate felt she'd waited long enough. A decision had to be made. Hadn't Dinwoodie said her scheme could work, but that it would depend on how capable she was? Strange that. She who rarely confided in anyone had told him her problems. There was something about the man. He'd a vitality about him, sick though he'd been, and a strength and sureness that came from holding power. Anyway, a man who would bother about an injured nursemaid must be of the same ilk as MacNishe, McAlister and Fisher. Yes she liked him. Felt she could trust him. Well, she just had, by spilling out almost all of her life story to a total stranger.

He'd promised to keep quiet about the distillery problem and to help if he could. That was generous, though she did get the feeling that his convalescence was boring him. He was right though—no use alerting the workforce too soon. Or was it? Supposing Fisher either wouldn't agree or was unable to win the men over? What then? The timing was wrong. Already Bruce had the men disgruntled and, as for the women—well, they could be the key!

Remembering something from the hours she'd poured over history books in McAlister's study, a wild scheme began to form. She went over the idea on the way to the distillery. The men would react, but would it work? If only she could remember all the details of the story, or was it a play? She remembered it was from ancient Greece and the name was—Aristophanes. My, she could do with access to the library in Kevinishe, or McAlister's study, never mind the big ones in Glasgow. She'd been too busy of late to keep her reading up. Anyway, all the details needn't be exactly right. If it was good enough for a history book it was good enough for her, and what she couldn't remember she'd make up. She'd get Fisher to agree somehow. She would get into the whisky business, one way or another.

She'd waited long enough and so here she was, climbing the outside stairs again, ready to confront him. Knocking on the door, Cate opened it before she had time to change her mind. She'd timed her visit to perfection. Fisher sat in the office at MacNishe's desk, spread in front of him were countless pieces of paper. He'd the same frustrated frown she'd seen on Lady Jemima's forehead when confronted by the housekeeper's accounts. "Well now, you don't look too happy at all, so you don't."

"Unless you've something sensible to say, Cate, I've no time for you. Can't you see the work in front of me?"

"I see the work that needs doing. I just don't see you doing it."

"Well, you're right there. I've no time to be here while I'm needed below. I don't know where to start with this lot, the muddle they're in."

"You'd better listen to my plan then. It could help." Carefully she outlined her thoughts and tried not to notice the shake of the head and the look of disbelief on Fisher's face. She would make him see things her way. She had to.

"And you think, if the men refuse to work with you, they might be made to agree because of that? You're daft, lassie, plain daft."

"Let me try. That way we'll know for certain."

"It'll be a risk I'm no sure I can afford."

"Fisher, you can't afford to be going on the way you are. The whole village knows it's your skill that makes this place work. MacNishe always said you were the best stillman in the land. You've the experience and the nose for it. You've other skilled men throughout, but how long would they mind their tasks if you were stuck up here?"

"There're a few whose pride wouldn't let them make a bad job."

"True, Fisher, the ones who are proud of their own skilled jobs, but they're only a handful. The rest would soon become shoddy and sooner or later there would be carelessness, an accident, perhaps an explosion or a burning—a death even. Something this size needs your eyes to be everywhere and you know that, so you do."

"Aye, I do that, but I'm no so very sure."

"There's something I haven't told you." Actually there was quite a lot she hadn't told him.

"Let's hear it then."

"I've met a man…."

"God dammit, woman! This is no time to be considering courting. That's the whole thing in a cockleshell. Women's fancies! How could you even think to help here, when your mind's fixed on a man? That's it! Away an do the romancing and leave me in peace."

"Fisher—Rhoddy Cameron Macrae, or whatever your right name is—I was about to tell you I'd met a man who's a big ironworks owner. He owns foundries in London and Glasgow, men by the dozen working for him. He knows all about business, seeing as he started small but can now afford the letting at Laggan House."

"So?"

"I told you I'd been learning the figuring for some time now, but even I understand that the distillery is something else. This man is here for some time. He's offered to help with any business problems. I like him and I think we could trust him."

"You're away with the wee folk. You know as well as I do you keep your business to yourself. We might as well write out the making of Craeg Dhu and post it on shop windows in Glasgow."

"Fisher, the man is more than rich enough not to worry about robbing you. What's here would be like coppers to his silver. He'll advise me on a problem, should I take it to him. That's it. Do you know so little about me that you'd think I'd have all our affairs spread around? I've long kept my own counsel—take my letter from MacNishe for instance: I dare say you wondered about that—so why would I not keep yours?

"I'm sure if you wanted me to know you'd tell me."

"You'd have been curious all the same." Smiling as she spoke, she knew she'd guessed right. "Fisher, it was so strange. The Cailleach and the old tinker woman were my grandmothers."

"I'd thought as much. Why else would they have had the caring of you?"

For no good reason his reply made her bridle. Why indeed? If everybody had known, why hadn't someone had the gumption to tell her as a child? She would have belonged somewhere, to someone! He probably knew what else MacNishe had written, so she wouldn't bother to tell him.

"You're very quiet all of a sudden?" He could sense the change in her, but had no idea what it was about.

"I was thinking about the letter. Anyway, back to Dinwoodie. Listen to me. I could learn at his expense. Not of money, but time. I could find answers from him that I'd get nowhere else, or would take too long to understand. We've now got two sets of lawyers to work with, yours and mine. Again, we can use their knowledge. We can do it, Fisher. I feel it. Won't you try?" There, she'd done all she could. Dinwoodie had been her masterstroke. He could provide what she lacked, and she'd meant what she'd said. A great man who could still care about those well below him. Yes she trusted this foundry man, and she was right, of that she was certain.

Now back at Kevinishe, Bruce could barely believe what, Peyton, his factor, was saying. His grandfather's death had not turned out to be the good news it should have been. The title was his, but he was spending the money fast, while the problems just multiplied. Now here was this man telling him he couldn't carry out his orders.

"They just haven't got the funds. Put them out and I'll have trouble with the workers. I haven't enough as it is to run this estate properly, sir."

"I hired you to manage the men, Peyton. Surely you can do that. You're supposed to be experienced."

"I am, sir."

"Then use your experience and sort this estate out. No more of this letting a clodhopper like Fisher see to things. I'm the one who makes the decisions now."

"So I'm to evict them, sir?"

"If they won't pay up. Of course you are—those are my orders."

"There'll be real trouble, sir."

"Then use the workers to deal with it. I'm away to Edinburgh and I expect to hear you've solved this and any other problems, by the time I return, otherwise you may have one of your own."

Peyton went back to the estate office and wondered if his ambition had got the better of him. He'd managed men before and done a good job. This time he'd been tempted by the size of the estate and the number of workmen available. Yet he'd no sooner arrived than he'd found a large portion of the work force was not his, as the new Laird no longer controlled them. The remainder were surly and un-cooperative.

Now, with this eviction business, trouble was all he could see. What kind of man was this new Laird anyway? He'd been all affability at the interview in Edinburgh, but here he'd become a different person. It was as though he didn't like these villagers. Fair enough he could understand the man's disappointment in having the distillery, a good business by all accounts, left to a great uncle he'd no idea about. But his new master seemed to have no real knowledge of this glen or the people in it. The only thing the young MacNishe showed any interest in was how much he could get out of the estate. Another thing—the Laird was a drinker. No wonder the few domestic servants, the ones who hadn't already left, never looked overly content when he saw them.

As they watched the disgruntled men file out of the Old Barn, Fisher shrugged his shoulders and turned to Cate. "Aye well, you were warned. What else did you expect?"

"I don't know, Fisher. I thought when you explained you couldn't be doing your job and the office work, they'd see sense."

"They did. They're no bothered about getting an office worker, they just don't want you."

"But why? I'm here. I can do the job."

"You're a slip of a lassie in their eyes and some still think of you as a tinker, and tinkers have never been held in much regard by the villagers. Crofting women don't work in offices. Though you weren't even a true crofter, let alone being a tinker."

"The old Laird thought enough of me to trust me with his grandchild."

"Why wouldn't he, Cate? That's woman's work."

"Dammit, I should have told them their distillery and you needed me more than I needed them."

"Why didn't you?"

"And shame you in front of them? Really, Fisher, have some sense."

"There's some as would have done."

"Well I'm not one of them. You've always been kind to me. Anyway, if we're to work together, we must stay friends."

"So you're going ahead with it, despite their opposition?"

"Of course, Fisher. What choice do we have?"

"How long do you think you'll need?"

"We…ll they've stamped off home, having said no way could they work with me. We've said no me, no work. Fisher, I don't know. Will they come tomorrow?"

"Most probably. They'll think you'll back down."

"I won't. This distillery needs someone from the glen to stand with you against Bruce. No one has more desire to see him bested than me. I know the glen, the people, and I'll make damn sure I learn how to do all the office work—and you needn't pay me until I can. Where else are you going to get someone who can offer all that?"

"If they walk out? What then, Cate? They've heard of the miners and the shipyard workers making trouble. Why not them? An they're no in a good frame of mind anyway, what with Bruce's carrying on an all."

"Well, I suppose we'll have to depend on the women."

"Then God help us all, Cate, for I canna see it working."

The quiet knock at the outside office door brought Cate's head out of her books.

"It's yourself, Kirsty. Oh, and Morag too. Come away in. What's happening then?"

"Cold porridge in nearly every house, that's what's happening. Wives, mothers, girlfriends, daughters, not a one of us has lifted a pot to the fire for three days now."

"And?"

"Donald Uig's mother is saying he's fretting after his malt floor. Cursing something terrible, what with that an the bellyache." Kirsty laughed. "Imagine us being like those women in the history books."

"No quite like that, Kirsty. Not after what Cate was telling us."

"Morag, as though we would speak of that! Although Johnnie's supposed to be suffering more than a bellyache."

"Never! Sheena's never gone and put him out of her bed?"

"That she has, Morag. Five bairns to feed and she told him flat. 'No work, no money, no comforts'. I'm telling you, Cate, there'll be others before long. The women are mad that the men are no standing against the Laird, who's a real scunner, and here's you offering help. It's the women that'll suffer in the end."

"Kirsty, you'd make a great rebel. Thank you both for your help. I meant it when I said I wanted to do something for the women of the village in particular. But first we have to get the men back to work."

"I give Donald Uig no more than a day. Told him this morning I'd have nothing to do with a man who wouldna work. Said I might look elsewhere for another 'intended'."

"But, Kirsty, he's a good man and there aren't many single men in the village, and you might lose...."

"Och I know, but I'm safe enough. Who else would put up with that bitch of a mother of his, now I ask you?"

A sullen Fisher interrupted their giggles. "Glad I am that you have time and the inclination for laughter, so I am. Cate, we're nearly out of time."

"Give me one more day and I promise you they'll be back."

"Aye well. If what I'm hearing is to be believed, I'm ashamed of you."

"Fisher, if it works will you still be so?"

"I'm no even discussing it with these lassies in the room. Just see you get my distillery working properly again. Not a wink of sleep have I had these past few days. I can't go on any longer, even if I'm no eating cold porridge. By the way, since no a pot has been lifted, where's all the cold porridge coming from anyway?"

"I'm not saying, Fisher." Cate felt it was safer not to tell him of her part in the plan.

"Another of your evil schemes, no doubt, Cate. If the men come back...."

"Not if—when, Fisher."

"Aye well, if you're still here, God help the buyers. You'll have them struggling like the herring in the nets, not knowing which way to turn. What's that? Listen! Someone's come in. Here, get these lassies out of here. The men'll no stand for three of you being here, considering one was too many. Quick now. I'll away to my work and you get your head in those books, Cate. We canna afford to lose everything now."

Fisher made his way to the malt floor picked up the paddle and started turning the barley. If he knew his workers, it would be Donald Uig making his way up. He tended his barley like a mother tending her child, turning and watching till the first green shoots appeared. He must have done it thousands of times since he took over from his father, and still his face creased with pride when he announced they were all but ready to be moved. As the footsteps drew nearer, Fisher knew his guess was correct.

"It's yourself then, Donald Uig? "

"'Tis so, an I'll thank you to give me my paddle."

"Well someone had to be turning the barley." Fisher handed over the prized paddle.

"I'm here now and here I'll stay." Donald Uig caressed the handle as he spoke. "Groomed for this since the day I was born. Father never had any doubt I'd be here. Wee paddle and a corner of my own he gave me when I was but a lad."

"Aye, it was a sorry day when he was lost at the fishing."

"Mind the sea might have been easier than the old woman, Fisher. She's a mean tongue on her, so she has."

"So, you're back to stay with your barley then?"

"Cold porridge and losing an 'intended' is a high price to pay for putting a woman in the office. Though mind, she'd better stay there. I'll no have a woman on my malt floor."

"The others— will they'll follow?"

"Slowly, slowly, Fisher. If the hunger doesna get them, the dirty bowls, or the space next to them in bed will. Sooner or later they'll be back. Keep her out of the way and we'll see. Put a foot out of place and they'll no stand for it. So see to it, Fisher. As long as you're no to be ruled by a petticoat they'll thole it, I've no doubt.

Cate looked at the mess that was now her office floor. Somehow she must get all these papers sorted. MacNishe had kept only a few here in the office, the remainder he'd locked away in his study at

Kevinishe House. Fisher, having been instructed by a sick MacNishe, had brought them to the distillery and simply piled them on the floor. The all-important figuring books were neatly stacked behind the whisky bottles in MacNishe's drinks cabinet. At least it was locked.

Knowing Bruce as she did, the rest of these papers must be locked up too. Had Fisher all the distillery keys? Should Bruce have even one, it could mean trouble. Had the two men really managed to clear all the papers from the house? Nothing could be left to chance where Bruce was concerned. Although she'd understood, quite early on, that Bruce had no great intelligence, only once had she underestimated his natural cunning, but that once had cost her dear.

On the good side, they'd finally had most of the men reporting, in dribs and drabs, for work. She'd won, even if it did mean furtive visits to the old barn when she needed to relieve herself. The only other convenience was in the heart of the distillery. Forbidden territory for the foreseeable future, according to Fisher. Ah well, it was a small price to pay for victory.

Cate checked the table once more. Why was she so nervous? Both were good men, why wouldn't they get on? She'd arranged to use Fisher's house and had done everything herself. It had to be right. Dinwoodie must not feel he was dealing with people who didn't know anything. Fisher must appear to be the brilliant whisky man he was. For God's sake, they'd be fine! Wouldn't they?

"The old house used to look just so when MacNishe and his wife lived here. Beautiful you've made the table, so you have, Cate. It's a lot of bother to go to for a business meeting though."

"Oh. Do you think it's too much?'

"No. No. Though I'm wondering what sort of man needs all this carry-on for a wee look at the books."

"Fisher, this is important to me. I need his help."

"Ah, so you can't do it yourself? I could have told you so."

"Don't you dare say that! I've made more of a fist of it than you did. I don't mean I can't do the job. It's that I need to learn other things than what we buy and what we sell and wages and all."

"Alright! Alright! There's no need to be coming at me like a wild cat. I'm no saying anything."

"But you were. You're like all the others. What can a woman do outside the house? Well I'll tell you…. Oh! The door! He's here!"

"I'll open it then, while you choke on your rage. It'll no do to show the Iron Man what a bad-tempered besom you are." Smiling to himself as he made his way to let the newcomer in, Fisher couldn't help thinking that she had the right of it though. He had to admit she did seem to understand what the distillery needed. Yes, with the three of them in harness, always supposing he and the Iron Man dealt well with one another, the distillery would be fine from now on.

22

"No! No! No!" Alashdair thumped the editor's desk to emphasize his words, the draught sending papers flying. It was that simple action that was to change the course of his life.

James Scott, 'Scottie' to his employees, owner and editor of the Glasgow Gazette, stubbed out his cigarette, lit another and regarded the younger man through the smoke. Alashdair usually gave the impression of being half asleep, but today the steel-grey eyes flashed beneath the broad forehead with its cow's lick of black hair as the reporter reacted to the assignment he'd just been given.

"You know, I've fired men for approaching my desk, never mind rearranging the papers on it, and refusing to go where they're told. You've gone too far this time, Alashdair. You'll go on this job."

"Come on, Scottie. This whole idea is mad. For once your nose is playing you false."

"I see. Now you're a better newspaper man than I am?" The words carried a warning. No one was a better newspaperman than Scottie. "The Dewars have the world alerted to the power of whisky. Don't you read what others are writing about?"

"Fine. Send me to do a piece in London or Perth, wherever the famous 'Whisky Tom' is at the moment, seeing as how he does all their publicity. I'm damned if I'll go traipsing off to the Highlands to interview some unknown woman, who may or may not know something about whisky. Not every one is such a lover of the amber liquid as yourself."

This was dangerous ground, as drink was a sore subject between the two men. They both knew pursuing it would open a wound that had long festered, but Alashdair was too enraged to care. This was one assignment he didn't want and bloody well wouldn't do. The boss's instinct was wrong for once.

"I've never known you turn down a chance to interview a beautiful woman before. And may I remind you we need all the advertising we can get." Scottie knew of the younger man's various entanglements. Didn't approve of them but understood the need.

"So she's a beauty, produces whisky, is a descendant of The Lord of the Isles and presumably was gifted to us by the fairies! Man, you're out of your mind. Just get the secretary to post an advertisement form and leave it at that." The words, laden with sarcasm, and what amounted to an order, were the final blow. Scottie's famous temper flooded his face. The hue alone should have warned the younger man. "You'll take yourself off, interview the woman, write your piece, get the advertisement order and hand it in, or you needna come back. D'you hear? Now get on with it!"

Alashdair waited. Scottie continued to glower. For a moment neither moved, each gauging the other's response.

"Are ye deaf as well as insolent? You heard ma last word. Do as you're bid or clear your desk. Go on. Awa wi you!"

The lapse into his native Glaswegian was enough to convince Alashdair that his boss meant what he said. His own temper now well and truly aroused, he left, every movement showing his rage.

Fingering the glass door to check it was still intact, Scottie watched Alashdair storm through the newsroom, heedless of startled looks and oaths, as he scattered notebooks, knocked into chairs and tables. Theirs had always been a tempestuous relationship, ever since he'd discovered the boy trying to drag his drunken father back to their cramped two-roomed tenement dwelling. The youngster had hated him for seeing the level they were reduced to and had insisted he required no help. However, the sight of the small figure trying to persuade a great ox of a drunken man homeward had made Scottie shoulder the heavy body anyway.

Well, they'd weathered many a fight since then and were both driven by a determination to be the best in this cutthroat trade of theirs, about which they were equally passionate. This time he'd maybe been a touch hasty with him. Perhaps he should have sent someone else, but he'd be damned if he'd let any of his scribblers threaten him. Banging on his desk indeed! Anyway it was probably just the usual generation thing. Truth was their lives were too interlocked in other ways. Well, no time to let his mind dwell on all that or he'd get no work done. Alashdair would get his piece, and they would rub along until the next time they disagreed. Cigarette alight, editing pen in his hand, the true love of his life took over. Nothing existed but the Gazette.

Alashdair knew he should be out and about asking questions, finding leads. Instead he sought comfort as usual on the Broomilaw quay, lulled by the rhythm of the riveters' hammers as they worked on the hulls of great ships bound for foreign shores. He'd spent his youth waiting outside the dockyard gates for the striking figure of his father, always enthralled by stories told on the way home of ships being built and where they sailed. That was before his mother died giving birth to a stillborn child, and his lion of a father had taken to drink. The Clyde and the yards were in his blood. They'd been his schoolroom, his gateway to a wider world. Yet, he had to admit, it was Scottie who'd finished his education, slipping him a few coppers for information gathered, giving him papers and books to read, finding him lodgings when his father had died. Then given him his first job, as the errand boy in the newsroom of the Gazette.

Shoulders hunched against the wind, he flung his stub end into the river, then turned to make his way back to the newspaper offices and his research. He'd find out about the woman, go to the distillery in some godforsaken place in the Highlands, write the damned thing up with as much flair as he could, get the order, and then perhaps Scottie would listen to an idea he'd had for his next piece. First he had to go to Kelvinside. The thought depressed him. Most of the time he tried to forget the house even existed, never mind the tragic figure hiding there from reality. He'd not paid a duty visit for some time now. Perhaps Scottie knew.

Alashdair stood outside the station looking warily at the bus. Mr. McBrayne might run adverts in the Gazette but they never featured this broken down old wreck. The trip so far had been terrible,

317

mainly because he didn't want to be there. Frankly it was all too quiet and the space intimidated him. Glasgow, the newspaper, the tenements and the shipyards all had a constant comforting background of differing noises, teemed with people and were above all incredibly busy just being. A broken-down bus, a deserted station, and three passengers sitting on bags gazing in awe at the driver with his head under the bonnet wrestling with the wonders of the engine, and the deserted station made him feel he'd come to the end of the known world.

Rolling hills, deep wooded valleys, water and sheep. That was it! To make matters worse, it was raining. Fair play, it rained in Glasgow but, by the time it had splattered on myriad roofs, shipyards, factories and the thousands who worked and lived there, it just seemed, well, damp. Here, and Alashdair looked in disgust at the coat, which had weathered many a Glaswegian downpour quite satisfactorily but was now a poor sodden thing. Oh the stuff had started light enough. 'Just a little soft rain' the old fool in the station had said, but it had never stopped. What he wondered, did they call proper rain?

Dear God, why was he wasting valuable words and time on the bloody rain when he should be thinking about his assignment. His legwork in Glasgow had produced nothing more than bits of gossip from one or two of the buyers who'd visited the distillery. The woman was there, but no one knew anything about her. Still it wouldn't be the first time he'd turned up to a job with no angle. He'd be sure to think of something when he got there, although, by the time the bus finally spluttered into life, he was seriously considering returning to Glasgow empty-handed and risking being jobless. Except there was no train, so his only option was to take the now-mended bus. At least it would be dry.

The watchman banged on the distillery office door and entered. Then stood watching the woman, till she raised her head, before explaining his errand.

"There's a what outside? Angus, get Fisher to deal with it. I'm right in the middle of the books and if I stop now I'll never get

318

finished." Though she continued to work, Cate sensed the watchman's determination to stay put until he'd delivered what he'd come for. "Away you and get Fisher now." She attempted to return to the accounts. However, sensing the stubborn presence still hovering there, Cate looked up again and frowned at him. "What's the matter, Angus? I told you...."

"Well now, that's chust it. He says to take the wee paper mannie to you. Seems he, that's Fisher you see, aye does the distillery jobs and there's a lot of other things he'll have to be doing. Mind you...."

By this time Cate had lost all hope of remembering where she was in her figures. "Angus, please tell me what he said before we both forget what it's all about."

"Well and I never said I'd forgotten. I was chust telling you." Angus' cheeks puffed in indignation.

Irritated though she was, Cate knew that whatever she did, Angus, like all the older glen folk, would not be hurried. Resignedly she waited till he'd recounted the myriad reasons why she must see whoever it was. Sighing, she nodded in agreement and watched his careful tread as he left to resume the sweeping of what he considered was his courtyard.

All the waiting about had not improved Alashdair's temper. The stone distillery with its distinctive pagoda, the mountain with a collar of mist, the rushing of the foam-capped burn speeding towards the loch and the tiny lime-washed village but and bens hugging the shoreline, did not interest him. At last the wizened old man, still clutching his witch's broom, reappeared.

"Well, well, she'll be seeing you now." Duty done, Angus made for the exact spot he'd left minutes earlier and resumed his slow methodical sweeping.

"You! Where in the hell am I supposed to go?"

This was too much for Angus. "Don't you be shouting and swearing at me! Where else would you be going now but to the office?" With this, accompanied by a vague wave heavenwards, he returned determinedly to his broom.

Alashdair controlled the desire to wrap the broom round the teuchter's neck and instead made for the door the man had used, hoping to find someone more helpful on the other side. Although he was no stranger to the smell of brewing yeast it was usually diluted with all the other Glaswegian odours. Here it engulfed him and, by the time he'd followed the unwilling gestures of more than one taciturn distillery worker, the noise, the overpowering odour and the endless narrow staircases twisting and turning as if he was climbing the bloody mountain itself, he felt ready to do battle with anyone.

Cate regarded the sullen man dripping on her carpet, and smiled. "You look as though you've been for a swim."

My God, the bloody woman was laughing at him! Returning her stare, Alashdair cursed for not heeding Scottie's words. Those green eyes seemed to rob him of coherent thought. She was beautiful—no, not truly beautiful. The eyes and the hair were too dominant, the face not quite the perfect oval, the mouth over generous, but by God she was striking. Her speech and dress, though not fashionable—a simple cream shirt with tucks following the curve of her breasts—would grace any city drawing room. The red hair, tied back in one of those bun things at the nape of the neck framed the paler contours of her face to perfection, and for a moment he wondered what it would be like hanging free.

"I believe you wanted to see me about something? If it's work you're after, I'm sorry but we only employ men from the glen. Local industry is what keeps the life in it."

"I already have a perfectly good job." Collecting his thoughts he continued. "My editor wants a piece on your whisky and suggests you take an advertisement in the Gazette. Seems the whisky is suddenly becoming fashionable. Perhaps I should be speaking to Mr—er?"

"There is no Mr—'er' or otherwise. I deal with office matters." Typical male! They all had the same idea of the woman's place: pregnant and in the home if a lady, in service in the big houses of the well-off or slaving long hours in the factories if common. She didn't need this bad-tempered arrogant newspaperman. Well actually, she did. In fact he was exactly what she, or at least the distillery, needed. Still she'd much rather be concentrating on the bills and receipt books on her desk, than sitting here trying to placate the dour figure on the other side of it. However, they needed to advertise their Craeg Dhu, and, new to this sort of work, she'd just have to get used to it. Here was her first opportunity and she must hide her distaste. Too many jobs in the glen depended on it. Fisher had never let her down and she in turn mustn't fail him now. She turned her attention back to the intruder.

"So what do you want?"

"You haven't answered my question. Manager then. You know, the one who actually gets the work done." His eyes surveyed what he could see of her above the desk. " Though you're a very pleasant sight front of house."

Damn him he hadn't even bothered to hide his insolence. "You couldn't possibly expect a mere woman to be involved in the business, except as a distraction for passing males." Cate's words were icy.

"Needled are we? Okay, time to get down to business so I can get the hell out of here. Let's start with the real reason I'm here. Who exactly runs the distillery and why are rumours circulating in Glasgow?"

"Really. Are they discussing Kevinishe's whisky in Glasgow? Then perhaps I don't need you after all." Oh she'd seen his meaning in those grey eyes. A red-haired doxy, a male plaything or worse, damn him! She forced a cold smile and prepared for the fight, if only for the distillery's sake.

"Look here. Let's not waste any more time. If you want some publicity and adverts, then you've got to give me something worthwhile." He took his eyes off the woman and tried to rescue his notebook from among the myriad of other things in the sodden depths of his pocket.

"Worthwhile for me would be a simple piece about the distillery and our single malt, Craeg Dhu, but somehow I have a feeling that's not why you're here."

"Right first time, lady. You're the story I want. What's behind you being here, who are you and why are there whispers abroad? That's the sort of thing that sells newspapers, not one more whisky trying to break into an already crowded market."

"Does your editor know what an extremely rude man you are? Or is this how all newspapers go on? Well, let me tell you what we want." She could feel her temper stirring. "A picture with a caption describing the whisky and the distillery will do to begin with, and then perhaps something bigger should the first advert be successful. If you can't do that, even though we would be the ones paying for it, then I suggest you leave."

"We? Well. Well. Seems we're getting somewhere at last. Who is 'we' exactly, and why is he hiding behind you? That's what the readers want to know. What's the relationship? Why has he put a young woman up front? To distract the excise man perhaps? Or is it simply a rich man pandering to his mistress's whim?" Alashdair began to write in his notebook.

The object, whatever it was, clipped him on the side of the head and left him reeling. Only then was he aware of the change in the woman facing him. Standing up she was almost as tall as he was, and right now she was as mad as hell.

"Get out of my sight or I'll do you some real damage, so I will. Get out! Do you hear me? Out or I'll...." As she moved towards him Cate halted as the door opened and Fisher entered.

"Cate!" The roar echoed round the room. "I hear you want to see the distillery then?" Towering over the bruised journalist, now holding the side of his head, Fisher smiled. "Well then are you coming?"

Alashdair knew he'd no option. The huge partner's desk in front of the woman could well have been hewn from the oak that had been this man's twin. The face atop the tree-like body appeared carved from the ancient rocks littering the surrounding countryside. Was this the 'protection' man? Something was definitely going on here and he'd find out what it was and pay that red-headed bitch back somehow. For now he'd let her know she hadn't rattled him. "Thank you for your time, 'Cate' was it? How exactly do you spell that?"

As the door closed she stalked round and round the office. Why? Why had she let his taunts get to her? Stopping in front of the huge portrait on the wall she appealed to it. "MacNishe, will I never learn?" Studying the time-worn face of the old Laird, memories of their first meeting all those years ago made her walk to the window. The slopes of Beinne Nishe rose starkly in front of her, the Laird, his mountain, the distillery—the keys to her past and future.

Fisher watched the paper man make his way out through the distillery gates to wait for the post bus that would take him to the train. Now he'd better go to Cate. She'd wanted to do some advertising, saying they could no longer depend on their reputation, and the Iron Man agreed. Fair play to Mr. Dinwoodie, he'd been a godsend to them both. Hopefully he'd stay long enough to get her new plans in place. Well he'd away to the office with the post and see what she was like.

Fisher found her, back to the door, unaware of his approach. She was deep in thought looking at Beinne Nishe. She might be really upset. He'd better go careful here. She'd more than proved her worth since taking over the office. A nip here in working practises, a tuck there in wastage, and figures for everything at her fingertips. Now this advertising fellow had likely upset her. "Cate?"

Turning from the window, Cate came back to the present. "I'm sorry, Fisher, I didn't hear you come in. I was thinking of MacNishe. With that big painting up there, I sometimes feel he's in the office with me. Don't you mention 'women's fancies' either!"

"Truth to tell there's many a day I've had a wee craic with him myself in here, I miss him that much. This came with the post. What do you want to do with it?"

"What is it?"

"The annual Whisky Ball Invitation. MacNishe always went."

"And yourself?"

"No me, I'm needed here. The dancing is no for me, never has been."

"Fisher I couldn't go. And certainly not alone, what do I know about society balls." Look at the mess I've just made of my first press interview."

"The Ball will be different. You'll be among like-minded people. Though you're right, it's no fitting to go without a partner. What about the Iron Man?"

"Dinwoodie? Why would he want to go?"

"Ask him. That way you could get a wee drive in his new automobile, so you could."

"I couldn't Fisher. It's—well it's no seemly."

"So be it. Now this boundary fence you and the lawyer fellows are so keen on. We need more timber and at a better price, as you pointed out, but there's a problem."

"Bruce?"

"Aye. Peyton's desperate to offload some of that felled timber, but Bruce'll no be reasonable over the price."

"We'll need to source it elsewhere then Fisher. Though that could be as dear."

"True enough, Cate, but once we've fixed a price they'd likely stick to it, unlike him. Mind, if rumours are right, Master Bruce is scratching around the estate for things to sell. I hear tell it was Jupiter that was on the market last week."

"Well, I hope he went to a better owner than Bruce."

"He never went anywhere. The poor animal's never recovered from a hiding Bruce gave him. Gregor should have sneaked that animal away when he himself was kicked out. With MacNishe gone, those two belonged to one another."

"What will Gregor do now, Fisher?"

"He's above my stable, but keep that to yourself. Bruce would harm him given the chance."

"And the horse?"

"Still there."

"Would they put him down?'

"More than likely—Oh no! Definitely not! I can see your scheming mind at work. We don't want any more trouble with Bruce. The horse will just have to take its chance. You just put any thought of interfering right out of your mind, Cate."

"Fine." Cate quickly changed the subject. "Look, Fisher, you'd better go to Fort William and see to the timber and I'll get myself to the Glasgow do, though I don't fancy it one little bit."

"You'll be grand when you get there, so you will, and the Iron Man will make sure you're okay. Seems to me he has a soft spot for yourself!"

"Fisher—I've done damage to one man today already!"

"I'm away out of danger then." Fisher laughed as he left.

As he waited for her in the hotel foyer, Dinwoodie couldn't help wondering what she would look like in formal dress. So far he'd seen her bundled up in a shawl and in the shirts and the long straight serge skirts she wore for work.

"Dinwoodie, will I do?" She came towards him and did a pirouette. "Well?"

"You look…." Words really were inadequate. The hair, piled high on her head, added height to her tall figure, making her truly statuesque. The cream dress was startlingly plain, save for the MacNishe sash pinned with an enormous silver clan brooch, all so simple but breathtaking in effect. "I'm lost for words, Cate."

"My mouth's in the same state, I'm that nervous."

"Come, my car is here."

When they arrived, Cate found the huge ballroom overwhelming, with its beautifully decorated plaster ceiling, glittering chandeliers sparkling in the light, ruby red velvet drapes at the windows and gold and red seats. Chiffons, satins, and materials she'd never known about adorned the seated ladies.

"Come along, let's get in the line."

"You mean we've to queue to get in, just like the butcher's?"

"Wickedly put, my dear. We're being formally introduced to the President of the Whisky Association. He's the host for the evening."

"Who are the others in there? Surely to God we don't have to shake hands with them all? My bonnie white gloves will be black and the hand inside will be as limp as the seaweed on the shore."

"No, Cate! Only the welcoming party, come on, deep breath and you'll be fine."

Dinwoodie smiled at his earlier words. She was not only fine—she was turning out to be the belle of the ball. She seemed to have an inexhaustible source of energy and an ability to follow what others were doing. Nobody would think this was her first real social occasion. Would she remember to go into supper with him, or had some handsome young man appropriated her? No she was heading his way.

"Dinwoodie, I thought I'd never find you in this crowd. You've barely danced with me."

"I'm not used to having to queue for my partner."

"Well I wish you would. Some of these—well, they've too much whisky taken and no very sensible conversation. You try to talk business with them and they laugh at you." She didn't want compliments. She wanted ideas, facts, and practical thoughts. She was a businesswoman now.

"Supper first and it'll be my pleasure to claim more dances afterwards. Cate, here's the Lord Chief Justice coming our way."

"Dinwoodie, I'm glad to see you among us again. You've recovered?"

"I have that. My partner sir, Mrs. McAlister, from the Kevinishe Distillery."

"A charming addition to our Glasgow scenery. Will you both take supper with me?"

"I hardly think we'll be on your table."

"I know all of the others. Fresh company will be welcome. I see you've been occupied with the distillers on the dance floor, Mrs. McAlister."

" Yes, but I'm afraid they're mostly concerned with their numerous drams."

"You're hard on them, Mrs. McAlister. It's their reward for a long year's work."

"I'm not so very well acquainted with all your fine rules, sir. This is my first ball, so perhaps you'd be doing better than seating yourself with me."

"Your smile and the twinkle in your eye make me think we'll have a most enjoyable meal. What do you say, Dinwoodie?"

"You'll not be bored. Of that I'm sure, though other tongues will be wagging."

"That won't do either of you any harm. Distilleries and foundries can always do with more publicity. Don't you agree?" Having rearranged their table to his satisfaction, Lord Monroe studied the young woman talking animatedly to one of the Grants.

Leaving the supper table, they were hailed on numerous occasions by others greeting Lord Monroe. Cate felt the curious glances but simply smiled at them.

"Mrs. McAlister, I've rarely been so enchanted at a 'duty' ball. You've a keen wit and your command of mimicry kept our table thoroughly amused."

"If I've been that out of the ordinary I may just have broken an awful lot of polite society rules." She'd been surprised by the pleasure gained in their animated conversation, though some of the men clearly thought she was too forward. Still, she'd learned a lot and thoroughly enjoyed herself. She'd paid little attention to the food, but the crystal and the silver on the table had held her gaze.

"Perhaps, but you were a spring breeze in an autumn evening. Now may I have the pleasure of the next dance? It's the Dashing White Sergeant so Dinwoodie and I will be your partners. What do you say?"

"I would like that very much though…."

"Come now, why on earth not?"

"Dancing, like many other things, wasn't part of my learning sir."

"Shame on the establishment then. You were wronged."

"Well sir, there was no 'establishment', unless you count Life itself. I'm but a tinker girl, though working my way up as hard as I can. So you see sir, no dancing lessons, but if you'll guide me, I'm willing to learn. Indeed I've learned a lot already this evening. However, now you know my background, to save any embarrassment, I'll go and freshen up. If you're not here when I return, know that it has been a great pleasure supping with someone as distinguished as yourself. Sir, Dinwoodie, please excuse me."

"Well now, Dinwoodie, just where did you find such an extraordinary woman?"

"Originally as a result of an accident. She was a nursemaid then, must have been all of eight or nine. Then again half way up a mountain last year, while I was recuperating in the Highlands. She is indeed an unusual and talented young woman."

"Well, if you're agreeable, I think the Dashing White Sergeant, don't you? Tinker or no, though I find that hard to believe, I'm not willing to forego my dance. Then I must leave. I have another event I must show my face at this evening, before I can seek my bed."

Watching Cate as she wound her way through the group of young men jostling her, Dinwoodie was suddenly alerted to one particular fellow who looked as though he was about to be a nuisance, but then could hardly stifle his mirth as Cate brought her high heeled boot down sharply on the fellow's foot, smiled sweetly, and came across the floor towards him.

"Dinwoodie, time to go I think. Is that alright?"

"Certainly, if you're sure you're ready. A spot of trouble, over there?"

"Nothing I couldn't handle. Too much drink taken makes most of them unsuitable partners and I'm quite ready to leave, but one last dance with my preferred partner, I think."

As they circled the floor Dinwoodie couldn't help a somewhat triumphant glance at the young blades.

23

Although she'd come out for a walk to clear her head, Cate was still wrestling with distillery problems. Stupid really—the whole point of the walk was to forget them. Looking round she realised she'd lost the dog. This Labrador was truly hers, unlike young David's one she'd looked after. That one had gone back to the gamekeeper once its injuries were healed. She'd bought this Rory with the hope of pleasing Rhoddy, but he'd lost interest once he'd learned that he had to look after it, so the dog became her close companion, sleeping at her feet, beneath her desk, while she worked. Now, not only had she lost it, but looking round, Cate realised she was on the edge of the Kevinishe estate. She'd no wish to trespass, especially since Dinwoodie was away in London.

She was so involved with her thoughts she'd gone much further than she'd intended, and she was not familiar with this area, it might even be the beginning of the Laggan estate. An excited barking to her left made her groan. Damn dog had chosen to disappear in a thicket of brambles. Whatever he was chasing the barking indicated he was far too excited to worry about returning to her, so she'd have to go after him.

As she struggled out into the open, Cate was both annoyed and intrigued. Rory came bounding up to her, tongue hanging out from all his exertions, but tail poised to sink between his legs as soon as she scolded him. However, she was far too interested in her surroundings just at that moment. They were in what looked like a garden, but it was so wild it was hard to tell. "Now then, Rory, what have we here?" The dog, realising her interest was elsewhere, wagged his tail energetically and made to move on. Intrigued, Cate followed and was rewarded by a glimpse of what must originally have been a fine house, but what she could see of it now was in a sorry state, almost strangled with wild briar roses and ivies.

Circling it, pushing her way through shrubs that had grown into and through one another after years of neglect, she wondered why anyone would have let it get into this state. The windows were so covered with algae and shrouded in creepers and brambles that it was almost impossible to see through them, but she caught sight of the occasional piece of furniture. "Why, Rory? Why would anyone leave it to get into this state?" Suddenly Cate felt cold. *Then a mist swirled around her and out of it appeared the red-headed woman. Passing Cate she smiled, walked through the overgrown tangle of creepers, and vanished through the door of the house.* As the mist left her Cate heard Rory whining. Puzzled, she turned to him. Then, remembering suddenly how she'd got here, fixed what she hoped was a fierce look on her face. "Don't you be running away on me again! You're a bad dog." The rebuke was too late and they both knew it. The dog slunk to the ground for the required moment of penitence, then, as her gaze wandered to the house again, was up ready to be off.

Why had the woman appeared? Cate pulled at the bushes where the woman had passed through, but was only able to squeeze her arm through to the door, which she could not open. She stood there as the creepers began to swing back into place. Was she seeing ghosts? If she was, this one had been happy. Eyes shut, Cate felt, she knew it was foolishness, but she wanted this house. Without knowing why, it seemed right. Somehow predestined. Here she could make her remaining dreams come true. She knew exactly what James Wiseman would say to her. 'Another impetuous decision, Cate, you do seem to hurtle into things. I must admit it worries me'. The dog cocked his ears in surprise as her laughter echoed round the tangled scene. Patting him on the head, Cate knelt down and spoke to him. "Can you just see the lawyer's face, Rory, as I explain in all seriousness that I want this house because I '*saw*' an image of a red-headed woman? Though it did look as though she was inviting me into the house and she seemed pleased to find me here. Perhaps, Rory, I'll keep those thoughts to myself. The man already thinks I've made some funny decisions and not given them enough thought."

Actually, that wasn't the case. She considered everything very carefully these days. McAlister's money had enabled her to take charge of her own future and there was no way she was going to let that security disappear now. Her first use of the money had enabled her to begin her fight back against Bruce. His decision to oust the old folks from their cottages provided her with the perfect opportunity to begin her revenge and help the village. She'd used some of her inheritance to buy the cottages and let the elderly of the village die in peace in the homes they'd always known. At present the distillery didn't need extra funding, so she'd been able to help, without worrying James Wiseman too much.

Back at the distillery she went in search of Fisher. By saving the old ones from eviction she'd gradually won the workers round and now moved freely throughout the distillery. This was a necessary learning for her anyway and one she thrived on. To understand every process from the delivery of the barley to the casked whisky in the warehouse was as essential to her as digesting the figures or understanding the whims of the buyers. As usual she found him in the stillroom. Cate loved the shining copper shapes of the stills with their bright brass locks and the bubbling liquid within, reassuring her that both she and the distillery now had a future.

"Do you know anything about it?" She asked, having told him about her find.

"Well now, I do and I don't."

"And?" Cate could see Fisher was determined not to say any more as he peered at the wash still level, wiping the spotless glass unnecessarily. "Fisher?"

"Och it's no a very respectable house and that's why it's been left in ruins."

"It's not exactly in ruins. Neglected, mind, but it looks more or less whole." Someone must own it, Fisher."

"I believe a MacNishe at one time rented it from the Laggan estate."

Cate shook her head as she watched the stillman busy himself doing nothing in particular while making it perfectly obvious he'd no wish to tell her any more. She knew she owed him her life after he'd spirited her away to Glasgow following her rape by Bruce. Then, when she'd returned to the glen, penniless and hungry, with young Rhoddy, he'd helped her again. Now that he owned the distillery and she worked full time with him, they were business colleagues, as well as dear friends. Mind he was a thrawn man when he wanted to be, and he certainly didn't want to say more on the subject of the house.

"So, it could be bought." Cate simply couldn't let it go.

"Dear God, woman, what would you be wanting with the Harlot's House?"

Cate sent a triumphant glance in Fisher's direction. There was a story here.

"Well there would be no harm in mentioning it to the Laggan factor, or even Dinwoodie, would there?"

"There are times when I think you'd be better off still travelling with the tinkers, Cate. All this working business and buying things is getting too much talk about you, and this would be the worst thing you could do."

"I see. I can buy the villagers' cottages, but not one for myself? Well, if the glen wants to see me as a harlot, it's no worse than what some of them accused me of in the early days." She paced up and down angry with him, the villagers, and herself.

"And what would you be doing with the Black House now?" Fisher asked when she'd finally stood still.

"I've a a scheme in mind for that, but I'll need a visit to Glasgow first."

"By yourself then?"

"Fisher, stop it. Dinwoodie has become a very dear friend, just as you are. So ignore the village gossips. Anyway I'm a grown woman and fancy free, so there." She had noticed though, since the ball, Dinwoodie was spending a surprising amount of time at Laggan House, considering he was the sole owner of such a huge business, and, as she knew, businesses didn't run themselves.

As she watched the outskirts of Glasgow go by, Cate was amazed at how they'd grown since she'd first made the journey. So much had happened since then. So many fine people had died: McAlister,

MacNishe, the old tinker woman, the Cailleach, old Mr. Wiseman the lawyer, all of them good friends and sorely missed. Friends were, of course, the purpose of this visit. Despite her many appeals to Maggie, Lizzie had never ventured to the glen. Hopefully now she would be able to change that. But first Gordon Wiseman!

He too was becoming a slight problem. On his father's death, Gordon became her lawyer. A few business lunches, two theatre outings, and now his invitations were becoming a little too pressing. Like his father, he was an excellent lawyer, and had suggested doing her buying in Solly's name and then transferring the deeds to hers? That way Bruce had no real knowledge of the buyer of his village houses.

The further she travelled from her brief marriage to McAlister, the more aware she became of two things: what a good man he'd been in every way and how much she'd liked him. He'd be a hard man to replace. Anyway, she'd no desire to marry again, so she'd have to distance herself a little from the lawyer.

Just at the moment her life was filled with her work in the distillery. Even in her younger days work had always been her strength and her security. Now she took a real pride in providing work for others. Her promise to the village women was long overdue and she might just be about to fulfil it, but it all depended on Dunoon.

Seated in front of the young lawyer she concentrated on the purchase of the house. What do you think, Gordon? Have I the money for it?

"You certainly have enough funds at present for the purchase, Cate. Your income from your annuity is increasing. You appear to be a very frugal woman. Unusually so, I believe, compared with what I hear from some of my clients, whose wives seem set on bankrupting them."

"I bet my houses cost more than their dresses!" Cate laughed. "Seriously, please remember that, as soon as the distillery needs funds, they will have to be found. On that I'm determined. Nothing must threaten that."

"I've been meaning to speak to you about your position there, Cate. It seems to be that, with your work and ideas, you are improving the viability of the business. Perhaps it's time for you to persuade Mr. Macrae to let you invest some of your capital with a view to a partnership."

"Wouldn't that be a bit forward of me? He knows I've said, if he ever needs it, financial help from me would be there."

"I understand that, Cate, but, as you are the one with the true business sense, it seems...."

"Wait now, Gordon. Without Fisher, there'd be no whisky to sell."

"Yes, but without you the business wouldn't be growing as it is. Both of you are essential to the continuing prosperity of the distillery."

"Aye, but what if he doesn't want a woman as a partner? Look at the trouble I had being allowed to work there in the beginning."

"Well, just think about it. Remember, he's an older man and if he were to...."

"Don't even think it. Kevinishe would be nothing without Fisher."

"Look at it this way, Cate. Should anything happen to him, you do realize who would inherit the distillery as next of kin?"

"Maggie I suppose, or his other sister Jessie. Maybe even Lizzie."

"More probably the only other MacNishe, your enemy Bruce."

Cate sat, her mind trying to come to terms with Gordon Wiseman's words. Fisher was the distillery. Any of these possibilities would mean ruin for them all. Though she was fond of the three women, she was only too aware they couldn't cope with the business. Bruce—what a catastrophe that would be, not only for the distillery, but also for the entire glen! That must never happen.

"I see I've given you much to think about. Please do so, Cate. I don't want to scare you, but you've already been through an unhappy experience due to sudden death and I do know how much Kevinishe means to you. Now about this house?"

"Well, I'm not so sure I can afford it if we're thinking of putting money into the distillery."

"I'm not saying you need to do that immediately. Just think about it. Tell me about the house."

Cate rose and walked to the window, watching as the people of Glasgow hustled and bustled about their daily life. This would never be for her. She felt a growing longing for the hidden house. She wanted to restore it, provide it with beautiful grounds, like Balvourie House, and inside create the restful interior she'd dreamed of since she'd first seen Lady Sarah's room as a child. Somehow, there, she knew she'd find true peace and security.

"It does seem a large house, Gordon. It might be dear, although it's badly run down."

"It all depends on whether the Laggan estate wishes to keep it, is aware of its existence, or could do with the funds. Incidentally, talking of funds rumour has it that Bruce MacNishe is being hounded for gaming debts."

"In Edinburgh?"

"No, he's currently gambling in Glasgow. Apparently he's been forbidden his usual haunts until he settles the outstanding sums."

"Nothing that man does would surprise me, he's bad through and through."

"Well there's a good many folk agreeing with you now, for there are some unsavoury accounts of him, not fit for a lady's ears."

"In that case, I'll not listen. Gordon, I've another plan to let you look at." Taking the roll from her bag, she unfurled it on his desk. "I'd value your advice on this. See if you can find any problems and if I can finance it."

"You may not be spending money on yourself but at this rate you'll have a business empire of your own."

"Hardly that, and, with what you've said about the distillery, I may need to think again. Anyway, I'm off on the boat to Dunoon. I'll call in on my way back and hear your thoughts on house, distillery and the new plan. See if I can afford any, or all, of them."

"So you're not staying in Glasgow? Pity, I thought we might dine."

"I'm sorry, Gordon, I've business in Dunoon. If I'm not kept there too long we could perhaps dine on my return."

"I'll hold you to that. Have a good journey, Cate, and I'll get to work on your proposals. I look forward, as always, to seeing you again."

On arrival in Dunoon, Lizzie, as usual, was overjoyed to see her, Maggie less so.

"You mean I'd be making other lassies sew? I coudna do that, Cate. They wouldna do it."

"Not make them, Lizzie. Teach them. Show them how it's done. The really difficult bit will be that you'll have to do most of the cutting, finishing and probably re-doing most of their work to begin with."

"Oh Mammy, it's what I've dreamed of. Cate doing the designs an me the sewing—no, I'd need to be calling it 'the dressmaking', eh Cate?"

"You remembered. Well done you, Lizzie."

"It'll be too much for you Lizzie, seeing as you'd likely be doing all the work." Maggie spoke in a cold voice.

Cate stared at her, astounded. This was so much more than the market stall idea for Glasgow; this was a proper business for the women of Kevinishe. It was a dream in the making.

"Maggie, it's what we'd always planned. Lizzie would be doing something she enjoys, making a good wage and a life of her own.

Maggie changed the conversation. "I see you've got yourself in the papers these days, Cate." Right enough she'd got to where she'd always told them she'd be, but her Lizzie was going nowhere near the Highlands. Why would Cate no just let go? Maggie refused to listen to the uncomfortable thoughts at the back of her mind. She'd made a decision and she couldna go back on it now.

"Maggie, what has that got to do with us here? Yes, I was at the Assembly Rooms and, if as Solly says, there was a picture of me in the Glasgow Gazette, it wasn't my doing."

"I've cut it out, Cate. Mrs. Cameron—you know the old woman I sit for some times…?"

"Lizzie, what would Cate want to know about her for?"

"Maggie, what's the matter with you? This is silly. You used to be like a mother to me. Surely you can't hold my mistakes against me forever? I'm doing what I always said I would. You just never really believed me, did you?"

336

"Well, that's mebbe so, but Lizzie's no going."

"Mammy. You don't mean that. I know you wouldna let me go for a visit, though I'd like fine to meet my uncle. But this would be work. Proper work, no just helping out here an there."

"I do mean it. I've told you both before. It's no for you, Lizzie."

'Why, Mammy? Why, 'cause you're no invited? You canna go because you upped an married Bert. I was taken to Dunoon because you wanted that. Well I want this. You never gave Cate a chance. Just believed whit folks told you. I hate you, so I do. Just hate you an Bert an Dunoon." Lizzie took her tears to the box-room.

"Now see what you've done, Cate, set mother against daughter."

"No Maggie. I've never done that. You have. Oh, in the beginning your fears were possibly justified. I was young, foolish and probably selfish. I did what I felt was necessary, but the one thing I never did was forget my promise. Even when I was wandering the roads, heartbroken and starving, I never ever forgot the two of you. I just—there's something not right here, Maggie."

"You're right there, an it's you. You dinna belong here. Get back to your grand business and stay away from my Lizzie."

"That's it, is it? 'My Lizzie'! Do you really think I'm trying to steal your daughter to replace my own? I've come to feel for that girl, crying her heart out through there, more than I've ever done for anyone. She's the sister I never had. If this feeling is what real love is like, then I love Lizzie. My only wish has always been to share her future and yours."

"My future's Bert's."

"Exactly, Maggie. Then why deny Lizzie hers? I've tried to do this with your approval, but I warn you, I'll not leave it alone. Think about it. When you and Bert are gone, Lizzie will be alone in the world. Is that what you want?"

"Lizzie'll no suffer. I'll see to that."

"You're wrong, you know, and I hope to God you understand that some day. She'll always be your daughter, but she'll always be my best friend as well. Nothing can change either of those facts. Goodbye, Maggie. I'll write to Lizzie." As she shut the door behind her, Cate had to suppress the urge to go back and shake some sense into Maggie. How could she be so stubborn? Why?

"Here, would you look where you're going."

"I'm sorry, I…."

"It's Lizzie's braw friend Cate, is it no? In the papers an all you were. The lads on the boat—listen to me chattering on! You'll come away back in?"

"I'm, I'm in a hurry, Mr. Green."

"Now then, less of the Mr.—'Bert' to any friend of Lizzie's. Well, I'm sorry to have missed your visit. Here's my hand on that."

"Good bye, Bert, and thank you." The seaman's hand seemed enormous and—the mist was there again and then the sea. *Huge waves crashed one upon another. Tossing a man between them again and again, playing with the body. Then it was over. Only the stormy sea remained.* The mist and cold receded. Her hand still in his, Cate shivered."

"Here, you're no well. Come on back indoors with you."

"No, no I'm tired. I've had a long journey and another one in front of me. I must go, Bert." She had to leave, and quickly. She had to get away, think. Something made her turn again to the man. "Take care, Bert. Take great care."

Back in Kevinishe, as each week passed, Cate felt the danger to Bert, must have passed. How could she warn anyone without revealing how she knew? Did she know? Wasn't it all just plain superstition? Something the older generations believed because their forbears had done so? She'd always been alone as a child, lacking friends. Was the red-headed woman just wishful longing, and the battle incident just a dream? Imagining at the time of the funeral, Fisher and Bruce fighting was easily explained. After the will reading they were bound to be enemies. Well, as far as Bert was concerned, they'd heard nothing, so he was still very much alive. She knew herself to be a practical, logical woman. The whole thing was nonsense. Fisher's entrance was a welcome interruption.

"We appear to have a problem."

"Surely you mean another problem? Broken windows, tools going missing, more than usual spillages—the list goes on. You've no new hands taken on, have you?"

"Not a one. Why?'

338

"It doesn't make sense, Fisher, that's why. The distillery has kept its people in work. They've not even got a complaint with me. I've kept to the office, and I explained why I had to be let into the distillery workings because I couldn't sell the whisky if I didn't understand how it was made. There's been no problem with that. Why would any of them want to make work more difficult?"

Fisher shook his head. "If I knew that, there wouldn't be a problem."

"What is it this time?"

"Timber again. I'm trying to run a distillery here, Cate. I've no time to spend running after planks of wood."

"Timber? What do you mean? We've no need for more just now—it's all bought and paid for. What's the matter with it, Fisher? You said the delivery was fine."

"So it was. As long as it was here."

"You mean it's going missing? Come on, Fisher. Tools being misplaced, young lads breaking windows, raw spirit being stolen—not good but it's understandable. How in God's name can someone put a plank in their boot or under their coat at knocking-off time?"

"Exactly so. I've no answer for you, but I'm telling you it's going missing."

"So we've a thief among us. That's not so very pleasant." If she didn't know he wasn't at Kevinishe House, she would suspect Bruce. Oh, the incidents had been small at first, easily explained by lack of care, but this was something different. "Do we need to get help for Angus? In fact, is Angus too slow-witted for the job anymore? Surely he's not involved?"

"Never. As you say, he hasn't the wits to be in on the likes of this."

Cate rose and looked out of the window. "You know what I'm thinking, Fisher?"

"Aye, Bruce. But how?"

"I have a nasty feeling we'll find out soon. We'll just have to be on our guard. I've a scheme in mind for the women, so I'll have a craic with them and see if anything comes up."

"You've more faith in them than the men?"

"Yes, I do. If it does have something to do with Bruce, a MacNishe would more easily persuade the men. For generations they've done the Laird's bidding. It'd be a hard habit to break."

"But the women?"

"Fisher, it's the women who keep everything going. What do they care about the Laird's wishes? Their home and family are their main concern. They would never put those at risk. Why do you think they helped when the men wouldn't work with me? Not because I meant anything to them. No—because their way of life was being threatened. I know you men are supposed to be our superiors, but sometimes you don't see where things are going. Women can see round corners. We've to do so many things, sometimes all at once, that it's not difficult for us to look forward and see what's going to happen."

"Away with you. You'll be saying they've all got '*The sight*'!"

"No I won't. What a stupid thing to say, Fisher! I'm surprised at you. If you're going to make a fool of me, I'm away." She made for the door and was down the stairs before he had time to work out why.

Now what in the name of God had he said? Making his way to the stillroom, he thought she was right in one thing. Women certainly did see things men didn't. Otherwise what was that outburst about?

Having sneaked into the Kevinishe stable, Gregor could see it was almost over. The stallion, Old MacNishe's pride and joy, lay listless in the filthy stall. The beast could not be kept alive with titbits on an occasional visit. Too many whippings, lack of care to injuries and no one allowed near the house, meant the end of the beast. A gun, that's what was needed, to give some dignity and release to the once noble horse. The bent old man went to the distillery for help.

Looking for Fisher, Gregor found Cate in the office.

"Hello, Gregor, I've been meaning to see you. Jupiter—I hear he's bad?"

"He is that, Cate. I'm here for the loan of Fisher's gun. No animal should suffer like that."

"He's really bad then?"

"Dying, but slow like. Broken hearted and neglected. We're forbidden near the stables an I canna save him, nor can I abide seeing him wither away in discomfort."

"Surely even Bruce must care, Gregor?"

"Him! He'd watch you and me die before his very eyes and laugh. What makes you think he'd care for an animal he could never control? It was always Jupiter's fault, never his, when he was unhorsed. That one was born cruel, Cate, and will likely go to his grave even worse."

"Who's there now?"

"Well there's the Englishman in the gatehouse and a rough-looking type who's supposed to be a butler in the house. If that one's a butler, I'm the next MacNishe!"

"What about the stable boys and gardeners? Surely they're still about? Don't they see to the horse?"

"Not a one of them. All been sent out on the estate. Lady Sarah would weep at the sight of her flowerbeds. He's sheep on the lawn, dirty beasts that they are."

"Bruce?"

"I'm no sure, Cate. Might still be around. He was a few days back, but there was no sight of him this morning, an he never goes near the beast."

"You say Jupiter's beyond saving, Gregor?"

"Aye, poor beast. He just needs an easy death."

"I'll speak to Fisher. Away home with you now! Keep out of sight. Go nowhere near the Big House, do you hear?"

"I'm away to my bed this minute. It's the rheumatics, as you know fine well. I canna move with them."

Watching the little bowlegged man leave, Cate raged. All his life that one had done nothing but love the animals his family had tended for generations. Now Bruce's cruelty to one of those noble beasts was breaking the old man's heart. There was no way Fisher would let him have a gun. Gregor couldn't do it and she couldn't shoot, but something had to be done for the horse and the man. What had she got that could be given without causing more distress?

When he heard the news from Peyton, Fisher was relieved. Next morning he went straight to the office to tell her.

"I hear he's gone then." Fisher just knew she'd had something to do with it. Though Peyton had said the beast just upped and died. No surprise, the Englishman felt, considering the state of the horse. He'd tried to feed it when he could, but Bruce refused to take action when he'd asked for the vet. Anyway the man had said he'd enough troubles trying to run the estate, never mind seeing to the Laird's horse.

"Bruce is gone?"

"The horse, Cate. Seems he just went to sleep and never woke up. Hardly surprising according to Gregor, seeing as the poor beast was that weak."

"How do you know, Fisher?"

"Peyton told me. At least that settles my mind."

"Your mind Fisher? Why? What were you worried about?"

"Gregor, or mebbe even you, Cate" He looked her straight in the eye, but not a flicker.

"Why me?"

"Because, Cate, you've a way of getting done what you want and sometimes you're either no very sensible about it or too brave for your own good. Anyway, the horse wasn't shot, and that's all I'm worried about. I'm in the stillroom if you need me."

The stallion had needed little of the laudanum she'd brought back from Glasgow to ease the pain of two of her dying villagers. She'd spent the night easing his sores and using her hands to draw some of his pain as he faded. He'd gone, head on her lap, her whispered words of comfort his last memory.

Bruce again! When was the village to be rid of his wickedness? The thought reminded her of Fisher's words about Rhoddy—the idea of sending him to school away from the glen. He was eight now and she couldn't ignore the snippets that filtered through to her about bullying smaller children. They'd got off to a bad start. She'd been too young, too full of rage, and dragging him with her from one situation to the next hadn't help. They had an uneasy relationship and shipping him off to school wasn't going to help, but it might be the best for both of them.

The distillery would be shutting down for harvest soon. The men needed on the crofts to gather their hay and those that weren't would be fully occupied in the servicing and repairing of all the distillery machinery. That should give her at least a couple of weeks when she wasn't needed. She'd take him to Fettes and enrol him for September. Bruce, as far as she knew had no idea that Rhoddy was his son, nor of her involvement in the distillery and that's the way she wanted it to stay.

24

Once again Bruce was at odds with his factor. Damn man didn't get results. "What do you mean, they won't buy, Peyton? Since they've decided to erect that ridiculous fence they must need the timber!"

"They've had it brought in from Fort William, sir. You wouldn't sell, remember?"

"Well I want those felled trees sold. They'll do no good lying in the wet. They're a harvest and should be heading to the mill."

"They were sir, till you changed the agreed price. Mrs. McAlister said she wouldn't stand for that sort of double dealing and cancelled the order."

"McAlister did you say? Tall, with red hair?"

"That's her, sir."

"What's she got to do with the blasted order?"

"Surely you know? She's now working in the distillery with the new owner. Rumour has it that she's even a partner."

"Don't be ridiculous, Peyton. She's nothing but a bloody tinker. Supposed to be roaming the roads selling heather." Bruce couldn't believe it—not her!

"Then I think we must be speaking of a different woman, sir. This Mrs. McAlister runs the distillery office. Rather like an accountant, sir. Nothing is bought or sold without her say-so."

"Then it's definitely not the woman I'm thinking of. Anyway, get that timber moved and at a good price. See to it, Peyton." Bruce turned on his heel, mind racing. No, it simply couldn't happen. How could she have laid her hands on money? He was finding it hard enough to thwart the distillery as it was. Damn servant man he'd brought to Kevinishe was supposed to be making things difficult for Fisher. Enough trouble and he'd soon give in. Should never have had the distillery in the first place. What the hell had his grandfather been thinking? Everything on the estate ought to be in MacNishe hands. The man was a by-blow, not fit to own anything.

It couldn't be her. If she were still in Kevinishe she'd be scratching a living out in that hovel on the moors, plying the usual witchery to the stupid villagers. Should have evicted her first. Not too late though. Peyton wouldn't have the stomach for it, but the newcomer might—a man with a criminal background he'd brought up for just this kind of task. A frightener here and there, and then she'd be ready to quit. Or would she? Always ready to put up a fight in the past. Now that occasion, high up on the moors when they were young, had been enjoyable. Not much of it about at present, with his funds drying up. The way he liked his sexual pleasures cost a great deal of money. Yes, let his man soften her up and then he'd finish her off himself. For the first time this visit he felt good about something.

He'd waited over long for the miserable old man, his grandfather, to die and, as he watched him lowered into the MacNishe vault he'd had so many plans. Then they'd all gone wrong. First he'd lost the distillery. That meant he'd been cheated out of estate labour. Then the money was nowhere near what he'd expected. They'd always seemed to have so much. Where had it all gone? Those two scheming old men—they'd never liked him. They'd defrauded him. Damn them both, his grandfather and his bastard friend, Fisher.

His new lawyers had searched every angle. Come to that, he'd fallen out with several sets of lawyers, but none had answers. It had to be the damned distillery. That was the root of all his problems. If he'd any spare gambling money, he'd bet it on a connection between his poor inheritance and the distillery's apparent success. It was his money that Fisher was using. The bloody little tinker girl couldn't have anything to do with it. She was probably just sleeping with Fisher. He'd get rid of the two of them, one way or another. Then he could live the proper life of a Laird.

Although there was no bad news from Dunoon, Cate couldn't stop worrying. Surely Bert had to be safe? She had at last admitted to herself that these events that came unbidden to her mind had the mark of 'The Sight', though she'd long denied it. What was she now supposed to do about it? Write or go back to Dunoon? Cate walked to the window, her mind unsettled.

There was no peace to be found there. The wind slapped against the office window as if the glass was the sole reason for its fury. The storm had been working itself up all night and there would be some real damage done before the day was out, unless it slackened soon. She'd weathered storms before. Why was this one making her uneasy? Probably because these were the very conditions she'd seen in her moment of 'Sight' as she bumped into Bert Green that day in Dunoon. She returned to her desk, mind still preoccupied with Bert. She had to stop this! Cate shook her head as if to rid it of the worrying thoughts.

Precious little sleep she'd had last night worrying over Bruce and the distillery problems. That's what was ailing her surely? Still she couldn't seem to settle to her books. Turning to look out the window again she saw nothing but black clouds and rain in runnels on the glass. The storm had completely removed the familiar world. That increased her tension. Getting up, she paced the floor, willing herself to shake free of her foreboding. Fisher's entrance startled her. "What are you doing here? What's wrong?" Her tone was sharper than normal.

"Well now, it's as much my office as yours."

"I'm sorry, Fisher. That was rude of me. I just felt there was trouble brewing."

"An why would there be anything wrong? Woman, you're as skittish as a horse in this weather. Surely you're no feart?"

"Of course not. It's only wind and rain, but— oh!" The lightning startled her.

"Aye that was a mighty flash, the thunder'll roll next. That's why I came up to see you, Cate. Someone was no afraid of the storm last night. They were out cutting the wire in the fence."

"Fisher, this picking away at us is getting me down. I can't abide things going on and no action being taken to stop it."

"Well now, short of patrolling the grounds, what can we do?"

"Couldn't we use Gregor to do just that?"

"What, in this weather? And him crippled with the rheumatics? Away with you! It would be the death of him."

"I suppose so. Though I do think we need to get Angus some help. It's gone on too long and they're getting more brazen."

"You've the right of it there. I'll have a word with Angus. He can't be in two places at once, so I'll put someone else outside, though I'll wait till this weather's over. No man should be made to go out in this. Anyway you'd best away home or you'll no find your way across the moor."

Shutting the door firmly against the storm she was glad to be home. She had it to herself now since Rhoddy was away at school in Edinburgh. What a problem that had been! Another change, another reason to dislike his mother, another move from friends he'd made, home he'd known. She didn't feel hungry, so a good cup of tea would do fine. Cate stacked the fire with some of the dried driftwood she still collected on her shore walks. Topping her tea up with a dram of Craeg Dhu, she settled in front of the now blazing fire and stared intently into it. As the sticks spat at her, flamed and then crumpled into glowing red embers, she felt her lids drooping. Too comfortable to move, Cate drifted into slumber.

Hours later she stirred, but could find no ease. Stretching her stiff limbs, she made for her bed, the fire now nothing but a few grey ashes with a flicker of red here and there. As she began to undress, the wariness of the morning seemed to take hold again. The wind still whistled round the house, but the rain had eased.

Later, in the darkness, Cate woke. Something had disturbed her sleep. Since she was alone, it must have been the wind. Listening now, she realised the storm had not blown over yet. Well, she was safe and warm. Maybe it would be gone by morning. Snuggling down again, she tried to sleep, but it was useless. She might as well get up, and go over those figures, as lie waiting for sleep.

With the fire built up on the embers and hot sweet tea in her hand she debated whether another dram of Craeg Dhu would be advisable. For sleep perhaps, but for figures no, so she set out the papers on the table and worked away, only raising her head at intervals to sip the tea. The crash, when it came, sent her scurrying outside. She'd known she'd heard a strange sound earlier. Battling the wind, still a true gale, she swung the lantern high as she made for the shed, but no damage had been done in this wild October storm. Turning, to return to the house, she gasped in horror as she saw flames leap from the back of it. She ran to do what she could. Stumbling, she dropped the lantern and with no light, it took her some time to reach where the flames lit her way. If only she had her shawl to cover her mouth. In desperation she ripped the end of her nightgown, tied it round her face and braved the smoke at the door, she had to save the house and all that was in it.

Fisher wasn't sure whether it was the howling of the wind or his horse's neighing that woke him. Gregor would see to the beast, so there was no need for him to rise. Try as he might, though, he couldn't sleep and the horse was now kicking the stall. Was Gregor in trouble perhaps? The animal was close to the wee man. Mind, with all the other night-time shenanigans, he'd better investigate. Dressed, he made his way to the back of the house. Then he saw it. Flames, jumping this way and that, buffeted and fuelled by the wind. The Black House was on fire.

The villagers had all turned out and fought till dawn. They'd had to hold back Fisher and the other one from Laggan House, when he came, from entering the burning building, till even they became resigned to the loss. As the sky began to lighten, wearily they surveyed the dying flames. Many a mind was uneasy as they thought of harsh words or deeds towards the body that surely had burnt along with the now ruined house. The lad, away at school, had now lost his mother as well as his father.

It was Gregor who found her, out beyond the shed, the house cow's halter by her side. As they bore the almost lifeless figure to Fisher's house, the villagers following, they could only marvel as to how she'd escaped in her nightclothes and those half torn away and burnt. She'd cheated being burnt to death, but most of those present could feel evil hovering still.

They all needed sleep, yet somehow no one was prepared to be the first to leave. The men and women, wrapped in their shawls against the wind, moved uneasily about waiting for instructions. Fisher, who'd led them for years, would tell them what to do. But it was the Iron Man who came out. Doubtless Fisher was with her. He'd be that concerned.

"One of you run to Laggan House and...."

"I'll take the horse, sir, it'll be quicker."

Dinwoodie wondered if this little gnarled old man could even mount a horse, but the idea was good. "You can ride?"

"All my life and yon lass was good to me. I'll ride fast enough."

The crowd parted and within minutes Fisher's big roan was pounding across the moor with the tiny figure of Gregor head to head on the great horse.

"Is she...?"

A curt shake of the head and Dinwoodie turned to enter the house. Thinking better of it, he spoke to them. "Look, you've done all you can for the moment. Go home, get warm and dry and thank you all for your help."

"Why would we no help?" asked Donald Uig. "Wasn't she just one of us."

Kirsty moved to the front. "I'll come in and see to her clothing and make a sup for the two of you, sir."

"That would be most kind."

"She was a good friend to me."

"An who's to make a sup for me, Kirsty? You're my intended."

"You've an old crone tucked up in bed. Away an wake her, Donald Uig. I'm no your wife yet. Morag, would you away and get some dry clothes for her and a shawl?"

Later Kirsty joined the men. "I've wrapped her in your blanket, Fisher, till Morag comes back. Her burns look sore and the hair's burnt. Frozen she'll have been in that storm, never mind the hurt of the fire. She had bitties of paper in her hand, half burnt, figures and such like on them. If that's what she ran out of the house with I dinna know why she bothered. She'd have been better bringing her shawl. I've left them by the bedside, Fisher. I dinna know what we'll do for her. See we've always had the Cailliach, or Cate herself, to tend us and now the one's dead and the other both burnt and near frozen to death."

"Aye, Kirsty, and with Callumn retired to Edinburgh and the nearest doctor miles away, a journey's the only hope."

"Don't lose heart now, you two. If I'm not mistaken, the horseman—what's his name, Fisher?"

"Gregor, sir. A jockey in his youth he was and could ride like the furies. He'll get the chauffeur here in no time. Will I come with you to Fort William, sir?"

"I don't think so, Fisher, you're needed here. The villagers will look to you and everyone must be on their guard. I've a feeling that fire was never an accident. We've no idea what went on last night, but I've a premonition there may be more to come."

Only now was Dinwoodie beginning to understand how he'd merged into this community—thank God he'd been at Laggan House—and how much the stalwart Highlander beside him had gained his respect. Patting his shoulder, Dinwoodie gave what comfort he could. "I'll see she has the very best of medical attention, Fisher. Trust me to take care of her for you."

"You're a good man, sir."

"Come now, after all this time surely 'Dinwoodie' would do?"

"You've the right of it, Dinwoodie, and here's my hand."

On his way to Dunoon, the policeman wasn't looking forward to his task. Announcing a death was never easy. He knocked, while preparing his words.

Maggie opened the door and the sight of the policeman, visibly uneasy, alarmed her.

"We've never been in any kind of trouble. I don't know what you want with us."

"I'm afraid I've some bad news, Missus. Can we go inside?"

Following the two women, the constable wished himself elsewhere

"What kind of bad news?"

"Your man, Bert Green, seaman aboard the fishing vessel 'Island Girl', wasn't he?"

"What about him? He's no hurt?" The look on the constable face gave her the answer.

"I'm sorry to have to tell you he's been lost at sea."

"No, that canna be right, not my Bert. Are you sure? How can we manage without him? Not my Bert. He can't be drowned, he just can't!"

Maggie stared at the policeman as he answered her with a nod and described how Bert had fallen on the deck of the 'Island Girl' during a storm, knocking himself out, and then been washed overboard.

In a whisper she asked, "His body?" She needed his body, to bury him. Somewhere she could go to mourn.

The constable shook his head. "No, I'm afraid not. As we understand it, they tried, but the weather was too bad, and the boat itself was in danger for some time."

Lizzie broke the awkward silence that followed the policeman's explanation. "You're sure then? There's no mistake? I mean…"

"No. There's no doubt about it. I'm sure the fisher lads will see you and answer any further questions when the boat gets home. Do you want me get anybody in the meantime—a relative, the minister?"

"It's alright, I'll look after my Mammy. Thank you." Lizzie answered since Maggie remained silent.

"I'm so sorry for you both. Are you sure there's nothing more I can do?"

"No, we'll be fine." Lizzie just wanted rid of him.

"Goodbye then."

Lizzie closed the door as the policeman left, and, as her mother hadn't moved, she made some tea and took it to her.

"Here, Mammy, drink this."

"What use is tea for us? You know what this means. No Bert, no future for us, Lizzie."

"Shsst. now, Mammy. Come on drink your tea, an I'll make a bite. We have to eat an then we can think."

"Lizzie, tea an food will no give us answers—it won't bring my Bert back! Two of them I've lost, Lizzie, two husbands! Dead, Lizzie, my Bert's dead!" The words were too much for her. She rocked back and fore, keening for the man whose shroud was the restless waves.

Lizzie felt her world slipping from her. This screeching woman in front of her was her Mammy. She'd best get her to bed and stay with her.

Later, Lizzie raised herself on her elbow and looked at the woman by her side. They must finally have slept—in the big double bed that Bert would sleep in no more—but now the older woman lay awake but silent. She could think of nothing other than tea, helped by a good drop of Bert's brandy, to give to her mother. Taking it back into the bedroom she persuaded her mother to sit up and, putting the cup in her hand, left her to go and light the fire that had gone out overnight. As the flames flickered Lizzie cradled her knees in front of them, frightened by the uncertainty of their future.

As he left the nursing home in Glasgow, Lord Monroe was surprised to see Dinwoodie.

"Now then, Dinwoodie, you're not ill are you?

"Indeed no."

"Glad to hear it. Hopefully not a family member then."

"No, a good friend. And yourself, Lord Monroe?"

"Busy as usual." As he made to leave, the Lord Chief Justice turned back to Dinwoodie. I may be overstepping the mark here, but as I'm a patron of this nursing home, my mother died here, why don't you let me have a word with Matron, make sure your friend is well looked after?"

"I know one shouldn't ask for favours, but I am anxious about Cate…"

"Not the charming Mrs. McAlister, Dinwoodie? What's happened to her?"

A concerned Lord Monroe, interested in the friendship between the Iron Man and the Fascinating Widow, listened to Dinwoodie's account of the storm and the woman's injuries, and then insisted they go in search of the matron to ensure that everything possible would be done for Cate while she was there.

Back in his office catching up on his backlog of work, after a tour of the foundry with the manager, Dinwoodie realised he'd have to leave for London as soon as possible. First he'd have to find someone to stay with Cate, who had now developed pneumonia while recovering from her burns. He'd start by using Monroe's offer of help. By the end of the day he had the name of the firm where the clerk now worked. Giving his secretary the letters to sign and instructions for contacting him, he made his way to the car where Morrison was waiting.

As they drew up in front of the lawyer's office, Dinwoodie dismissed the chauffeur. "This'll do fine, Morrison. I can get a cab to the nursing home. You need to get me to the station in the morning, the train leaves at eight."

Climbing the steps to the lawyer's office, he felt rather guilty taking up the man's time, never mind asking to borrow his clerk, but, if it would help Cate, he'd wallow in guilt.

As he was expected he was shown straight to the office where the lawyer rose to greet him. "Mr. Dinwoodie."

"Good of you to see me at such short notice, Mr. Wiseman."

"Not at all. How can we help?"

"I'm afraid it's not your legal services I'm after—been with my firm since the beginning and wouldn't leave them. No, let me explain." As he related the facts, Dinwoodie was surprised at the effect the news had on the young lawyer.

"Just how badly injured is she, Mr. Dinwoodie?"

"You know her?"

"Indeed I do. She's one of our clients, and a personal friend."

"As I said, she's been hurt, but now the pneumonia is the problem and the doctors want someone by her side. I've been doing that, but I have to go…."

"I could certainly help out."

"In truth I was after your clerk, Mr. Wiseman."

"Solly—of course, they've been friends for some time."

"She'd told me that, so I thought he would be the ideal candidate. You see I was unaware that you also knew her." So here was another admirer in the Cate camp! Dinwoodie felt it was getting somewhat overcrowded.

"I'll arrange for Solly to have some time. When would you need him?"

"I'm leaving in the morning, hopefully only for two days, but these politicians can never be trusted to keep to a timetable."

"Between us we'll cover your absence, Mr. Dinwoodie. Have no fear of that. Perhaps you'd like a word with Solly? He's in the outer office."

As the door closed the lawyer was already planning flowers, fruit, and spending time with a captive Cate.

Dinwoodie explained the situation to Solly. "So there you are. Will you help?"

"Sir, I'd do anything for Cate, believe me. I…can't bear the thought of her lying…."

"Now then, lad, don't upset yourself. We'll bring her back to health. Trust me. Your part will be to sit at her bedside, chat to her, so when the fever breaks she will have someone familiar close to her."

"What about Lizzie, sir, she means more than anyone to Cate. They're like sisters."

"You don't happen to know…?"

"Yes, in Dunoon, sir. I visit her sometimes. She lives there with Maggie and Bert." Solly couldn't wait to be of assistance.

"Capital. Write it down for me and we'll bring her in as well. I leave Cate in your hands, young man. Now I have the address, may I make a call? I've let my chauffeur go home, but I'll need him back here now, if I'm to go to Dunoon. The politicians would have to wait for another day at least.

When she heard the knock on the door, Lizzie didn't want to open it. The horror of the last visitor three days ago was still with her. Had it been a neighbour, they would have called and come in. Her mother sat by the double bed beside the empty space, and even the more insistent knocking didn't arouse her interest. Slowly the girl rose and made for the door. The man standing there was a stranger, though she thought she'd seen him once before.

"I'm sorry to intrude like this. You know, you're just as Cate described you."

"Cate!" The name exploded in her head. Cate would help them. She wasn't here, though. And who was he?

"I've startled you, I can see. May I come in? Your mother, Maggie isn't it? She's at home?" To his horror tears began to slide down the girl's face as she shook her head.

"Her Bert…" She could say no more, before the tears took over.

"Look, I think if we went inside, perhaps you could tell me what the problem is and I could tell you why I'm here." Seating them both by the fire, he listened as Cate's friend sobbed her way through the drowning of her stepfather, her mother's grief and their uncertain future. When she'd finished, he took her hand and began. "I'm not surprised it's all been too much for you, but I can help." What a nightmare! Poor girl left on her own, mother prostrate with grief, and the thought of losing their home.

Lizzie, comforted now by this man, suddenly remembered his words about Cate. "Is…is Cate in Glasgow then? I could do with her here. She'd tell me what to do."

"I'm sure she would, but Cate has had an accident…."

"Not Cate, she's not dead too?" Lizzie's lips trembled and the tears began again.

"Come now, I need you to be strong. Here, have my handkerchief and dry your tears, while I explain about Cate and then I will talk to your mother, offer my help in solving your future problems, and persuade her to come with you to the nursing home."

By the end of the next day everything was in place. With the widowed mother, and her daughter Lizzie installed in temporary lodgings, and Solly and the lawyer on hand as well, Cate now had plenty cover at her bedside.

As he packed his briefcase for the morning, still worrying over Cate, he felt he'd done all he could for the present. Now he must empty his mind of her so that it would be clear for the meetings, already delayed by a day. Warring politicians and the threat of war itself along with the lack of preparation, all meant long and heated exchanges, and he'd go over his notes during the train journey.

Throughout the following days her friends took it in turns to visit Cate and on his return it was Gordon Wiseman who detached himself from her bedside and tackled Dinwoodie as he entered the room.

"I need a private word, Mr. Dinwoodie. I have a problem I'd value your advice on."

"Then let's leave the two young people with Cate and find somewhere to eat, while we talk.My club, I think, would be best, if you agree."

"That would do just fine. Thank you."

Once seated, Gordon Wiseman explained his predicament about the house, Cate had instructed him to buy for her, and his uneasiness about his future move, while they looked at the menu. "And that's my problem. One of ethics really."

"So what you're saying is she instructed you to purchase the property, and the Laggan estate has agreed."

"Yes, but with her ill, should I go ahead? I would normally consult her first, about the price, any conditions and so on, but obviously I can't. I wouldn't want to lose the house. It seemed to mean a great deal to her."

"My advice is to go ahead. You have the funds at your disposal?"

"Oh yes, we handle all her affairs."

"Where exactly is this house? It's just that I can't think of a vacant house on the Kevinishe Estate." He hoped she wasn't thinking of moving away, but then he knew only what Cate deigned to tell him.

"That's because it's next door on the Laggan Estate. Apparently it's an old ruin, hidden somewhat, so what she wanted with it I really couldn't say. Anyway, we have the option on it and at a very reasonable sum. Thank you for the supper and your advice, I'll proceed immediately, and we'll hope the fever breaks soon."

The following week, Maggie sent the two young ones out for a break from the hospital. Truth was she needed time alone to think about Bert's death, and the coolness that had been between Lizzie and herself since Cate's last visit. She'd been wrong to deny her daughter the chance to join Cate in the Highlands, but she'd had her reasons. A family who'd disowned her. A church she'd been cast out from, all because she'd broken their rules.

Of the long-ago passion she'd no regrets. She'd loved him. Those summer evenings had been warm and beautiful. Nestled in the dunes of the machair they'd been in a world of their own with only the quiet murmuring of the waves on the shore. Two months later the cruel scene in the church could not have been more different. Being called to the front to face first the pulpit and then the congregation. To be shamed before them all had been too much. That memory, of the beautiful times with her man and her faith in him, had her raging at them all, denying her God, her family and the place of her birth, while inside her, their child grew. After that there was no place to go, no living in the village, so she'd left, vowing never to return.

Lizzie knew nothing of her shame and so she'd denied her the homeward journey, to join Cate, because she couldn't risk losing her daughter's respect. Now, with Cate injured and Lizzie's heart breaking at the loss of her dream, she was losing it anyway. Cate had the right of it. Whichever way her thoughts turned, Maggie knew she'd been at fault. Fearful, but somehow feeling better, she knew she would now explain to Lizzie why she had denied her and sent Cate away.

The next day with Solly absent from the bedside, Maggie knew this was as good a time as any to talk to Lizzie and their voices would still be there for Cate in her delirium.

"Lizzie I've things to say to you, that should have been told long ago. Mind, they're no any easier after all this time."

Lizzie, holding Cate's hand, thought she knew what her mother was going to say. She'd been wrong about Cate. What good would that do now, with Cate getting no better?

Maggie began. Painful though it was, she relived the scenes for her daughter and by the time the story was told she could hardly bear to look at Lizzie's face for fear of the shame she might find there. When she did she was taken aback by Lizzie's unexpected anger.

"That's why you wouldna go back? 'My Lizzie's no goin to the Highlands. I'll look after her. She'd be doin all the work'. It was nothing to do with me. It was for you! Whit do I care aboot meenisters, churches an the like? My daddy loved me, so what difference did it make if you were wed before or after?"

"But Lizzie…" Maggie tried to interrupt.

"No. You let me speak! You were the one no wantin to go back. Fine, but that doesna mean I couldna go back! Do you think Cate would have let them be bad to me? Look at her—she went back and she'd a bairn! She was brave. Do you think she wasna feart? 'Course she was! She went back, but you didna. And whit was worse you spoiled it for me! How could you do that? Make me miserable for some reason of your own?"

Maggie couldn't believe this raging girl was Lizzie. She'd expected shame, a little anger—yes, but only now did she realize how blind she'd been! All those months of close companionship and Lizzie's idolizing of Cate had formed an unbreakable bond between them. By trying to split it, she was losing her daughter. What's more, the shame that had been burning inside her for years was of little concern to the girl. Cate had been right, and now she might well lose Lizzie too.

"Oh Lizzie, my Lizzie!" Maggie moved to hold her, but Lizzie turned away.

"Don't you 'my Lizzie' me! That's whit it's all aboot—you, Mammy, only for you! Cate, Cate she…" Distraught, Lizzie leant across Cate's bed sobbing. "I'm that sorry, Cate, I ken you were right all the time. I believed you when you said we'd get on together. Niver mind I wis no allowed to. I knew you'd no forget me. Cate, please get better. Please! I need you, Cate. I canna do the braw frocks and the speakin and I dinna want to live in a place where there's no you. And you near deid. Dinna die, Cate! Please dinna die! Or at least take me wi you."

"Lizzie, ma bonnie wee Lizzie, dinna wish for death. Oh God, not that. I canna bear it. No you too, Lizzie." Maggie's sobs joined her daughter's.

Alerted by the loud voices, Dinwoodie and the sister, who'd been discussing Cate, came hurrying in. The main cause of their concern still lay in her fevered world. The rest was bedlam. Tears seemed to be the order of the day. Even the duty nurse was vainly trying to hide her tears.

"Nurse! Stop that this instant! Look to your patients." What had been going on here? "Excuse me, Mr. Dinwoodie. I must remove that girl—she could do damage lying like that on my patient. Heaven knows what matron and the doctor would think."

At that moment the doctor hurried through the ward, motioning the sister away from his patient's bed. "Leave her, Sister."

"But Doctor, with all this—I'm sorry, the noise...."

"Yes. I heard it too. A pitch of emotion surrounding her like this could perhaps touch her. We've no real idea what a fevered brain does, but we need something, some stroke of luck, to help break the fever. Leave the girl. Let her weep and implore—you just never know."

He beckoned the others to resume their duties, while he took Dinwoodie to join Maggie, who'd also moved away from the bed, leaving Lizzie, still sobbing as she clung to Cate.

While they spoke, Dinwoodie was the first to see the change in Lizzie. The doctor gripped his arm. Maggie stood, hand to mouth. Then they heard her.

"Cate? Oh Cate! Yir lookin at me! You're no goin to die! You're no! You aye said you would niver leave me. Oh Cate!" Lizzie kept shaking her head, unable, even now, to believe that Cate had come back to her.

"There you are, Mr. Dinwoodie! The fever appears to have broken. Probably just coincidence, but you never know. Right, just a couple of minutes while we enjoy the change and then I want everyone to say goodnight and let sister see to our patient. A good night's sleep, and we'll see what morning brings—hopefully no relapse."

25

Fisher urged the stallion through the tangle of bushes and surveyed the old house that had all but disappeared, but she was right. The house was neglected rather than being the ruin he'd expected. Quite why he'd come, he wasn't sure. Mebbe the lawyer fellow had done nothing. It might still belong to the Laggan Estate. He'd have to wait to find out. Riding for home, he saw Dinwoodie approaching.

"Ride a bit with me, Fisher, I've news."

"Is she…?"

"She's making headway at last." By the time Dinwoodie had told the whole story, Fisher's face was sombre.

"Come on, man, apart from Bert's death, it's good news, on the whole."

"Ach, Dinwoodie, it's just that it should never have happened to her. I blame myself."

"Now that's nonsense. Both you and Cate were concerned and, you told me yourself, a new guard was being employed. Even you can't control the heavens! Bad storms are just that. Anyway, though we have our suspicions, about the fire there's no real proof. She saw no one at the Black House."

"Well, I doubt she'll ever live up there again, even supposing we were to rebuild it. She had a fancy, you know, for a different one."

"Yes, I know that."

"She told you?"

"No, Fisher, she didn't." Dinwoodie could spot jealousy when he saw it. "She rarely confided her personal wishes to me. Her lawyer, in Glasgow, was part way through the purchase and asked for my advice."

"Well enough, with her lying half dead. He might have thought not to bother. What did you tell him?"

"Buy it. Once we start assuming she won't come back, somehow I feel that's what might happen. Though it'll be some time anyway and the offer from the Laggan estate could be withdrawn if the lawyer doesn't proceed."

"You're right." Fisher smiled. "She'd be in one of her rages if she thought we'd given up on her. Damn, it makes me feel better just to think of it."

"Where exactly is it?

"Well nigh on the border between Kevinishe and Laggan."

"Good God! On my doorstep and I've never seen it."

"Dinwoodie, it was built no to be seen. It was a long time ago. A MacNishe had a wife he didn't agree with—forced to marry her, as I remember the tale. Anyway, he loved the Glen, but not the wife, so he rented the old dower house from the Laggan Estate, for the woman of his choice, where he could take his comfort without it being too obvious, if you take my meaning."

"My, my! What a reputation it has then!"

"I told her straight, but...."

"She wouldn't listen."

"Dinwoodie, as I mind it, she had one of those rages I was speaking about earlier and near took the ear off me!"

"I can imagine that. How much of a ruin is it?"

"Well, I've just been riding that way and there's no doubt there's work to be done on it, but it's in good fettle. I thought about mebbe taking the overgrown cover off for a start, before she comes back."

"I think it's a capital idea, Fisher, and I'd like to help. We can sort the labour out when we're ready. Another thing, I've a retired accountant sitting in Edinburgh, could you do with his help till Cate returns?"

"I could at that Dinwoodie."

"Good."

"By the way, you've my grateful thanks for all you've done for the women in Glasgow. I'll need to settle...."

"No, Fisher. Cate and you have given me a friendship I now value highly. I've become accustomed to the Highlands. Though I'll always have to see to the foundries, I find peace here."

"My hand on that, Dinwoodie. You're a gentleman." And one with more than an interest in the young woman he'd been teaching business practices to, Fisher thought.

"As one to another then, Fisher, here's my hand."

"Well now, I still see myself as just a stillman, I've never had leanings for more. I'm content with my station."

"That's a happy state of mind and many would envy you. I'll call on you next week when I've thought some more about it. In the meantime, you take care. I've a feeling this story has a way to go. Which makes me think of something else."

"No more trouble, surely, Dinwoodie?"

"It could be. Now don't think I'm being pessimistic here. I'm convinced she's on the way to recovery. But this episode has set me thinking—of you and Cate."

"As a gentleman I'd not expected you to speak of village gossip. God, man, the girl is like one of my own. How could you think such things?"

"I was about to say, Fisher, that, if Cate had not recovered, it would have been difficult for both yourself and the distillery."

"Well, we'd miss her for sure, and sorry I am that I snapped at you, but the gossip gets to me now and again."

"I was thinking along more practical lines. I know her financial help is available to you should you need it, but what if she'd died? Now think purely of the business. No emotions here. Indeed, if anything happened to you, Cate would face the same problem."

"We'll have to trust the good Lord spares us both then. You'll be having a thought as to how we should be going on, I've no doubt?"

"I'm the outsider here, but, if it were my business, Fisher, I'd take her into partnership. You would gain her assets and she'd gain the distillery. Hopefully Bruce would get his hands on neither. Now that's she's making headway, I don't foresee either of you going to your maker, but it never does to leave anything to fate. Meantime, be on your guard."

"Not you too Dinwoodie! Haven't I half the distillery clucking round me like a pheasant with chicks? Good day to you now." Fisher rode on with an easier mind.

She'd made rapid progress and now Cate was restless, longing to be back in Kevinishe. Dinwoodie's appearance in the ward was timely. "I've just been thinking about getting out of here and back to Kevinishe."

"Cate, the doctor says you're not strong enough. Orders, my dear, and you have to obey, or he'll not let you out."

"Dinwoodie, I'm needed and I want to go back."

"Mmm. I rather feel those reasons are the wrong way round."

"Alright, I just want to get home."

"My dear girl, you haven't actually got one, you know."

"I thought you said Gordon Wiseman had bought it."

"Bought it, but not made it habitable. There's a difference."

"Dinwoodie, it's me we're talking about! I grew up in campsites, under bushes, in caves. I can live anywhere."

"Possibly, but you're not going to. That, my dear, is my final word."

"I do so hate to be bossed around. I'm sorry, that's rude after all you've done, but…."

"No. No. Cate. This is what you're going to do." What luck he'd held onto Michael's town house. Somehow, when his son died, it was too upsetting to dispose of it, and now, in these uncertain times, it was as good an investment as anything. When he'd explained, her refusal came as no surprise.

"But I can't just go and live in your house."

"You're not listening, Cate. It's not my house. You need to stay in Glasgow, near the doctor. Lizzie wants to stay with you. There's a perfectly good housekeeper cum cook there and you'll be—well—chaperoned."

"What? Did you think we'd get up to no good then?" The corners of her mouth formed the teasing smile he so enjoyed.

"Cate, be serious. The doctor will do some more tests on you tomorrow and, if he says so, you may leave on condition that you have a companion—Lizzie—and are within a short distance of his consulting rooms. It's all arranged, so stop being difficult and, for once, do as you're told."

"Yes, sir. Sorry, sir! I've lived alone too long. I'm not used to taking orders. Actually, I never did like doing as I was told."

"Really? You do surprise me! Now then, by the end of the week you'll be installed and I must be off to London again. I've neglected my business for too long."

"Dinwoodie, forgive me, and thank you."

If she continued to look at him like that, it was just as well he was needed in London. "Look, here's Maggie visiting. I'll leave you together. It's alright, Maggie, I was just leaving."

Giving her time to sit down, Cate was wary of this visitor. "Maggie, I thought you'd gone back to Dunoon. Have the neighbours kept an eye on it?" Why did she have to be here today? With no one else there it was going to be difficult.

"Everything's fine there, but no between us. I canna do more than say I was mistaken, Cate, but it's no enough for you is it?"

"There's something I can't explain. Or if I did, you'd either not believe me or hate me."

"We'll never know till you try, now will we?"

"It's Bert, or at least his death."

"If you're thinking your visits and the arguing upset Bert so much he worried about it while working on the boat and didna pay attention, and drowned, you're wrong. More like because of my holding back, but my Bert never got worked up like that, said his piece and that was it. Mind, he was mad at me over Lizzie, and he had the right of it, though it's all behind us now. Yon Mr. Dinwoodie offered me a bed with you and Lizzie, but I said no. I'm going to Dunoon for a bit and then I'll go back to Kevinishe. I've things to settle. I just came by to say that. Mind you take care of my Lizzie."

"Maggie, will you be alright on your own?" Maggie's departing nod removed the chance to bring up the matter of Bert again. "Give's a hug then Maggie."

"There you are. Hugging in public indeed! Right, I'm out of here before I start bawling. Mind what I said. Take care of yourselves."

As the door closed behind Maggie, Cate could have wished that her memory had not survived. Oh, the night of the fire was still a mystery. She remembered the flames, trying to save the distillery papers, the house cow, pain, darkness, then nothing else. Unfortunately, everything before that was crystal clear. When they'd told her in the nursing home of Bert's death, she'd become so upset the nurse made her friends leave. That hadn't helped the guilt and the fear of what her mind had done to her. How could she have known? What could or should she have done? Said 'I think I saw your man drown, Maggie. Don't let him go to sea again'. Should she have said that? No one would have believed her. Could she have warned him somehow? Was it just a coincidence? Fishermen drowned all the time, didn't they? The questions were never ending and the answers few. She'd have to tell someone somehow or her mind really would be affected. But who, and when, and would they believe her, never mind help her?

At long last she was getting out! Oh, she'd always be grateful for all that everyone had done for her in the hospital, but to be out in the open again! How good that would be! "I can't thank you enough for all you've done for me, Doctor."

"You look after yourself out there. You were lucky. Most of the burns have healed and the few remaining marks will fade, though never go. It's lucky none of them were on your face. The pneumonia, though, could well have damaged your lungs indefinitely. I've a feeling that coughs and colds will trouble you more in the future, so don't ignore them. Take precautionary action. In the immediate future, I want you to live quietly and give your body time to heal. Remember our appointments. I'll see you then. Goodbye, Cate. I see your car is waiting."

Having collected Lizzie first, then Cate, Morrison drove the girls to the house in Hyndland and waited while they got over the excitement of the drive and the sight of the house as he pulled up in front of it. He took the baggage in and introduced them to Mrs. Shaw before returning to the garage to work on the automobile while Mr. Dinwoodie was away in Edinburgh on business.

Once they'd unpacked and explored their rooms the girls ate in the kitchen with, Snowy, the cook's preferred title, and listened while she told them about the house, the area and herself. Then they chatted about their own plans to set up the sewing circle in Kevinishe until it was time for Cate to rest.

In the Gazette building, Alashdair was wondering just how long some of his fellow hacks would continue to believe there wouldn't be a war. More to the point, when would Scottie allow him to write what he wanted? So far the Gazette followed the herd in believing that nothing would come of it. Was he right in thinking the politicians were simply ignoring what the Kaiser was up to? For years now the man with the withered arm had watched his English and Russian relations build up their empires. Jealousy is a powerful tool. The Germans had been building their nation into a powerhouse for years, whereas Britain had barely scraped through its last colonial war. If a German challenge arose, we'd neither the men nor the armaments to meet it. But would anyone listen? Maybe if he tried Scottie again he could persuade him. Scraping back his chair Alashdair made his way to the office.

When he'd finished, the bored look on Scottie's face was the answer. What was the use? He'd done his spiel. It was the same old thing: none of our business. Why couldn't Scottie see what was likely to happen? Mind he wasn't alone in that.

"You can take that look off your face and pay attention." Scottie wanted none of his warmongering. "I've no idea what your hunger for war is, Alashdair. Let the politicians sort it out."

"That's the point, Scottie. If you read between the lines…."

"Do you no hear me? Let the government sort it out and you get on with what this paper needs."

"Which is what precisely?" God, Scottie used to be the best newspaperman around. Why was he being so blind?

"You take note of this. The public's fair fed up with the likes of you and your warmongering. They've enough labour troubles, with talks of strikes and unions, to make them sick, and women encouraged to try for the vote and God knows what else. What the public want is a bit of good news—light relief if you like."

"I suppose you've something in mind?" Alashdair tried to contain his irritation as he waited for Scottie to deliver his next assignment.

"You remember that piece you did on the distillery?"

"God, not another trip to the wilds. Not me this time, Scottie, please."

"Well, you didn't make an awful good job of the last one. It was nothing like your usual standard. I wonder why?"

"You know damn well. The woman was a hellion and the last person in the world I want to see again."

"That's a great shame."

Alashdair leant across the desk. "You wouldn't?" As he glared at the editor scratching away at the side of his face, Alashdair knew that he would.

"However, it's no the Highlands, so that won't be so bad. Listen carefully. Seems she's had some sort of accident an…."

"Good. I hope it hurt. No chance it was fatal is there?"

"You'll have to lose that attitude for a start."

"So I'm to find out what's wrong with her and then what? Who in God's name will care whether the woman is alive or dead?"

"Try Lord Monroe."

"The Chief Justice? Away with you! Why would someone like him care one way or the other?"

"An you can throw in Dinwoodie for good measure."

"The wrought iron man?"

"The very same, and that one is rumoured to be in line for honours one of these days. There's your interest. The wee tinker girl keeps some right posh company. An another thing…."

"Oh aye, Lloyd George has her as his Scottish fancy. You've been reading too many fairy tales. All you're missing is the big bad wolf a…"

"Ah, but I'm no forgetting about him. You've heard of Bruce MacNishe?" Scottie could see the younger man's interest quickening. Right enough he could never pass up a good lead. "Well then, apparently he's to do with your distillery—or he should be."

"Well, if he is, there'll no be much of the amber stuff left. The man's damn near a drunkard and a habitual gambler, plus the fact that he's into some nasty habits where women are concerned."

"Listen here now. I've heard he rants an raves in his cups about the old Laird leaving the distillery to a bastard, and what if your tinker girl is the one the wrong side of the blanket? Two highly placed men, a Highland Laird with a bad reputation and bad debts, plus a mystery redhead: that should be enough for a story. If not, here's your heading. 'Where's the Fascinating Widow'?"

"We don't even know if she is a widow, never mind fascinating."

"Another twist! See to it. I'm telling you, even if there is going to be a war, telling the public we're no ready for it is hardly going to help matters."

"Aha. So you agree war is likely?"

"Nothing of the kind. Frightening our readers isn't going to help circulation figures, but a juicy bit of scandal should!"

In the stillroom, Fisher was uneasy. He was not one for imagining things, but he couldn't help feeling it was all going too smoothly. The Laggan labourers had cleared the grounds of the house. Dammit, what had been the name of the place? Ah well, it'd come to him when he wasn't thinking about it. There'd been no more trouble at the distillery. Dinwoodie had brought up the retired accountant from Edinburgh and the three of them had sat up nights to keep the books all balanced and proper. He'd even done a trip to Glasgow and Edinburgh himself—Dinwoodie's idea. But looking for new customers was not for him. Sitting around chatting, telling them why they should be buying Craeg Dhu, when they were not that interested, made him irritable. He knew he made good whisky, but he didn't have the gift for selling it.

God knows what he'd do if she didn't come back. Lassie she might be, but she'd talked a good few of the lowlanders into trying the whisky and hooking them. Aye, he'd make it and she'd sell it, keeping them on a tight rein where the money was concerned. God, she was almost better at that than MacNishe had been.

Well, he'd better get back to work or they'd have no whisky to sell. He met Donald Uig on the stairs.

"I'm thinking I've the answer to the stealing and such."

"It's been quiet of late and he's no come back so mebbe it'll no be a worry."

"I'm thinking you're wrong there, Fisher."

"There's no trouble?"

"Let's away back to your office an have a craic."

For Donald Uig to leave the malt floor, never mind spend time in the office talking, was unheard of. Fisher knew his feeling of unease this morning had been right. Once in the office he poured a dram for them both and waited.

"You mind Johnnie?"

"Since he cuts my hair, why wouldn't I?"

"Right you are. He's got a cousin, up to no good for most of his life that one, been in and out of prison. Well he's back here."

"You're no telling me he set fire to the Black House?"

"I'm not, but he was telling Johnnie, who told me to tell you that yon butler at Kevinishe House was in the prison with him."

"Was he now? Gregor said he was a rough-looking character. You think he might be our troublemaker, on Bruce's behalf?"

"There's more."

"You've never been able to prove he set the fire, Donald Uig?" Fisher felt he'd throttle the fellow, given the chance. Cate could have died in there.

"No, no, Fisher. Do you mind the wee lad who picks up the splinters for the coopers? Well, he's one of the cousin's sons. The lad keeps the wife and God knows how many other bairns fed and watered, while the father is in and out of the jail."

"Not on what he earns here, he doesn't, so I suppose he's been taking extra to cause us a wee bit of bother in the distillery."

"Thing is, Fisher, the lad's done wrong, but sack him and the family starve."

"Right enough, but watch him carefully, while I think about it."

"He'll no be the one for the fire, though. He's away home to help out as soon as he finishes and he's way on the other side of the village. So it probably was the lightning."

"Possibly. Now away you back to work, or they'll be gossiping at you being up here that long."

Later, Fisher found the lad, arms full of old staves, making his way to a handcart. Skinny little thing he was, but working hard. "A word, laddie. So your father's home again."

"Aye sir, he is that, but for how long with the people no friendly?"

"Well, you can't blame them, for no employing him here, with his record."

"Without a job he has to go back on the thieving. We've six bairns, never mind myself."

"So it would no be very wise of you to put the kindling and your pay at risk then would it?" The lad was quick, no doubt about it. His face fell. He put the staves on the ground and shrugged his shoulders. Fisher knew he was waiting for the sack.

"How much did the Laird's man pay?"

"Coppers."

"Was it the factor, Peyton, or the butler?"

"The one from the jail."

"Well now, you and me don't have to fall out over this, as long as you understand it was wrong and worth a sacking."

"I'll no fall out with you sir. I was just that tempted. The bairns needed food, but what he gave me was no enough anyway."

"Right then, from now on you'll stick to your cart, but there's another wee job you can be doing for me as well. What do you say?"

"I'm no afraid of work, but I need to be home too, the bairns need seeing to and…."

"Surely your mother can see to that."

"She's dead, last summer."

Dear God, mother dead, father in prison, bairns to be cared for and himself working! No wonder the lad was tempted. "Right then, here's something in advance, away and buy some food for those bairns."

"We've no need of charity, I've kept them alive without help before."

"Dammit lad, have you no been listening? I've a new job for you, to bring in more money. Surely to God I can give you something for a pack of wee bairns, going hungry and cold no doubt? So think about that, and get something bought for them at the post office."

Striding back to the stillroom, Fisher fumed. Why in the hell had the villagers done nothing about this? Bairns in need on their doorstep and no help given. How could they! Donald Uig would most likely have the whole story, so it was no use cursing the villagers till he had the full facts.

Fisher tackled his malt man as he was leaving the distillery.

"It's no use raging at the village, Fisher. The father has had jobs but he either didna turn up or helped himself to others' belongings. Folk got fed up. No word was said about bairns in need. Mind, Johnnie used to feed the lad, now and again, but never a word about hungry bairns did anyone hear from him. Though, now I come to think about it, the lad never seemed to eat when he was here. As to the wife, I doubt anyone knew. The women usually stick together, though they didna like the father. Too ready with his hands according to Kirsty! Then the house is a way out of the village itself."

"Well, the lad'll work with the coopers in the morning from now on and then see to the bairns. I've a wee job for him as well. That ought to make a difference. See if any of the women could mebbe give a hand, though he's a touch prickly at the thought of charity."

"Aye, we're all a bit like that, and you can't blame him. You'll need to see the father doesn't take the lad's coppers. I'll have words with Johnnie as well. By the rights of it he should have done more, him being a relative an all."

As the two men parted, Fisher couldn't help wondering what had happened to them as a community. In the past, MacNishe, Rab, Callumn or himself would have been around the estate and something like this would have been uncovered. MacNishe dead, the doctor retired from the glen with his liver soaked in Craeg Dhu, Bruce uncaring, and himself with no time: that was no way to run the glen. Things would have to change.

26

Sitting in the pub, a disgruntled Alashdair flicked open the evening paper and stared into his beer, three weeks and not a whisper. He'd gain nothing by going back to the Gazette at this time of day, so he might as well read the one he had. The beer lightened his mood and he scanned the print. It was only a paragraph, but it provoked two thoughts. What had the Iron Man been doing in London and was his return anything to do with the woman?

Alashdair was certain that the country was under-prepared for a war. If it were inevitable, then Dinwoodie and his foundries would be prime targets for the government. With war on the horizon, folks could do without their fancy railings. So, was the foundry man returning to gee up his workers? Fair play to the man, there'd been little or no unrest in his works, unlike the other firms, such as the shipyards. Or was he returning to see the red-head?

There was only one way to find out. He'd do a rough draft of the article Scottie had turned down and beard the man at the foundry. Who knows, perhaps the big man would agree with him? If he kept his wits about him, he might even get a lead on the woman. Whistling, he waved a cheery goodnight to the barman and left.

Next morning he was outside the foundry gates. He hated all the waiting around his job entailed. It was amazing how often the weather was bad. Luckily, weather-wise, it was one of those 'nothing' days today, a bit like his wait at the locked gates. The gateman had been distinctly unhelpful, so now he had to hang around to see if he could nobble a likely suspect to pump. One with a boozy face would do fine, so they could retire to the pub. Beer slaked their thirst and loosened their tongues. Staying discreetly away from the gates, he watched as they filed out in twos and threes. He spotted the group immediately: young ones, jovial now the shift was over. They'd be for the pub. He waited till they'd gone in and then made his way to the bar.

"Busy now aren't you? Hardly a seat left."

"Thank God for it in these times. See you away and shove in wi they noisy lot. They havena got the old bones that need stretchin. Aye youse yins, haud on, can you no see, I'm busy with this mannie here. Here you, watch yir mooth! Aright, aright I'm comin. You'll be aright over there, pal. They young yins will no mind you shovin in, so they'll no."

Alashdair approached the group and spoke using the patter of his youth.

"Him behind the bar said you'd no mind, seein as how there's nae room."

"Shure, hae a seat. See here, are you from the works pal? Naw, didna think I'd seen you afore. Here Jamesy, this wan needs a seat."

The talk was of the heat, the smelting, the beer, the yards and their troubles, and, of course, women. Who they'd had, who they'd like to have, and a catalogue of intimate details. He'd chosen his victim, drunker than the rest, and seemingly in no hurry to leave. By the time he'd bought the fellow a couple more beers, the rest was easy. Not productive, but easy.

So the great man had been there, but had left early with his driver. "Gone to London has he?"

"Naw. Aye waltzing off to yin or ither of his braw hooses—twa at least in the posh end o Glasgow."

Alashdair rose to replenish his informant's glass. Forcing his way back to the table he handed it over.

"Thanks pal. Cheers!"

So that was the gist of it. Not a lot of help here. He might as well leave. As the fresh air hit him he found his legs were a touch unsteady from the unaccustomed quantity of beer. As he made his way homeward, he suddenly remembered Alec, the doorman at the Courts of Justice. He'd used him before, when following court cases, to gather information. A great man for the racing was Alec. Right, armed with a good tip from his racing man he'd go to the courts tomorrow and find out about Monroe. Having worked out his next move, he was feeling pleased with himself until he remembered why he was having all this bother—that bloody woman!

Next morning Alashdair peered at his reflection in the mirror. Good job he was off to the courthouse—he wouldn't look amiss amongst the riff-raff up before the beak today. He needed two things for his day to go right. Alec to be forthcoming and for the horse to win, then everybody would be happy. Well, even though he was no a bonnie sight, he'd better get there early.

When he did collar his man, and explained his errand, the fellow was less than pleased.

"Well now, last time the beast was placed, sure enough, but he didna win."

"Come on, Alec, I never said he would. 'A sound tip', that's what I gave you."

"Och, man, anything else I might manage, but Jesus, Alashdair, Lord Monroe himself?"

"I'm no asking you to burgle his house. Just a few wee questions asked around the courts—his driver mebbe, his secretary or even the cleaning woman. Don't tell me you don't know them all, Alec—social body like yourself, all this time on your hands opening and shutting bloody doors. You've to do something to pass the time."

"Aye well, you're right there. Fourteen years I've been doing it an I'm hoping to make it fifteen, so I'm no getting into trouble for you."

"I see. Well no more racing tips then—that's fair."

"Now there's no need to be hasty. I could mebbe have a word here an there. The cleaner often has a wee chat an I daresay a few coppers would come in handy for her."

"Good man, Alec. Any ideas where he gets his papers?"

"Not a one, but he gets his pipe baccy at yon wee shop roond the corner. Could be worth your while trying there."

"Fine, I'll do that. See you in the pub, end of the week, Alec." Now he'd better get back to the paper and then the library. If the Iron Man had two houses in Glasgow, he'd find them—wait outside all night if necessary.

Cate and Lizzie enjoyed just walking the streets surrounding their temporary home. Snowy had told them this district of Glasgow was called Hyndland. As they explored they were delighted to find it was in the fashionable West end, perhaps not quite as genteel as Kelvinside, but a paradise nonetheless. Without the roar of the city centre, the streets, lined with trees, were quiet and although there were red sandstone tenements, they were far removed from the squalid ones of the Gorbals. These had gardens in front, stained glass windows, and pretty carvings on the face of the buildings. There were also individual townhouses like Dinwoodie's. The whole area spoke of money and a better class of resident. The shops may not have been as grand as those in Argyle, Buchanan and Sauchiehall Streets, but they provided all the adventure the two of them needed. Today they were on the way back from the hairdresser's.

"Lizzie, I feel as if my head's been cut off. It's so light."

"No wonder, she's no left hardly any hair on it. Mind it's nice. You've wee curlies round your face, but, Cate, you don't look...."

"It's no good telling me I don't look alright now."

"No, it's no that, it's just—you're no like yourself anymore."

"I know, I saw that in her mirror. Mind, with my hair half on and half off my head when I went in, I wasn't exactly tidy, was I?"

"No, but it's right short. Women well—it's no right."

"You, Lizzie Balfour, are stuck in the last century. I'm going to be a modern woman from now on—though yours is pretty rolled up like that. You didn't want it cut?"

"No me, I'm too feart."

"Here, give me your arm. Next shop for clothes!" Cate laughed at the look of horror on Lizzie's face. "I know we make our own, but I've a fancy to see what's on offer and, if we like something, we'll buy it. Remember, I've barely a stitch to cover me, since it's all burned. No, Lizzie, no arguments. I've money of my own and I need clothes, bought or made. Talking of buying—I've bought a house."

"You've done what? A whole house! Whit for?"

"To live in, of course, since the last one is but a ruin now. And before you ask, you're coming with me. Oh, Lizzie, I told you this would happen, remember?"

"Cate, you're going too fast for me. I mean getting your hair cut and mebbe buying a frock or two, but a house with just the two of us together? Where, Cate?"

"Where have you wanted to go all these months? Who did you want to get to know?"

"The Highlands? Uncle Fisher? Oh, Cate, I dinna believe it. The Highlands, my uncle, the sewing and you—but my Mammy?"

"That depends on her, Lizzie. What she wants to do. We've no right to decide for her. Remember when she decided for you? You didn't like that, so how can we do it for her?"

"You're right, but I wouldna like to leave her in Dunoon, with the rent to pay and no help."

"We'll see she's alright, Lizzie. Now come on. We've shops to explore."

The next day, with Cate resting, Lizzie and Solly went for a walk in the park and fed the swans.

"I can't believe I'm throwing good bread to the swans, Solly. When you think of all those bairns going hungry in Glasgow."

"It's not only in Glasgow, Lizzie, there's hungry bairns everywhere. That's why we must always be grateful to Mr. McAlister for what he's done for you, me and Cate."

"You know she's bought a house in the Highlands. Well I canna seem to…"

"To think of Cate in the same way we think of Mr. McAlister or even Mr. Dinwoodie—the sort of people who buy houses?"

"That's it exactly. Solly, we've had fine times in the house here, what with hairdos and new frocks, but it doesna seem right, no working like."

"What are her plans? Do you know?"

"I'm no so sure. I think she's waiting for the doctor to say she can go home. She was all for it in the beginning, but now she's away to libraries an offices asking questions or has her head in half a dozen newspapers."

"She needs to use her mind, Lizzie. Keep improving it. She has money to look after as well."

"Has she—has she an awful lot? Of money I mean?"

"I don't know, Lizzie, but she must have got a tidy sum for the house here in Glasgow. I don't know what kind of house she's bought in Kevinishe."

"Oh, it'll be one of the village houses, I think. My Mammy used to tell me all about them, though they're quite small. You know she's gone back there now?"

"Maggie's left Dunoon? Does Cate know?"

"Aye, we both saw her off. She went all that way with Morrison. He was taking things to Laggan House so he took Mammy with him. She was feart to go back I think."

"Right then Lizzie let's go over there to the tearoom and have a sit down, we've walked far enough, and I could do with a cup and a bun".

Although supposed to be resting, Cate was in fact in the public library, choosing her day's reading. The yelp of pain came seconds after she'd stepped backwards. "I'm sorry, I didn't...."

"Obviously." She was a looker. Short red hair curled fashionably round her face, a decidedly modern miss. "Here, let me collect your papers. Pretty weighty stuff this—finance, labour riots. Your boss must be a heavy thinker."

Afterwards she could never tell, but the arrogant way he dismissed her as a secretary fetching stuff for a male employer reminded her of the Distillery incident. Yes. It was him and still belittling women! Well this time she'd charm him before telling the newspaperman exactly what she thought of him.

"Have I said something wrong?"

"Not at all. Thank you for my papers and sorry about your leg." Cate walked as sedately as she could to the reading room and settled down to her task. When next she raised her eyes to the clock, he was there. Smiling briefly, she gathered up her things, returned the papers and left.

"Look, I don't want to be a nuisance."

"Then don't be."

"Let me introduce myself: Alashdair Stuart. And you are...?"

The sooner she ended this the better. "The name is Cate, and I believe you couldn't spell it. Though your head is still on your shoulders I see." In later years she continued to wonder why she'd suddenly had the urge to laugh. It might all have been different if she hadn't.

"I'm sorry about the paper weight. It wasn't exactly ladylike, but you were so rude it was unbelievable. I've had the hair cut off, that's all."

"Shall we start again? Let me prove my good faith."

"Have you any?"

"Doesn't the condemned man always have the right to prove his innocence?"

"You were guilty before you were condemned. Now I must away home."

"That's a long walk back to, where was it?" As he hurried to match his steps to hers, Alashdair was thoroughly enjoying the verbal sparring.

"Kevinishe. Why are you here?"

"I work here. And you?"

"I'm recuperating from an accident."

"I'm sorry. Were you badly hurt?"

"No, burnt, hence the haircut. And now I'm recovering from pneumonia."

"Good God. Are you all right? Should you be out? Let me walk you home."

"Yes, yes, and no thank you." He really had looked concerned.

Catching up with her again, he continued, "Look, I was sent up to the Highlands against my wishes and when I saw you—well, I was wet through, mad, and you laughed at me, then refused me a job you knew I hadn't asked for. That amounts to provocation. No. Don't walk away. Wait! Please listen. It was all a bad mistake. I was rude and I'm sorry. Let's walk and you can tell me your side of the story, since I had it horribly wrong. Looking back I can see that, but you did hurt my pride, as well as my head, and…."

"And?"

"You set that mountain of a man on me."

Now, she didn't try to conceal her amusement. This broke the ice and, by the time they reached the Hyndland Road, Cate had learnt of his path from tenement boy to newspaperman, and he hers, from tinker girl to property owner and distillery accountant. She was not to know that, just as she had withheld details, so had he.

"I'm fine here, and surely you should be out there gathering news?"

"Cate—you don't mind me calling you that?"

"It's better than some of the things you called me in Kevinishe."

"Please! Can't we forget that first meeting? Before I go, I've enjoyed talking to you and I want to see you again."

"Really?" At his nod, she relented. "I'm in the libraries most days. Thank you for walking me home. Goodbye."

The reporter haunted the library over the next few days and his persistence was rewarded when he finally saw her coming towards the reading room. When she'd finished there he led her outside and on their way back to Hyndland he told her of his latest assignment. Her reaction was predictable. In her fury she turned on him.

"You ought to be ashamed of yourself. You're not a serious newspaperman—that's just gossip you're looking for."

"Exactly! I'm supposed to be writing about a fascinating widow and I really want to write about the threat in Europe."

"There's nothing fascinating about me. So concentrate on Europe and the likelihood of war." She'd really looked forward to seeing him again, and now this!

"You think there'll be war?"

His expression showed his astonishment.

"There you go again—how could a woman keep up to date with foreign affairs? Apology or not, you're still arrogant and condescending.

"Okay! I apologise again! Going back to the assignment, you've been seen with two notable men and the editor thinks the public will want to know why. And pared down like that, the quest seems shameful, even to my ears."

"You're sure you don't want to write it, or are you wondering whether I really am a widow or just the doxy from Kevinishe?' Studying his face, Cate could see the discomfort, so she'd guessed correctly. "Here you are then. Here's your news. I went to the ball with a neighbour and good friend, Mr. Dinwoodie. He introduced me to Lord Monroe. The papers have already printed pictures of the event, so why the interest now? Compared to what you said you wanted to write about, it's…."

"Trivial?"

"Something like that—to people reading it anyway. They've better things to be thinking about than pictures of a ball."

"You'd be surprised. In fairness to Scottie, the editor, people who have miserable lives often want to read of those who live the kind they dream of."

"I dreamt of what I would do with money when I was homeless and starving, but it wasn't to dress up and go to a ball."

"What was your dream?"

"Still is. To have a home of my own, a family of my own and to live and work in my Highland community, using the money to help those that live there."

"Those are pretty lofty dreams. I see they don't include the fancy dresses or the hairdos."

"I make most of my own clothes—well I draw them and help Lizzie cut them out. But she finishes them."

"Lizzie?"

"She and Maggie, her mother, are the people in the tenements I told you about. Took me in when I needed it. You never forget that. Just as your Scottie did for you."

"That's true enough."

"But you were telling me why the editor wanted to know about the ball."

"Because pictures may sometimes tell a story, though as often as not they don't, so Scottie wants to know how a tinker girl came to be keeping such illustrious company."

"I see. I'm not good enough for that according to your editor. We're back to the same old story. Am I the mistress of one or both of them? Is that it? That should keep me right busy. If that's the kind of work you do, you'd have done better to stay in the tenements. At least the filth there is honest-to-God grime."

"I'm sorry. I know it sounds bad. But I had to tell you. Can you understand? I'm not surprised you're hurt. Both you and I have been insulted like this in the past, because of our lowly birth? Right now you look the better human being than either the editor or myself. And I can only apologise."

"Away and tell your editor, or, better still, take me to him and I'll tell him the facts. If he prints anything else, I'll set my lawyer on him."

"You've a lawyer? How many more surprises do you hold?"

"There you go again—your face says it all—a tinker with a lawyer! I told you I was married. He was a lawyer. So, before you ask, I inherited on his death. Not as you so crudely put it, 'for favours'."

"I'm sorry. Look here, I told you I was not only mistaken but also thoroughly rude. To make amends why don't I meet you in the library tomorrow and we'll go to see Scottie together."

"Right, until tomorrow then. Maybe I'll have a go at him for not making a good job of that advert of mine. I could have done better myself. Goodbye." As she made for Hyndland she thought about the meeting with the reporter. He was an interesting character and she'd enjoyed their talk.

The next day, Scottie watched the pair as they left his office, walking through the newsroom, Alashdair pointing things out, her nodding and smiling, and the rest of them open-mouthed. Right enough, she was a handsome woman and not to be taken lightly, demanding a re-run of the advert with a bit more of a sparkle about it and threatening him with her lawyer unless he stuck to the facts about her. Disappointing though all that had been, it was Alashdair he was disconcerted about. For someone who had no right to be, the younger man was showing a great deal of interest in the fascinating widow. It would need watching, otherwise it could spell serious trouble for all concerned.

Out on the pavement, Cate extended her hand and smiled. "Thank you for doing that. At least I know if he still wants to make a story out of nothing, you won't do it. I'm glad. You could be writing so many other things that need writing about."

"Don't go, Cate. Remember I promised you the Glasgow tour. Of course, we can't do it all today, but we can make a start." He couldn't let her walk out of his life, not now he'd found her. He merely filed his conscience in the in-tray, to be dealt with some other time.

Hours later Cate's head was awash with facts, figures, pictures and varying smells. "I must go now. I've seen so much I didn't know about. It's all there in the things I read, but it's so different actually seeing it."

"I told you it would be interesting. What about a tour of the parks on Sunday? Are you free?"

"Yes, I suppose, oh…"

"Am I still not really forgiven? We've had a great day today. Why not, Cate?"

"It's, Lizzie. I simply can't neglect her any more. And there's Solly"

"Who is he? A boyfriend? Come on, it's only been one day."

"No. They're both good friends. Oh, It's just…I've been bored with this recuperation. We'd fun to start with, but it's gone on too long. So now I go to the libraries, the museums, reading and learning, and…well it's not really Lizzie's world. Trouble is I so enjoy it and get immersed in it. Late home. Forgetting promises. It really isn't good enough, so I'm sorry…"

"Why not bring her with you?" Anything would be better than not seeing her.

"Of course, why didn't I think of that? Where shall we start? I know Lizzie likes the Botanic Gardens."

"By the glass house, two o' clock then. See you tomorrow, Cate."

"I've enjoyed today. Thank you, Alashdair, for my lunch and everything. See you in the gardens."

Cate hurried back from yet another trip out with Alashdair, her conscience bothering her about abandoning Lizzie, who'd cried off because of her leg being tired. She found her friend in the kitchen with Snowy.

"Lizzie, I'm so sorry about your leg—I never thought—all that walking in gardens and standing around in museums. Come on now, the truth—you were bored as well, weren't you?"

"Just a bit, but the leg does get sore. And anyway…"

"Anyway what? Out with it, Lizzie."

"Cate, yon newsman is mad about you, anyone can see that."

"Lizzie, I'm so glad you've said that. I've been trying to hide it. I thought you'd be cross."

"You daft thing! C'mon, tell us all about it."

Shy about revealing her feelings Cate hesitated.

"Well, c'mon, Cate, tell us!"

"I wish I knew the words, Lizzie. I don't know what's happening to me. I mean, I didn't even like him in the beginning! I've never felt like this. I don't know! I just—well, like today, when he was near, our hands touched and it made me sort of all tingly. I can feel his eyes on me, even when I'm not looking. It's—oh, Lizzie, it's like everything is brighter and I want to smile all the time! Heavens, for the first time in my life I look at myself in the mirror, properly, staring at myself. Are my feet too big? Am I too tall? Should I have cut my hair? What shall I wear? I can't wait for our next outing. We talk and talk and I never want to stop. I think about our days as I fall asleep and as soon as I wake. He's in my head, Lizzie, and—I'm sorry it all sounds so…"

"Forgive me for interrupting, but if you were to ask me, Cate, I would say you've a good dose of love sickness." Snowy smiled at the two young women.

After dinner when they'd all gone to bed, Cate sat on the window seat and looked at the night sky. This was not what she'd planned. She'd never really been easy around men and, given her early experience, it was no wonder. Yet, when she thought about it, look at the good ones she'd come across: MacNishe, Fisher, McAlister, Dinwoodie, Lord Monroe, Gordon Wiseman and his father, the distillery men—these good people were so unlike Bruce and that other one. And Alashdair, where did he fit in? Perhaps this was the time to play safe and go back to Kevinishe—after all. If she was well enough to go gallivanting with Alashdair she was fit for work. But she simply didn't want to. She must steal some more time. She was too happy here with him. So happy she couldn't sleep.

Cate couldn't believe the view in front of her. All these outings they'd had in the previous weeks had been in Glasgow, but this was the best of the lot. They'd taken the train and it had all been such a surprise. "It's just—you've no idea how wonderful this is for me. The parks are fine, but to be out in the country again!"

"Cate, it's only a bit of water with bushes round it!"

"Alashdair, what are you saying? It's so beautiful. The huge expanse of calm water, the sun reflected in it, the…what? You're laughing at—you never meant it did you? Come back here, you coward. Just wait till I catch you!" Unheeding of her tight ankle length skirt, Cate gave chase and launched herself at him.

"Alright! I was teasing! Loch Lomond is beautiful, so please stop pummelling me. Is that always your response, to 'beat the bejesus out of me', to quote the Irish?" Holding her hands this close to his body stilled the laughter. Those extraordinary green eyes searched his face, asking questions. Their lips met and all the nearly touching moments of the past weeks exploded in wonder. Stunned by the intensity of that first kiss, they sank to the ground. For a long time they lay wrapped in the magic of the moment. Then his hands moved hesitantly to the buttons of her jacket and still her eyes held his, unblinking, as it covered the swell of her breast. Where he led she followed, until their bodies fused length to length answering her questions.

As the outskirts of Glasgow came into view, Dinwoodie couldn't resist the urge to see how the girls were getting on with Snowy. "Hyndland first for a short visit Morrison and then across town and home."

"It'll be a pleasure to see the young ladies again sir."

"Indeed it will. Here we are then. I'll not be long."

Morrison waited till the door opened and closed and then set about cleaning the windscreen, while he waited.

"Snowy, I'm not interrupting am I?"

"Good heavens no, sir. Come away in. Lizzie's in the kitchen sewing."

No mention of Cate. Did that mean she'd gone? Of course not! She'd never have left Lizzie. Perhaps she was resting. "Lizzie, busy with your needle I see."

"I never sit idle, sir. It's a dress for Cate. Oh, we've had such a fine time, Mr. Dinwoodie. We went into some right posh shops, looked at their dresses and then Cate came home and drew them so we wouldn't forget. She chose this bonnie green velvet and cut her pattern out and I'm doing the finishing. I'm better at the sewing than Cate is, though she's right clever at everything else."

"How is she, Lizzie?"

"Better, sir, though she's no here now."

She'd gone. But why leave Lizzie behind? "Where's she off to on her own?"

"Cate's made friends with a young newspaper man, sir. He's taken us all over, so he has."

"But not with you today?"

"No sir, they've gone off for the day to Loch Lomond. It was too much walking for my leg an it was really a surprise for Cate."

Dinwoodie turned to the housekeeper. "It's a long day for Cate, Snowy. She mustn't overdo things yet." So the inevitable had happened—there was a young man on the scene. Well, what did he expect?

"Oh, she's right fine now," Lizzie interrupted. "Thanks to you and Snowy here. You've both been so kind."

"Delighted to be of assistance, Lizzie. What about a quick cup of tea and one of your delicious cakes, Snowy? And this young lady can tell me about all their adventures." Hopefully by that time Cate would have returned.

She arrived like a whirlwind. "Whoa there, young lady. Take a breath at least. Sit down and tell us about your day. Did you like Loch Lomond?" Silly question—she was glowing, shooting sparks of radiance with every word. Dinwoodie didn't need anyone to tell him. The girl was full of that very particular brilliance that comes from being in love. She deserved some good luck, but her joy struck a sad chord for him. Thankfully he managed to feign interest in her day's adventure, but took his leave as soon as he could, promising to return soon, to discuss their future plans. "Mustn't keep poor Morrison waiting too long. Goodnight, ladies, and thank you, Snowy. You've done a good job as usual."

"Miss Cate looked ever so well, sir. Though I barely recognized her when she waved to me on the way in. It was the short hair that did it."

"Do you know, I can't say I noticed, Morrison, I'm tired and ready for home."

Summer was over, and Cate's conscience was troubling her. All the fuss she'd made to get into the distillery and here she was spending time in the most pleasurable way with Alashdair. She had to get back to work. She was fully recovered, and, if she didn't go soon, the men would think they'd been right in their opinion of her. How could she have forgotten her dreams of distillery, village and—Fisher now, what must he be thinking after the risk he took letting her work in the distillery? No, she'd have to work out a way with Alashdair to visit each other somehow. She couldn't give him up. Not now. Not after finding a man she could truly love. She'd speak to him today. He'd been neglecting his work as well. Yes, decision made, Cate put her hat on and, with a quick glance in the mirror, left.

Later in his flat her decision, when she'd told him, shocked him.

"My dearest girl, you can't go now. I won't let you. We've only just discovered this new world. I'd be lost without you."

"Alashdair, I've work to go to! I should have gone home before now."

"Cate, give it up. Stay in Glasgow with me. I can't lose you.

"You won't. The Highlands aren't the end of the world, I can come down to Glasgow and you can come to Kevinishe. Dinwoodie does it all the time. He even goes to London and then to Laggan House. You're making too much of it all. Seeing problems where they don't exist." This was their first disagreement since falling in love and she had no wish to prolong it and ruin one of their last days. "Come on, be positive. If our feelings can't stand a little distance, they're a poor thing altogether. We've a lovely day ahead of us and there's my surprise at the end of it. Let's have a wee smile for Cate now." She pretended to pull his mouth wide. "Come on—that's no a very pretty face you've on you just at the moment." He really was making too much of her intended departure for

Kevinishe, whereas she was beset with guilt at the thought of the time she'd been away. She knew Fisher would think less of her and he'd be right. She'd let both Distillery and him down by staying away so long. Yet these weeks had been magical. Never before had her mind and body been so attuned to another's. A new phase in her life had begun and now she must integrate it with the other parts of her world. She had friends to see to, a house to make into a home, a business to help expand, and she knew they needed her. Thinking of it all, she was suddenly aware of a huge surge of energy and optimism. Now her life had all the necessary ingredients—well almost.

She'd kept herself well informed during her stay in Glasgow. Bruce was doing a good job of destroying himself, but still she could not rid herself of her very real dislike and fear. Somehow she would reduce him to where he was no longer able to threaten anyone, especially her and those who mattered to her.

As they made their way along the street the atmosphere between them was strained.

"I don't know what you've been thinking about, Cate. You're quiet all of a sudden."

"Alashdair, I was back in Kevinishe for a moment."

"There you are. Even walking beside me you're not thinking of us. Imagine what it'll be like when you're gone."

"Now we really will argue if you speak like that about my home. I don't like many things about Glasgow, but I don't picture it as hopeless. I am a Highlander, the person you fell in love with, or so you say…"

"Cate, you're the one looking for a fight. 'So you say'—what's that supposed to mean? I love you! God almighty, haven't I shown that over these past weeks?"

"I'm sorry, Alashdair, but we have to go on with the other parts of our lives. How many good articles have you written lately? How many extra days' holiday have you used up? How much of your editor's good will have you lost?" Cate knew the answers, because she'd already been over her own sins of omission in the same period and the debit side was full to overflowing. "Come on! Let's forget the walk and meal. I'll take you straight to our surprise." As she led the way to the car Morrison had hired for her, Alashdair's surprise was exactly what she'd hoped. "This is my good friend and driver, Morrison. He's taking us for a drive to a special place and he'll pick us up tomorrow. Come on, let's go."

The reason for this weekend jaunt was not lost on Morrison. With Miss Lizzie away to stay with an old neighbour in Dunoon before they left for Kevinishe, Snowy off to relatives, Rhoddy staying for a large part of the school holidays in Edinburgh with a school friend, and his boss in England visiting his daughter, this was to be a lovers' trip, if ever he'd seen one, and somehow not one Mr. Dinwoodie would have wanted. He was very protective where Miss Cate was concerned. She knew it too— why else would she have insisted on hiring a car instead of using his?

As they headed north, Cate kept up a conversation with Morrison, but Alashdair had more uncomfortable thoughts to contend with. This love of his had come a long way from her origins. She used just the right amount of familiarity and authority while speaking to the chauffeur. Appeared to attach little importance to the business of car hiring. God alone knows what else she had in store for him today. For the first time, he saw beyond the childlike enthusiasm and energy, with its equally ready humour and temper, to the innate ability of the grown woman and the core of steel that would handle any crisis with an instinctive honesty that could rob him of her love. Yet he knew it was because she was that woman, he'd fallen for her in the first place. Even in that first meeting, beset by his own bad temper, he'd admired her, though he'd never have admitted it. She'd never been simply an easy conquest to join the others. He wished they'd simply gone back to his dingy flat and made love. Well she was right. Time was short. He'd enjoy the moment and leave worrying about how he was to keep hold of this forbidden love for another time. "Where exactly are we heading, Cate?"

"Oh, I thought you were asleep, you've been that quiet. Anyway we're here. Let's see what you think of my surprise. Just by the gate, Morrison, and I hope you'll be comfortable in the inn. See you tomorrow at five. Thank you—I couldn't have arranged it all without your help. Come on, Alashdair carry that case, my turn to surprise you."

"Well at least it's not…"

"Don't you dare say it's not the Highlands! Look, this is beautiful. The view is tremendous and —hurry up! I want to show you the river. Come on. Catch up! Move those townie legs of yours." Cate was so happy she ran straight to the riverbank and, removing her shoes and stockings, plunged her feet into the water. Even in September it was a chilly shock, but once that was over, her feet tingled and she splashed them vigorously. Her joy at being in the open was immense.

"You're a mad, mad woman and no a very discreet one, waving your bare legs about in the air! You're like a little girl, though I'm more than fond of your woman's body. I adore the grown-up passionate creature that entrances me in my bed."

Later she had another surprise for him: a beautiful home-cooked meal. Sitting back, Alashdair stared at her. "I never realised cooking was one of your many talents."

"When you're in service you can learn a lot just by watching. Oh, Alashdair, I've known so many good people who've taught me so much. I used to copy out recipes for the Kevinishe cook and then I'd write them down for myself. In Glasgow I learnt more fancy dishes. I tell you, one day I'll have a big kitchen all of my own."

As she rattled on about the house in the Highlands, Alashdair began to wonder just how big it was. Her descriptions of the Black House had placed it as a typical small village house. Were these just overblown dreams about what she'd do to the new house? He certainly hoped so. He was no longer poor but his money would never support the kind of dreams she appeared to be having. What was the matter with him today? Everything she said or did seemed to depress him.

"Right then, Mr. Paperman, the dishes. We're not leaving the place like a midden for the morning. Wash or dry?"

"It's woman's work! How the boys in the newsroom would laugh, if they saw me now! I'd be better off down the pub with yon Morrison."

"Well, you're not going, so dry. Here—one clean tea towel."

390

Cate woke just after midnight, rose quietly, and pulled the drawn bedroom curtains. Curling up on the window seat, she studied the stars and smiled. The cottage had been another surprise in McAlister's letter that he'd given to Solly for safekeeping. Fancy the deeds in her name, sitting in Solly's dresser all that time and her with no roof over her head! Since then, she'd kept the cottage a secret from everyone, especially Alashdair. She wasn't quite sure why, but somehow owning two houses seemed a little extravagant and not quite appropriate for someone like her. She'd sell it if it became necessary, but not unless she had to.

Speaking to the starlit sky, she whispered, "Thank you, McAlister. None of this would have been possible without you, the first man to show me how a woman's body should be used. I know it seems silly to come back here and mebbe not the right thing to do, but I feel it's the perfect time to say my own special thank you for everything." As the tears welled up, she hugged her knees and thought of their time together. Alashdair had a lot to live up to. "I wish I could've had more time to tell you how much I appreciated everything you did for me and how my feelings towards you grew. I've kept the hurt of Sarah deep inside me, but one of these days I'm going to find her and bring her back, for you and all you meant to me as much as for myself. I think I came back here to tell you in my own ignorant way that I did love you. I hope you knew that. I'm taking some of your furniture to my new house for the study there, so it will always remind me of yours. That's where it all began really. Sleep well, dear McAlister, and watch over me and mine."

"Cate? Who're you talking to? Come back to bed. It's the middle of the night."

"Shhsh. Go back to sleep, I'm talking to the stars."

"Crazy woman, you'll freeze!"

Cate waited until he fell asleep and then continued her vigil. This night was as important to her as her time with Alashdair. She'd no chance to grieve for the good man and it was long overdue. She'd said her words, and now her silent wait till a new dawn broke would be her final mark of respect before she returned him to the place in her heart he would always inhabit. Now she could move forward, knowing that she must uphold the standards her husband had set for her, while admitting that would be hard. She knew only too well that her character possessed some less than lovable traits and her decisions were not always the best, but she would try. His memory deserved no less.

27

Doug sized Kevinishe House up as he went round the back. Ron had done all right. Must be a good few classy bits nobody would miss in a place like this? Ringing the bell he waited, till his old cellmate, opened the door.

"God, Ron, it's cold out here"

"Here then, Doug, this'll warm you up. That's best single malt that is—in fine crystal. I've got a real nice thing going here. I'm the butler. I've the keys to the whole damn place. Silly bugger of a laird!"

"C'mon then, 'Butler Ron', what we after?

"There's plenty bits here we can help ourselves to later, for now we've a job to do. The boss wants the distillery out of action. Tomorrow's pay-day so we're to remove the wages and that'll mean the workers will walk out." No need to tell Doug about the other—the fire. After all it had been meant as a frightener, not to burn the bloody place down with her in it.

"What's he want to do that for, Ron?"

"He reckons his governor should have left it to him. So now he's for making trouble. We'll be paid for our work, and we can always help ourselves to a little while we're there?"

"So how do we get in, and what about the guard?"

"What's going on in that head of yours, Doug? Who's done so many stretches in the jail for burglary? Do you think they all invited me in?"

"I never thought."

"The old watchman goes round every half hour. So we need to wait till we see him go into his hut, and then we move fast. Right then. A few more drams, an off we go. Are you sure you weren't followed, Doug? What about that son of yours? He's always skulking around."

"Charlie? He won't follow me—I've seen to that."

In the small cottage on the far side of the glen, the bairns all stood eyes wide with shock, looking at the battered boy. Many's a time before now they'd all felt the back of their father's hand, but never anything like this. Charlie, their big brother, was bruised and bleeding on the floor. They'd no idea where to go for help or what to do for him. One of the girls put a ragged shawl over him and they knelt beside him and waited. For what, none of them knew.

The pain in his head, as he opened his eyes later, nearly made Charlie pass out again, but he knew he had to get help. Could he make it over the moors? They were up to something, him an the other jailbird at the Big House. He'd heard them planning a few nights ago, when they'd met on the moor. He had to get to Mr. Fisher. He just had to.

Having locked the bairns into the house. Charlie staggered along the heather path, picking himself up so many times, each one more difficult than the last. By the time the village was in sight he knew he'd never make it to Fisher's house, on the moor, but his cousin Johnny's was close. He leant against the door and banged his fist on it, before sliding to the ground.

In his nightshirt, holding a candle, Johnny opened the door to find no one there. A groan made him look down.

"Jesus, God in heaven, lad! No, no—dinna try to speak."

"Mr. Fisher—someone must get Mr. Fisher."

"But look at you. Who did this to you, Charlie?"

"Father. He's with the other one from the jail—need to tell Mr. Fis… "

"Aright lad, aright. The two of them up to no good—where lad?"

"Distill…".

Within minutes, Johnny had Charlie inside and the lad next door, still tucking his nightshirt into his trousers, running for Fisher.

The two criminals waited until they saw the watchman lock the distillery door and return to his hut. Giving the man a moment to settle, Ron picked the lock on the main gate, and with no sign of the old man, they made for the main door and were soon inside. They searched floor after floor, till they found the office. Once Ron had opened the safe, they stuffed the loose money, documents, and account ledgers, along with the wages bag, into the sack. Not forgetting to grab a bottle of whisky, they tried to find the still itself, but it took too long, and thinking they heard sounds from outside, they gave up and made for the main entrance.

But finding the way out again proved even more difficult as the numerous winding stairs were confusing, and they often lost their way before reaching the front entrance.

By then Fisher, Johnny and several of the distillery men had arrived outside the gates, and after an initial chase in the distillery grounds, had no problem overpowering the criminals, removing the spoils, and locking them up in one of the storerooms to await the arrival of the police.

Drama over they made for the distillery, now lit up. Fisher pointed to the bag of stolen items and said, "That was well done! Thank you— there'll be some extra in the wages bag. But first we'll have a dram all round, and then to your beds. Donald Uig, you and Murdo take a couple of men each and search every floor. Leave the stillroom to me."

"Fisher, the lad, Charlie—he's hurt."

"Where is he now, Johnny?"

"In the house. It was him raised the alarm, no me. I just knocked the village doors after he'd told me to get you. Mind, he tried to make his way to you, but collapsed at my door."

"Poor lad. He and the other bairns have made right good wee watchers. Charlie did say he thought they were planning something, but since not a word was said about tonight, I thought we'd be fine."

"That's because he's been lying at home, near beaten senseless since the middle of the day."

"Right then, Johnny, you get back to him and see the women tend him. He's saved the distillery for us. God knows what other damage they might have done had we not been warned." Fisher set the men to their tasks and made for his beloved stillroom, praying that they'd touched nothing there. While his thoughts were on the injured boy, it made him realise that this was the very time they needed Cate. If she'd been here she would have known what to do about Charlie, given him one of her concoctions for the pain and set him right. What was keeping her all this time in Glasgow? She should be here. The glen needed her more than she needed recuperating. Of that he was damned sure. Just what was she doing? Was she coming back?

Dinwoodie and Fisher rode in companionable silence. They'd met up while out riding, but by mutual agreement they'd turned their horses towards Cate's house and, once there, dismounted to check on the work done since they'd last been there.

"I've had the men leave the walls as they are for the time being. She's always on about gardens and her plans. In fact she's been doing a fair bit of gallivanting round parks and gardens, looking for ideas. Been with Lizzie and the reporter. You know the one, Fisher? I believe he came to the distillery for a less than harmonious interview."

"Dinwoodie, you're telling me she's out and about with him? She couldn't stand the man. Damn near took his head off with a paperweight!"

"Well, they seem to have put all that behind them. They've covered all the parks and gardens in Glasgow, as far as I can tell, so she'll have her own ideas as to what she wants done here. Still, it's all neat and tidy."

"Aye, your Laggan men have done a fine job. With the windows sparkling and the wood oiled by the distillery coopers, she'll be right pleased I'm sure. You're to pick her up this week, are you?" About time too! She should have been back long ago. The news of the paper man was most unwelcome. He wouldn't be at peace with himself till he'd seen her with his own eyes. She couldn't have changed that much surely?

While they walked the grounds, the conversation continued, Fisher bringing Dinwoodie up to date with the happenings in the glen. "So, with them back in the jail, mebbe there's an end to Bruce's mischief, but I doubt it. Have you time to spare, Dinwoodie?"

"I do that. Why? Surely there's no more of his troublemaking?"

"Yes and no, and I would value your advice, as usual."

"Fisher, I'm glad to help in any way I can. You know that."

Mounted once more they left the house and made their way to the distillery. Once in the office Dinwoodie began the conversation.

"Now then, Fisher, what's your problem? Everything looks very much in order."

"Thing is, with Cate being away I've had time to think. I've had some papers drawn up by MacNishe's lawyers, the old man's that is, in Edinburgh. Though now I'm no so sure about them?"

"There's a problem now?"

Aye, Dinwoodie, there might be, after what you've been telling me this morning, what if Cate's no for coming back to the distillery anymore? With the burning, the new house, and now this paper mannie, she might not? So what use would a partnership be to her then?"

"If I know Cate, nothing will mean more to her, Fisher. She'll be that proud you trust her. She's always had the feeling that we, as men, underrate her. I believe she'll be very pleased indeed."

"Right then, can you see to the signing of them. I've no mentioned her putting in the money—what with all her work, we've still no need of it. She's no one to go back on her word anyway. We both know that."

As he rode home, Dinwoodie wondered if he'd been wise advising Fisher on the partnership. Love did strange things to an individual. His only hope was that Cate would remain the woman that both he and Fisher believed she was. The will had been a surprise, but then why not?

Papers signed, Fisher put the copies in the distillery safe. He too was troubled, but his worries were not with Cate. She would be safe now, and, with Dinwoodie having the signed originals, should Bruce attempt anything else on the distillery, he'd find only the copies. No, he'd no worries over Cate. She knew where her destiny lay, never mind the wee paper mannie. She was like his own family, and, if what he'd garnered from the Cailleach and MacNishe was true, she could well be just that.

Sitting opposite his bank manager in Edinburgh, Bruce couldn't believe what he was hearing. How dare the damned man threaten him! He simply couldn't lose the town house here. Well there was nothing for it—he'd have to have another go at Kevinishe. Perhaps try that fellow—what was his name— Dinwoodie. Rumour had it that he was up and down regular to the Laggan Estate. He might be persuaded to rent Kevinishe house instead.

Now that could provide him with enough to quieten the gaming club's demands for a bit. Give some spare funds for another trip to London. Some of the Kevinishe pictures might be worth getting rid of as well. A few gaps here and there wouldn't be missed, should Dinwoodie take the bait. It all came down to not having the distillery. Why were they making such a success of it? If only his grandfather had not disliked him so much. If only his father hadn't died. If only—'If only', wouldn't pay his bloody bills! Well, he'd be sure of a good dinner this evening at Stuart's. After all, he was a cousin and might well be good for a few sovereigns. As he looked up at the windows in George Square, the rooms seemed to be full of people. Damn, he thought it was to be just a quiet family dinner with his Edinburgh cousins. Hopefully none of the guests would be people he owed money to.

Once inside, Bruce was thankful he couldn't see any of his creditors. Nevertheless, he was nervous when, after supper, a man tapped him on the shoulder.

"Hello there, I was just wondering. I hear you're from Kevinishe? Your name's not McAlister by any chance?"

"The name's MacNishe" What the hell did the man want? He'd made straight for him, and now it looked as though he couldn't get rid of him.

"It's just that my son has a friend at school with that name and he comes from Kevinishe. Wondered if you knew him or were related?"

"No relation of mine in Kevinishe" As the man melted into the crowd, Bruce tried to find the significance of the name, but the drink had fuddled his mind. A son at school, that would be something, to keep up the family tradition though, but he'd need a wife first. Of course! What a fool he'd been! There was his answer.

Been done for generations—marry money. Did the Dinwoodie fellow have any daughters? Would have no good blood, of course, but money. He'd made a few discreet enquiries earlier in the evening and the man was apparently extremely well breeched.

He'd better start paying attention to the assorted company. That's what he should have been doing all along. It was just that nothing seemed to come near the thrill of the gaming tables, and a moneyed daughter would have a powerful father on hand, who most certainly wouldn't stand for him taking his pleasures, the way he liked them. He'd have another drink or two and have a look for a likely candidate anyway. It was about time he had a bit of luck.

Bruce had spent weeks looking for a bride without much success. Trouble with these damn tradesmen was money. You'd have thought that, with all their wealth, it wouldn't bother them, but it seemed most of them wanted to hang onto it. They were keen enough to begin with. He'd danced, made pretty speeches, sat through social gatherings, but all for nothing it seemed. One or two of his choices had seemed promising, till their fathers investigated his prospects and, finding none, removed their daughters. One damn grocer had even stated quite plainly that he'd be willing enough to give the girl for a title, but he was after more than 'a small time Laird'. Damned impudence! Take the man from Laggan House—he'd married his daughter to an English Lord and he was just a bloody tradesman, albeit a wealthy one. He couldn't compete with that. He'd tried but, since once again his funds were low, he needed more money to continue his chase for a wife. He simply had to keep the Edinburgh house. He couldn't bear to live in Kevinishe—hadn't done so since his father had died. He'd leave the social scene for a bit and put his proposition to Dinwoodie. He'd let the house to him, and sell the land. Then he'd have enough money to do what he liked. That way he'd get married when he was good and ready. After all he couldn't let the MacNishe name just disappear.

With all that had been going on in the glen, Fisher was concerned solely with Bruce MacNishe. For some time now, the estate manager, Peyton, and himself were in the habit of having a wee chat when they met out and about on the moors. The man had been horrified to hear about the break-in, though not truly surprised. In fact he was about to give in his notice now that Master Bruce was back for one of his rare visits. Peyton seemed a decent man, Englishman though he was, and out of his depth here. Mind he appeared to know his job. The orders, after all came from Bruce. You couldn't hold that against the factor. With Cate in mind and the worry over what Bruce might do to Peyton, or any of them really, Fisher knew it was time he took some action. In fact, by his reckoning, it was long overdue. Master Bruce had been allowed to cause quite enough trouble as it was. Now was the time to put an end to it.

Some days later, leaving his horse by the stable block, sadly run down now, Fisher made his way to the front door of Kevinishe House. It seemed such a short time ago that he'd been an almost daily visitor here. While waiting for his knocking to be answered, his thoughts sped back to the days when the three of them, himself, MacNishe and Callumn had grown to manhood here. Even their love of the same woman had never split them, though Calumn and himself had never married. Well, why would you, when you'd never love like that again? Now they were all gone, leaving Bruce and himself. For all those ghosts he must try to sort young Bruce out. Make him aware of his responsibilities and end this bitterness, before more harm was done.

When he opened the door, Bruce couldn't believe the clodhopper was actually on the doorstep. Looking at the size of the man close up, however, made him aware he was alone with the stillman. Better to take this carefully. See what the oaf wanted. "So, have you come to admit defeat then? You know the distillery is mine by rights. No bastard ever claims a rightful heritage. You're as aware of that as I am."

"Master Bruce...."

"MacNishe to you."

"I've only ever used that title for your grandfather. Even his father barely got the word from my lips, feckless Laird that he was."

400

"How dare you criticise your betters! At least he wasn't a bastard like yourself."

"See here, name calling will solve nothing. I'm here to settle this business of you and the distillery and the village and to...."

"Ha, you've finally come to your senses then. The Glen, and all in it, is mine, as you know full well. Mind it's not your fault your mother lifted her skirts for my great grandfather. Prostitutes do that."

Had he been able to, Fisher could never have said why the foul accusation from the blackguard's mouth upset him so much. All he knew was he'd had enough of Bruce MacNishe. It was obvious words would mend nothing. Because of his size, other than in competition, Fisher had only once used his massive strength, in a temper. Since that youthful episode, the boy lying damn near dead, he'd vowed never to do so again. The incident had so shocked him that he'd never allowed himself to repeat it. Now he could feel that iron self-control slipping. It was time to go. He could do no good here.

"I see the truth has silenced you. Think about it man! I'm the last in a long line of noble Scots. Where does that leave you, eh? A bastard, a whore for a mother and a tinker whore for your mistress. What makes you think you're worthy of all this?" Bruce waved his arms to include the estate. Had he not been drinking, he might have avoided the other man's lunge.

Fisher could only hear the vile words from Bruce's mouth resounding in his brain. He had to silence them, even if it meant killing him. He grabbed Bruce by the shoulders and forced him to the ground. As he lay on the steps, Bruce wondered if his last moments had come. His cries, his strangled sobs imploring Fisher to let him go, were useless. He was held fast and he saw the huge fist aiming straight at his face. With a whimper he felt his bowels void and knew it was all over.

As they lay on his bed in Alashdair's flat, he realised, Cate was no longer concentrating on him. "You, my lovely, are not entirely with me tonight. Not good for a man's ego, being unable to hold his lady's attention."

"I'm sorry. It's just the school holidays didn't turn out to be the success I thought they would be." What an understatement! Even Lizzie could get little out of him during the time he stayed in Hyndlands with them, though Snowy's cooking met with favour. Rhoddy had made them all uneasy, slipping away for hours on end, secretive about his movements and, she had to admit, bolder in his petty disobedience. Most of her good intentions had evaporated by the time Fettes beckoned. "I just thought he'd enjoy Glasgow and Lizzie so much more than the Highlands, and he didn't."

"There you go again. Do I come such a poor second to your son and your Highlands?"

"Of course you don't. It's jus…."

"That the boy, your friends, your house, and the distillery keep your mind away from me. I don't like it Cate. I desperately want you all to myself."

"Well, that's not possible. Be reasonable, Alashdair. I share you with the paper and the all-powerful Scottie."

"That's another thing. Why don't you like him? Good God, Cate, I owe my career to him!"

"True, but he shouldn't rule your life, making you write what you don't want to, refusing to listen to your new ideas. He doesn't seem over friendly to me anyway. It's almost as if he's jealous of…."

"Well, if we're going to talk like that, what about your group of hangers-on? Fisher, the ox, for a start."

Pushing his weight to one side, Cate sat up, eyes flashing. Don't you ever speak to me about Fisher in that tone of voice! I've never hidden the fact that I probably owe my life to him, and you gain nothing in my eyes by being rude." Somehow their lovemaking had suddenly turned sour. She might as well have stayed at the library.

"This is ridiculous. It's all this coming and going." He pulled her close again. "Cate, please look at me. I want you to be with me all the time. I need you here close to me, not now and again, but permanently."

She'd wondered as time passed whether he ever intended to ask her, but she shouldn't have doubted him. "Alashdair, you know the answer, I've never felt like this about anyone. Oh, I'm sorry I've been a disappointment tonight, but I do have worries at home. Still, once we're all in the same place it will be so much less complicated. Just imagine, when we're married you can come to Kevinishe and write that novel you've always dreamed about." Suddenly Cate was aware of his lack of response. Shouldn't he be gathering her in his arms, sealing his proposal with a passionate kiss? Wasn't that what he wanted? "Alashdair? Say something. Anything. Don't just stare at me."

"I, well, I thought we'd stay in Glasgow and…." Why hadn't he kept his mouth shut? This had always been what he'd dreaded. Tell her now and he was doomed.

"It's selfish I know, but look at this little flat. Despite me putting in extra cushions and things, you must know it wouldn't be suitable. I daresay it's fine for you on your own, but I can't live here."

"Oh I see, not good enough for Her Ladyship."

"That's unkind and you know it. I'm offering you a chance to do what you really want. I already have a house big enough for us all, and, before you start, yes, Rhoddy and Lizzie will always come as a package with me. Heavens, what would you think of me if I suddenly abandoned them. What kind of person would do that?"

"Well that's it. If you don't love me enough to put me first, what sort of relationship would we have?" He couldn't believe life had been this cruel to him. To have her, even with her responsibilities, tucked up in the peace and quiet of the new house, where he could at last write and fulfil his dream—the pain of the loss of that, as well as her, was hard to bear.

"Alashdair, it needn't be like that. It's not a question of being first or last. I love you, Rhoddy and Lizzie in totally different ways. Let's leave the whole thing for now. I'm tired after my long day and so are you. Get a cab for me and I'll go. Snowy's probably waiting up for me anyway, and I don't like her having to do that. She worries if I'm late. Dinwoodie made her responsible for me when I was ill, and she's never stopped caring about me."

"There you go again. Now I'm even further down the line, behind a bloody housekeeper. Then there's the rich iron industrialist—how could I possibly compete with him?"

"Alashdair, what's happened to you? Have you any idea how downright nasty you are being about the people I have in my life? I love them. They're my family."

"See, now apparently you love the bloody Iron Man! Two minutes ago it was me you loved. How many more men don't I know about?"

The hard smack on his face caught him unexpectedly and brought back their first meeting. He'd have to remember that the passion she showed in his bed could easily turn into fury.

"Never insult me like that again!" Leaping from the bed, Cate retrieved her clothes. "How could you accuse me of that sort of thing? You're supposed to love me. I'm leaving, and the way I feel right now I may not return!"

"Cate, no! I'm sorry. I was upset. I didn't mean any of it. We'll talk again tomorrow. Please don't go." The thought of losing her was unbearable as he watched her leave.

When she finally got to her own bed she must have gone over the scene in the flat a hundred times. How had a proposal of marriage gone so wrong? She loved the man, and her body had a will of its own when he was near. Despite that, and the care he took in their lovemaking, she was well aware she was vulnerable. She'd already had an illegitimate child. Sometimes she couldn't believe she'd let her body dictate her actions with Alashdair. Life dealt harshly with those who broke the rules. She still remembered the feeling of panic that washed over her, listening to Maggie's story. The instant relief she'd felt, when Alashdair told her he needed her always, had lifted an unseen burden from her shoulders. Apart from that, their quarrel was spoiling her sleep. None of it made sense. He'd proposed to her, not in so many words, but he had said permanently. She lay till dawn came, trying once more to work out how to make the jigsaw pieces of her life fit together.

The ringing of the telephone roused her just as she was finally slipping into sleep. Shrugging into her dressing gown she ran downstairs, hoping to quieten the wretched thing before it woke anyone else, her mind still full of Alashdair's bitter words. At this hour it could only be him on the phone and, as yet, she wasn't ready to accept his apologies. Grabbing the instrument, she let her annoyance show in her words, "What time of night is this to be ringing? Oh I'm sorry, Dinwoodie, I thought it was someone else. There's nothing wrong is there…? No! You're mistaken. You have to be. It can't be true! How…? Why…? Where…? Oh my God, Dinwoodie! Yes, I understand. Obviously that must be our first concern. Oh, Dinwoodie, I can't believe—It's barely possible. No, no I'll be alright. It's the shock. What must I do? With Morrison, you say? Coming to the Infirmary? Right, I'll be waiting."

She left the phone dangling and tried to stop the screams of horror and outrage that were building inside. Taking a deep breath, she knew she had to be calm for the others. Knew, but felt only the dread in her stomach, the heartbreak ahead and the deep love, that she'd never really understood was there, for the man.

As the ambulance drew up at the Infirmary, Cate tried to come to terms with what had happened. Could she cope with all that it meant? She knew the answer. She had to. There was no one else. The fight to keep the tears from flooding her face was lost, but as the stretcher with the prone figure of the man, with the twisted face, spittle dribbling from the corner of the mouth, hunted look in his eyes came level with her, she stifled the tears and in a cheery voice leant over him. "Fisher, I leave you alone and look at you! C'mon let's get you inside and see what they've got to say and then we're away back to Kevinishe. Man, we've a distillery to run, you and I." Taking the lifeless hand in hers she bent to kiss the wet corner of his mouth. "I'm here, Fisher. I always will be." Her reward for her action was the change in his eyes. She knew he trusted her not to leave him in the hands of others. God knows how she would manage it, but keep the promise she would, whatever it cost her. She could do no less for the now-broken Fisher. Her giant of a man had been felled by a stroke. Kevinishe and all it meant to both of them would now have to be defended by her alone.

Part Six

The Homecoming

1913

28

A moment or two for goodbyes and, with their luggage in the car, Cate and Lizzie waved to Snowy as Morrison headed for the Highlands. Both women were saddened at the thought of leaving the housekeeper. She'd taken such great care of them and was always ready with timely advice. But the sadness of their parting and having to leave Fisher in the Infirmary, was tempered by their growing excitement about the journey, the new home at the end of it, and seeing Maggie, who was already back in Kevinishe. Eventually, tired by all the emotion, they slept for most of the long journey.

Cate's slumber was peopled by an irate Alashdair, a stricken Fisher, a sullen Rhoddy and a malignant Bruce, all worrying her with their individual demands. She was grateful when her eyes finally opened. The fraught situation she had left behind in Glasgow she must and would deal with, but now, with Kevinishe approaching, she gave herself up to the pleasure of seeing the house again. It had been such a long time since she'd first found it. Gordon Wiseman and Dinwoodie had completed the purchase while she was in hospital, and that had included the furniture, though what state that would be in was hard to tell.

"We're nearly there now, ladies. About another thirty miles to go."

They sat in silence for a moment or two and then Lizzie turned to Cate.

"You are bringing him back? You're no leaving him in the Infirmary, Cate? See, I've never even met him and Mr. Dinwoodie thinks...."

"I know what he thinks, Lizzie, and so does Maggie. We have to keep hoping. It may be foolish, but what else can we do? There's one thing I'm sure of—he'll just give up if he's left to moulder in

Glasgow. That's why we must bring him home, as soon as they say we can." Whether that would be alive or dead she wasn't sure. Whatever it was, she'd have to deal with it. Painful though it had been to leave him in the Infirmary, she had to get back to the glen. Someone had to keep the distillery running, and God knows if the men would let her, but she was determined for Fisher's sake.

"Cate, my Mammy says he'll never be better."

"Maybe not, Lizzie. Look, let me try to make you understand. If Fisher hadn't come along that day, long ago on the moor, I could have died. He and the Cailleach tended me and then he sent me to you and Maggie. Neither of us would be sitting here, Lizzie, without his action that day. There would be no big house, no saved distillery, and no village being cared for. Come to that, you and Maggie would still be in the tenements and your poor leg couldn't cope with the work you would've had to do."

Lizzie shook her head. "But if he's no to be well..."

"That, Lizzie Balfour, is the point. Can we desert him now, just because he's locked in a crippled body? He's still Fisher and nothing changes the debt we owe him—you and I and the others. Now then, I've explained. If anyone asks, he's coming home and we're all to look after him. That's my last word on the subject."

There was silence again, both women occupied with their own thoughts, until Cate, realised they were approaching the glen. "Lizzie, look, that's the road on to Kevinishe. There's the mountain, but you can't see the village yet. We turn off here onto the Laggan road, so we're nearly at the house. Though we'll have to make do there until we've sorted it all out. Last time I saw it you couldn't get through the door for bushes!"

Thinking about the door reminded her of the red-headed woman passing through it and she just knew the house would be fine. Her dreams were about to become a reality, and they would be shared with Lizzie.

Lizzie's mouth had hung open ever since they'd swept in through the gates, after leaving the track that was all that remained of the road.

"Cate, we—we're never living there? That's surely no it?"

"Lizzie, do close your mouth. You look like a herring in the net. That's our new home ahead. You'll like it. I know you will, especially since we'll never have to move again if we don't want to. Oh, Lizzie, at last we've a place all our own—and no one can take it from us."

"I'm no really sure I can believe it Cate. It's even bigger than the one in Hyndland! I'll be lost."

"I'll tell you a secret, Lizzie. We'll both be lost. I've never actually been inside."

"Surely you never bought…"

"Oh but I did! I couldn't even see through the windows when I found it, all overgrown, walls and windows hidden by creepers, everything dirty with peeling paint. But look at the outside now. I see Fisher's hand in this transformation."

The mention of his name hurt unbearably. Only he would have thought to please her like this. Would he really survive? 'He's had a massive stroke, Mrs. McAlister. It's doubtful he'll recover and he'll definitely never be a whole man again.' She pushed the consultant's words to the back of her mind. Dragging her attention back to Lizzie, she forced herself to be cheerful. "See now, we've both had a pleasant surprise. Home, Lizzie, that's what it'll be, truly it will."

As the car slid to a halt at the door, Cate leapt out to hide her distress. "Enough of this talking. I'm that excited—I'll see to the cases in a minute, Morrison, if you don't mind waiting."

"You go ahead, Miss Cate, I'll start to unpack, while you look round."

"Have you the key, Cate?"

"No. But I expect Fisher…" There it was again. When would she get used to it—this new gap in her life? "He'll have left it open for us, give me your hand, we'll go over the doorstep together. It's really happening, Lizzie! It's all ours, thanks to McAlister."

As she opened the door, Lizzie's gasp alerted her. There, waiting for them, were Dinwoodie, Maggie, and a group of the villagers. When the cheering died down, Cate simply couldn't stem the tears. She just stood shaking her head in wonderment that these good people had provided such a welcome. This time she had no doubts. She'd come home, and soon she'd bring Fisher home too.

Seated in what had once been the drawing room, Cate looked around. Some of the furniture was faded, the curtains had lost almost all their colour, and the strange array of chairs must have been collected from the rest of the house as none of them matched. The blank spaces on the walls spoke of missing paintings, but it didn't matter. It still felt wonderful, and it was all hers.

Later, while Cate said goodnight to those from the village, Morrison was driving them home, the 'family' gathered round the kitchen table. As she rejoined them, Cate tried to explain her thoughts. "I've never been so—I mean I can't explain what all this—the people, their kindness, the work that's been done…"

Dinwoodie answered her. "We worried slightly, I must admit, Cate, in case you'd think we'd taken too much on ourselves, clearing and cleaning the house, but everyone wanted to do something for you. What started out as Fisher and myself quietly getting the grounds cleared soon ballooned into a small army descending on the house. 'Help getting ready for her coming back', seemed to be the password, with every one of them doing something."

"Dinwoodie, you're right. I would normally have wanted to come in and explore and see to everything myself, but coming through that door tonight, I think, I really understood for the first time what being part of a community means. Though l have been in a position to give, tonight I learned how important it is to receive as well." Almost overcome again with emotion, she went round the table, bestowing a hug and a shy kiss on each of them. Dinwoodie, who appreciated this new, softer, Cate, was first. Then, when she finally faced Maggie, she hesitated. As their eyes met, the silent passage of emotions was for them alone and ended in the biggest hug of all.

Dinwoodie rose to his feet and drained the last drops of Craeg Dhu into their glasses. "We're pleased to have you home, Maggie already back living in the village, and now you and Lizzie. I know we all have the big man in our thoughts. So here's to him and all of us. Slainte mhath! I hope that's the right pronunciation. After all, I'm only a lowlander!" As one they rose and swallowed the remains of the fiery liquid that embraced their world, each wondering how this same world was going to fare in the future.

"I, Cate…."

"Yes, Lizzie?"

"Well, I was thinking that we're no all here. What about Solly? He's part of what has happened to us. He's been there from the start."

"You, Lizzie Balfour, are not only clever, you're brilliant." Cate wondered why she hadn't thought of it herself. Looking at the puzzled faces, she explained.

"I know you've all had doubts about bringing Fisher home, but we'll do it. We'll care for him between us, but I'll need your help and that's why your mentioning Solly is fantastic, Lizzie. I can't run the distillery and do all the accounts. This is a family business, and Solly is nearly one of the family. I'll speak to him. You never know, he might just come and join us." She could sense Dinwoodie's worry before he uttered it.

"Cate, admirable as all this is, aren't you forgetting what Fisher's prime task in the distillery was?"

"How could I? That's the next important step. I need a first class stillman to satisfy Fisher before I let anyone into the distillery."

"I think you're forgetting that Fisher is no longer part of the real world."

"Oh no, I'm well aware of that. But what did you think I was doing all the time we were waiting for the doctor's results?"

"Without being too rude, Cate, we thought—well I thought— you were…" Suddenly Dinwoodie felt embarrassed.

"I'll tell you what I was doing. Concentrating on finding a stillman, and I believe I may have done so. I'll let you know what's happening about that as soon as I can. We're all tired now. It's time for bed. Morrison's back, Dinwoodie and thank you so much for all your help."

As Morrison prepared to take Maggie back to Fisher's house and then himself and his Master to Laggan, Cate and Lizzie watched the lights until they disappeared. Tired, but still excited they went to bed.

Cate wandered into the stable block, her mind busy with the problem of her excess furniture. 'Craigavon'—Fisher had remembered the name of the house, Dinwoodie told her, and she saw no reason to change it—had been furnished by a woman who was used to surrounding herself with beautiful things. True some had been spoiled, and she'd need to replace them. The room she'd chosen as a study was now indeed a replica of that comfortable room in Glasgow, and her private sitting room almost an exact copy of Lady Sarah's. In fact it looked better, because Craigavon, though not as large, was a much more feminine building than the sturdy Kevinishe House. Otherwise she'd replaced faded drapes, added a few personal touches and that was all. Part of her was reluctant to change much, as though she was keeping faith with someone. *The red-headed woman* had practically invited her into the house with her smile, and Cate could feel her presence in every room. Of course it was all rather silly, this feeling of harbouring the past, not upsetting anyone, but she was happy with it and that was all that mattered. Anyway, the letter from MacNishe, that the lawyers had given her after the funeral, might have been burnt, but she could still remember his spidery writing and, if it was true, then she had indeed come home. What a pity she hadn't told Fisher everything that was in it. Once again her quick temper, and her hasty decision at the time, had left her with yet one more regret.

Deep in thought she hadn't noticed where she was going. She'd arrived at the summerhouse in the furthest part of the garden. It badly needed painting. The men had obviously not ventured this far in their clearing. She dusted the seat, moved a nest and a pile of leaves and sat. Almost as if she'd expected it, *the woman appeared from the tangle of bushes, but there were no welcoming smiles this time. Her face was creased with grief and she held out her hands beseechingly to Cate. Then with a shake of her head, she faded.* Cate shivered as the December air penetrated her cloak. Always the woman had been a source of comfort and now what was she to make of this? '*The Sight*', if that was what it was, had unsettled her. On edge now, a crackling in the undergrowth had her darting towards it.

"Just what do you think you're doing?" Her question was directed towards a boy she'd grabbed as he tried to make his escape.

"I was watching you."

"That's as may be, but you're trespassing." Mind, he was only a boy and hadn't she done the same herself all those years ago. As she released her hold she saw he was limping. "What happened to your leg?"

"I was hurt, but I had to use it and it's no mended right."

"Are you…?"

"Charlie's my name. You're no supposed to see me. I never thought you'd come down here."

"Why am I not supposed to see you?" The way he framed the words, made it sound to her as though he had permission to be there, but not seen.

"We-e-l."

Suddenly she remembered. "Fisher. You're spying for Fisher, aren't you? You're the boy from the break-in." Of course, how silly she'd been, wrapped up in her home-making! Trust Fisher to have remembered the danger from Bruce.

"No spying. Just to keep a watch. See if anyone comes round who's no supposed to. We canna be doing with you having the head of you bashed."

"You're right there, Charlie. We can't be too careful." Were they never to be free of Bruce's threats? "Come on, we'll away back to the house and I think we've some scones left over from yesterday's baking. You'll take some tea with us?" Cate could barely suppress her smile as the ragged boy looked thoughtful for a moment, considering whether he would care to take tea with them.

"Aye well, as you like."

He could have been a very small version of Fisher. The speech, the serious nod and then the direct stare belonged solely to that giant of a man, or at least the man he'd been. "He's coming back you know, Charlie."

He understood but was puzzled. "Whit —here? But they said he was as near dead as could be, so he was."

"I'll no lie to you, Charlie. He's very ill, but I'm having him brought back here and I need all the help I can get to care for him. Can I count on yours?"

"Oh aye, missus. I'd do anything for him."

"Right then, tea I think." They made their way back to the house, deep in conversation.

"Lizzie, we've a visitor for tea." With some discreet questioning Cate knew all about the boy before the plate of scones had disappeared. Lizzie identified with Charlie's limp immediately and the two of them walked him to the gate and watched as he disappeared over a stone dyke.

Two weeks later, back in the distillery, Cate watched as the men shuffled uneasily into the courtyard, the women hovering outside the gates hoping to catch a word or two. They all knew what was coming. Hadn't she been in Glasgow all this time? If she hadn't come back to Fisher when he was here, she wouldn't be staying now.

"Miss Cate?" The McAlister had been dropped in the usual Highland way for a widow. She'd become one of them after the fire.

"Yes, Donald Uig?"

"Are you to tell us...?"

"That's why I'm here. Please listen carefully as I want to make mine and your positions quite clear."

They all knew what this was about. A buy-out, that's what and him lying like dead in the big city. Dead was what the village would be from now on. Those big city fellows would use the stock for blending and that would be the end.

"I can see, by the looks on your faces, the thoughts that are going through your minds. Forget them! My plans have nothing to do with closure. I have an accountant arriving soon to take my place in the office. I believe I've also found an excellent stillman from Speyside. With his and all your help we will continue our production. I shall go on with my sales work, advertising our Craeg Dhu and trying to increase our share of the market. This distillery is neither going to be closed nor sold. That's the most important thing." She waited while the shuffling and murmuring stopped.

"Now I want to tell you about the changes.'

Donald Uig nodded his head. Aye, they'd had the jam, now here was the stale tasting bread. As like as no he'd tended his last germination. It would be another hand nursing the wee green shoots. Well he'd better pay attention as she was speaking again.

416

"I intend to do two things. First, and most importantly, I'm bringing Fisher home. What has happened to him is as bad as can be. There's no getting away from that, but as soon as they'll let me, I'm bringing him back. We shall care for him at Craigavon and, for whatever help any of you can give me in this, I will be grateful."

Once again Cate waited till the murmuring subsided. Then clearing her throat she continued. "The second, perhaps unwelcome news for all of you, is that I intend to run the distillery myself, to the best of my ability, and to care for the village and those in it, just as Fisher has always done. Please be aware that this is not something open to discussion—it's what I intend to do."

Once again there was a ripple of conversation, a great deal of shuffling feet, and she waited till it stopped.

"I understand your uneasiness. Knowing the resistance to my working in the distillery in the beginning, I am quite aware that some of you may wish to leave rather than work with me. In that case there will be no hard feelings on my part—just a sorrow that you have no stomach for the fight ahead."

"There's no much wrong with our stomachs, Miss Cate. But it's…

She cut the distillery worker off before he could finish. "It's a man's job. Isn't that what you were about to say."

"Aye, it was that. No petticoat can…"

"Oh yes, this one can and will! Donald Uig and Murdo did the right thing shutting down production after Fisher's accident."

Again there were rumblings in the crowd, but this time she knew the anger was not for her, but at the word accident. They no more believed it was an accident than she did.

"The distillery will remain closed for another two weeks. That should give me enough time to settle both accountant and stillman and bring myself up to date. Angus, thank you and any of the others who kept watch and cared for the business during Fisher's hospitalisation and my absence. There we are then, the distillery will re-open in two weeks. I hope to see you all then. In the meantime I will be here daily if you need me."

Later, at MacNishe's desk, still shaking after the stress of the meeting, she turned to MacNishe's portrait and immediately decided to somehow get a painting of Fisher to hang beside it. She needed them both here. Speech completed, she'd raced to the safety of the office, before her trembling became obvious. The task in front of her seemed Herculean and today she wasn't up to fighting the men. Well, over the next few days she'd no doubt hear from many of them, probably the women as well. Now she had two weeks to get up to date with the books, and settle Solly and Stuart Monteith in Fisher's house. Helping herself to a dram, she swirled it round the glass and spoke to MacNishe on the wall. "We've come a long way from the gambling Laird, Black Craig, and his illicit still. Your ancestor knew what he was doing when he named the whisky after himself, Craeg Dhu in the Gaelic. For generations it's been lucky for the village, with only your father bringing the gambling back and nearly losing everything. But black's what it's been round here lately, MacNishe. Can I do it, do you think—the distillery and the tending of Fisher?"

Settled in the office once more, Cate had a long week with Dinwoodie's retired accountant, going over everything with him. Although she'd done a great deal of studying in Glasgow, she seemed to learn more from this old man than from any books.

"I think that's the lot, Mrs. McAlister, and I must say, for a woman, you have a surprisingly good mathematical brain. It's been an unexpected pleasure to work with you."

Cate listened as the old man spoke of finding new markets, playing the numbers, looking to the Dewars, the Grants, Mackie with his White Horse brand. Although they were blend merchants, it was not their product he was recommending but their sales tactics. He emphasized the need for bottles on retail shelves, reminding her that wholesale or private didn't matter, as long as her Craeg Dhu was out there in the market place. He counselled her to be on the lookout for growth opportunities. Warned her that that business was an uncertain thing, and taking his spectacles off he rose and held out his hand.

It's been a pleasure, Mrs. McAlister, and an enjoyable change from my pipe and slippers."

Cate took his hand in hers and held it for a moment, letting her eyes say all that she didn't utter for fear of embarrassing the old man. "Goodbye and thank you. I'll remember your words and all your lessons. I'll do my best."

She saw him out and determined she'd do better than her best if need be. So far only a couple of the men had given in their notice. All the rest had followed Donald Uig and Murdo, their view being that they'd give her a chance, as she was all they had. Not exactly an overwhelming vote of confidence, but these dour Highland men had never been ones for complimentary words and she could tell they expected her to fail. Well, and didn't Dinwoodie and all those at Craigavon think the same? Oh, how she wished she knew what Fisher was thinking, locked in that crippled body, jailed in the alien Infirmary.

29

Bruce couldn't believe he'd let himself be talked into going to a school concert. Still, Isabel's young cousin was in the orchestra and she'd wheedled him into escorting her. Unless her father came up with some sort of approach soon, he'd try his luck with someone else. Three months and he'd seen no sign of the tailor being ready to settle his daughter. Not just any old tailor though—a chain of shops and some sort of factory into the bargain. He'd do his bit. Sit through the school thing, then supper somewhere, and who knows what might happen.

When it was over he had to admit it had been no worse than he'd imagined. At least there were refreshments being served, so that would save him from providing a supper later. The spotty scholars were making a beeline for the food though, so he'd better urge her to the tables.

Isabel was pleased that he'd come to the concert. She realised she wasn't the best-looking woman around, and was well beyond marrying age, but Bruce was attentive and could be her last chance. Of course she understood only too well that her father's wealth was an obvious inducement, but then so was Bruce's title, she did so hope her father would come round.

A week later, holding the note in his hand, Bruce couldn't hide his delight. This was it then, the tailor's invitation to discuss 'a personal matter'. Old man Brodie was ready to deal. Checking his appearance carefully, Bruce donned his hat and topcoat and whistled his way to the hired car. As he drove up the drive to the house in Crammond, he'd no time for the view of the choppy grey waters of the Firth. His mind was fully occupied with the plans for spending Isobel's money. At last he'd get his hands on some real wealth. Oh, it might be a bit sticky in the beginning, but she was his only child, and the old man wouldn't last forever. For the first time in many months, Bruce felt it wouldn't be too hard to be pleasant and mean it.

Thank God he'd escaped from Kevinishe in time! He'd thought it was all over for him, and then the big man had staggered and fallen on the steps. Thankful for his escape, he'd got in the motor and headed for the anonymity of London. Hopefully no one would remember he'd been back. Leaving the fallen Fisher on his doorstep could perhaps benefit himself even. If his luck held, the stillman might have lain for days outside the empty house. Might even be dead. Then the distillery would be his. His luck may have deserted him on the gaming tables, but it had certainly returned in London, where he'd met the spinster, Isabel, and her aunt looking for a cab outside the theatre. Now that too was all to be signed and sealed tonight.

He was shown straight into the study. No sign of Isabel, so the old man obviously meant business. "Good day to you, sir. Delighted to see you again."

The stocky little man behind the desk studied the visitor. Title be damned! He was nothing but a near penniless Highland Laird, a gambler, a womaniser and now this last piece of information he'd ferreted out. Oh no, he'd have no bastard from God knows where inheriting his fortune. True the boy went under a different name, and from his enquiries he'd discovered the boy actually lived in Kevinishe with the mother. He'd had them investigated, and it'd been an interesting story—no definite proof, but all he needed to get rid of this unpleasant suitor.

Offering Bruce a cigar, and with a pleasant look on his face he opened the interview. "You've squired my daughter about town a great deal these last few months. She tells me you've a decent house in Charlotte Square."

"I have that. Been in MacNishe hands for centuries. Of course I will eventually inherit my stepmother's country house in Berwick, and then I have my own estate, Kevinishe House, along with the distillery, village, and the estate, which boasts some excellent shooting. I believe Dinwoodie—you know, the Iron Man—is interested in buying it, but of course it's not for sale."

"I must admit it does all seem very impressive, though I did hear it was a neighbouring estate Mr. Dinwoodie was renting. That would be because of your refusal to sell, no doubt."

"Most likely, sir. He was very keen on Kevinishe, I can tell you."

"I believe your stepmother, Lady Sarah, has retired to her late father's residence in Dorset. Seems she's kept you in the dark. The Berwick property was on the market some time ago. I know because I looked over it myself. Beautiful house— fetched a goodly price. This one's more convenient for me though. A little hobby of mine that, going round viewing the houses of the great and the good who're too damned broke to keep them. A bit like yourself, lad, wouldn't you say?"

"Well, you know what women are like—pique easily. To tell you the truth sir, we never really got on. Didn't like her replacing my mother, you see. Still I didn't think she'd cut me off like that. I'd better go down to Dorset and make my peace with her. Perhaps a wedding invitation might oil the wheels of reconciliation. What do you say sir? I believe Isabel is more than willing."

"She might well be." Brodie rose and walked round the desk. Leaning on the arms of Bruce's chair, he leant into the arrogant, and to him unpleasant, face of the younger man. When he spoke the words were short and brutal. "Get out. You do my intelligence a disservice by even remotely thinking I'd leave my daughter in your filthy hands! As to my fortune, I'd rather give it away before a penny reached your soiled hands. Away with you! Collect your bastard from Fettes and have your merry Christmas in your run-down estate. You may well have an heir the wrong side of the blanket, but you'll soon have nowhere to lay your head, never mind property to leave to him. He's better off with his mother. You should have married the lass. That was your big mistake. She's the one keeping the best company and no short of a copper or two, if the rumours are right. You're a wastrel. Now get out and, before you ask, my daughter's in Rome with her aunt, and you're the last thing she wants to see. Good day to you."

Isabel would make a fuss, but she was well rid of this one, good looking in a swarthy sort of way though he was. And she didn't know the half of it. Did this arrogant young wastrel really believe that he, John Brodie, would turn his wealth over to scum like him?

Leaving the house, Bruce rammed the car into gear and drove. He didn't care where. All he knew was his inside was churning. That bloody little whore again! He should have had her burnt to a cinder in that hovel of hers. God dammit he'd so nearly solved his problems at a stroke. Isabel would have been putty in his hands. Now what? His dismissal would be all over Edinburgh soon enough. He'd better remove himself to Kevinishe. Would it be safe there though? What had happened to the stillman? Bruce hated the place. Yet, was it true about the boy? Brodie wouldn't have quoted information without it being accurate. So what if that immature coupling had produced a boy? He was his then. He was a father! Had an heir—another MacNishe!

So, she'd enough resources to send the boy to the best school in Scotland. Hmmm. Pity he'd been thrown out of it himself—not likely to welcome him there now. But the boy would be in Kevinishe at some time. Of course, the doting mother would give anything to keep the boy. Now then, this situation could be used to cause her more pain than being charred, and it could continue for as long as he wished. Suddenly the leaden waters of the Forth didn't look so gloomy. Yes, he might just provide a less than 'Merry Xmas' for the tinker whore.

Kicking his heels along the shore, Rhoddy watched the rider galloping towards him. Using the crop, the man forced more speed out of the animal, and the sight of the foaming mouth, the rush of the wind as they passed him, made Rhoddy look with longing at the now distant rider. Kicking his toes into the sand he stared at the deserted shore. Everybody was in church, except his mother of course. She never did the same as everyone else. It was all her fault his school days were spoilt. Why couldn't she look like the other mothers? Nobody ever noticed them. Not her, she always had other people looking at her, whispering things about his father. Everybody else had one, so why did his have to be dead? Then there were the names. 'Highland bastard', for one. How could he be a bastard? He'd looked it up in the school library. He did have a father. He was just dead. Then some of the older boys shouted other things. 'Son of a whore!' 'Who's got no daddy then?' Splashing a piece of driftwood in the waves he didn't hear the rider behind him.

"Hello there. Bit lonely all by yourself aren't you?"

"I like it by myself. Who are you?" It was the rider again.

"I'm the MacNishe. I own the shore you're standing on, the distillery, the land all around here—everything really. Even the people of the village are mine. What's your name?"

"McAlister, Rhoddy McAlister. I'm on holiday from Fettes College."

"Now there's a coincidence! I went there. As old school chums sort of thing, you deserve a treat. Come on, it's boring for you here. Want some real excitement? Up you come in front."

"But I can't ride, sir." The horse was huge and the beast had strange eyes.

"Not afraid are you? You don't have the look of a coward—big boy like you. How old are you?"

"Eleven, sir and I'm not a coward." He was afraid of a lot of things, but he wasn't going to tell this man. "How do I get up?" Once the man had yanked him up into the saddle the ground was miles below.

"Right, we're off. I'll show you a real gentleman's home. Kevinishe House. Hold tight. Here we go. Tally ho!"

Never before, even in the times he'd been dragged from what he knew to strange places and people, had he been as terrified as in the ride from the shore to the beginning of this place. It was worse even than when the older schoolboys had stuck his head down the toilets, or made him drink his own piss. He felt if he opened his mouth he'd vomit.

"Now, keep your eyes on the bend in the drive ahead and you'll get a first glimpse of a real gentleman's home. Now that will be something to boast about at school. That'll make them sit up."

As they rode up the drive, scattering pebbles as they went, Bruce almost told the boy the truth, but stopped himself just in time. Little by little he'd win the boy over, let him do the damage. Inflict the pain bit by bit. "There you go, just look at the size of that. Beats those cramped little village houses that you live in, now doesn't it?"

"I don't live in one of those. My mother's just bought a big new house. It's not as big as that." Rhoddy nodded in the direction of Kevinishe House, now in full view. "She's pots of money, just had the house done up and everything. Oh lots of stables and—well other things."

"Has she indeed? Whereabouts?" There were no other sizeable houses around. "On your own there, just the two of you?"

"No, there's Lizzie and some man from Glasgow, Solly something. I don't like him."

So she'd a maid now and another man. All this garbage about her having money was just as he'd thought. Like a leech she was, clinging onto anyone who'd support her in return for the usual favours. My God what a tramp! How could she have fooled everybody? At the thought of proving others wrong, plus the added pleasure he'd get out of manipulating the boy, Bruce felt like riding off with him altogether, making her go through the agonies of loss, all at once. Better not—he'd stick to the original plan. More painful in the end and at least it would amuse him while he was avoiding Edinburgh after the Isabel fiasco.

Where on earth could he be? Cate had tried all the outbuildings, searched the grounds, even the shore was deserted. One thing was for certain now—she'd have to get a horse. Beautiful though Craigavon was, it was just too far away from the distillery, the village and even Laggan House, never mind Fisher's house on the other side of the village. Dinwoodie had suggested a car, but somehow that didn't appeal. Anyway she'd always loved riding, ever since Gregor had taught her. Thing was she still felt that McAlister's money shouldn't be used lightly, and somehow buying something for her own pleasure seemed wrong. But this covering of distances quickly was certainly a problem, which brought her to why she was out. Well he wasn't here. She'd have to go back home, check he wasn't there. As the light began to fade Cate felt a sudden fear that had her running full tilt home. Rhoddy had to be there.

"You're sure you've searched everywhere?" Lizzie asked when Cate arrived home.

"All the obvious places. Where he used to play. I thought he'd just wandered off because I was displeased with him being rude to Solly. I mean he is our guest and, though there's no reason Rhoddy should like him, he simply can't be rude to people."

Cate had to admit that she couldn't please the boy these days, however hard she tried. Then it was a difficult balance to get right, this trying to get along with her son and preventing him turning into another Bruce. Whatever the reasons, she'd just have to try harder with Rhoddy. Right now she'd have to find him.

"Look, Cate, he's coming up the drive."

"Lizzie, for a moment or two there I thought something dreadful had happened to him—I really did."

"Well, don't they say 'bairns will be bairns', though it's no like him to wander far from home. C'mon let's go and meet them. I know he's had us all worried, but don't scold him now, Cate. Let's just be glad he's back."

"You're right, Lizzie. I'll hold my tongue."

Rhoddy wasn't the least bit sorry that he'd upset the women. "I don't know what all the fuss was about. I just walked further than I thought. Walked right up to some big house. Miles away it was. Have I missed lunch?"

That evening, standing on the front steps, Cate searched the blackened sky, seeking reassurance. There was something wrong. She could feel it. Mebbe she hadn't always understood Rhoddy, but he'd a new wariness about him tonight, and at times she'd caught him looking at her with—what? Once again she was letting her mind run away with her. Somehow that last sighting of the red-headed woman in some kind of distress was still unsettling her. Slowly Cate was beginning to come to terms with this secret part of her world. Not that she really believed in 'The Sight' but certainly she appeared to conjure up these meetings, and the 'Bert' incident, plus Fisher's stroke at Kevinishe House, still disturbed her. She'd tried to discuss it with Maggie, but it was all too late now, so she kept it locked away and tried not to dwell on it. That's what she should be doing about the Rhoddy problem. Somehow, however hard she tried; she couldn't dismiss it or shift her uneasiness. She knew the boy was lazy: he'd never have walked to the gates of Kevinishe House by himself. Either he was simply boasting for effect or—no, it was too horrible a suspicion even to consider. Time she went to bed.

As she watched Rhoddy go through the school door for the Spring term, Morrison following with the trunk, Cate could almost feel her shoulders straightening. Rhoddy's disappearances during the Xmas holidays had really disturbed her. She'd considered following him on one occasion, but spying would only result in even more arguments and disobedience. The boy was growing up. Some of the taunts he flung at her, like ignoring him, preferring work to him and having that creepy Solly around, made her mad, but uneasy at the same time. As his school reports showed, Rhoddy wasn't the brightest of pupils, and sometimes the way he spoke during the holidays didn't seem quite right coming from him—too adult really. Well, she'd a busy week ahead of her, so she'd have to leave Rhoddy and his behaviour at the back of her mind till she'd time to think about it.

Time—there never seemed to be enough these days! Although her thoughts were constantly on Alashdair, the distillery still filled most of her waking hours. The remainder were spent overseeing Lizzie, Kirsty and Morag preparing the dresses for the new catalogue. She'd finally kept her promise to Lizzie. One of the outhouses at Craigavon had been converted into a large sewing room, with several machines. Lizzie soon had the other two doing the basic seams, and both Maggie and herself lent a hand when they could. This visit would also have to include a visit to the printers for the catalogue. The extra work was difficult to fit in with the claims of the distillery, but she'd promised the women, and that meant she needed to expand the sewing business if she was to employ others from her waiting list. Maggie now looked after Stuart Monteith, the Stillman, and Solly in Fisher's house, so everyone was settled. Only Fisher was missing and that was one of the main reasons for this visit. He was coming home. They'd done all they could for him at the Infirmary! The other reason was Alashdair—she couldn't wait to see him again.

Cate was discussing one of her adverts with Billy in the advertising department of the Gazette. Studying his draft, she was nodding in approval when Scottie walked past.

"Good day, Mrs. McAlister, I thought you were away to the Highlands."

"I was until today, but I've things to see to in Glasgow. Actually, Billy and I are finished here. Might I have a word with you about another project I have?"

"We'll away upstairs then—get Mrs. McAlister some tea, Billy."

Settled in the editor's office, Cate sipped her tea and wondered again why the man didn't like her. His words were polite enough, but she could sense his hostility. Making an effort, for Alashdair's sake, she smiled and began. "I'm very pleased with the advertising you've done for Craeg Dhu, but today I'm in need of some advice."

"What kind of advice?"

"I wanted to ask you about printing a catalogue. I'm not sure if it's the sort of thing you do, but I'm starting up another small company, and, if you wanted it, I'd be delighted if you could do the printing."

"An what kind of business is that then?"

"Don't laugh: a dress catalogue! Lots of young women can't afford to go into the big shops. Many of them live too far away anyway. The travellers come round the outlying places with their catalogues, but they stock everything, and the clothes section is usually pretty poor. You know what young women are like, Mr. Scott. They want to look pretty, go dancing, make their boyfriends fall in love with them, dress their babies nicely when they come along. Why shouldn't they have the opportunity to do all that? Anyway I've done a rough design and would like your advice about the printing." Unaware of the change in the Editor's expression, she placed the draft in front of him. "There we are, see what you think of it."

Her cheerful words and the happy pictures she conjured up had Scottie on his feet, his anger rising. He thumped the desk, startling

Cate. "Because most of them don't bloody deserve it! I've never heard anything so selfish in all my life. What about the ones who don't go gallivanting about? Don't have bairns? Don't have a man? Don't have a bloody thing! Just get out. Go on with you."

Cate was astounded at the man's outburst. "What—what did I say? What have I done? We're talking about a wee book with frocks in it! There's no need to shout at me like that, Mr. Scot. I was only enquiring..." Cate rose and paced round the office, then put her hands on the desk and faced him. "Look here, why the outburst? What on earth have I ever done to you? You've never liked me since I first set foot in this office with Alashdair. Yes, I may be distracting him from his work, but take that out on him. Just be careful you don't lose my custom—or indeed Alashdair."

Now Scottie jumped to his feet and leaned his face into hers. "Alashdair this and Alashdair that, as if you owned the man..."

"Well, if you must know, we may soon be..."

This he didn't want to hear. Leaning ever closer, he thumped the desk in anger. "Just you remember this later. You asked the question! I'll damn well give you your answer. 'What have you done to me?' I'll tell you. You've stepped right into my life. You've taken advantage of a damnable situation and you're no fighting fair. That's what you've done."

"I'm sorry, I've no idea...."

"You're right about that, Mrs. McAlister, you haven't, so I'll give you the truth of the matter. See here. There'll be no 'we may soon be' anything. Whatever Alashdair's promised you, it'll no happen. Do you hear? There's something you should know about your fine Alashdair. That one's married to my daughter and has been since she was sixteen. Wed to her and to this paper and I'll see to it he never leaves either!"

"Married?" Cate stared at the red-faced man and felt a fleeting stab of pity at the misery beneath his anger. "But he lives in that small flat, alone. Where is she? Why?"

"She lives in Kelvinside, but make no mistake—wed they are! My beautiful young girl, a mental wreck she may be, but she's his wife and I intend to see she stays that way."

Cate felt her knees trembling and knew she had to go. Picking up her bag she slowly retrieved the catalogue design from the desk, and only then could she trust herself to speak. "I see. Well, I don't think I'll—goodbye, Mister Scott." That was all she could manage. Very slowly, Cate turned, head erect and walked, placing one foot in front of the other very carefully, lest she should fall, out of the building, neither caring nor knowing where her leaden feet were taking her. Eventually she found herself in one of the parks staring blankly at a solitary duck on a pond.

The pain was unbearable. She never, for a moment, doubted the man. Every word had had the ring of truth, as he'd spat them at her. She could feel the pain in her body but her mind seemed unable to function. It was over. What should she do? Where could she go? As she watched the duck swim in circles, first one way then the other, ending in exactly the same spot, her mind echoed the useless circles. Round and round, the one word—married!

She sat unmoving until dusk fell and the park keeper rattled his keys at her. Somehow she rose and her feet functioned. She was supposed to be saying goodbye to Snowy, collecting Fisher at the Infirmary, and travelling back to Kevinishe. She could do none of it. Like one of the injured stags on the hill she needed to hide, to explore the wound in private and hope that she wouldn't die from it.

Cate had no memory of what she'd done as she left the park. It was only hours later that the guard's words 'Balvourie Station, Balvourie'. Finally penetrated her numbed brain. Why had she come here? What instinct had sent her to seek shelter with that wise woman? Well she might as well get out. She had nowhere else to go. The long walk seemed to pass unnoticed. Carefully picking her steps up the drive, forcing her body to move, using the bushes either side to keep her straight in the darkness, she headed for the stables. Once inside she climbed into the loft, felt for the hay bales and lay on top. Then, at last, the sobs racked her body, while below, unaffected by the human heartbreak overhead, the horses chewed contentedly at their hay.

Next morning, Alashdair slung his coat on the desk and pulled his chair out. As he began to sort the chaos in front of him, he became aware of the silence. The newsroom was never silent. "What's the matter? Isn't anyone doing any work in here?" No one met his eyes or answered his question. "What?"

His next-door neighbour nodded in Scottie's direction and then buried his head in his work.

"I see, like that is it? What's set him off this time?" Now the newsroom became a hive of activity and Alashdair recognized the signs. There had obviously been a row, a fairly regular occurrence, and usually he was the only one who could handle Scottie. With all the time he'd been taking off lately, he could well be the cause of it. He decided to wait it out. Scottie would pounce on him in his own good time. The call came almost immediately.

The words echoed in his brain as he struggled to make sense of them in the editor's office. She'd been here. Why in God's name? What had happened here? As Scottie continued, Alashdair felt everything was moving too fast. She'd been in the flat yesterday. They'd made love before she left for the Infirmary. He'd tried to persuade her to leave Fisher there and they'd argued, but she couldn't have been here. Some business, the Infirmary and then back to Kevinishe, that's what she'd said.

She couldn't have been here. Not alone with Scottie. That was dangerous. He'd never have disclosed their closely guarded secret surely? Would he? But he had! That was exactly what he was telling him. Alashdair could hear Scottie's voice raging at him, but all he could think of was losing Cate. It couldn't be! He couldn't let her go. There would be no life for him if she left. He must see her, explain. Finally it penetrated. Scottie had told her. He'd sent her away. Rage poured through him. Leaning across the desk he grabbed Scottie's shirt and shook the man violently. "You did what? You told her? How could you? I finally had a chance at true happiness and you couldn't stand it, could you?"

"Your happiness! What about my daughter's happiness?"

Alashdair couldn't bear it. There was no answer to give Scottie. She would never find happiness. They both knew that. He hurtled out of the office, his one idea to find Cate, explain the situation and beg her to stay with him.

Meanwhile, back in the office, Scottie could feel his world collapsing around him. Alashdair had seemed so right, a young man needing a lift up. Why wouldn't he jump at the chance of the boss's daughter? That that same daughter was motherless, spoilt and insanely unstable because, like her father, she'd developed a liking for drink, he'd refused to face. She'd been pretty in a fragile sort of way then. He'd hoped, oh how he'd hoped, that marriage would be the answer! Of course it never was. She'd an unnatural fear of childbirth—her own mother had died in it, for God's sake! Unbeknownst to Alashdair she'd sought a back street abortion when she'd found she was pregnant. The incident, and Alashdair's wrath, had tipped her over the edge, back to her prams and her dolls. So she remained to this day, a woman with the mind of a child, who, when she ranted and raved, could only be pacified by drink or drugs and had to be kept in the big old house in Kelvinside with her jailer of a nurse.

Hours later Scottie raised his bleary eyes to the clock. A new day and the knowledge that Alashdair, having vented his wrath, had stormed after the woman and would probably never return. He was alone with the paper he'd sacrificed his daughter for. And on his death, what would happen then? The man the newsroom feared bent his head on the desk and wept, the tears turning items of copy into spidery blotches, as dawn crept through the window.

Lizzie was alone in Craigavon. Cate and the ambulance with Fisher in it had not yet returned from Glasgow. The house appeared even larger in the dark and the frightened girl sat in the kitchen rocker concentrating on her stitching, avoiding the shadows the light threw, waiting for the others to come home.

The knock, when it came, frightened her and she was unable to move. The tapping on the kitchen window sent her screeching to the far side of the room. Only when she heard Mr. Dinwoodie's voice did she stumble to the back door and into his reassuring arms.

"I'm sorry, Lizzie. I didn't mean to startle you."

"What's happened? Where are the others?" Lizzie asked.

"I thought they'd be here by now. I only came across to see if she needed any help with Fisher?"

"Surely nothing's happened to them, Mr. Dinwoodie?"

"I shouldn't think so. Look, why don't you make us a nice cup of tea, Lizzie, and I'll away and help myself to Cate's Craeg Dhu. That'll teach her to change the arrangements." While Lizzie made the tea, Dinwoodie was also wondering exactly why Cate, Morrison and Fisher hadn't returned. It was so unlike her. The Infirmary would be none too pleased with their preparations being changed. Was she simply lingering on in Glasgow with the reporter, he wondered? Making his way back to the kitchen, he decided to keep his thoughts to himself.

Having finished their tea, Dinwoodie rose. "Lizzie, there's no use worrying. We'll just have to wait and see what happens. Now off you go to your bed and I'll keep the fire going down here, and stay with you till the morning. I expect we'll see them all tomorrow. Goodnight to you now." Left alone, he helped himself to another dram. As he swirled the amber liquid in the glass, his thoughts were sombre despite his cheery words to Lizzie. She wouldn't be the only one whose world would be rocked if anything had happened. Dammit, village life would be empty without Cate. They'd all had a taste of that, and hadn't each and every one of them constantly wondered when and if she'd come back? The welcome home had been a joyous affair, and a relief to have her back. With the distillery, the sewing, the buying of the old folks' cottages and the other schemes she kept drumming up, she was turning the whole place into a living breathing community again. Somehow she'd replaced Fisher, strange though that might sound. She was also worth a hundred of the present Laird. He had to admit his own days would indeed be glum without her, so they'd just have to hope she turned up soon

30

Stevie looked at the Balvourie stable door. The bolt wasn't across. No wonder it didn't look right. Someone had been at it since he'd shut up last night. Easing the door ajar, he armed himself with a pitchfork. This early it was difficult to see, but the horses seemed fine, shaking their heads, ears pricked for their morning tasty bite. "Well now, you're all safe and sound and I'm imaging things so…" A sound from the loft had him climbing the ladder. "Come out or I'll lay into you with this pitchfork." With no reply he edged towards the hay bales and the sound. He couldn't believe his eyes when he saw her, curled up, covered in straw, face tear stained and swollen. What in God's name had happened to her?

"Stevie? Is that you?"

"That it is, Miss Cate. What're you doing here? Look at the state of you. Are you in some sort of trouble?"

"No, It's just that I arrived very late and I didn't want to disturb anyone. Do you think I could tidy up in the tack room?"

"You go on down there. I'll get word to Cook and she'll have a breakfast ready for you. Only, Miss Cate, it's her Ladyship."

"What Stevie? She's not—oh what?"

"She's sinking. Never really had the heart for it after his Lordship died, although your arrival got her going again for quite a while. Still rode out a little then, but took a fall a few months back and seems to have given up. You might just be the answer we've been waiting for."

Was everything in her world falling apart once more? Cate dragged herself to the tack room, hurriedly washed her face, though nothing could improve her swollen eyes, and made her way to the kitchen, ashamed that she'd thought of her problems instead of Fisher. And now Her Ladyship too was in trouble. Surely that brusque voice couldn't be silenced so soon? Almost as though the old lady would fade before Cate could see her, she quickened her pace. Personal problems would have to be shelved. She owed this friend a great deal. Whatever help was needed she'd have to find a way to provide it, and then get back for Fisher. He'd think she'd let him down, and of course she had.

In the kitchen, Cook was glad to see her. "And aren't you the welcome sight! Come away in—tea's made and I daresay a bowl of porridge would be welcome. Mercy me, lassie, what've you done to your eyes? No, don't tell me, that kind of weeping could only be for a loved one. A man is it?"

"Nothing I can't get over, Cook, but it'll take time. Her Ladyship is bad, Stevie tells me."

"She is that, Miss Cate. That leg of hers just won't heal. Strictly between ourselves mind, she just can't be bothered, and it irks her that the bossy nurse the doctor sent treats her like a baby."

"Mmmm. This is delicious. I can see being treated like that wouldn't go down well with Her Ladyship. Was the leg broken?"

" Twisted and cut, I think. Then the gash got infected and now the leg is the size of a boulder."

"Is she still in the same room?"

"Just the same and young Bella is with her—that's if bossy boots has let her stay. Orders Bella about like a servant, does that nurse. It's no right. Her and Guthrie are too close and you know what I think of him."

"Right, the nurse first then. I could do with a good battle this morning. I think the tears are about to give way to anger—make me feel better at least!"

Knocking lightly, Cate entered the room, to be met with a wall of stale air. A fire smouldering in the grate, curtains shut against the daylight and from the smell the chamber pot still held its contents. With deft movements, she soon had the curtains drawn back, windows opened and chamber pot outside the door. Then she turned her attention to the bed. Her Ladyship was hot and flushed.

436

The nurse had her wrapped up like a parcel, in garment after garment. About to remove some of them, she was interrupted by the screech from the door.

"Just what do you think you're doing with my patient?"

"Letting her get some good fresh air. This room smells like a midden. I'm going to change, wash and dress her, but first I want you to tell me how you're treating her."

"We're not. The old woman's dying and the doctor says, since that's what she wants, we might as well let her get on with it. What's it got to do with you anyway?"

"I've come to look after her and I have no intention of letting her die."

"Mr. Guthrie will soon stop your nonsense. I'll get him immediately."

Cate ignored the woman as she flounced out the door. Guthrie she'd deal with later. Right now she had to get her patient more comfortable. As she pulled back the numerous blankets, she saw a flicker of the eyelids. "Well now, this is a fine how-do-you-do, My Lady. Just what's been going on here then?"

"Cate?"

"Yes. Now I'm here to look after you, and by the look of things, it's not before time. Come on now. Let's sit you up. That's it—hup-sa-daisy. Right, I'm just going to get Bella to give me a hand and..." She was interrupted as the door was flung open and the nurse returned with Guthrie.

"There she is, and look what's she's doing. Cold air! Sitting her up! Just you tell her, Mr. Guthrie."

"Good morning, Guthrie. Her Ladyship sent for me to look after her, so you can let the nurse go, immediately. I'll want to see the doctor, of course, and then I can report to Lord Albert. I trust these arrangements will be satisfactory. I'm sure you agree it'll be quite in order. However I can telephone Lord Albert and you can speak to him if you prefer."

With a baleful look, Guthrie turned and left. Closely followed by an exasperated nurse who could see her easy billet disappearing fast.

"Cate?"

"Don't talk, save your strength. I've rung for Bella. We'll make a start in taking some of these clothes off, and then we'll freshen you up. Bella?" Cate turned as the door opened once more.

"Cate, whatever are you doing here? Where's that bully of a nurse? Guthrie's just as bad. Neither of them will do as I ask. Oh, it's so good to see you!"

"Time to catch up later. Can you get a jug of hot water and we'll start by giving her a wash. Pity she can't make the bathroom, but there it is."

Washed and with clean nightdress and bed jacket on, Cate unwrapped the bad leg and stared in horror at the suppurating gash and the filthy dressing, barely covering it. "Bella, when did the doctor last come here?"

"I don't really know. I think the nurse just says she's about the same and no one seems to do anything."

"She's tired now. We'll leave her for a bit. You go down and get Cook to give you a little beef tea and some bread. We must get some food into her. I want to have a good look at this leg." Cate wondered if she could do anything about the wound. That was obviously causing the fever. By the looks of it, with no food and even less will, the old lady was in a bad way.

Bella brought the bread and tea. Patiently, Cate fed Lady Jemima, small spoon by small spoon. Tiny bits of bread soaked in the good strong tea. A minor battle of wills, but Cate was the stronger and her patient simply didn't have the strength to refuse.

"Told you we would clash." Lady Jemima whispered, her gnarled hand searching for Cate's.

"I know, My Lady. You see I've learnt you were right. Now we've got some food into you, I'm going to see to the leg, but it'll hurt."

"Useless thing anyway. Brandy?"

"In the cupboard, Cate, I brought some up here when she first fell." Bella pointed to the washstand.

Taking out the empty bottle, Cate showed it to Bella. "Not Her Ladyship, I don't suppose. I'll away and get some and I'll need some hot water and whisky. Don't let that awful woman back in here. I'll be as quick as I can."

Hours later, Cate eased herself out of the fireside chair and went to check her patient's breathing. Gently replacing the cold compress on the hot brow and tucking the bedclothes in, she studied the lined face. To lose a mother, then a beloved brother, followed by an arranged marriage, the death of her children and husband, and finally to be a prisoner in the home that was no longer hers—no wonder the old lady wanted to give up. Cate was uncertain whether she could heal the wound, or even if Her Ladyship would ever walk again, but she would do everything in her power to make the end, if that was what it had to be, as pleasant as possible. Fisher and Kevinishe would have to wait and she would have to learn to live without Alashdair. Stolen love was not for her. She knew that now—however hard it might be to accept.

In the darkness she'd time to wonder where Alashdair was. Had he seen Scottie yet? What a fool she'd been to think he'd proposed marriage when all along she'd been nothing but a dalliance. Yet even now she couldn't really believe that. They'd both been in love—she could have sworn it. Strangely enough, it was the deceit, as much as anything, which hurt. Why not tell her the truth? Of course, she understood why not. He knew she could no more have taken someone else's husband than steal anything at all. He would follow her till he found her. She knew that, but it was over. Had to be. She couldn't bear the emptiness, the future without him, but she must. The tears began again and she slid behind the curtain, cool glass on her face, beseeching the dawn to come quickly so she would have something to occupy her mind and stop it from remembering the unexpected love of these past months—a love that was now not only beyond her reach, but also put there by her own rules. How quickly her dreams of a wonderful love and marriage had been shattered by the angry words of a bitter father! How could she carry on without that love? Where would she find the necessary strength?

Next morning, Cate telephoned Snowy. She knew it was cowardly, but she could speak neither to Lizzie nor Dinwoodie. The housekeeper would tell Morrison about Balvourie and he could let Craigavon, the distillery and Laggan House know. The infirmary phone call she had had to do herself. The matron had been fairly frosty, but having reassured her it was only a temporary delay, she'd thawed slightly. Necessary chores done she headed for the kitchen and some food.

"Cook, I need some strong tea and porridge. Yesterday was trying enough, never mind setting my own affairs to rights this morning. It's all but robbed me of my strength."

"How do you think Her Ladyship is today?"

"Don't expect too much too soon, Cook. We'll have to take it day by day." Hour by hour as far as her personal pain was concerned, Cate thought. How long would it hurt like this? "They talk about bread being the food of life, Cook, but give me a strong sweet cup of tea any day. Mind, a wee dram of Craeg Dhu might give me more strength." Seeing the puzzled look on Cook's face, Cate explained.

"Now then, Miss Cate, a drop of sherry is what I'm partial to, but only at weddings, christenings and funerals."

"Well, neither whisky nor sherry will do for her Ladyship. She'll need some more beef tea and perhaps a mouthful of fish later. She's only managing a little at a time, so not too much. Oh and I'll need a wee basket if you can spare one. I've to collect some herbs from the hedgerow later today."

As she entered the bedroom, Cate was pleased to see Bella reading quietly, and her patient looking a little more alert. "You look the better for that sleep, Your Ladyship."

"Don't think I'm going to let a slip of a girl like you bully me for long." The voice was a little stronger this morning.

"That's exactly what I'm counting on. I never thought you'd let me get away with it. Let's have a look below here." As she pulled back the sheets, Cate remembered the tea. "Cook is preparing some more beef tea, Bella. Would you slip to the kitchen and get it while I check the dressing?"

"Damned indignity of it, people poking about where they've no right to be. I treat my horses better than that."

"Your Ladyship, that's the point of it all, to get you back on your feet and riding again. They all look in fine fettle this morning. I had a quick look at them with Stevie. Major's a bit stiff, but I gave his fetlock a rub down."

"Now you're going to do mine, I suppose. Another bloody old mare."

"That's more like the woman who hoofed me back to the Highlands. Now then, brandy or bravery, My Lady?"

"Brandy, girl. What's the point of being brave at my age? Thank you."

"You don't know what a small glass I'm going to give you."

"No, you're damnably mean with my own liquor. It goes without saying, you know, my thanks for all this. I really had just given up— what's the point and all that?"

"I know, My Lady. Here drink this and grit your teeth. I think you're up to me doing a bit of digging down here. I didn't like to do too much while you were still weak, but now your strength is slowly coming back with the food, I'd really like to start properly on the leg. It looks pretty bad."

"You mean if I was a horse you'd shoot me. Quite right too...good God above, girl, are you sawing the damn thing off?" Lady Jemima twisted the sheets in her gnarled hands.

"Oh, Cate. I can't bear the look of it." Bella put the tray down and turned her eyes away.

"Hold her hand and don't look. I can do without you being sick all over me! First put that bowl by the bed, on the floor there, Bella, and those rags. Take care—the water's hot" Cate carefully cleansed the wound. The bread poultice she had put on the previous evening had drawn some of the poison, but she had to get to the bottom of it. She knew what to do but would such a high-ranking lady agree? Checking her patient, she saw she'd almost had enough. Well she'd cleansed the wound, and now for the spirit. "Hold her tight, Bella. This will hurt." As she dripped the whisky into the wound she could almost feel the pain herself. Topping it with a fresh poultice she bound it firmly. "Now then, food, Bella, please, while l ease the pain in the rest of the leg." Unlike her '*Seeings*', as she called them, her ability as a healer she'd always been grateful for. Slowly she worked on the leg and the familiar warmth suffused her hands. By the time the food was gone, Cate could feel the tension in the leg slackening and knew her patient would sleep soon. Then she could go and gather her herbs, first in the garden and then in the woods. For now she'd done all she could.

Arriving at the distillery, bleary-eyed, after travelling overnight, Alashdair opened the door and confronted the two men in the distillery office.

"Yes, can I help?" Solly got up from the desk.

"Where is she?"

"Look here…"

Dinwoodie had been waiting for this. He knew it had only been a matter of time before the reporter put in an appearance. "Good afternoon, this is the distillery accountant," indicating Solly, "and my name is Dinwoodie. I'm helping out here until Mrs. McAlister returns. I presume that's who you're looking for.

" Mrs. McAlister returns! I'm no fool. I don't believe you. She was coming back days ago. So where is she? Where are you hiding her? I have to see her, talk to her. She must be here. She must."

"Look here, we've no idea why she didn't return as planned. By the look of you there's been some major upset. Solly, a dram I think—never have I seen another human being more in need of one."

"Here then, it's the best single malt there is." Solly sat, eyes furious.

"Please, I beg you, I have to see her, to explain. I can't lose her. She's my life now. Without her there's nothing." He pleaded.

Dinwoodie could stand no more. No man should have to bare his innermost emotions like this. "Believe me, I give you my word, we've not seen her since she left to take her son back to school for the spring term. However, we do know where she is. First, I need your word that you will behave like a gentleman if we tell you her whereabouts."

"Damn you both, I knew…."

"Wait until you've heard me out, before damning us. She should have come home days ago, but I believe something happened in Glasgow and the manner of your appearance has confirmed that. Whether she was running or whether she'd already received the other news, only she knows. At present she's with a very dear friend

442

who is seriously ill. Cate is tending her and I'm not sure that your sudden appearance will do either of them any good. The lady is elderly and Cate's healing skills may be her only hope. I trust you understand the gravity of upsetting Cate in the circumstances."

"What rubbish! Oh, she told me all about her healing, but it's all poppycock. What could she do for a sick woman? You're lying. Where is she? I'll get into every corner of this godforsaken place till I find her. Out of my way."

Dinwoodie held the man firmly as he tried to pass. "How dare you doubt my word! Why should we lie to you? None of it is our business anyway. She is at Balvourie House in Argyle. I suggest you come to Laggan House with me. Travel weary, unkempt and sleepless is no state in which to resolve anything. When you've attended to all of those, my car and driver will be at your disposal. Now then, Solly, we'll leave you to your books, but might I suggest we postpone the other matter until Cate returns?"

"You seem sure she'll be back." Momentarily Alashdair envied the Iron Man's certainty.

"I don't know what's gone on between you, young man, and it's certainly none of our business, but rest assured, whatever happens, Cate belongs here and will most certainly return. Now come along, this is very much a working distillery and we're preventing Solly here from going about his business."

In Balvourie house, Guthrie made his way upstairs. He didn't bother knocking, simply pushed the sick room door ajar before speaking. "There's a person to see you."

Cate ignored Guthrie's tone of voice and the look. She'd recognized the car. She was so glad Dinwoodie had come. Hurt though she was, Dinwoodie's reassuring presence would help. Yes, he was exactly what she needed right now. Tripping down the stairs her words of welcome froze in her mouth as the figure in the hallway turned to face her.

Alashdair was afraid to begin. "Who's this friend you've run to? Another man? Here in this great house? How can I compete with that?"

"Alashdair!" Then a painful silence that seemed to stretch forever, before her feet moved of their own accord and she was almost in his arms before she regained her control.

"Cate, my dearest girl, I…."

"NO!" The cry, wrenched from the bottom of her despair, steadied her. She sidestepped him and went out the front door. Once in the open space she felt safer. Here, with distance between them, she could send him away, but it had to be quick. She could not hold herself together for long.

"Cate, wait. I should have told you. I kept meaning t…."

"But you didn't. You allowed me to believe you intended to marry me—that I was the love of your life!" Here her voice broke.

Seizing his chance, Alashdair narrowed the gap and reached for her, but he was not quick enough. She walked away.

"I will never understand why you thought the fact of your marriage wouldn't come out. I suppose you just thought a stupid Highland girl like me would be only too willing to be your mistress."

"How can you say that? After all we've meant to each other. Dear God, does that now count for nothing? You stand there, beautiful, proud, but wounded. I can see your face shows the same pain as mine. Cate, I made a mistake. I hid the fact of my marriage from you, but there were extenuating circumstances."

"Yes, I know. And those circumstances are just why you must leave and never see me again." Crying openly now, she met his eyes, shoulders sagging, despair in her every breath. "How could you ever have expected me to take my chance of real love at the expense of anyone, never mind some poor unbalanced woman who will need your care for the rest of her life? You obviously never really understood me, never mind loved me." Stifling her tears as best she could, Cate straightened her shoulders and continued. "Go home, Alashdair, back to that weak and damaged soul, her grieving father and the paper. That's your life—go now." Cate moved within earshot of Morrison. "I think the gentleman is ready to leave, Morrison."

"Cate I can't…." Alashdair couldn't stop the tears. You can't—I can't…."

"You will have to, just as I will. God alone knows how, but I must. Go back to your wife and care for her in that lonely world she inhabits. Make your peace with Scottie. Go, I can take no more. Like me, you must bear this dreadful pain. God I wish I had never...."

"NO, Cate! Don't say it. Let me at least keep the memory of our love. Don't destroy that too." The anguish in his voice was as distraught as hers, as he made his last desperate plea.

"Goodbye, Alashdair." Cate turned her back on him, climbed the steps, shut the great front door and disappeared.

Alashdair heard the clang of the door as the end of his world. He waited, even knowing it was hopeless.

"The car, sir. Get in the car, sir." Morrison could barely speak, as he urged the man into the vehicle. Never had he seen two people so distraught. The reporter slid into the back seat. Closing the car door, Morrison, with one last look at the big house, took his place in the front and drove off, knowing that he'd never forget the sight of that despairing face in the upper window.

By the end of the next week, Cate hoped, the bandages would be ready to come off.

"Well, have the wretched things done the business? I can't believe I let you do this. Revolting little things!"

"They have, My Lady, better than I could ever have done. The wound is clean. The maggots have eaten all the dead and rotting flesh. Now we must clear them, pack it and let it close slowly."

"What an extraordinary woman you are! Where has all this knowledge come from?"

"The Cailleach, mostly, the tinkers a little, books, and something inside myself. I've healed for as long as I can remember. Even as a child. A broken bird's wing, a stoat from the moors, a barn owl that was sick. Later, it was people and horses. My hands just seem to know what to do."

"By jove you're a useful individual! There's no doubting that, my gel. Come now, the dratted leg is on the mend, which is more than I can say for you." The girl's inner struggle had been obvious during her stay despite her brave attempts to hide it. "Man trouble by the looks of it. That's always the worst kind."

"It's just something I..." Despite her trying to stem them, the tears flowed.

The older woman let her weep. As Bella opened the door, she waved her away. Much, much later she prised the reason out of a despondent Cate.

"You could have done what others have done before you. The invalid was no real threat to you."

"How can you of all people say that? It would have been a lie. Do you think I could have lived with myself, knowing he was not free and she was unable to care for herself? How dare you think so little of me!"

"Good—that's the first painful step over."

"What are you talking about, My Lady?"

"Temper, rage, call it what you may, my dear, always works wonders for a broken heart. Doesn't heal of course, but stops the weeping and wailing. Just you remember that. Oh, don't look so astounded. Don't you think I know of heartbreak? Dear Lord, I've buried much more than lost love. Take it from me: anger, exercise, fresh air, work and ambition are the way forward. Fill your life. Exhaust yourself and, ever so slowly, the pain will recede. Of course, it never goes completely, but you manage it, instead of the other way round. Now, off with you, I need to rest. Go on! Fetch one of my riding habits—far too big off course. Doesn't matter. Take Major, get the wind in your hair and let your senses rule. You'll feel better. Now go on—do as you're told for once! Do you the world of good."

31

As they finished dinner in Laggan House, he studied the drawn, pale face before him. Cate had always been slender, but she was bordering on the skeletal at the moment. Never one to worry about her looks, the clothes hanging on her appeared to have escaped her notice. Lizzie was right. Something had to be done or she'd make herself really ill.

"Don't you think you're overdoing things a little?"

"No."

"Cate, in the three months you've been back you've done nothing but work, work, work and you dance attendance on Fisher. That's what he's got a nurse for."

"Yes, but she's a miserable besom and she'll be leaving soon."

"Cate, be reasonable. He needs nursing." It came out more harshly than he'd intended.

"Don't shout at me, Dinwoodie. I'm bringing Sister Mary Anne up from the infirmary in Glasgow. She's ready for a change. She'll be here in a couple of days."

"Good. I'm sorry, my dear, but you can be so exasperating. You cannot, simply cannot, do everything yourself. Why, for heavens sake, with all your other commitments, are you still without someone in the house?"

"I have Lizzie."

"You know that's not what I mean. Dammit, woman, using work as a hair shirt won't help if you kill yourself into the bargain. Yes, your summer love seems to have come unstuck…."

"How dare you examine my feelings? What do you know about anything? My life is just that—mine, and I'd thank you to leave me alone! I'm going home."

As she slammed the front door, he shook his head. Well, he'd made a fine mess of that! Oh Fisher, good man that you are, what an evil day it was for all of us when you were struck down! Now you would have been able to make her see sense. I always fancied the bond between the two of you would blossom into love, despite your age.

In the distillery office, Cate drew another set of figures towards her and wished she didn't feel so tired. The knock at the door was almost a relief, despite the fact that it was bound to mean another problem demanding an answer. Maggie's appearance meant at least it would be a domestic one this time. "Maggie, what are you doing here?" Her words lacked any sense of welcome.

"As I remember, we used to be friends, Cate. That's no a very bonnie face you're showing me. I hear it's the same for any other body who dares to ask you the time of day. Seeing as how I'm no welcome, I'll take the telegram back to the post office an you can get it yourself."

Meeting Solly on the stairs, she gave him the telegram. "Someone had better do something or she'll do herself damage so she will. We've all tried. Your turn now."

He made his way to the office, knocked, opened the door and dropped the telegram on the desk. As she did not respond immediately he waited, before speaking, till she did. "Cate, Maggie's brought this telegram for you and she seemed upset. She'd gone out of her way to help and a kind word for that wouldn't go amiss. When you've read that," he pointed to the telegram, "we need to talk." He waited as she read saw her colour drain, and her hands clench the flimsy paper.

"What Cate? Is it bad? Tell me!" She hadn't looked well for weeks but now she seemed on the point of collapsing.

"Her Ladyship, Solly, she's—she's—dead!"

"But I thought the leg was healed?"

She'd been much better after the leg incident but now she was gone, leaving emptiness where there'd been a staunch ally.

"Cate, they say the Gods never give us burdens we can't handle."

"Damn them then! All of them! They don't seem to care over much for those of us still below. What about your father's death, McAlister's, Fisher felled by a stroke, my baby girl stolen? Have I to be thankful for that, glad of the burden? Now another good soul gone—and they didn't give her an easy life either, for all she was a rich, high-born Lady. Hasn't the Almighty given me enough woe without having Lady Jemima die as well?" Tears of rage and sorrow mingled on her cheeks.

Taking his handkerchief out of his pocket, Solly went behind the desk and took her in his arms. "Shhhh now, Cate. Here, wipe your eyes. It was just her time. She'd had a good life. I know she'd had her sorrows, but they would have been balanced with better things. No life is all one or the other. Take yourself, they tell me you were fair blazing with the joy of it in the summer, but the New Year brought you grief. Now you're setting the rest of us back, witnessing your struggles. Remember, she could have gone back then, when she was injured, and no proper medical care. Your healing meant that she passed away in a much better state than she was in when you found her. Keep that thought. You'll need to go to the funeral. Now, a dram and get off to make your arrangements."

"Solly, I understand what you're saying about the distillery workers, villagers, Maggie and the rest of you—but I didn't know losing Alashdair was going to hurt so much. It just eats away at me and.... "

"Well, you'll not sort it on your own. You've made yourself ill. Get yourself back here fast and give us a chance to help. Away with you now! My tongue's not had this much work since I left the legal world."

As the coffin was lowered into the family vault in the Balvourie church, Cate stood with the other servants mourning the passing of the woman who had intervened on her behalf. It was this selfless act that had obtained the legacy McAlister had left for her. As the dignitaries departed, servants hurrying behind to see to their needs, she walked to the vault dropping her simple heather bouquet onto the lavish wreaths of the gentry already on the coffin.

Much later, sitting in the kitchen with Cook and Bella, they were interrupted by the entrance of Lord Albert. Having made the obligatory curtsies they waited for the great man to speak.

"Mrs. McAlister, meant to thank you for looking after Her Ladyship, but quite slipped my mind, don't you know. She left this letter for you. That'll be all then." Duty done, Lord Albert left.

"Cate, what'll happen to us?"

"I truly don't know Bella, but I have a shrewd suspicion that Guthrie will and he won't be long in telling you. Listen, here he comes." As soon as the butler appeared, Cate knew her friends were doomed. The smug smile on his face meant he was safe and delighted to be the bearer of bad news.

"Lord Albert has informed me that the house is to be shut and in future he'll bring his staff with him, as and when he visits."

"And us? What's to happen to us?"

"Ah, Cook, I'm to return to England with Lord Albert. You and the other staff are to remain until the house has been closed up and then your services will be terminated."

There was no comfort Cate could give the women. In those two sentences the domestic world of Balvourie house was removed as surely as death had taken it's custodian.

Later that evening, Cate opened Her Ladyship's letter, and when she'd read it, her eyes filled with tears. Why had she thought the servants would be forgotten? She should have known better.

Dear Cate,

There's no saving me this time. My only sorrow is that I cannot wait for your return. However heavy your heart, please try, for my sake, to leave the past behind and look not only to your own future, but also to that of those I leave in your care. Unlike you, they are not masters of their situation and thus require your help. Know that I leave you having been glad of your friendship. My lawyer has my instructions and will pass them to yours. Life is to be lived, dear girl. I implore you to do just that.

Yours affectionately,

Lady Jemima Hartley-Porter.

Once more Cate spent the night, forehead pressed against the cool glass, looking at the stars, searching for the Heaven that was supposedly there, listening in vain for the brusque voice that belied the warmth of the speaker.

Having left Balvourie and its staff after assuring them that their future was secure, she caught the morning train to Glasgow and Gordon Wiseman's office, where the lawyer informed her of Lady Jemima's wishes. As she sat listening to the terms of the will she understood that once again the wiser older woman had solved, not only her servants future problems, but also hers, by thrusting the burden of responsibility for them onto her shoulders, ensuring that she would be too busy to go on wallowing in the loss of Alashdair.

Gordon Wiseman understood why the woman before him was quiet as he tried to interrupt her thoughts. "I know this must be a bit of a shock for you, but I understand Lady Jemima has explained what she wished you to do with the funds she has put at your disposal."

"Yes, Her Ladyship has done just that."

"Cate, forgive me, but as I understand it, the domestic servants, horses, equipment, grooms and outside staff are willed to you, in return for her care and friendship. You appear to be collecting a menagerie. What on earth are you going to do with it all?"

"I have no idea, but obviously I'll have to think of something. I owe Her Ladyship more than I can ever say, so I will have to find a way of carrying out her last wishes. It's the least I can do for her memory. Thank you, Gordon. I must now get back to Balvourie and make a start on it all."

"Cate, you look too tired to travel, why don't you rest in Glasgow?"

"I must get back, Gordon. Could you arrange for her Ladyship's funds to be put in a separate account and let me have the details and I'll sort out her personal belongings between the staff."

As he watched her leave, there was something about the wan figure that told him he would remain the friendly lawyer and nothing else. Closing the files he crossed to the window and let his eyes dwell on her diminishing figure until it was out of sight.

Back in Kevinishe, with important news to tell, Angus hovered near the distillery entrance till he heard the clatter of hooves on the road. Hurrying to open the gate, he waited for Dinwoodie to dismount. "She's back then, sir."

Dinwoodie needed no other explanation. "You've seen her?"

"Well, I have indeed. Her, and what you would be calling the travelling show she has brought from wherever she's been this time." Since the other man did not answer the unspoken query, Angus continued. "In the dawn it was, she came traipsing in with carts, animals, boxes and boxes of things and people. She was not alone, indeed she was not." As Angus had known he would, he watched the Iron Man turn his mount and ride towards Craigavon. He knew the village men were betting on the newspaperman to become 'Mr. Cate', but with the interest the Iron Man was showing, Angus would put his money on him for a wedding.

As Dinwoodie rode up the drive at Craigavon, even having been warned by Angus, he was taken aback. What was she up to? Hadn't she already done one flitting, moving McAlister's furniture to Craigavon? What was all this? People, noise, chaotic movement— now what had she done? Finally he saw her, still thin and wan, but clearly in control of the situation, ordering strangers, giving directions. Then he saw them—my God, what a set of beauties! Now, his curiosity needed satisfying. Where had she found horses like that? Dismounting, he strode over to the centre of activity and addressed its ringmaster. "I see you're back then and busy with it. All you need is a top hat and tails!"

Cate knew he'd never ask, so she drew him aside and briefly explained the sudden multiplying of her household. "You're just the man I need."

"Aye well, if it's the humping of boxes, I've better work to do."

"Dinwoodie, don't laugh. Just look at it all. I haven't worked any of it out. I need to get some of these outbuildings converted, but, in the meantime, I've four men—well three at least—who have to be housed until their families can join them. Any ideas?"

452

"I daresay they could be lodged for a while at Laggan, while I'm still renting it. I'll see what's available, but I need to know why they're here."

"Let me get them unloaded, fed and somewhere to sleep for the day, and tomorrow I'll come over and tell you the whole story. I can see it's not the muddle or people you're interested in, but you can wait till the horses are settled before you start inspecting them." With something of her old laugh she turned away, and then, as he mounted, she called after him. "Dinwoodie, it's good to be back, and thank you." She knew he understood it was not his help this morning she was thanking him for, but the comfort and the talking to that he'd given her before she left for the funeral. Like Lady Jemima had been, Dinwoodie had become a cornerstone of her existence and she hoped he'd be there for a long time. She couldn't see herself ever doing without him.

Next day, as she settled herself behind her desk in the distillery office, Solly was taken aback by just how tired she looked. "Never mind seeing to all those you brought back with you—it's your own bed you should be in. You look worse than when you left."

"Now that's exactly what a girl wants to hear, I'm sure."

"Don't you go bandying words with me. You know what I mean, Cate. You really do look ill."

"I know. Oh it's not just Alashdair, though that pain doesn't seem to get any less. I'm just so tired and I have to confess to feeling decidedly green this morning. Funnily enough I fancied a dram when I came in, but the smell didn't seem to agree with me. Anyway there you are. Dinwoodie was on at me to get some help in the house and now, courtesy of Lady Jemima, help is in all corners of my house and stables."

"Exactly how many are there?"

"At present, Cook, Bella, Stevie, the groom, and three gardeners, but the men will have to have their families brought up as soon as possible and I can't remember just how many children there are."

"It's not my business, but workers have to be paid."

"That's the least of my worries. Lady Jemima sold her really expensive jewellery and cashed in her personal financial holdings to put in a trust fund for their keep and re-housing. I'll employ them at Craigavon initially and we'll have to see whether they settle or not. At least Dinwoodie should be pleased."

"We're all pleased, Cate, but you have to worry about yourself. An employer can't function without good health. You'll need to sort that out and soon." He'd done all he could! Now the books needed his attention.

Maggie rose from her bed struggling with the problem of the new arrivals at Craigavon. They'd need food when they woke, so she made her way downstairs. Standing in the kitchen doorway she stared at the scene in front of her, as the woman addressed her.

"Good morning to you, Mrs. Maggie. See I've tea made, will you have a cup?"

Maggie nodded in amazement. The cheery little woman, as round as she was tall, had a roaring fire going in the range that Maggie had never quite conquered, the big kitchen table laid with enough places for an army, and enticing smells coming from the copper pans.

"Don't look so surprised, I managed to sleep on the overnight journey and I always get up with the dawn, so I hope you don't mind. I just got on with it."

"Well I'm very glad you did. You have to be Cook."

"I am that and if Miss Cate thinks she's going to house us all here and not have us take care of her and her home, she's mistaken. Now as housekeeper, wouldn't it be a good thing if you and I had a wee chat and sorted out who was going to do what, before Miss Cate arrives?"

"Well, I'm not really the housekeeper."

"You should be then. This house was spotless when I arrived. My bed was clean and no musty smells in the room. That means you're a good housekeeper. You know what it's like. These young ones need looking after and, if you ask me, Miss Cate most of all. I've a word to say about her, but you might think it not my place."

"I'll no have words spoken against her. She's been that good to my Lizzie. Oh I know she can be hasty—we've fallen out before…."

"Look, I think the world of her. I'm not after miscalling the lass. Well, I'll speak my mind and just hope you and me won't spoil this good start we've made. That one, though she doesn't appear to know it, to my mind has fallen. There, make what you will of it."

Maggie couldn't believe she'd been so blind. What with the break from the paper man and the funeral of the old Lady, they'd not thought of another reason for her being off her food, tired and ill-looking all the time. Making up her mind immediately, Maggie faced her new friend. "I think you may well be right, and she'll need us both. Welcome to Craigavon, Cook. As to being the housekeeper, well I've only been here while Cate was away, but I think you've the right of it—housekeeper I'll be, if Cate's willing. I'll get one of the village women to see to young Monteith and Solly in Fisher's house. I'll tell you all about them over tea. I think you and I'll get on just fine. Now then my Lizzie does the sewing in the stables, and that young Bella will be very welcome there. You'll have to tell me about the wives that are coming later and we'll sort them out between us. Craigavon has just become an even bigger family home, and we'll make it a right good one. Thank the Good Lord we've all those extra rooms! Now to your tea and porridge."

Cate made her way to the summerhouse, hoping for some peace after the busy weeks. Thankfully, Craigavon had absorbed her newly extended family. She was particularly grateful that Maggie had asked to stay on as housekeeper, as it was good to have her here. Dinwoodie had found a builder to make a start on the remaining outhouses for accommodation and the sewing women had been moved from the stable block to another outhouse, as their former workroom now housed Lady Jemima's beautiful horses, with Gregor delighted to be helping Stevie.

Satisfied with her mental inventory, Cate finally turned her attention to the problem she'd shelved for weeks. Pretending it wasn't there would soon no longer be possible. As if losing Alashdair wasn't cruel enough, he'd left her with a child to be born out of wedlock. That she wanted it was never in doubt. Should she tell him? What was the point? Even if he acknowledged the child, he couldn't marry her She'd made her decision and, hard though it was, it would be a great deal more painful to see him but not be his love. She cradled her stomach and allowed herself the luxury of a few moments of what might have been—Alashdair here, a child to share, and each successful in their chosen work. It was a fairy tale of course. He would never have settled to the Highlands, and city life was not for her, but oh how she wished the dream could have been reality! Work filled her mind, but if she stopped, even for a moment, the pain of losing him was still there.

The arrival of this child in a small community would not make her road easy. Not much had changed since Maggie had been turned away from church and home. Church would not be her problem, but the glen would. With a substantial older population against her, she could still be made an outcast. True she could skulk in Craigavon, but what of her work, her other plans? She knew she could not just sit idly at home. Well she'd just have to brazen it out, but it would be hard, especially if the distillery workers turned against her. Rhoddy, what of him? How would he take the news? More importantly, what of herself? She'd hardly been a roaring success as a mother to the two children she had already. She'd made a mess of bringing up Rhoddy and she still felt guilty over Sarah's abduction. She'd been too wrapped up in her grief over McAlister's death, giving Caroline her opportunity.

Somewhere across the ocean her Sarah would be going to school now. Please God they were being kind to her, loving her, making a home for her and giving her the security her mother had never had. Cate felt she now had so many painful memories bottled up inside that she doubted she'd ever be happy again.

Three days later, Mary Anne knew as soon as she entered the room, Fisher was gone. Crossing to the bed, her thoughts were not of the man whose struggles were now over, but of her friend. Could Cate cope with yet more bad news? Leaving bed and erstwhile patient neat and tidy in true Infirmary fashion, she went to find the woman she'd befriended, knowing this news would be unbearable for her. At this early hour she'd be in her study.

As she knocked on the door, Mary Anne would have given anything to be able to turn round, but she opened the door and faced Cate's welcoming smile.

"I thought it would be you, Mary Anne, this early. How is he this morning? I'll be up in a minute."

Somehow her cheery words were too much for Mary Anne. The tears betrayed her. "Oh Cate...."

"No, please no." Cate rose and, confronting her friend, shook her by the shoulders. "No, Mary Anne! No! You can't have let him die! I promised him!" With that she ran sobbing, up the graceful, winding stairs, into the room that now held the end of her hope. As she closed and locked the door, her speed and noise ceased. Slowly, she crossed to the bed, stroked the withered hand, caressed the cold cheek, and laid her head on the broad chest. "Oh Fisher, I should have been here, holding your hand. I let you down again. Too busy doing other things, but I was on my way up. Why didn't you wait? You should never have been allowed to go to the hereafter on your own. We would have made things better for you, we would! I just know we would. F....I....S....H....E....R! The strangulated cry echoed through the house and those who were not already awake were dragged from their beds by it. As one, whether dressed or in nightclothes, warned by Mary Anne, they made for the door and the wounded human being within, but the lock foiled them. All they could do was stand and listen to the intense pain of the woman inside. Would this new blow finally fell her?

32

Villagers and visiting mourners alike were confused when the lone piper sent his melancholy notes drifting over the glen as he led the coffin and assembled male mourners, not to the graveyard, but to the distillery. The minister hurried after the woman in black, wondering just what she'd done now, heathen that she was. Through the distillery gates, beribboned in black, they went, onto the newly created garden, stopping over the yawning grave in the middle, as the men of the distillery lowered the man they'd known and respected from childhood into his final resting place. The minister would take no more part in this, for hallowed ground it was not, and so he left. None of the villagers was surprised when the black-robed woman stepped forward, though it caused a shuffling and whispering among the visiting mourners.

Head held high she felt inside her cloak and, drawing an ancient flask from its depths, held it aloft. This time it was the villagers whose shocked murmurs split the silence. Unheeding, Cate spoke loud and clear. "Fisher, we've placed you as near your beloved distillery as we could. It may not sit right with the church, but this was your holy place. You guarded and guided it to prosperity and now you go to join MacNishe, brothers in life and now in death. As you were christened in water on your birth, Fisher, I now send you to the hereafter with the precious liquid spirit of your ancestors. Slainte mhath!" With these words Cate brought the flask crashing down on the coffin, over which the precious liquid dribbled from the broken container, bowed her head and signalled to the piper, who took up his lament again. She stood there as the shocked assembly, one by one, muttered their own ashes to ashes, sprinkled handfuls of good Highland earth and left.

With a final worried glance at the woman, standing statue-like at the grave, as the men began to fill it in, Dinwoodie, understanding she'd be dammed by the world for her unorthodox funeral, led the mourners to the Old Barn.

Cate knew they'd all gone. She'd asked Dinwoodie to take care of the proceedings at the wake, her wounds too raw to join them. She'd no idea what would happen now. They'd trusted one another, Fisher and herself. There'd been no need for a partnership agreement to be drawn up. What now? Would that oversight spell the end of the distillery?

The by-now completed mound at her feet reminded her of all those other deaths and how each and every one of them had meant a new direction for her, chaos and trouble. This one would be no different. Nodding her head, she made yet another promise as she stood by his grave. "I'll fight him, Fisher, so I will, with every penny I have, and Dinwoodie and the village will help. Bruce will not destroy all you and MacNishe worked for. I told you we'd be back at the distillery together and here we are, whatever the world thinks of it." Brave words she thought, but how she would manage it she'd no idea. Turning, she felt Morrison's hand on her arm.

"I'm to take you back to Craigavon, Miss Cate—Mr. Dinwoodie's orders.

Back in the Old Barn the wake was rather subdued. Those from outside the glen, for Fisher had been well known, not only for his skill as a stillman, but also for his prowess as a thrower of the hammer and the tossing of the caber at the annual Highland games, were confused by the unorthodox burial. The villagers, like all Highland people, who from birth were brought up on tales that owed more to myth than truth, were outraged at what she'd done. Oh, the burying wouldn't sit well with the church and no doubt herself would go straight to hell for doing it, but it was the precious flask that had them muttering dire warnings in their drams. How could she? The flask had sat in its glass case facing the main distillery door, since being moved there, with much ceremony, from its place in the old distillery. The story had come down the generations. It was the last of the illicit whisky, distilled, God knows where in the mountain, by their ancestors. As long as it was there the distillery would prosper. Even generous measures of Craeg Dhu did little to quell their fears.

As he left the stragglers to lock up the Old Barn, Angus in charge of the keys as usual, Dinwoodie sank into the car. "Better make it Craigavon first, Morrison. I need to check on her."

"Right you are, sir. Will she get away with it, sir, the grave in the distillery, I mean?"

"Truly I have no idea, but it would be a braver man than I who decided to dig it up."

"You're right there, sir. Miss Cate has a temper on her and no mistake. Not wishing to speak ill of her."

"I know, Morrison. Like many others, you like and admire her. Still it's not the grave that worries me—it's the arrival of MacNishe. Word is out now that Fisher's gone. I had expected the man to gatecrash the funeral. I'll not rest easy until he makes his move, as he surely will… Ah, Craigavon. Leave me here, Morrison. I doubt she'll have any sleep tonight. I may be needed. You can come back for me in the morning. Goodnight to you."

He found her where he expected, in Fisher's room. Taking a chair by the window he said nothing, waiting for her speak.

"I suppose you're as shocked as the rest. Are you, Dinwoodie?" Looking at him, she felt this man was perhaps the only one who would truly understand.

"Taken aback, yes, and disappointed that you didn't trust me enough to give me the details."

"You know why, Dinwoodie, I'm sure."

"Yes, I believe I do. You knew I would try to dissuade you. Only because I fear you have caused unrest in the village and distillery and lost some of the goodwill you've worked so hard to create. Mind you, I must admit it was truly theatrical, though I'd have liked to see that glorious red hair of yours flying in the wind!"

"Dinwoodie, how can you laugh at such a time?"

He rose and, sitting on the bed beside her, spoke. "Cate, we've both done all of this before. Yes, the pain and the grief are immense, but others need us, and so we put our feelings to one side and manage as best we can to move forward. It's the only way, and even forced laughter helps."

At his words the will, that had carried her through ever since she'd unlocked Fisher's door, crumbled. Dinwoodie held her while she wept. Held her, his arms growing cramped, and finally laid her on the bed of the departed man. Covering her gently, he held her hand until the eyelids closed and then quietly resumed his seat by the window. He would be there for her when she awoke. Afterwards, who knew what would happen, but the original will nestled in safety with all his other legal documents in his solicitor's office in Glasgow and he'd already informed them of Fisher's death. They would now take the necessary steps to inform her, and by God he'd use all his means to ensure she had what was now rightly hers, even though she didn't know it yet.

The disturbance was so loud that, even deep in conversation with Monteith in the stillroom, Cate heard it. As she made her way down to the ground floor, she couldn't begin to think what it was, but nothing much would surprise her at the moment. Since the funeral, she'd encountered silent opposition from both distillery men and the other villagers. Her own fault really! Oh, they'd thole the grave in the distillery grounds, knowing how Fisher would have liked it. The flask was a different matter. Should she tell them? No. Let them think badly of her. If she could win them round on this, then, when the real battle began perhaps they'd back her. Thinking of battle, she'd better hurry up and see what all the fuss was about.

At the sight of him she knew the fight was here and now. Angus, bless him stood, broom across the front door and Bruce was trying to push past him. Others had left their tasks and formed a phalanx behind Angus. She collided with Donald Uig as she reached them. He took hold of her shoulders and pushed her back. "We'll see to it, Miss Cate."

"No, Donald Uig, this is my job, but I'll do it the better for knowing you're behind me. Are you behind me, in spirit as well as body? I need you to be." At his nod, Cate pushed her way through the group and there he was. Pasty-faced and fatter, how could the years have reduced him to this?

"Don't just stand there, you tinker whore. Get out of my way and call this rabble to order. I demand entry to my distillery."

"We don't know yet that it is yours."

"Don't be ridiculous! It's always been mine and now that dolt of a man…"

"Speak no ill of the dead here, and not that one in particular. Fisher was given this distillery by your grandfather and until such time as Fisher's lawyers tell me otherwise, you are not welcome here. Trust me, I shall have you removed by force if I have to. The choice is yours. Go quietly and let the law take its course or force the issue and my hand will be the first one to strike you."

Eyeing the silent men behind her, Bruce re-mounted. "It's mine, do you hear? I'll take it when I'm good and ready, but not before you've all paid for this, everyone of you, and especially this brazen whore in front of you! This distillery is mine. Kevinishe is mine, and be damned to the lot of you. I can't believe good Highland men would put up with trash like her on the premises. Call yourself men? Throw her out. Back me and together we'll run this distillery. We'll do much better than the bastard Fisher…"

She moved so quickly the horse's head was held firmly in her hands before he could move the beast aside.

"I warned you! Mind your tongue! Get out of here! How dare you—a drunkard, debtor and debaucher. I never want to hear you sully your uncle's memory, here or anywhere else in the glen. MacNishe may have been heartbroken at the thought of you, but you'll break no hearts here!"

Bruce took aim with his crop, but he was too slow.

"I see you've still clung to your boyhood, bullying ways." With a scornful laugh and a darting arm she'd wrested the crop and laid in to him—Alashdair, Fisher, Lady Jemina, McAlister, Sarah and that dear MacNishe, his life's end made miserable by this unworthy grandson—Each stroke of the crop on the bloated body hammered out her bottled-up heartache, anger and grief at the loss of these dear friends. Finally, she threw the crop on the ground, let go the horse and spat her final words at him. "Get out of this place! It's hallowed ground now, and you deface it." Turning she made her way back through the men to Donald Uig, who nodded his approval and, taking her arm, led her to the office.

Bruce watched her go and made to speak but the look on the men's faces changed his mind. Turning the horse's head he galloped out of the distillery, wordless. As he rode his fury increased. That bitch! Was he never to be free of her? He simply hadn't reckoned on her being there or the men not obeying him. Dammit, they'd always obeyed the Laird. Did they know about Fisher and the fight? That he'd left him for dead on the steps of Kevinishe House? That must be it. They'd never stick up for a woman, even if she had been Fisher's whore. That bloody man Peyton must have seen him. Yes, that was it. If they knew about his part in Fisher's death, those men would seek revenge. He'd be better out of the glen for now. He'd bide his time. Go to his grandfather's solicitors. They'd know about a will. Since Fisher had died unexpectedly, bet the dolt didn't have one. Pity he'd been so dammed rude to them when he dispensed with their services. Maybe they'd be sweeter when, as the only remaining MacNishe, everything reverted to him. Of course he wasn't quite the only one, but that would be his secret, till he'd estranged son from mother. How sweet that would be! After this morning he'd have no pity on the whore. He'd destroy her bit by bit, until she begged for her life.

Things would change as soon as the lawyers made him the rightful owner of everything. With the wealth of the distillery behind him, he no longer needed to go around with his begging bowl. Could afford to pay off his debts. Maintain Kevinishe House. Yet, why bother? He hated the place, always had done. No, he'd sell the land and Kevinishe House, and get something down south, even London, perhaps. Right, Edinburgh next and the lawyers! The tinker whore had given her last orders and now he'd hold back no more. The boy was his for the taking! She was the first one he'd deal with on his return as a wealthy man.

Shaken by the scene at the distillery, Cate was uneasy, though she knew Bruce had left the glen. Young Charlie, continuing Fisher's instructions, always let her know Bruce's movements while he was in Kevinishe. Now another problem had to be confronted.

Having made her decision, Cate let her gaze wander round the drawing room at Craigavon. Before she carried on her fight for the distillery she must speak to her friends. Now the moment had come she was nervous, yes, embarrassed indeed, but it was the fear of losing the respect of this close group of friends, who'd shared so much of her life, that really worried her. Dinwoodie, Maggie, Lizzie, Solly, Bella, Cook, and Mary Anne, getting ready to leave as she no longer had a patient. They were all there, the nucleus of her home. Only Rhoddy, still at school, was missing and that was another conversation she dreaded. She put the drinks on the central coffee table and wondered how to begin.

Dinwoodie had no idea why she was behaving so strangely. Two weeks was perhaps too soon after the funeral to expect her to be back to normal, though normal was the last thing the funeral had been. Not a word of explanation had she given, nor had she mentioned the brouha at the distillery. That he'd found out from Donald Uig. Patently she was uneasy about something now, but not of those in the room surely? All present were as close to her as if they'd been her natural family, so why the hesitancy? To cover the awkward silence he began to tell them his news.

"Bruce MacNishe seems to be in even deeper trouble these days."

"What's he done now?"

"Oh, more of the same, Cate. His financial assets are disappearing fast. Kevinishe and its acres have been mortgaged to fund his lifestyle and it seems his bank is uneasy and may be about to foreclose."

"Does that mean, Dinwoodie, that the estate is for sale? What about the distillery?"

"There was no mention of the distillery Cate. Just the estate and the main house."

"Are you willing, Dinwoodie?

"I could be interested. It would be a good investment for business purposes."

"Surely you're not starting smelting up here? Polluting our lovely Highland air?"

He rose, walked to the window, remembering. He'd wanted no part of the craze of following the Royals in their love for the Highlands, but he'd been mistaken. Others had followed their lead and interest in these lands had grown. The rail and road links had expanded and more would no doubt follow. The rich and famous had no desire to share the wilds with the ordinary man in the street. They looked for large estates, where their privacy was guaranteed. Turning to the waiting group, he did his best to explain

"So you're saying, Dinwoodie, that Kevinishe, if you bought it, could provide what the English and foreign landed gentry required?"

"Exactly, Cate, Scotland has become fashionable, people, especially the aristocracy, are willing to travel up here now, and those who take advantage of this can make a tidy business out of it."

"Will you take the bait then?"

"I might at that. If I can find the right partners, I could well be interested."

"And we'd get rid of Bruce?"

"No, Cate, he'll always be the Laird. No one can take that away from him, save the Good Lord himself."

"Yes, but, he would be unable to threaten us from afar. Perhaps the distillery might still be safe, and the villagers in his houses would certainly be so. Think of the increased jobs you could offer. You must do it, Dinwoodie—I mean if you can afford it."

"Well, we'll see. Now didn't you want to tell us something, Cate?"

"I don't really want to say anything, Dinwoodie, but, in all fairness, you must all be the first to be told."

Maggie stepped in with her invitation. "Well, come on then, Cate. Don't keep us waiting. I hope it's no bad news."

"I'm, well I'm...." She could see her hesitancy had set them all worrying. She'd better just say it. "I'm going to have a child." She couldn't fail to notice the conspiratorial glance that passed between

Maggie and Cook. How long had they known? She could almost have guessed the variety of reactions to her news. The two older women had already worked it out. Lizzie and Bella were excited. Solly looked thoroughly embarrassed and worried. Dinwoodie was like the sphinx she'd read about. She could tell nothing from his expression and feared she might have lost his respect. That would hurt her dearly. "Well there you are. I'll leave you all to decide how you want to react to my unwelcome news. Enjoy your tea. I'm away to the study."

As she made her way there, she collected the mail with a shaking hand. Seated at McAlister's desk, she made a brave attempt to sift through it, but her problems seemed too burdensome today. Well, she'd told them and that could add to her worries. Although Bruce was no longer in the vicinity, she still felt his evil in the air. Shuddering, she picked up the largest of the letters. Might as well get the biggest one answered first.

The house seemed to stifle her and, changing her mind, letter in her hand, Cate made for the summerhouse. Whether it was that so much had happened of late that her system could cope with no more, or whether she simply couldn't bring herself to believe what she'd just read, she wasn't sure, but her mind seemed unable to come to terms with this latest twist. Seated in the summerhouse, she almost expected it and wasn't disappointed: *Slowly the mist appeared, and then out of the bushes she came, a smiling red-headed woman this time. A touch on Cate's cheek, a wave and then she was gone.* Cate put her hand to her face and wondered what it meant. Never before had the figure been anything but insubstantial, but the touch, almost too light to feel, had been real.

Much later, the letter read again and again, Cate began to laugh, so loud and for so long, that the hidden Charlie rushed to the house for help.

After Cate had gone out and the others had left, Maggie tackled the one person she thought could solve the pregnancy problem. "It'll no go down well in the glen, Mr. Dinwoodie, and, after the scandal of the funeral, the visiting minister will have a fine time with his 'whores of Babylon and the like'."

"I agree. It's not a very comfortable situation to be in. Look here, Maggie, can I pry into your personal thoughts?"

"I've just given you them, have I no?"

"This is damnably difficult."

"Aye well, you'd just better spit it out then and hope for the best, sir."

"Damn it all, if she's to hold her head up in the glen and elsewhere, she needs a husband."

"True enough sir, but she'll have no more to do with the Glasgow fella— unless she's changed her mind on account of the bairn."

"There's a problem with that, even if she wanted it. He's married, remember."

"Well, there you are then. Short of raffling her at the next ceillidh, I've no answer for you."

"Solly?"

"Mr. Dinwoodie, we canna dispose of people like that! Oh, I'm no saying he wouldn't be overjoyed at the idea, but it's no fair. She'd be too much for him, no matter how he fair worships her."

"Well if you have any other thoughts, Maggie, please let me know. I'm determined to save her any unnecessary pain."

Watching him ride away, Maggie couldn't help wondering if the solution wasn't in his own hands. Now that would be tidy. There's him, all but owning the glen now and rattling around in that big house, and there's her needing a good man's name. Then the distillery problem—he'd be the man to sort it. They dealt pretty well with one another. Why not? It could work. Look at herself and Bert. Come to that of it, what about McAlister and Cate? Aye, it could be done. Tidy indeed, but who would have the gumption to suggest it? No her anyway.

With that thought Maggie wandered over to the window, only to see young Charlie running as hard as he could for the house. More trouble? Hadn't they had enough?

"Missus, it's Miss Cate, she's…." Drawing breath he managed, "the summerhouse."

Before he'd finished the word, Maggie was away, calling over her shoulder, "Get the others, Charlie." Reaching Cate's special hiding place, Maggie stopped and stared. The girl was out of her wits surely? Laughing and crying at the same time and making no sense! Maggie did the only thing she could think of. Cradled the hysterical woman in her arms, while looking for signs of an aborted pregnancy. Was that why Cate had hidden herself here?As the others from the house arrived, Cate's laughter ebbed and she shook her head at Charlie. "I was fine. There's nothing to worry about." She swept her arm to include the others. "I'm fine. I've just had some news to share with you, but first I must wait for Mr.Dinwoodie, so be patient with me. Let's go back to the house and have some tea.

A week or so later, seeing the size of her, coming up the steps to the front door on her return from work, Maggie determined to have a word, though no doubt it would result in her having the head bitten off her again! Sighing, she tackled Cate as soon as she was seated.

"Cate, about working, well it's no seemly, and...."

"Maggie, are you telling me I'm no use to them any longer? The distillery can do without me, is that it? An unmarried pregnant woman is not suitable for you all anymore? Even if the place does truly belong to me now."

She still couldn't believe what had happened. Not only had Fisher drawn up papers for a partnership, which sadly they'd never signed, but he'd also left the distillery to her in his will. Her right to run the distillery was now legal.

"I don't know what you're thinking about, Cate, but pay attention to me. I'm just saying, it's no seemly. You may own the place, but it's full of men who canna thole the sight of a swollen belly, though it's them that swells it. Can you no see that?"

"Don't be silly, Maggie what difference does being pregnant make to my work?"

This was too much for Maggie. "You're the one being silly! Always ready you are to make your own and other people's decisions. You're the one that's got us in this pickle, not me, not the men in the distillery, not Dinwoodie, nor the lot here at Craigavon. Sit there and listen for a change!" Maggie, visibly angry, continued. "I was about to say you'd be the better of taking the work home and tending to it here till it's over. You won't be the first or the last in these circumstances, but if you'd a brain in your head you'd see it's no right to flaunt it in the men's faces. It's no decent. Now then— see what you've done. I was never going to fall out with you again, and here we are shouting at one another!"

"Maggie, I'm sorry. You're absolutely right. I've only myself to blame. You'd think, after Rhoddy, I'd have had more sense."

"Aye well, I was no so sensible myself if you remember. That's why I worry about you and the village. Oh, you're no likely to catch it the way I did, for the village needs you more than you need them, but, all the same, the older ones and the men will find it hard. After all, it's no as though you're little is it? You could be carrying one of them whales in there."

"Yes, I'm large. I'm sure I was never like this with Rhoddy or Sarah. Thank you, Maggie. You're right. I'd better work from home till I'm confined."

"Aye, you're being sensible now. It'll no be easy, you know, Cate."

"I do, but then I have little choice."

"Look now, there through the window. If it isn't himself, coming up the drive. I'll away and get cook to put some scones on for him. I'm sure they don't take enough care of him at Laggan House. That's why he's so often here. Needs a wife that man does." As she made her way to the kitchen, Maggie told herself at least she'd tried.

As she opened the door for her dear friend, Cate was thoughtful. Did he need a wife? That would change everything. She turned her attention to the man. "Dinwoodie, come on in. Needless to say, Cook and Maggie are determined to feed you. Anyone would think you hadn't a perfectly good cook at Laggan House."

"Ah, but it's the company while I'm eating that makes the difference. How are you?"

"Thoroughly chastised. Maggie's just been putting me in my place. Suggesting I work from home in future. Apparently I'm no a bonnie enough sight to be in the distillery."

"Not the pair of you falling out again? I always thought the peace might be fragile."

"Why?"

"You are sometimes a little uneasy in her company."

"Dinwoodie?" Dare she share this with him? She'd tried with Alashdair and he'd simply mocked her. Funny that. Only now did she realize how his scorn should have warned her. "I do have a problem with Maggie, but it's to do with Bert."

"Bert? I thought he was dead."

"Exactly." Cate rose and stood behind her chair, gripping the back, while telling him about the Bert incident and her other pictures, visions, whatever they were. "Now you may laugh."

"My dear girl, why would I? It's always been known that certain people, Highlanders in particular, have a kind of sixth sense, an ability to be more aware of things than others. After all, we must assume that the Cailleach was related in some way to you."

"I've never told you about the letter, have I?"

"Which letter are we talking about, Cate?"

"MacNishe left me a letter when he died. He left a small inheritance for Rhoddy and...."

Dinwoodie interrupted before she could finish. "I fail to see why. You, I would understand."

"Oh, Dinwoodie, way back on the mountain, when I told you my life story I omitted one fact. Rhoddy was not as you assumed, McAlister's child. He's Bruce's."

"But, he can't be! You've always hated Bruce. Surely you never gave yourself to him. I don't..."

This time Cate cut him off. "Please Dinwoodie, don't think of me like that."

"But Cate, I don't understand."

"Then listen. He knocked me out, raped me and left me helpless on the moor. Fisher found me and saved my life. Now you can understand the bond I had with Fisher and my deep hatred of Bruce." Cate waited for Dinwoodie to speak. Would this be the end of yet another close friendship? Was she doomed to lose all those who meant much to her?

Dinwoodie rose and went to the window. The lawns, manicured now, stretched in front of him. She'd been most insistent on that—wanted to recreate the picture of Balvourie House. Was it true that the line between love and hate was so very narrow? Had she loved Bruce? Exactly what had the immature Cate felt during her time in Balvourie? More importantly, what difference, if any, did this make to his emotions where she was concerned?

"Dinwoodie, your silence bothers me. I was young and very definitely the victim. Fisher understood that."

"Ah well, Fisher would. I suppose you're now going to tell me that he was the real love of your life, not the reporter after all." Why was he saying this? For so long now he'd managed his emotions as far as Cate was concerned. He must bury his jealousy. Continue to do so. "Forgive me, Cate, your words startled me. I interrupted your discussion about the letter. Please carry on."

"I don't think I can now, Dinwoodie. I'm a little tired, would you mind going?" As the front door banged behind an irate Dinwoodie, Cate couldn't work out quite why she felt so hurt. What had made him say those things? Never, since she'd met him had he been other than kind and considerate. Look at all the things he'd done for her. Maggie's exclamation as she saw the uneaten scones brought Cate out of her thoughts.

"I never thought Himself would turn down a good plate of scones, Cate. Has he gone?" The other's silence alerted Maggie. "Cate, you've no started? Surely it's way too soon?" Crossing to the chair, Maggie pulled Cate down and sat in front of her. "Come away, lass, what's the matter now?"

"I don't know. It's Dinwoodie, Maggie. He was really angry with me and I so wanted to tell him something."

"Would he no listen?"

"Oh yes, it was just that, after what he said, I didn't want to tell him."

"If you left him as puzzled as I am now, I'm no surprised he left with such a stout bang of the front door. There are times when you can be hard to handle, Cate. You have to admit that. Mind, he seems better able to handle you than anyone other than Fisher, bless him. I could fine do with my brother walking through that door right now."

"Maggie, I'm sorry. I sometimes forget, in my own need for Fisher that you are also grieving for him. Actually, I was telling Dinwoodie how much Fisher meant to me, when he accused me of loving him!"

"Who now, Fisher or Dinwoodie? You're no making any sense, Cate."

"Don't be daft, Maggie. You know what I mean. I'm fond of them both. Fisher saved my life, gave me the opportunity to work. It's affection, not love—I'm finished with that."

Maggie knew this was the chance. "Cate, I'm going to say words you'll no want to hear, but let me finish them."

"I'd be rude not to, after all you've done for me."

"You've aye had the ability to solve all sorts of problems. Right clever you are, but there've been times when you don't see what's in front of you. Now take the newspaper man..."

"I don't wish to talk about that, so stop right there, Maggie."

"What happened to letting me finish, Cate?"

"I had no idea you'd be talking about my personal life."

"So that's me put in my place as the housekeeper then, is it?" She might have known the temper would take over.

"Maggie, it's just...."

"I'll tell you what it's just, Cate. You're so bothered about work and doing the right thing, caring for others, getting on, and God knows what else, that you pay little heed to either yourself or others around you. As one woman to another, I know about love, lust, and heartache. And if that bulge in front of you is anything to go by lust played a part in yon relationship too. I've no doubt your heart has been broken, but it'll mend

"Maggie, I loved him, like I've never known love, or ever will again."

"That, Cate, is nonsense. Oh, you might not think so now, but everything passes in time. Think about this for a minute. You'd never have lived in Glasgow—you hated it. An he couldn't be doing with the Highlands. Think of all the other things that were different.

In the long run it wouldn't have worked and, if Fisher was here, that's what he'd tell you. He never liked the man, you know, and yet my brother was the only one who really believed that you'd never leave the glen, never desert us. He knew the affair wouldn't stand the cold breath of dawn, Cate."

"Maggie, I've never heard you make such a long speech." She was right though.

"Since we're into saying some honest words, here's some more. Despite what the glen thought, Fisher did love you, but like the daughter he never had."

"I know that, Maggie, and he was my missing father."

"Aye well, but you've no idea that Solly there thinks the world of you, has been in love with you since the day you met. The lawyer man in Glasgow hasn't been squiring you all over town because you're a client, or did you no notice that either? And close your mouth—you look like a dead guppie!"

"I'm not daft, Maggie. Of course I knew Gordon Wiseman was interested in me."

"You're maybe no daft, but at times, as I said before, you canna see what's in front of you. Mister Dinwoodie's been running after you for years and you treat the man like you do the servants in this new house of yours…No, don't stop me, I'll no hear a word from you till I'm finished. The glen may have backed the wrong man in the beginning, but it's like a horse race, so it is. Fisher may have been the leader, but they knew as well as I did that the newspaper fellow and Solly would always fall at the first bend. Well, they were wrong about Fisher and so that leaves only one winner…"

"Maggie, shut up before I lose my temper with you. Haven't I just had Dinwoodie blethering on about Bruce in that fashion! How could you of all people…?"

"There you go again. For a clever woman, it seems, despite all the figuring you do in that office of yours, you still canna count. It's Dinwoodie, as you call him, though God knows why you never use his christian name, I'm speaking of." Maggie saw the truth so clearly in that moment that it dismayed her she'd never understood before. Clasping Cate's hands, she said. "Listen to me. The trouble with you is you never received love as a child and if you've no been loved then I reckon you canna either return it or recognise it when it's showered on you. The Iron Man's been in love with you for years, but my thoughts are he's put it aside because he believes you'll no have him. There, I've said my piece and it's been overlong, but it needed saying. I'll away and get you a glass of Craeg Dhu, by the look on your face, you need it." Scooping the tea things up, Maggie left, knowing that Cate's silence meant she'd shocked her.

33

Dinwoodie looked at his untouched evening meal. The glen might call him the Iron Man, but he'd lost his grip on himself earlier. There'd been too much emotion in these past few months for all of them. Remembering that he had to leave for Glasgow in the morning, he thought he'd better return to Craigavon tonight to make his peace. Was it too late? Dammit, he didn't care! He couldn't leave without putting this right.

As he knocked on the Craigavon door he was glad to see the lights still on."

"Dinwoodie? What brings you out at this time of night?" Cate was glad he'd come. She'd no wish to be at odds with him and yet, because of Maggie's words earlier, she was uncomfortable.

"A bad conscience, my dear. Cate, I'm truly sorry for speaking sharply to you earlier. I'm afraid we're all a bit out of sorts with all that's happened lately. I'm sorry. Am I forgiven?

"Of course, come into the drawing room and help yourself to a dram. Maggie keeps the decanter full at all times." Cate followed him into the room and waited while he poured them both a dram. Seeing him so soon after Maggie's lecture was a little unnerving. Was Maggie right? As he handed her the glass she knew that he needed an apology for his summary dismissal that afternoon.

"Dinwoodie, I...."

"No, Cate, no need to say it. Let's just go back to your letter from MacNishe. I am interested, truly."

"I've told you about the money for Rhoddy. Even MacNishe never knew about him, you know, not until the Cailleach told him when she was dying."

"Understandable, since you kept your secret well. Cate, this is not idle curiosity. Does Bruce know?"

"Of course he doesn't, Dinwoodie." Here she was being sharp again. "I'm sorry, I didn't mean to snap, but the very thought of Bruce knowing makes me nervous."

"It would make me nervous too. That knowledge would give him a perfect weapon to use against you. Perhaps even remove Rhoddy from your care."

"He couldn't do that, Dinwoodie, could he?"

"I think it's a possibility we ought to explore, just in case. What else did the letter say?"

"Answered questions I'd given up asking when a child. You remember, earlier today I explained about Bert. Well one of the other '*Sights*' I saw was not of the future but the past. Dinwoodie, it was so strange and frightened me." Cate crossed to the window and pointed. "We can't see it from here but Beinne Nishe was in that picture, vision, whatever you call it. Like a story of long ago it was. A battle, a wounded Highlander and the *red-headed woman* I told you about. On the mountain, in my cave, the woman gave birth."

Cate resumed her seat facing Dinwoodie. "MacNishe wrote that the woman was a tinker and the young Highlander her lover. He was also the Laird's only son. Quite how all the family lines intertwined since then, even MacNishe was not sure, but, as he saw it, the tinker's, the Cailleach's and the Laird's families were all descended from there."

"So you have a remnant of all three in your blood. That makes you part MacNishe, surely then?"

"More than part, Dinwoodie, The letter also said that the Cailleach had a bairn to MacNishe's father, and she gave her to the tinkers. That woman was my mother and so the Cailleach was my grandmother. My father was a tinker and, when my mother died, he vanished."

"So, you're not really a tinker girl after all?"

"I was brought up as one, but why, Dinwoodie, why would no one tell me? Why leave me to think I was nobody's. Why did no one care for me?" Cate turned her head away as tears threatened.

"As I understand your story, two elderly women shared your early upbringing. Unless you were related to either or both of them, why would they undertake that?"

"Then they couldn't have been very pleased with me if neither of them would own me."

"Dear girl, you really are defensive, aren't you? You immediately jump to the conclusion that you were unwanted. Why don't you admit to yourself just how angry you are about your birth? "

"Well, what else am I supposed to think?"

"Those two old women gave you the strength to stand up against the world. Do you think you could have done that, had you been spoiled and coddled as a child. No, my dear, they knew they were old and you would be alone eventually. Who knows, perhaps your existence was best kept hidden. There could have been someone out there who might have harmed you."

"Nonsense. Dinwoodie. Why would anyone care enough about me to do that?"

"There you go again. Cate, if you don't value yourself for what you are, rather than for what you can do, you'll never be at peace with yourself."

This was too much for Cate. Rising, she made for the door. "First Maggie, now you. I'm fed up with you both."

As Maggie entered the room, she wished, on sensing the mood, that she hadn't bothered.

"Good evening, Maggie. Your entrance is timely."

"Why's that now, Mister Dinwoodie?"

"I've been arguing with the mistress of the house."

"Well, and you're not alone in that, sir. She'll have the heads bitten off us all before that whale appears! If it's arguing you are, I'll just leave you to get on with it."

As Maggie left the room, Dinwoodie looked to Cate for enlightenment.

"She says I'm so big this time, it must be a whale. Anyway, did you come over earlier today to lecture me or with some news?"

"Remember I told you about Bruce and the banks? It seems your fine Laird, Cate, put his money on marrying a tailor's daughter, or at least borrowed on the strength of it, but the tailor would have none of it. So Bruce came up here to lie low till the rumours died down. Trouble is that all his creditors are demanding instant payment now that his prospects are no longer bright. With the distillery legally yours, the bank, the biggest creditor, wants to foreclose."

"The rumours were right then. So, it'll mean selling either Kevinishe or the Edinburgh house?"

"Exactly. Now, if it's Kevinishe, what would you say to coming in on my scheme for it?"

"Dinwoodie, what use would I be, like this?" Cate glanced disdainfully at her swollen figure. "I'm no exactly a bonny sight for the holiday makers."

"Once again you're making decisions too quickly. Firstly, you won't be in that condition for much longer. Secondly, look around this room. For that matter look around any of the rooms in Craigavon, or the grounds—you've transformed the place. We'd need your skills for fixing it up, staffing, that sort of thing. The distillery would have somewhere to show your Craeg Dhu and we could have the travellers come to us instead of you traipsing off to the city. What do you think?"

"I think you've been doing a lot of thinking, and most of it makes good sense. What about the distillery, the Glen, the sewing and all the other domestic things I have to care about?"

"Cate, you're a master of organization. Use that skill. You've Lizzie longing to be nursemaid and, before you ask, Bella is easily good enough to see to the village women and their sewing. You've Lady Jemima's personal servants, who'd be glad of a proper job and more money. Dear God, woman, you've a ready-made staff to do the work! They just need to be organized."

"What about the foundries? You can't neglect them?"

"I'm not going to. I've good men in charge of the day-to-day work, good sales and administrative staff and excellent foundry managers. They only require me for the organization, ideas, financial support, my high-level contacts, and to drive the business on."

"It seems a lot of investment. How much would you need from me?"

"I don't want your money. I want your expertise. You can work for your share."

"Dinwoodie, why are you really doing this?"

"Difficult to say. You and Fisher care so much about this village and somehow I've been made to care as well. Like you, I feel sure Fisher's death can be traced back to Bruce. Like the fire, the break-in and everything else that's gone wrong here, it's all down to him. Somehow I too feel committed to getting the better of him, and also, my dear, to protecting you, not to mention the extraordinary household you've accumulated!"

"That's very thoughtful of you. And you're right there. For a homeless tinker girl, I've gathered a few to my lonely bosom, as the books would say. Let me think about it, Dinwoodie."

"Right, but don't take too long. The creditors are circling and the banks are anxious to settle the matter. We wouldn't want another set of bad landlords in the village, would we? It's late, time I went."

"Dinwoodie. Wait. Don't go."

"Now what? If it's your time, I'm not your man!"

"Dinwoodie, you should see your face!" She simply couldn't help smiling at the thought of this distinguished man assisting at the birth.

"Seriously now. I'd never thought of that."

"Which particular 'that', Cate?"

"Well, if Bruce sells and you don't buy, someone else will and they could be worse than Bruce."

"It has taken you some time to work it out, but yes, that's my main reason for the purchase. We've had quite enough of someone else interfering in our lives. Let's be masters of our own destiny."

"Right, we'll do it. I'll get to work straight away, do some drawings, make plans, and—Dinwoodie, where are you going?"

"Away, before Maggie starts on me. No extra work for now, Cate. Dammit all, I haven't bought the place yet!"

"Well then—hurry up!" She waved him off with a laugh. How comforting it was to be at peace with him again. It was a shame he was leaving the glen in the morning, but he had to look after his business. She knew that, but she'd miss him. He'd truly become one of them. The remaining thoughts about the man, she pushed firmly to the back of her mind. It was time for sleep.

The fear woke her, the dream still vivid in her mind. Struggling into the dressing gown that no longer met round her middle she made her way downstairs. Hot milk with a dram of Craeg Dhu should chase the fear away. It didn't. Restless, she went to the drawing room window and pressed her forehead against the pane. How many times had she sought this method of easing her troubles?

Almost as if she'd been waiting for it, the grey mist appeared and the dream repeated itself. *There was the bend in the road as it entered the next glen, the outer wall of the quarry rising steeply from it. As she watched, the wall crumbled and the vehicles were swept over the other side of the road amidst a hail of rocks. She saw them tumbling down the far side of the road into the valley below.* Cries of horror resounded in her ears as the picture faded.

Try as she might, she couldn't dismiss this. Twice before she'd had a warning and done nothing. Bert Green had drowned. Fisher too, she was sure had been fighting with Bruce before his stroke. Twice she'd been forewarned of tragedies and ignored them. Could Fisher still have been alive today? In her unwillingness to believe in the existence of *'The Sight'*, had she condemned Fisher and Bert to death?

Hours later, Cate understood, at last, that she had no choice. Unwilling though she was to admit either to herself or others that she possessed it, she must take action now. Knowing that making it common knowledge would distance her from all in the glen, making her as feared as the Calliach had been, she knew she no longer had a choice in the matter. The post bus would travel that road in the morning. Dinwoodie would have Morrison driving him to London along the same road. She had to act.

Never one to hesitate on a decision, she dressed, and even knowing it was unwise, saddled her horse. Not even bothering to dismount in the village, Cate banged on Donald Uig's door. Would he believe her? Would he help?

"What in the name o God do you mean dragging me from my bed? Is it yourself in the dark, Angus? Is it the distillery?"

"It's me, Donald Uig. I need your help."

"Miss Cate! Come you down off that horse, this minute. What can you be thinking in the middle of the night? Is it Kirsty you want?"

"No, Donald Uig, it's you I need. Come, help me down and walk with me." As they made their way along the shore road, Cate told him of her struggles with her 'pictures' and her decision that this time she had to act. "Will they laugh at me? Will they understand?"

"Of that I don't know, Miss Cate, but since my Kirsty is to be on that bus tomorrow we have to let them know. There will be no vehicles on the road in the dark so we have until daylight to act."

"You believe me then, Donald Uig?"

"Wasn't my old grandfather saved when the Calliach warned of the blow-out in the distillery? Why should I not believe you? Now you get to Laggan House and I'll to Wully. The post bus will no run tomorrow or any other day till we see what happens. Back to your horse you go, though God knows you should never be on the animal in your state. Now away with you and tell himself and I'll deal with Wullie. No one else need know for now."

At Laggan House, Dinwoodie watched as she wept into his handkerchief. Though she'd told him about her 'pictures' she'd not remembered the one of Fisher and Bruce. Now she was distraught at the thought she might have been able to save the big man.

"Cate, I don't know whether you could have done so. I don't even know if there is anything in this warning, but you have done all you can this time. I will postpone my journey and you've alerted Wullie. We can do no more for now. I do wonder why not admitting this ability of yours to yourself and others was so important?"

"You see, you think I was at fault—you're blaming me already. No, don't say anymore. I knew no one would understand. Don't you think I was odd enough—a homeless tinker girl, not even a true tinker, just some brat holed up with the Calliach in the winters. Damn it all, they were afraid of her as it was—how much more odd would I have appeared if I'd told them about *The Sight*? I didn't want it and I pretended that it never happened. Was that so awful? I just wanted to fit in, to belong."

Dinwoodie heard and understood the childhood pain in every word she spoke. He knew that it had taken a great effort of will to do what she'd done tonight. Not only would her secret be common knowledge now, but also her fear of having contributed to Fisher's death would be with her always. They must now wait and see if her vision was true or simply the fancy of a heavily pregnant, grief-stricken woman.

They waited in the houses throughout the village. The carter had been and gone back down the road in question and now, two days later, he would be back again. Wullie had also set his mind to getting the post bus back in service. All this upset of late had twisted her mind. Nothing had happened in the quarry and they would begin blasting again the next day, just a piece of female foolishness—that was what it was. He'd told them all in the village the bus was going, though so far no one had asked for a seat. Well he'd lose his job if he didn't get to the mail train tomorrow, so that was that.

As he wiped the windscreen next morning, Wullie wished he'd had a better night's sleep. It was all very well saying he'd go, but now the churning in his stomach was making him think twice. Well, he'd better get the engine started and be off before he lost his nerve.

The rumble of falling rocks was heard for miles around, and Cate knew it had happened. Thank God she'd stopped them from going. She knew some of them had begun to doubt her—indeed she'd wondered herself, but at least now they were all safe. Yet she still had an uneasy feeling. Something was wrong. Then she heard the urgent battering at the door. Pulling herself up she answered it. A distraught Donald Uig stood on the doorstep. One look at his face and she knew. "Who?"

"Wullie—he thought he'd lose the post bus if he didn't make a move. And the Carter will be coming back." We'll need you there in case—unless—can you tell—is he gone?

Shaking her head, she gathered her shawl about her as they waited till Morrison and Dinwoodie came with the car. Meanwhile

482

others, some walking, some running, others astride a horse, a cow, a bicycle, all made their way to the quarry corner, carrying what pitiful tools they had.

For hours they wrenched stones, and prised rocks out of the way, but there was no sign of the bus. They found the carter and his horse, both dead, protruding from the stone avalanche, cartwheels, crushed and broken. No one spoke of the bus or Wully. They ate the food brought to them, then continued scrabbling amidst the rock fall. Night fell and they lit their heather torches. By daybreak outside help had arrived. Each and every one of the assembled crowd kept at it, shifting, probing, searching. Word had come—the post bus had not arrived at the station. Somewhere under the tons of rubble, bus and Wullie were lost.

Now some of the villagers, exhausted, hope gone, were already leaving, slowly, regretfully. Surely there was no more to be done? Cate moved away from the crowd, further along to the bend in the road. She knew he was there. As carefully as she could, Cate began the descent. It was towards the end of the main rock fall and yet she knew it was the right place to look.

Dinwoodie couldn't see her. Where was she? In her condition an awkward step, a loose stone and she'd tumble into the unstable mass below. The thought of her in danger was unbearable. The strength of his emotion shocked him. She'd become part of his life. He should never have let her out of his sight. He found himself screaming her name frantically as they searched.

Cate kept on the downward slope, somehow maintaining her footing and balance. Then she saw it—a flash of red mudguard. Screaming his name she willed Dinwoodie to hear her. Again and again she called for help, knowing that the imprisoned man was barely holding on. She screamed till her voice broke and then she saw them at the edge of the road—Dinwoodie and the village men. She whipped the shawl off her head and pulled her hair loose. Standing on the nearest rock she waved her red flag of hair until at last she saw them begin the climb down. Then she began pulling desperately at the debris surrounding the bus.

It took them all the rest of that day, but just as evening closed in, they pulled an unconscious Wullie from his bus and watched as the ambulance bore him to Fort William. They had lost one man, a horse a wagon and the post bus. Wullie was barely alive.

Coming down the stairs a week later, Cate was happier than she'd been for some time. She felt full of energy today, and even clearing out Fisher's room to make way for a nursery hadn't dampened her spirits as she awaited the birth of this wretched child, that spent its days walloping her in all directions. How one set of tiny limbs could cause all that movement she'd never know. In fact this pregnancy was so unlike the others, she really couldn't understand it. Hearing hooves on the driveway, Cate went to see who it was. This late in the day a visitor was most unlikely. Delighted to see that it was Dinwoodie back from London, she went to welcome him.

"Well, you do have a serious face on you! All that politics is surely no good for you."

"My dear Cate, I'm so glad to be back. Though you're right—the news is pretty grim." Both nationally and for her personally, but she would have to be told. He'd certainly need the support of that generous measure of Craeg Dhu she was pouring for them. "Thank you. How have you been in my absence? No problems, I hope?"

"I'm fine now. Maggie, as you know, has made me work from home...."

"Should you still be working, Cate?"

"Oh, Dinwoodie, not you too! I love to work. What else would I do all day? Stevie won't let me ride, Maggie won't let me lift a duster and Cook screeches at me if I as much as lift a teaspoon. Doing the books and walking Rory are my only pleasures. No, that's ungrateful! They're all good company, but my brain will go soggy if I don't keep mentally alert. Were you able to get those books for me?"

"Yes, Morrison will bring them down tomorrow. Cate, I've news for you."

"Bruce?"

"No. I met your editor friend."

"He's no friend of mine."

"Well, I don't know about that. Would you have preferred to carry on in ignorance of the reporter's marriage? Somehow, I don't think so. He asked me to offer you his apologies. Not for the substance of your heated discussion, but for the manner of it. I believe he's truly sorry, though I rather get the impression you forced the issue by inferring that you were going to marry Alashdair."

"Yes, I probably did. I can understand how he felt, but his response was pretty brutal, nonetheless."

"He's a broken man, Cate. Alashdair has left the newspaper and Glasgow." The sound of her glass breaking had him leaping to his feet. He picked up the shattered pieces and wiped the whisky from her skirt with his handkerchief. Her face was waxen. He worried for the unborn child.

Where was Alashdair? Cate wondered. Somehow she'd taken comfort from knowing his routine, where he'd be, what his flat looked like, what he ate, how he slept. Now that too was taken from her. How could she visualise any of that in another town?

"Cate, dearest Cate, I didn't mean to upset you. I just felt you needed to know. I'm sorry. Truly I am. I'll leave you now. Take care till I see you again."

She watched him ride down the driveway and then fetched her shawl and the dog and made for the woodland. Once out of sight and earshot she lay on the mossy floor and wept. It was truly over.

Dinwoodie knocked on the malt floor door. "Have you a moment, Donald?"

"For yourself, sir, I could make one."

"First, I've news of Wullie. What's left of his legs will mend slowly, but it will be some months before he comes home."

"At least he's alive, Mr. Dinwoodie, though he'll miss his bus. Like a wife to him that bus was. Mind it's thanks to Miss Cate he's still here. How is she?"

"Over it I think, though she had me worried for a time. It took a lot out of her."

"The village is grateful to her. We could have lost many more. Seeing as she no longer comes to work in the distillery, we've never had a chance to thank her."

"A word of advice, Donald. Just leave it. I think she feels uncomfortable with *'The Sight'*."

"I can understand that, sir. It's a heavy burden to have, but she must know we are grateful to her, and why wouldn't we be? Didn't she claw at those rocks till her hands bled? She's not only saved Wullie—she's saved village and distillery. There's not one of us wouldn't do the same for her now. See you and tell her that, sir."

"I will, Donald. Now I need your advice about something else."

"Well now, I shouldn't think the likes of me could be advising a great man like yourself."

"Possibly not outside Kevinishe, but, without Fisher, you're my man."

"Well, there is that, with herself being—well, how will she be coping later on? We need her back here working. Mind, I'm grateful for your help, but you've your own concerns. I tell you, Mr. Dinwoodie, it worries me about later like."

"I understand your worries, but she'll be back, and the distillery will be in firm hands again. Don't ever underestimate her."

"Well no, after this last thing I'd never be doing that, sir. Twice before that she's taken the men of the village on and beaten us. The first time no exactly by yon Marquis of Queensbury's rules, but beat us she did. And there's not a man here will ever forget her besting the young Laird. Aye, that, the funeral and the Quarry disaster, will join all the other stories of the past. The red-headed tinker girl will certainly be part of the Glen's history, you can be sure of that. Man, Fisher would have been proud of her."

"You're right, though it would have been what he expected of her, I've no doubt. Now to the matter in hand—I've been thinking, Donald. While she's working from home, Solly up in his office, Monteith glued to his stills, you down here tending your barley shoots, do you think the men would mind if I walked round occasionally while I'm in the glen? Just to let the odd one, who might be thinking of taking it easy, know someone is watching."

"A capital idea, sir. I do what I can, but my floor here is my first concern. If they thought the Iron Man was checking up on them, it would keep their hands steady."

"That's settled then. I'll to the office. They're used to seeing me there, but I'll come in the front door after this."

"You do that, sir, and now I'll to my own work."

Dinwoodie made for the office. "Solly, how are you?"

"Good, Mr. Dinwoodie, sir. I'm glad your back. The glen seems safer, somehow, when you're here."

"Thank you for that, Solly, but I think our Laird has too many problems elsewhere just now to bother about Kevinishe. However, the news from London is less good."

"Will it be war, do you think, sir? The papers are full of it."

"Not immediately, some of our august politicians still believe that it's not inevitable. Quite why they are so unaware of Germany's feelings and progress, I have no idea. They are being very stupid, for war it'll be within the year. Mark my words."

"Is it true we're no ready for it?"

"Lamentably so. Germany has been forging ahead for years. I know. I've visited some of the iron foundries there and they're miles ahead of us. They want war. The Kaiser is sick and tired of his royal cousins and their vast empires. Envy is a powerful motive for a man with a withered arm. He struts around in military costume all the time and he's put territorial expansion at the top of his agenda."

"The country will be more than busy if we suddenly have to produce enormous amounts of military hardware, Mr. Dinwoodie. Though it's a sad fact that warmongering will benefit some, while others pay with their lives—Oh sir, I didn't mean you. I'm no blaming you. Without the weapons we'd be done for. Will you have a dram to take the taste of war away?" While he was pouring the dram, Solly casually put his question. "Any news of the paper man?"

"I have. He in fact is one of the few reporters who've believed war is imminent. He's left the Gazette and is now a roving correspondent in Germany and the Balkans."

"Does she know?"

"That he's gone, yes. Where, no, not yet."

"Well that's one less worry for me anyway. That only leaves Bruce."

"Nonsense, he's all but finished now".

"I hope so, sir. I worry about her, especially after that business of Wullie and what she did. It was madness climbing down like that in her—you know her condition."

"It was indeed madness, but then that's Cate—act first, think later. She did save him though. We all worry about her, Solly. By the way, with Cate not here and Monteith not a village man, I've had a word with Donald. From now on, until Cate is back, I'll walk the floors when I come to the office, just to keep any of the men from slacking. I know there's no need to worry about you here in the office, or Monteith in the stillroom"

"Thank you, sir. You're right, I'm tied up here and I'm no exactly the figure of a boss man, now am I?"

"Your skills, Solly, are in your head. Without your careful handling of the finances, the distillery would soon go downhill. Make no mistake, when Cate returns, there'll be no doubting who's boss, but you're every bit as necessary, so don't underestimate yourself. Right, I'll leave you to your books. I'll be in again tomorrow.

Today Cate was too excited about all the new plans she'd been working on for Kevinishe to sit still. With Rory at her heels, she set out for the summerhouse. Jim, the head gardener, had cleared all round it, so Charlie couldn't hide there from her anymore. Instead he helped Stevie in the stable or Jim in the garden while his younger brothers and sisters were at school. She was very fond of the lad and had plans for him. She must have fallen asleep, for she woke with a start at Rory's low growl as Dinwoodie approached.

"Call your hound off, my dear. I mean you no harm."

"Dinwoodie! Come and sit down. You know perfectly well he just warns you and then leaves you alone. He knows you would never harm me. You've been by my side often enough these past years. Whenever I'm in trouble, you're there for me. Mind, I wouldn't start beating me!"

Uneasy about raising the subject of the newspaperman, Dinwoodie searched for another topic. Remembering something he'd meant to ask for some time, he faced her. "Cate, were you really so sure you'd get away with smashing the old whisky flask? You know how superstitious they all are—even yourself come to that. It was a pretty daring thing to do."

"Dinwoodie, you didn't really think I would tempt the fates to that degree did you?"

"I did wonder, but I suppose you had your reasons."

"I did. Fisher had a good reputation throughout the Highlands, but he was just another man and time would have erased his memory. Not now! The story of the flask was well known in whisky circles and beyond. I've given them a new tale to pass on. They were there—part of it. Fisher and the flask will live on and it won't do any harm to the distillery's reputation either. Myth and magic, Dinwoodie, are a heady combination."

"But you risked alienating the whole village." Although he appreciated her desire to do the best for Fisher and the distillery, she'd taken a huge gamble. Looking at her now he saw the impudent smile, the mocking eyes. Now he understood. "You tricked them, didn't you? You cunning witch! How?"

"Filled the flask from my own decanter, having first transferred the old malt to a not quite so ancient flask I found in the bowels of the distillery. That's what gave me the idea."

"What I can't see, Cate, is why you've never spoken of it since. Just left them all believing you'd robbed them of a good omen— your pride! After the funeral you wanted them to continue with you in the distillery. Win them over by yourself. My God, what a gambler! You'll do well in business, my dear, but take care. Look where gambling got Bruce."

"I know, and I'm sorry, Dinwoodie. I meant to tell you, but with everything else, I simply forgot. As far as the distillery is concerned I'll let them know as soon as someone brings the subject up."

"I don't think after your last little escapade they'll worry about their good luck charm. You're that now, my dear, whether you like it or not. You saved Wullie and put yourself at risk. Their loyalty is yours for life now. Your feminine presence in the distillery has changed. Instead of being unlucky you are now their lodestar."

"Oh, Dinwoodie, I hardly think so. Anyway, how was London? What news?"

"Cate, I was hesitant to tell you about Alashdair the other day."

"I know, and thank you. Painful though it is, it's better I know about it. What is he actually doing? Working for another paper?"

"No, he's gone abroad, fact-finding, working freelance at the moment, but, when Germany forces us into war, he'll be in demand as a correspondent."

"How do you know? He might come home again."

"Cate," taking her hand in his he explained quietly, "I believe that war will come, and, when it does, it'll be bloody. We're not prepared for it and we'll fare badly in the beginning. There're all sorts of reasons why we're not ready, but the stark truth is we're not. Your Alashdair is using danger the way you used work when you first came back. Work made you ill, but his danger could very well kill him. I don't wish to distress you, but by your own admission, the relationship is over."

"You know it is. It had no future, once I knew he was married.

"There you are then. You're settled here, surrounded by friends. You do have his child to look forward to. I know how much you want to make a success of your children, providing them with everything you never had. Somehow we'll make it right between you and Rhoddy. Oceans are no longer the barriers they used to be. I know one day we'll trace Sarah. I know we will. Then there's this child, conceived in great love. Yes, there was betrayal, but dwell on the love, Cate. The deceit will only poison you. It happened. Struggle through it. You now have another chance at motherhood, and this time you're neither alone, nor poor, nor homeless."

"Sometimes I wonder if life wouldn't have been simpler if I'd just stayed a tinker girl. What are you laughing about, Dinwoodie? It's not funny."

"My dearest Cate, it is. Look at you! What have we just been talking about?

"I know all that. It's just...."

"Just what? You now know, thanks to the late MacNishe, your immediate heritage. Indeed you can trace your line, albeit somewhat fankled, all the way back to The Forty-five Rebellion. A poor, unwanted, unloved, homeless, orphan you are not. The little tinker girl has grown into the flame-haired woman, one who's made her own little empire here, a wealthy woman in her own right. The future holds much for you. You've defeated Bruce. By your own admission your summer love is over. The distillery and the villagers are yours—every one of them. You've conquered everything."

"For a great man you can't see what's in front of your eyes, Dinwoodie."

"I've just told you what I see."

"Well, now, wait you just a minute." Getting onto her feet, Cate removed her shawl, and placed both hands on her pregnant bulge. "This'll not be conquered. Even with all that you say. There's some in the village think I'm the right one to be living here—in the Harlot's House. When this child is born there'll still not be a ring from the father on this finger!" She waggled the ring finger in the air. Smiling now, she looked up at his serious face and mocked him. "Just how do you suggest I overcome that?"

"Well, you could marry me."

The End